Strebor ON THE Streetz

The Grind Don't Stop

Also by L.E. Newell
Durty South Grind

The Grind Don't Stop

A NOVEL BY

L.E. Newell

STREBOR BOOKS

NEW YORK LONDON TORONTO SYDNEY

Strebor Books
P.O. Box 6505
Largo, MD 20792
http://www.streborbooks.com

ISBN 978-1-59309-364-8
ISBN 978-1-4516-1771-9 (ebook)
LCCN 2011928058

First Strebor Books trade paperback edition January 2012

Cover design: www.mariondesigns.com
Cover photograph: © Keith Saunders/Marion Designs

10 9 8 7 6 5 4 3 2 1

Manufactured in the United States of America

For information regarding special discounts for bulk purchases,
please contact Simon & Schuster Special Sales at 1-866-506-1949
or business@simonandschuster.com

The Simon & Schuster Speakers Bureau can bring authors to your live event. For more information or to book an event, contact the Simon & Schuster Speakers Bureau at 1-866-248-3049 or visit our website at www.simonspeakers.com.

To my brother James "Jimmy" Newell Jr.,
and the real love of my life, my mama, Mama Marion

Acknowledgments

First of all, I'd like to thank GOD for not allowing me to give up on myself—for inspiring and continuing to inspire me through the trials and tribulations to keep pursuing my dream. For without GOD's guidance I couldn't have developed one word, one sentence, phrase or idea toward the beginning and the ending of this project.

I'd also like to thank my mama, Mama Marion—how she likes to be called—for birthing me and my sisters, Janet and Debra, who have continued to support me despite my hard-headedness to do the right thing; and my brothers, Jimmy and Mike. I'd also like to thank my nephews and nieces who've stuck by me, too.

To Robert, we call him Bobby, "Hollywood" Washington; you would, too, if you ever met him. He's a character, my main man, adviser and manager, who has certainly played a pivotal role in getting all this done.

To my buddies from back in the day, who traveled hand in hand through the triumphs and failures of surviving the street life. I choose to leave them unnamed for obvious reasons.

Special thanks goes out to all the writers I have used to teach me about how to write by reading their works over and over again until I got it right. Nikki Turner, Zane, Michael Baisden, Omar Tyree and countless others. Oh yeah, and Charmaine Parker, thanks, lady. Thanks, guys and gals, for without your brilliant styles I wouldn't have been able to develop my own.

And finally to Sister Michelle Renee Donaldson, my inspirational adviser, who has continuously encouraged me throughout the years that I could accomplish whatever I set out to do despite the odds as long as I put GOD first and foremost in my life. She's always saying that GOD is in my corner and heart, and with Him, all things are possible. Thanks, Chelle, you are wonderful.

The Prologue

Sparkle's breath came in raspy gasps in the stifling humidity as he struggled to keep his footing with each uncertain step in the soggy terrain. The light breeze slithering through the dense foliage gave him little comfort as he swiped at the sweat that stung his eyes as it rolled down his face. His knees ached from what seemed like hours of squatting on the sloped embankment. He needed to keep out of sight of the passing cars and late-night strollers along the sidewalk some twenty yards away.

The pungent odor of damp, dead vines and tree roots had him bending over on the verge of puking several times as he waited patiently for his boy Rainbow's signal. They'd split up after entering the mini jungle. He sighed in anguish, silently cursing the spur of the moment plan. But let Rainbow tell it and he'd swear to God it was one of his most masterful ones; as he did with all of his crazy ideas.

One look around and it was obvious that it definitely wasn't. But naw, I had to go on this crazy shit with him anyway, even when I knew it was fucked up. As far as he was concerned they could've easily walked into the club and blasted Black Don's grimy ass, gangster style, for all the static he'd caused them lately. Imagining the wannabe godfather's gorilla grit dissolving into a bitchy sob as he blasted his kneecaps with nine-millimeter pellets was like a rush of top-grade cocaine.

Sparkle leaned against a slimy tree, flexed his legs and moaned under his breath. Suddenly he jerked toward a flicker of light from the other side of the house. Shifting around for a better view, he slipped twice in the muddy leaves and branches, cursing angrily when his boots got snagged by some thorny vines.

The more he tried to free himself, the more his anxiety mounted. He began concentrating on any movements wondering if Rainbow was signaling him or if it was a reflection off of some shiny object like a car bumper. Worse still, was it his imagination playing para-noia tricks from the effects of the cocaine he'd snorted earlier?

He wasn't sure, so he got on his hands and knees and crawled closer. Almost immediately his black fatigues got snagged by the thick vines. Grimacing, he tried to jerk free. "Aw fuck," he cried out when a thick branch whacked him violently across the face. His trembling hand cupped his mouth as the pain shot sharply down his neck.

Gagging from the repulsive taste of acrid mud that coated his tongue, he grimaced. "Godayum, Nnnngggg." He grunted as mucus shot from his nose. He grinded his teeth in pain.

"Yo, man, you aight over dere?" Rainbow's voice whispered through the tingling in his ears from several yards away.

Sparkle jerked toward the sound, not realizing that he was that close. He blinked several times before he was able to focus on the look of concern on his boy's face. Sparkle muttered through clenched teeth, "Yeah dog, I'm aight."

"Whatcha say, man? You've gotta speak up." Rainbow hissed as he edged closer.

"I said that I'm aight."

"Don't sound like you aight."

Sparkle moaned in a strained voice, "Shit, man, I could've sworn you gave the signal from over yonder dere." He nodded to the other side of the house and rubbed vigorously between his eyes. "Dayum, dog, this coke's got me tripping, seeing all kinds of stuff. You sure you want to do this here, this way, because I'm jittery as hell," he stuttered through the pain.

Feeling the stress himself, Rainbow scratched his chin with his thumb. But since they were out there now he felt they might as well get it over with. He turned away from Sparkle's strained expression and looked toward the house. He noticed an eerie mistiness developing.

A watery-eyed Sparkle, still grimacing, flinched when he saw Rainbow's shoulders tense. The pain was all but forgotten as he followed his gaze toward movement in the backyard. They gave one another an intense look before they began creeping on their hands and knees toward the edge of the woods for a better look. Their senses dulled to the slaps of wet branches and sharp thorns as they went on full alert. Both of them flinched when the metallic click from cocking their guns echoed through the night air. Anxious to blast away, their eagerness faded when a lone figure emerged into the halo of light glowing from the open doorway. Simultaneously, they snorted with disappointment as a middle-aged lady wearing a flowery apron wrapped around her rounded waist dropped a garbage bag beside an overflowing trash bin.

Rainbow bumped Sparkle's slumped shoulder and cursed in a low voice full of tension. "Aw godayum, man, who da hell is that?"

Sparkle wheezed just as confused and his disappointment quickly turned into a sigh of relief. He was disappointed it wasn't Black Don so they could've gotten this thing over with once and for all, and he was relieved they hadn't opened fire on the old lady. He tapped Rainbow on the shoulder and nodded toward the way they had entered. It was time for them to make their retreat.

Rainbow heaved with his mouth turned down in disgust, before resigning to the inevitable, then nodded in agreement. They crept silently towards the embankment, maneuvering carefully around and over the jagged rocks and jutting vines. The stench of the rotten foliage was less bearable and the muddy footing added to their discomfort. They cursed continuously on the descent down the messy slope, slipping and sliding, scraping their elbows, hands and knees before eventually making it to the sidewalk.

Sweaty, bruised, exhausted and frustrated, they mumbled and grumbled, wiping mud and picking twigs off their black fatigues. They made their way toward Rainbow's low-rider Chevy pickup truck. They pressed their guns along their thighs, tense and ready to fire at the slightest target as they turned the bend of the winding road. Once the truck came into view, they became even more anxious and started jerking their heads back and forth, aiming wildly into the darkness.

They finally made it to the truck parked a quarter of a mile down the dark, forbidden road. Wheezing heavy with frustration, they laid their weary necks on the headrests. An eerie mist of rain started settling on the windshield and added to the gloominess.

Sparkle rotated his neck on the headrest, cursing the nauseous effect the comedown from the coke, mixed with the empty feeling of their failed mission, was having on him. He took some deep breaths before squeezing his eyes shut and reached for the crumbled pack of Kool cigarettes resting on the dashboard. Taking a long deep drag, he exhaled the smoke slowly, exhilarating in the calming taste and feel of nicotine.

He looked over at Rainbow and huffed. "Aw man. Why I let you talk me into this dumb-ass shit, I'll never know."

Rainbow had rested his head and arm on the steering wheel. He cocked a wary eye at him. "What, I talked you..."

Shaking his head up and down, Sparkle cut him off. "Yeah. man, that's right, talked me into this commando bullshit."

Rainbow lifted his head off of the steering wheel, raised his hands in exasperation and rolled his eyes to the ceiling. "Well, I'll be damned."

Sparkle feigned shock. "You're being what?"

Bracing his back against the door Rainbow coughed and swallowed hard. "Well, I'll be damned if you ain't bitching about a little mud and..."

Sparkle cut him off again. "Nigga, please, a *little* mud...man, this here's a real live welt across my nose, *shit*." He hissed, then rubbed the bridge between his eyes.

"Let me see." Rainbow reached over and pulled his hand from his face. "I said, let me see." He leaned forward and squinted to get a better look in the dim light. His eyes widened before he jerked back and put his hand over his mouth to try to hide the smile he felt creeping to the corners. "Damn, dog, dat do look kinda fucked up, yo."

Sparkle turned his face in different angles in the mirror. He turned away and pinched his nose when he felt the laugh boiling in the pit of his stomach. It didn't do any good for as hard as he tried to look serious, he couldn't hold it and grabbed his side and laughed. His forehead was wrinkled as he stared at Rainbow for a full thirty seconds before sighing.

"Aw, fuck you, nigga," he growled at Rainbow, who had started rolling around in the seat, wiping tears out of his eyes.

Rainbow swiped his forearm across his eyes and folded it across the steering wheel. He moaned and looked at Sparkle one more time before putting the key in the ignition. While the car was revving up, he leaned sideways to dodge Sparkle's wild swing at his head and pulled into the street. They had only driven a short distance before he switched on the windshield wipers to clear the mist that was starting to blur his vision.

Sparkle was reaching over to cut on the radio when the harsh high beam lights of a fast-approaching vehicle suddenly flooded the interior of the truck. Before it registered, the vehicle was right on their bumper.

"What the fuck?" Rainbow grumbled when the stinging glare from the rearview mirror blinded him. He raised his hand to cover his eyes. Sparkle peeked backward but the pain made him jerk away. There was a shocking boom, as the invisible terror rammed into the truck, jolting them into the dashboard. *Boom.* Another jolt sent Sparkle head first into the windshield and forced Rainbow to put a death grip on the steering wheel, as he struggled to maintain control of the now swerving truck. No sooner had he managed to keep the truck from skidding when there was another sound that sent shock waves down their spines. *Plink, plink, plink.* The sound of hot metal piercing metal invaded their senses and then the rear window exploded, splattering them with lethal shards of glass.

Both of them hunched over as the shock sent them into near panic mode. The rarely rattled Rainbow was forced to steer with his head barely able to see over the dashboard. *Plink, plink, plink.* Another round of scorching metal screamed over their heads, eating up the roof's upholstery.

Fuck this, time to fight back, Sparkle thought and shifted his body and reached under the seat, where he had placed his gun. He maneuvered around for a better angle. He reached over the seat and started firing blindly. His confidence immediately soared when the blinding light was cut in half, followed by the sound of tires screeching as the charging vehicle swerved sideways and slowed down. Recognizing the bleak advantage with renewed energy, Rainbow sat up and wheeled the car into a quick U-turn. Both of them stuck their guns out the windows and blasted away.

They were still firing when their truck bumped onto the sidewalk and skidded sideways into some thick bushes. Their bodies jerked around for a moment before they gathered themselves, reloaded their weapons, kneed the doors open and sprung out of the truck. Kneeling behind the doors they pumped lead until their pursuers skidded into a U-turn, before righting themselves and speeding out of range around the winding bend.

With the scent and sight of gun smoke swirling in the air, they slowly rose up and face each other. The combination of sweat, fear and chilly rain had them trembling in their soaked fatigues. Sparkle closed his eyes and twisted his neck in short circles embracing the sound and feeling of the crackling release of tension. Sighing heavily, he stretched a weary arm onto the roof of the truck. "Whadda fuck; how in da hell did somebody know we were out here?"

Rainbow lifted his muddy shirttail and put his gun in his waistband, then leaned forward to put his hands on his knees. Steam hissed through his fingers when he wiped the sweat off of his face. His whole body screamed *ouch* when he straightened up and hunched his shoulders. He took a deep breath, eased out of the truck and started circling the vehicle for damages. After taking a head-shaking tour, he eased back into the driver's seat, leaving one foot on the damp road and the other on the running board. With mounting frustration, he braced an arm on his knee to rest his head and stared off into the darkness.

Sparkle let him agonize for about a minute, before he circled the front of the truck and leaned on the open door and faced his boy. Gasping between clenched teeth, he snarled, "Hey, buddy boy, don'tcha think we better roll up out of here before one of these neighbors sends the five-o to check out all of the gun play?"

Rainbow sat mesmerized for a while longer before he slammed the door shut and cranked up the bullet-riddled truck. The tires spun for a moment before he was able to back out of the bushes and pull into the street. Sparkle barely had the chance to close the door.

They were only about a half mile away from the scene when they heard police sirens approaching fast in the distance. Rainbow refused to let the panic overwhelm him when he saw the red and blue lights on the horizon and turned into the next alley. Since he had been driving with the lights out, he doubted if they had seen him make the turn. When he got halfway down the alley, he turned the lights on and pressed the pedal to the floor, zooming along the bushes and tree-laden path. He alternated between side streets and other alleys until they got into College Park. From there he mixed with the normal flow of traffic on Main Street, through East Point and headed to Lee Street toward his crib near Turner Field.

Both of them were stuck way too deep in their own thoughts of what had just happened for them to have a conversation. Rainbow eased the truck alongside of the gray brick house, into the backyard and parked under an often used, rusty tire rim basketball hoop nailed on the garage door. He laid his head on the headrest. He stretched the seat out and lay back. "Aaah."

Several tension-filled moments later, Sparkle pulled on the handle and kneed the door open. The only light available was the car's dim roof bulb. "My nigga, I've been wracking my brain all the way over here and I still can't figure out how they could've known we were out there."

Rainbow lifted his aching body. "Mmm, me too, partner, there's one thing fer sho: we must really open our eyes to anybody other than the two of us."

"No doubt, no motherfucking doubt," Sparkle moaned.

CHAPTER ONE

As The Hood Turns

The persistent staticky racket on the police band was really starting to get on Beverly's last nerves as she spun around the corner in pursuit.

In pursuit of what, who? Her thoughts were twisted in a whirlwind of scenarios. *Am I following Lt. Woo because Woo and her squad of police hoodlums were trying to bust one of her boys? Or am I chasing Rainbow to see if he'll lead me to that bastard Sparkle? Does he or Rainbow know or have a hint of who took out old man OJ? Or if the hit was actually meant for him instead?*

Woo was such a valuable asset to erasing the drug problem in the Atlanta Metro area, but she was winding up in places that didn't fit and Beverly couldn't help but to question why. Digging too deep would cause others to formulate questions that Beverly wasn't prepared to answer. For Woo to try getting on Beverly's good side to advance her career was commonplace in the police ranks. She well understood and couldn't really blame her. On the other hand, she wouldn't be able to face her own self in the mirror if she allowed Woo to crack down on her peeps without at least sidetracking her some kind of way.

And that damn Rainbow and Sparkle, UGH!! How much more could she take of their crooked activities? She couldn't protect them forever like she was a mother hen refusing to realize that these guys were plain no fucking good. She shook her head, disgusted with herself for even thinking that way about the guys who'd helped her attain her position as police chief. But hell, it was her hard work and dedication to her beloveth Atlanta that had gotten her there. Still without them putting their own freedom on the line, hustling in the deadly streets of the hood to get up the money to pay her college tuition, she wouldn't have even gotten the chance to go to school. And how many dirty muthafuckas had they beaten down back in the day to make life so much easier as she grew from child to adolescent to womanhood to Police Chief. Without them it could've never been accomplished.

Rainbow and his sweetheart of a mama had always been there whenever she had needed a guiding hand regardless of the circumstances. She'd taught her how to be a woman and he'd taught her how to deal with crooks and the antics of the red light district. And then there was Sparkle.

Sparkle, Sparkle, Sparkle. Naw, to hell with that. It's Larry, Larry, Larry. Why did I have to fall in love with that knucklehead, that fucking fool? His crazy ass will never change. But hell, he might. "Aw, who the hell am I fooling? That nigga ain't gonna neva change." She wheezed, so frustrated that she grinded her teeth so hard that they started aching.

And those two bitches rolling with him. *Hmmmm!!* She knew Violet and could understand why his so-called "playa-play-ass" would be drawn to one of the best boosters in the city because he loved being the flyest-dressed dude in the hood. Violet was the aunt of one of her best friends, Yolanda, and Beverly had been aware of her boosting legend status for as long as she could remember. *But who is that other little bitch?* She nodded with her mouth twisted downward. She knew she'd find out all she needed to know about her sooner thatn later.

"These bitches must really think I'm some kind of chump bitch or something," she muttered under her breath in frustration. Her eyes swayed back and forth to the pursuit in front of her and then to the rearview mirror. She snapped out of her trance when she heard wheels screaming in protest. The car immediately in front of her with Woo and her henchmen of a drug squad pushed through the intersection, barely avoiding the crossing traffic. She had to concentrate on what was happening and gather her police sense instead of pouting about these niggas. She rotated her neck, squared her shoulders and got back into super cop mode.

✠ ✠ ✠

It was a hit that Rainbow felt; naw, a hit he knew was meant for him. What other reason would that nigga Joker, the nephew of his other partner, "B," be sneaking gritty sneers at him while he was shooting the breeze at the store counter with Junior's brother, "Big Guy"? He was the longtime part owner of the store with OJ. The three of them had practically raised that little nigga from the diaper into the hustling life. Add that grit with watching Joker's reaction and facial expressions as he dashed from his and OJ's checker game right before the shooting had started. The circumstances and consequences added up to a hit, no matter how you wanted to see it.

It had been some time since he had seen Joker; not since he'd been sent to juvie for blasting lead at a couple of younguns about some slutty little ho. So what had the little nigga been involved in since then? He instantly recalled when Joker, snotty nose and all, used to hide their dope package in his nasty drawers while he, Sparkle and Johnny 'B' strolled the streets of their little drug turf when they'd first ventured into the game. He smiled to himself recalling the wide grin on his little face when they'd given him his first pair of Air Jordans. *How old was that little nigga then, around seven or eight?* "Damn, how the years fly by," he muttered under his breath as he recalled all that crazy stuff that little fool used to get into. They'd have to come to his rescue before the other little toughies smashed his little ass. What in the world had happened to him since getting out of juvie? He didn't have a clue, but he was definite he would find out now.

He shook those memories out of his brain for things had gone way beyond what had happened in the past. His present state of mind was now in killer revenge mode as he jumped into his Caddie and jetted in hot pursuit of those niggas. Mistakenly, he hadn't paid the least bit of attention to Lt. Woo and her drug squad hoodlums parked near the end of the block as his tires screamed around the corner. His only concern was finding out where those niggas were headed.

After screeching through the intersection with the pedal pressed to the floor, hoping to overtake them, he chanced a look into his rearview mirror and spotted that worrisome little bitch and her henchmen.

Oh shit, I got to shake this little bitch first. Because when I catch these little muthafuckas, dey asses have got to go meet their makers. Dey ass got to die, leave this earth. Try to take me out like that. And kill one of my childhood idols. Oh hell yeah, y'all niggas got to die, for sho.

Rainbow was way beyond being a little shaken. He had to get rid of the bitch and her hoodlums, no doubt about it. There was no way he could take the chance of them witnessing him blasting on those fools. He shot down the next intersection and sped up, hoping to lose them.

✠ ✠ ✠

Regardless of how things had gone so far, Beverly knew she had to get to the bottom of it. And do it without Woo or anyone knowing. Talking about skeletons in her closet, this mess was really getting out of hand. She had to make sure that Woo didn't see her. But how was she going to do that and keep up with Rainbow? She was tailing Woo who was following Rainbow while he was following the niggas who'd thrown down on the drive-by.

Oh shit, has that bitch spotted me? Beverly thought as she narrowed her eyes when Woo's silhouette angled upward toward the rear-view mirror. Had the little bitch slowed down to get a better look at who was following her?

Beverly knew she could no longer take the chance of being spotted. She made a quick left at the next intersection knowing she was giving Woo the worst possible angle to recognize her. As she was making the turn she saw the car of shooters make a right some three or four blocks ahead. She pulled to the curb, jumped out of the car and sprinted to the corner. She pressed her back to the brick wall of the paint store and did a quick peek and duck back around the edge of the building. She'd seen Rainbow make a right turn a couple of blocks away. She assumed he was either trying to cut them off or had spotted Woo chasing him and was trying to put a move on her. Either way he pressed the pedal to the floor board, speeding down the street way over double the speed limit. She could hear the rubber screaming and see the smoke spiraling in the air from his tires as he jetted away.

It shocked Beverly when Woo didn't follow Rainbow and zoomed down the street the shooters had traveled. Even though she was puzzled why Woo had responded that way, Beverly had seen enough and rushed back to her car.

From the sounds of the radio some of her troops had already arrived at the scene of the shooting. *What should I do now? Go back to the scene? Follow Rainbow to keep his crazy ass from getting into any more trouble? Follow Woo to find out what the little bitch is really up to? Or put some more troopers on their trails?*

While she was contemplating her next move, another familiar vehicle jetted past her and turned left speeding down the street. She shot the car into gear and pulled up to the corner in time to see the car following the path of Woo and the shooters.

She blinked several times at the antennae sticking out of the trunk, knowing it was a cop's car. She zoomed in on the license plate and the silhouette of the driver. It hit her like a ton of bricks. *That bastard.* She grimaced as it dawned on her that it was JR, the deputy chief. "What in the hell is he doing here? What's his connection with all of this?" she mumbled to herself.

The light was red. She'd normally flip on the siren and speed by all traffic signs. But her intuition kept those responses at bay because she couldn't draw any attention to herself. *So what should I do now?* There were definitely too many things happening here to handle all of them at the moment.

She took a deep breath and started across the intersection. For some reason her eyes shot to the rearview mirror. "Now ain't that a bitch," she cursed at the silhouette of Sparkle in the car trailing hers. Why had the fool jetted away from her in the first place? From what she could tell he hadn't recognized her. So what now? Should she keep going to see what would happen?

She concentrated on his face for several blocks before she decided to circle the entire block to get behind them. Violet and the other girl were both still in the car. For a brief second she considered pulling them just to fuck with them and display her power. To let them bitches know that she wasn't anything to play with. But she had to consider how the girls would react. Would they get loud? That would certainly defeat her purpose of secrecy.

Besides, she didn't really trust how her jealousy would make her act.

For after all she was not only hiding from the authorities but from the street gossip as well. Especially knowing how cops always maintained their own personal crew of snitches. She had an army of them herself.

She followed Sparkle and the girls to the house by Turner Field and settled in the parking lot. She pulled out her mini binoculars to check out the activities of the house.

A huge lump roughed its way down her throat as she watched Sparkle pull up to the curb in front of the house. He leaned forward in the driver's seat to let the other woman out. From where she was sitting it seemed like the girl pushed the seat forward with a little attitude. Violet jumped out of the other side and eased into the front seat with a smirk on her face. One that said, *Aw, little bitch, handle it.*

It only meant one thing to Beverly: both of these girls had to be Sparkle's woman. She shivered with jealousy as the car sped down the street. She followed them to a small set of apartments on Memorial Drive. She knew she couldn't park there so she drove across the street and stopped in the supermarket parking lot.

No matter how long it would take, she was going to find out what in the hell he was up to. Her heart pounded with grief and anger as she settled into the seat and pressed the binoculars to her eyes. *It may just be a long night.*

✠ ✠ ✠

Rainbow looked across the table wondering how long it would actually take the trio of young hustlers to master the art of the false shuffle.

Mercedes, the sexy little Vietnamese that had stunned Sparkle with her pole dance at the strip club a while back, was really getting at it. She was definitely concentrating a lot harder than Sparkle's nephew, Stacy, and his number two ho, Princess. He knew that Stacy was getting the big head since he'd been winning with the marked decks they'd schooled him to the last few times he'd played at Al's poker game in Lithonia. In a way he couldn't really blame him after getting skimmed by Al, probably for years. But there was so much more for him to perfect than marked cards. He'd have to bring him down a couple of notches for his own good.

He took a moment to study Princess. Her jet-black, eye-candy physique and intoxicating glare was still sexy enough after all these years to display her like a fine piece of jewelry. He'd yanked her off the ho stroll after only a few months when he decided that she was much more valuable to him than selling head and pussy. She had a sassy, no-nonsense attitude that had proven to be quite an asset when he'd allowed her to run his dope on the hotel route along I-20. She'd made him a mint in addition to keeping his other bitches on track. Her uncanny resemblance to Queen Nefertiti was definitely a plus as well. He picked the deck up and smiled brightly.

"Yo, Stacy, just because you've learned the easiest way to get your cheat on, doesn't mean you can run slack on the other stuff you need to keep racking up the cash, my man. Believe me when I tell you that marked deck thang's gonna run thin a lot sooner than you think."

He didn't give him a chance to respond before flipping a card upside down on the top of the deck and false shuffled six or seven times. He could tell right off the bat that they weren't able to keep up. It felt good to see that stunned look on Stacy's face. He knew they'd catch on sooner or later, hopefully sooner, so it was on to the next phase. He placed a mirror in front of him and started shuffling in slow motion. "My nigga and niggettes, I want y'all to get a mirror and practice like this until you can't see the move yourself. It has to look like your natural deal, feel me?" He waited for them to nod their understanding. "Then I'm gonna grind y'all wannabe slick asses at dealing seconds and off the bottom all with the same motion, okay?"

With faces eager to please the teacher they started gathering up the cards. Rainbow leaned back and shouted for Chef-bor-a-Lady, who was doing her usual throwdown in the kitchen. She was actually his very first girlfriend from way back in elementary school. After all these years of pimping, he'd never even considered putting her through the rigors of that kind of life and she'd stood by his side ever since. His forever bottom lady, was the way he saw it. "Yo, lady, how long did my nigga say he was going to be?"

Lady's cheery puppy-dog face leaned around the corner with her hands full of floured chicken and smiled. "He said something about picking up Yolanda and coming right over." She twisted her wrist around awkwardly to look at her watch. "That was about a half-hour ago, so they should be pulling up anytime now."

The words were barely out of her mouth when the car pulled into the driveway. Even before the doors slammed, they could hear Yolanda's and Violet's loud voices arguing about where they were going to off some of the stuff they'd stolen. Violet, Sparkle's main girl, was still considered legendary when it came to the boosting game. Short and thick she still reminded folk of a much older version of Toni Braxton. Back in the day she'd trained nearly all of the pimps' hoes, using numerous gadgets to aid in the art of stealing. Rainbow was still amazed at some of stuff she'd come up with. She was one strong-willed babe who didn't take trash from anyone. And Yolanda was like a darker, younger version of her Aunt Violet. She was actually an original member of the gang from their kindergarten days. She was Beverly's first and best girl buddy as well as being 'B''s bottom girl forever. There wasn't a nigga alive that could pull something over on her. Rainbow smiled at the sound of her voice as he recalled the many times that Yolanda had kicked ass right along with them for messing with Beverly.

Sparkle stepped through the door shaking his head and tossed his thumb back toward the yakking duo. "Damn, dog, why didn't you tell me these hoes would be going at it like this here. God-ayum, I've had to put up with this bullshit from the moment they saw each other."

He paused and broke into a brilliant smile when he saw Mercedes practicing in front of the mirror. Her concentration intensity took him back to the days when he used to do the same thing hour after hour while locked on segregation in the joint.

The glitter in her eyes and high-cheeked smile when she looked up made his heart thump. Shivers tingled along his spine when she purred, "Hi, baby, look at what Rainbow has showed me." Mercedes did the false shuffle awkwardly but her tiny hands seemed to be made for it.

He bent down and kissed the top of her head. "That's good, sweetie, how about standing up for me for a moment?" She looked puzzled but only briefly before she placed the cards on the table and stood up to greet him with open arms.

He turned to Yolanda and Violet and shouted over their loud chattering. "Hey, can y'all stop bickering long enough to look at her? Geez." There was an immediate ceasefire to their rapid-fire conversation as they walked over to Mercedes and started circling and spinning her around. Yolanda leaned back bossily and cocked a bejeweled hand on her wide hip before she spoke. "Damn, she little for a mug, but I think I've already got some stuff in the trunk that'll fit her just right."

Violet quickly added, "Mmm-hmm and I can easily, well not easily, but I can adjust the straps on the bubble. But can her little ass waddle?" She smiled warmly as she began turning the little honey around thinking of all the ways she was going to train her in the shoplifting trade.

Sparkle smiled and wondered if Mercedes really had what it took for all the illegal stuff he had planned. Then he looked over at Rainbow, who had been ho sitting for him every since he'd made her a part of their little crime family. "Do you think she ready, dog?"

Rainbow rubbed the side of his face and started massaging his chin before he gave a sniffled reply. "My nigga, baby girl here has been picking up on everything like a real pro." He rolled his eyes to the ceiling and pinched his nose before going on. "Hell yeah, she ready."

Reassured by the confidence his main man was showing, he smiled down at the little star. "You think you can waddle, baby girl?"

She frowned and shyly whispered, "Waddle?"

Sparkle smiled down at her and then began marveling at the resemblance between the two professional boosters as they studied Mercedes' reaction. Yolanda was a shade darker. They had the same high cheekbones and big almond-shaped eyes. Their hair was cut short with bundles of curls swirling on the top. Violet's hair was dyed blonde while Yo favored a dark mixture of red and brown. Yolanda's breasts were smaller but her hips and ass were much wider. She had one of those high-rise bubble butts. They liked to dress fly all the time; this could only be expected from two of Atlanta's best.

Violet grasped her hips and looked at Sparkle. "Baby, what I'm gonna do is dress her up like a pregnant little doll and just let her shop and observe while me and Yolanda here go to work. Is that cool with you?" She cocked her head to the side and spread her hands far apart waiting for his response.

Before he could reply the telephone drew everyone's attention. Lady picked it up on the third ring. She spoke briefly before poking her head around the corner and held it out to Rainbow. "I think you better hear this here, baby."

Rainbow snatched the phone out of Lady's outstretched hand and listened intently for nearly a minute.. "How much did they take: They did all that; even after y'all gave up the dope and the loot? Damn, where she at now? Go get her. Is it swollen real bad? You think you need to go to Grady's? He made you do that, too, whew." He continued to listen intently. "Naw, just stay there. I'll be out there in a little while. Uh-huh, in about an hour... Naw, don't worry about that. We'll make up for it. Don't open the door for nobody til I get there, okay." He tossed the phone back to Lady, arched his brow in Sparkle's direction and started gnawing on his bottom lip as he headed down the hall. The wall vibrated when he slammed the bedroom door.

Sparkle twisted his mouth to the side, sighed and eyed the crew's solemn faces before following Rainbow down the hall. He returned in a few minutes and frowned before directing his attention to Stacy. "Yo nephew, why don't you ride with the girls? Me and Rainbow have got to go and check on some things."

Stacy jacked his pants up and braced his shoulders. "Y'all sure y'all don't want me to ride with ya?" There was a sadistic smile on his face as he took his nine from behind his back and cocked it.

Sparkle smiled at his gangster display. "Man, put that away; you scaring the girls. Just gon' with them like I asked you to, man. I need you to get to know Violet and Mercedes a little better anyhow."

Sparkle started waving them out of the door. Mercedes reluctantly followed them. He couldn't worry about her feelings now. He looked at Princess, who had picked up her coat to leave with the rest of them. "Naw, black baby, you gonna ride with us." He took her jacket.

He noticed Mercedes frowning over her shoulder as she started out the door. He fought back the urge to call her back. He leaned against the door as they pulled away. He was closing the door when the phone started ringing again. Lady stuck her head around the corner again with the same worried look on her face. Sparkle took the call this time before he went into the bedroom to tell Rainbow what the deal was. There were loud yells and screams heard through the door before they came storming out. Their faces were stern with anger as they left the house.

Lady rushed to the door to watch their departure before she went back into the kitchen to wrap up the food for another time. Then she headed to the bedroom to place a call to an old friend.

✠ ✠ ✠

The driver smiled as he leaned his shoulder against the door of the late-model sedan parked across the street from the three-story house. Their prey had pulled out in their cars a couple of minutes apart and headed in opposite directions. They were certain the passengers hadn't paid them any attention, since they were parked among countless cars in the Turner Field lot.

The driver adjusted the sleeves of the baggy Falcons sweatshirt and glared angrily at the passenger. "Homie, I'm beginning to think that you may just be the wrong soldier for this job. After all, you've known these niggas a long time. Hell, all your life, as a matter of fact."

The passenger drew deeply on the cigarette dangling from the corner of his mouth and blew a steady stream of smoke out the window into the cool air before responding nervously. "I told you that I got this. Things have started to get troublesome for them already. I just got to make sure that I do everything right."

"Playa, playa, I ain't feeling that shit and I ain't got a lot of patience. You do realize that, don'tcha?" the driver spat in a low growl.

"Yeah, yeah, yeah, I know you need this done, but like you said yourself, I've known them for a long time. This means I know that they ain't nowhere near no dummies and I don't..."

The driver cut through his whining with a loud slap on the dashboard. "Nigga, stop playing games with me. Either you do like I told you or I do your ass." In a lightning-quick motion, he reached across the seat to put an extremely powerful grip on the passenger's shoulder blade. "Is my English plain enough for ya?"

As spittle sprayed the passenger's face to go along with the grip's paralyzing pain, a mixture of fear and hatred coursed through his brain and he gave the only answer possible. "Yeeeeaaaah."

✠ ✠ ✠

Beverly was putting her groceries in the trunk in the Kroger parking lot when her attention was drawn to the staticky police band. She automatically wondered if her boys, Rainbow and Sparkle, had answered the call of the wild with all the shootings along I-20. She knew there was no way that they were going to let that drive-by shooting pass without responding. She started reminiscing.

Deep in her heart she knew they'd pooled their mediocre bank-rolls to keep her in nice clothes and to get her in and through college. There was no way that her sweet old nana's social security check could have come up with all that money.

Beverly thought back to the days when she and her girlfriends would sit around admiring them at the dope hangouts. They called it their days of being so-called gentlemen of leisure. Pimping macks was how they jokingly labeled it. They became star protégés of the legendary queen of the con, Loretta. practicing the many scams she'd taught them in her basement on Auburn Avenue. It continued all the way to her tuition fees at Georgia State, where she began her quest for a law degree.

Neither ever volunteered to offer an explanation of the source of the money. She'd always had her doubts about all the different lies they'd tell. Whenever she would question them, as a group or one-on-one, they would never confirm or deny it; they'd stare at her blankly until she stomped away pouting. Sparkle was the only one who seemed like he wanted to tell her but even he wouldn't. The bottom line from way back was that she wanted to grow and make a difference in her hood, in her city and in their lives.

How could she ever deny any of them? From kindergarten to elementary, to high school to college, she always felt that she was nowhere near the brainiest hen in the flock. So, if not for their constant nagging and encouragements that she could really make something out of her life, she wouldn't be where she was today.

Talking about skeletons in the closet, she certainly had her share. She had to keep those skeletons hidden, well hidden. Actually, her career depended on it. Still on her oath to keep the streets clean, she certainly couldn't allow the violence to escalate out of control.

As she turned the key in the ignition, she looked in her eyes in the mirror wondering how far her loyalty could extend; and for that matter which way that loyalty would lean. As she pulled into the Candler Road traffic, she pondered her dilemma.

✠ ✠ ✠

Big Al was in a foul mood when he pulled up behind Don's car in his driveway. The heavy-set big man of fifty odd years was contemplating if he should run his usual poker game tonight. The past few days had begun to really stress him out; from dealing with all the different personalities that frequented his game room to test their luck at the card table to dealing with that crooked cop JR in their hijacking furniture trucks to supply the condos recently built to that punk Black Don. He'd helped run his dope investment and the many dope dealers that worked his product. He checked out the streets of his upper-class neighborhood before squinting into the rearview mirror. Was he really a celebrity look-alike as most folk had been telling him? *Maybe, except more handsome.* He smiled.

Lately, everything seemed to be grinding on his nerves. From the sound and feel of the gravel sprinkled along the entryway, to the raindrops that barely sprinkled his neck when he got out of the car, made his fist ball up in disgust. He even feinted at a harmless squirrel when it sprinted across his path on the way to scampering up a tree. The fresh smell of the opening skies mixed with the faint smell of the peat moss surrounding the two orange trees in his yard made his teeth grit. He fought the urge to stomp the rose bed along the front of the house because he felt that the aroma was too strong. *Damn, could he ever use a blunt to calm himself down.* He could almost taste the reefer and cocaine mixture rolling off of his tongue to invigorate his throat, nasal passage and brain.

He reached the door and started patting himself down before

throwing his hands up in frustration, realizing he hadn't taken the keys out of the ignition. *I've got to stop letting myself get so tensed up like this. The deal's gonna come through. I'm just letting the pressure get next to me, that's all. Just being too damn paranoid.* He grimaced and stomped back to the car.

"Come on, Al, get it together, man," he muttered under his breath as he reached inside the car to retrieve the keys.

As he was putting the key in the lock, he began shuddering. He turned around and scanned the neighborhood. He didn't see anything and took a deep breath, then shook off the eerie feeling and pushed the door open. He took one step inside and nearly jumped out of his skin when the shrill sound of the alarm shook him from head to toe.

"What the fuck?" Don screamed and jumped off of the couch with his fist balled at his side.

Black Don, the self-proclaimed ruler of downtown drug trafficking and strip club owner, hated being uncomfortable in any situation. Accompanying his aunt, Rose, the former Miami whore, to this money paradise of Atlanta all those years ago had certainly put him at the top of his hustling game. There was plenty of drugs, hoes and money to keep him satisfied, but it wasn't good enough for him. He wanted much much more and was determined as ever to get it. He wasn't comfortable the way Al had just barged in without a warning whatsoever and it showed.

Al could have cared less how this fool felt as he frowned and reached for the alarm beside the light switch. He punched in his code to silence it. He bristled up and turned around to stare angrily at Don. He massaged the bridge of his nose and stepped toward him like a stalking panther.

What the fuck is up with this nigga balling up on me in my own godayum house? Don thought.

Don felt Al's anger with each advancing step. There was no way he could've known about the fuck session he'd just had with Mona, Al's sexy-as-hell, freak of a woman. It had even surprised him how easy she'd been to conquer. And that pussy and head was bumping, grade-fucking triple A. She'd proven to be too hard to resist, not that he'd tried to. Actually, he was plotting how to hit it as often as possible or simply straight up snatch her from under Al's rule, toss her in the club and make a mint off of her sexy ass when Al entered abruptly.

Don took a couple of steps back and prepared for whatever. He felt his hands trembling, so he slid them in his pockets to keep Al from seeing the effect his attitude was having on him.

Al sensed his nervousness and stopped at the edge of the couch, He reached across Don's body to massage his neck and shoulder before he growled, "Where's mine, man?" When he took too long to respond, Al stepped around the couch and sneered even more menacingly. "Nigga, I asked you where my shit at?"

The tension deflated from Don's shoulders. *Wow, I'm not busted for my out of control dick play, after all.* He sighed heavily. "My nigga, you shonuff had me spooked for a second there. It's out there in the car. I was waiting for you to get here before I got it."

Al lowered his guard slightly. It didn't stop Don from watching him closely though. He patted him on the shoulder as he brushed by and whispered, "Damn, partner, what's got you so pumped up?" He didn't bother waiting for an answer and continued out of the door to get the package.

Al didn't budge an inch, letting him know that he wasn't for any nonsense. Al started nibbling on his bottom lip trying to bring his anger under control. He sighed and walked over to the bar and mixed a vodka and orange juice. He took a few sips, welcoming the sting as the alcohol scorched down his throat.

The sexy, sassy Mona suddenly appeared at the top of the stairs.

She secured the last button on a pink silk blouse with one hand as she made long brush strokes through her damp hair with the other. She was curious about her sister, Miriam, since she hadn't heard anything from her in the past couple of days. She'd really been worrying about that girl since she'd gotten hooked up with that so-called pimping nigga 'B.' She hoped that Al wouldn't recognize the afterglow of that hell of a fucking that nigga Don had put on her with his monster dick. *Damn, that motherfucka felt good.* Hell, it was the best dick she'd ever had, period. But right now she had to deal with this old-ass nigga Al and smiled demurely down at him. The tantalizing swell of her hips in a pair of skin-tight jeans caused his anger to subside momentarily with visions of sliding them off. She caught that look in his eyes immediately *This old muthafucka thinks it's all about him—good.*

Al felt his nape stiffen when Don came back through the door with an Addidas saddlebag draped over his shoulder. *Why I can't shake this bad feeling about this nigga?* Al continued feeling strange but he couldn't grasp what the bad vibes meant. He'd have to figure them out later on. He really needed to concentrate on getting this business with these high rollers taken care of.

He waited until Don had slung the bag off his shoulder and leaned it against his leg with the strap dangling across his Timberland boots. He flexed his shoulders with attitude and walked over toward him.

He felt Don looking past him but didn't comment on it and nodded for him to follow him to the game room. Don waited until he started up the steps before he reached down to get the bag. He raised his head and made eye contact with Mona. The lust in her eyes caused him to sigh. Luckily Al's back was to them because even Stevie Wonder would've seen the sexual tension between them.

Mona couldn't and didn't want to control the moisture damp-

ening her thong panties. She gasped silently when her eyes lowered to his monster dick as it expanded inch by pussy-throbbing
inch down his pants leg. Her pussy started convulsing while her
eyes budged every time it throbbed. She pressed her stomach to
handle the urges that were nearly uncontrollable.

She was thankful when Al began to turn around as he reached
for the doorknob. She immediately smiled at him. "Honey, you
want me to hook you up some greens and mashed potatoes to go
with this here chicken?"

Al's antennae bristled along his spine, but he stifled the urge to
grit on them before he turned around. "Whatever, baby. Ah, what
the hell, go ahead and burn a few of those catfish, too."

Don squinted at her and then gritted at Al's departing back as
he disappeared down the stairs. He looked back up at her, licked
his lips and winked as he silently mouthed, "I'm gonna tear that
fine ass up later." He followed Al into the game room.

Mona whistled a heavy sigh of relief and rubbed her pussy. When
the door closed behind them, she headed back for the kitchen.
Before she started preparing the meal, she went into the pantry
and finger-fucked herself to a spasmodic climax with the thought
of Don's gigantic dick digging deep into her gushing pussy.

✠ ✠ ✠

Beverly sighed heavily when the band reported a couple of arrests
as she pulled into her parking spot at the station. Thankfully, none
of her boy's names were mentioned. Of those she heard, she
knew that they were Jamaicans. That group was getting more
and more airplay as the weeks passed.

She grabbed her briefcase off the passenger seat and opened
her door. The first person she saw was RJ, the deputy chief. She

shivered with disgust at the sight of his pompous ass. What was he doing here this time of the day? Normally he worked the second shift, so she automatically became suspicious. There was something awfully strange about dude. He definitely had too much unearned, family-favored political clout as far as she was concerned. Damn silver spoon in his mouth from birth and all that. Luckily he was bent over in his car so he couldn't notice her. She veered the long way around to avoid him, certainly not in the mood to put up with his bullshit.

She slipped into the elevator and her mind drifted to Sparkle. Damn him, the way he kept her heart aflutter. *When am I going to build up the nerve to face him? Is he holding out to see if I'll reach out for him first? We know it's inevitable, so why all the stalling?* Without realizing what she was doing her hand slipped to her crotch. She massaged herself several times before she remembered that there were cameras in the elevator. Her hand froze and she looked around the ceiling trying to locate its location. She made a mental note to check.

The doors split and the first person she saw was Sarah, her secretary and friend. They smiled at one another and she headed for her office, knowing she would soon follow. She pushed her office door open and immediately became aware that her special phone was beeping in its special code to let her know that one of her boys was reaching out to her. She looked over her shoulder. Was anyone watching? She sighed, praying that it wasn't Sparkle. She wasn't ready for him yet. She slid her briefcase on her desk and stared at the phone, wondering if she should answer. *Aw, what the hell.*

✠ ✠ ✠

Kobe Bryant's soaring dunk had the Philips Arena crowd in an uproar when Johnny Bee, the third of the amigos, felt his cell phone vibrating on his hip. He'd always considered himself the flyest dresser of the crew, even when they were hooking junkies and hoes on the Ave back in the day, hoarding their ends to keep Beverly and Yolanda as the top girls in the neighborhood. He was dressed to the tee as usual in a gold silk lounging outfit with a brown felt fedora and matching brown gator shoes.

He was feeling much too dapper to have his lock-a-ho phase of the game disturbed by an unwanted call. He snatched off his designer shades and fumbled for it with his left hand, being that his right arm was pinned to his body by the wailing female he'd brought to the game. He felt an urge to yank her by the neck and scream out her name, but he couldn't recall it to save his life. *What was it? Ah, Mariah, Marisa, damn, it's Marsomething. Damn, aaaah what the fuck. What difference does it make anyhow?* As long as she could fit into his harem of boosters, it really didn't matter what her fucking name was.

Johnny Bee somehow managed to squeeze the phone from between their bodies. It was hard to hone in on the voice on the other end with her yelling to the top of her lungs and using him as a human teddy bear. All that wailing and the deafening sound of the crowd made it nearly impossible. But he did manage to decipher enough of the conversation to cause him to jerk angrily away from her.

The suddenness of his reaction surprised the hell out of her and she leaned away, frowning as he shouted into the phone. Her female curiosity was pushing her to say something, but the words froze on her tongue when she saw the fire blazing in his eyes.

It was like he was an entirely different person from the one she had met in Underground Atlanta when they had gotten caught up in a Michael Vick autograph frenzy at the bottom of the stairs. He'd been so gentlemanly and cordial. And in the weeks since, as he had wined and dined her, she felt herself falling in love with him without even realizing that it was happening. But now as she looked into his angry eyes, it seemed as though she didn't really know him at all. As the deafening roar of the crowd calmed, allowing her to hear her own thoughts, she realized that she didn't really know anything about Johnny Bee. With a mesmerizing jolt, it dawned on her that he had started dominating her time and thoughts as no man had ever done before. A mystery man had swept her off of her feet and now she couldn't figure out what to do about it.

As if he was able to read her thoughts, he quickly reverted back to his captivating mode. After all, he considered himself a practiced technician on matters of a woman's heart. Countless of times over the years of copping-a-ho, locking-a-ho, pimping-a-ho and blowing-a-ho, had certainly given him an honorary degree on the subject.

He put on his hundred-watt-dazzle-a-bitch smile as he measured the inner woman with the baby face features. Unbeknownst to her he was mentally calculating how her natural innocence would fit into the conning schemes that his other girls were at that very moment putting down somewhere in the city. He enjoyed this part of the game the most; the chase, the art of turning a honey out to the street life. So even though the news he'd received was disturbing, he forced it to the back of his mind and tried to concentrate on, damn, he couldn't remember her name. *It'll come to me sooner or later.* He pocketed the phone inside the vest of his brown raw silk suit, leaned over and whispered in her ear, "Yo, baby girl, I hate to tell you this but we've got to spilt."

Disappointment was written all over her face. It wasn't every day she got to wear one of her sexiest outfits to a Hawks game, especially one with her favorite player, Kobe Bryant, in it.

She blinked innocently hoping to change his mind for she was having a ball. But it only took her a few seconds to realize that the game was over, for her anyway. So she let out a heavy sigh, stood up, took his hand and allowed him to lead her along the aisles of screaming fans.

On the way through the Omni parking lot, he eased his car keys into her manicured hands. She looked over at him. She was surprised and disappointed. On one hand, it meant that he trusted her, yet it meant that he was about to depart her company. Even though she was wrapped in mixed emotions, there was a flow of exuberance because no man had ever put that much trust in her, especially giving her the keys to a luxurious, customized Chrysler New Yorker.

He knew the kind of effect it had on her. What she didn't know was that the car didn't really mean a damn thing to him since he'd gotten a crackhead bitch to lease it to straighten out a dope debt. It was something he did on a nearly weekly basis. What she didn't know couldn't hurt her. And it was good food for his massive ego, keeping a bitch locked on a magic carpet ride.

He smiled at her and placed his hand on her shoulder. "Sweetheart, something has come up that I have to handle immediately." She opened her pretty mouth to say something, but he quickly placed a finger on her lips. "Shhhh, just listen and do what I tell you to do, okay?"

She looked into his eyes and nodded shyly. He handed her a sheet of paper and licked his lips before he ran his hand across his mouth. "Go to this apartment in Candler East. A friend of mine named Yolanda is waiting for you. She'll tell you about some things you need to know. If she isn't there just let yourself in and make yourself at home. She'll be there shortly."

"What?"

He ran a hand down his face, then coughed in his fist to clear his throat. "Girl, just do like I ask you, okay? I wish I could tell you what's going on but I can't put that burden on you; you too new to the crew. I've got a lot on my mind right now and none of it concerns you, but I've definitely got to handle it." He kissed her on the forehead and he looked up into the sky impatiently as he waited for her to insert the key.

"I'll call you when I find out what's going on." He smiled and tapped the side of the door before he walked away. She watched stunned as he disappeared among the other cars.

She was wondering what kind of a dude she'd let herself get so emotionally involved with. That same curiosity soon turned into a smile as she pulled onto Houston Street and headed toward I-20 and the Candler East apartments in Decatur. She was excited with the anticipation of the unknown.

Being caught up in her thoughts, she didn't notice the dark sedan as it pulled out behind her, following at a safe distance. Its occupants conversed with each other while one of them took instructions on a cell phone.

'B' was locked in conversation with his boys on his cell as he headed for Five Points to catch the train. "Damn, man, y'all ain't got no idea who done that shit. Well, let's just go over there and brace his ass about it... Y'all on the way over there now. Good, I'm about to get on the train in a minute... Bet, see y'all in a few then. Hey, dog, don't you think you talking a little too much here? You need to go on the chill, for real, yo. Let's finish this up after we all get over there. I don't like talking on these cell phones. Which car is y'all in? In a few, then I'm out."

His thoughts were running wild as he started toward the turn-stiles. He felt a headache coming on and started wishing he'd put some coke in the heart locket draped around his neck. He'd left it behind because he was developing this new girl for the grind and wanted to hide that aspect of his life.

So here he was stuck with this oncoming nasty headache on the rise with no coke to curtail it. Hopefully Rainbow or Sparkle would have some on them.

The MARTA train to the Eastside had just set out when he sat up in the seat. "Man, what's wrong with me?" He took the phone out and punched some numbers. When a husky female voice picked up, he started shouting orders. "Bitch, who there with you? Okay good, meet me at the Krispy Kreme on Lee Street. I need a little something for this headache trying to crush my head. Hell yeah now, I'm almost there myself. Beat me there, bitch."

He clicked off, smiling before he shouted, "What?" to a pair of nosey women sweating him across the aisle. When they immediately diverted their attention, he resumed his relaxed position and muttered under his breath, "Damn, it still feels good to be a muthafucking king."

✠ ✠ ✠

On their way to rendezvous with Johnny Bee, Rainbow stopped to pick up the twins at his rundown apartment complex in Buttermilk Bottom where he used to sell dope. If nothing else, they would serve as a good cover if something unforeseen went down and the police felt like digging at a couple of fly niggas. The twins had proven to come in handy with gunplay in the past; especially Cheryl with her trigger-happy ass. Both she and her identical twin sister, Sherry, were gorgeous and had the heart of lionesses. Talking about spit-image lookalikes; hello to Diana Ross in her heyday. They also had the attitudes of real-life divas, to boot.

Sparkle was happy to be in the company of the twins again.

They'd been influential in getting him re-accustomed to the streets the first week he'd gotten out of the joint. They'd definitely come in handy when they'd introduced him to the many girl dope pushers along the I-20 hotel strip. At the time he'd really thought that their brother, Percy, and JJ, his sister Debra's ex boyfriend and former prison gambling partner, were running things in the dope game. Boy, had that ever proved to be a lot bullshit. Hooking up with the twins had proven to be quite beneficial in other ways as well. Rolling around with them had led to his getting locked in with Violet, his legendary boosting queen and main woman.

As they pulled into the club's parking lot they saw their boy's dark blue Caddie with its gold ragtop glistening under the street lamp. Two of 'B''s favorite boosting hoes, Pinky and Laurie, were sitting on the hood acting as if they didn't have a care in the world. They popped gum and snake-rolled their heads in the snappy, animated way that street hustlers did. Both Rainbow and Sparkle knew they were watch dogging the Caddie to make sure that 'B' wouldn't come out with his carriage setting on bricks. It was definitely that kind of neighborhood.

They had proven in the past that they would come in handy with some guns if it came down to that.

As they pulled into the club, they saw their boy's dark blue caddy with the gold ragtop glistening under the street lamp. Two of B's favorite boosting hoes, Cheryl and Laurie, were sitting on the hood acting as if they didn't have a care in the world. But they knew they were watch dogging the caddie to make sure that he wouldn't come out with his carriage sitting on bricks. It was definitely that type of neighborhood.

They had planned on easing into the club unnoticed, but Cheryl, with her shit-starting ass, had to say something. "What's up, hood rats? I see that B's got y'all stank asses just where y'all belong; playing watchdog."

"Fuck you, slut, ooops I mean sluts," Laurie, a petite sassy-mouthed, black-as-midnight vixen, replied in a voice full of venom.

"Y'all still licking those vanilla and chocolate lollypops for dime rocks?" Cheryl shot back with just as much nastiness.

"Mmmmm-hmmm, and saving the dusty Ziplocs so y'all can get a decent back," Pinky, a juicy-bodied redbone, clad in some shiny silver daisy dukes cuffing her donkey ass that matched the halter top and Hercules strap sandals yelped. She jumped off the hood and coiled up like a viper ready to strike. "Dat's right, bitch, I mean bitches. I said it."

Seeing her sister outnumbered, her twin, Sherry, quickly joined in the fray. "Aw aw, y'all, I smell a catfight. I just know yall funky hoes ain't ready to throw down, for real."

"Oh hell yeah we is, hissssssss." Laurie snarled as she lifted her long designer nails into a pair of deadly claws. They started circling each other, snarling and feinting back and forth.

"Man, why you looking all hype for? Dem silly hoes ain't gonna do nothing but act stupid," Rainbow shouted over his shoulder as he headed into the club.

Sparkle started to follow him when the girls started screaming and shrieking. He expected to see a real throwdown, but those crazy hoes were laughing and dancing.

"I'll be damned," he muttered, shook his head and turned away, mad because he was hoping to see female talons windmilling in large circles. He laughed at the clowning foursome and pushed through the door. As he swung through the Old West-styled swinging doors he was immediately mesmerized by the black and red blinking lights that made the undulations of the scantily clad dancers seem mystically herky jerky. He paused for a brief moment admiring their alluring movements. Won't nothing like a well-endowed honey shaking what her mother gave her. After a moment of lusting at their glistening bodies, he started looking around the club for his boys. He spotted them at the bar in a heated conversation with Bertha.

Now that was one helluva tough honey, that Bertha. Back in the day, when Rainbow was first getting his feet wet in the pimping game, she'd been one of the first real stud streetwalkers that he'd scooped. If the truth were told, which Rainbow would never admit, she was the one who had shown him how to be a real mack man. A big-boned, exotic redbone, Bertha had a squeaky little girl voice that shocked everyone she met.

"I done told y'all poor hustling muthafuckas that I ain't gonna be waiting no hour for y'all to be answering no godayum call," Bertha spat and rolled her eyes.

"And I told your fat ass that I was in a jam on I-20. My batteries ran out and there ain't no phone on the fucking interstate woman," Rainbow lied with a snarl between sips of Heineken beer.

"So whaddafuck you want me to do? The dude was in a hurry shit. Aw fuck you Rainbow I ain't gonna bend over backwards to try to please your yellow ass," she spat back immediately.

He pinched his nose and sniffled with a heartwarming smile. "You used to?"

She bucked her eyes and laughed. "Yeah, nigga, that was when I was young, dumb and full of come. I mean, cum, aw fuck you, man."

He stuck his neck over the bar. "Shiiit, looks like ya still toting enough to hold a whole lot of yo favorite treat." He licked his lips seductively before adding. "Uh, Rainbow pimp juice, uh-huh."

She wrinkled her nose and playfully mushed his face. "You wish." She turned away to pick up a tray of glasses.

He reached over the bar and slapped her big ass. It vibrated like a bowl of Jell-O. "Uh-huh, wish I could rock dat ass til you go to speaking in tongues like you used, too."

She blushed and stuck out her tongue. "Sho nuff, lover boy, as if that giant dick of yours could stay out of all this even if you wanted to." She was smiling seductively as she looked back at her massive butt and made it jiggle.

"Fer sho, jam ain't never shook like dat there." He winked.

The conversation came to an abrupt halt when her attention was drawn to the entrance. The guys' heads snapped in the direction she was staring.

A low moan hummed through the crowded room as all eyes followed the entourage of cops dressed in black riot gear stepping stiff faced towards the bar. Flanked by the half dozen menacing giants was the oriental black widow herself, the dreaded Lt. Woo, terror of the wards Red Dog drug squad. Even the hardest players in the joint turned away from the crazy bitch's cold-hearted gaze, giving her all the respect she expected. The conniving little monster deserved every bit of it too with the way she stretched the rules as dirty and hard as she could.

With her eyes narrowed to nasty little slits she walked straight up to Rainbow and hissed, "What's up, fellas?" in a low birdlike voice.

'B' responded to the unwanted intrusion. "Ain't nothing kicking, Woo, just us plain dudes and chicks enjoying a little drink."

She placed her talonlike fingers on his neck and squeezed. He hunched his shoulders grimacing in discomfort.

"Hold up there, Miss Kung Fu shortie. You can't just come in here harassing my peeps." Bertha snarled, obviously the only in the club willing to stand up to the little bitch.

Woo snorted, pinned her with angry eyes and snarled right back at her. "Whatcha say there, big momma?"

Bertha continued staring defiantly and spread her thick forearms on the bar gritting. "I said don't be bringing your slanty-eyed, wannabe gangster ass in here scaring my peeps; that's what the fuck I said."

Woo leaned on the counter and spit angrily. "And if I don't, then what?"

Bertha's nosed flared fire as she growled. "I'll call downtown and find out why the fuck not, bitch."

Woo smiled impishly and looked over her shoulder at her crew. "Mmh, Bigga mama here must can stand a shakedown." She turned her mouth down and snarled. "I heard that y'all got some underage girls dancing up in here, Miss Smartass. Whatcha gotta say about that?"

Bertha straightened up, folded her arms. "Underage my ass, either you produce some warrants right fucking now, or take these dumb-ass storm troopers of yours and make some tracks up out of here."

Woo casually lifted a Kool cigarette out of a crumbled pack in her arm pocket, took her own good time lighting it up and blew a stream of smoke into Bertha's face. Bertha didn't so much as flinch as she continued her fierce stare.

Woo cocked one eye. "I'm gonna let your big ass slide this time, girlfriend, but you can bet that I'm watching your ass really close from here on out."

Bertha turned her mouth down. "Whatever, get a microscope, bitch, do what you gotta do but do it legally—and right now since your little funky ass ain't legal, you can just ride on up outta here and take your fake-ass muscle heads with you."

Woo smiled slyly, stumped the cigarette out in a freshly cleaned shot glass, spun around angrily and exited with her crew. On the way out those nasty-ass troopers gave menacing stares to anyone who dared to make eye contact.

Rainbow spun around on the stool, leaned his back against the bar. "Whew, what in the hell was that all about, damn?"

Bertha wheezed tight little gasps of air to try to control her temper and began organizing glasses under the counter. She finally took a deep breath. "Aw that evil little bitch just be trying to catch a ho short. She been doing that dumb ass shit there every other week or so just to let a nigga know that she's running things, which I hate to admit but she damn sure is."

Sparkle picked up Rainbow's beer and took a large gulp. "Well, big sexy, all I can say is to keep it tight around this bitch, because I don't think that little monster took too kindly to you shining on her like that." He reached across the bar and lifted her face so he could look her in the eyes. "Especially in front of a crowded room like this and without a doubt in front of her goon squad. Shit, I'd watch myself if I was you, home girl." One could easily see and feel the pride swell up in the former street walker, who had seen it all from A to Z. She raised her head matronly. "And fuck her, too, especially in front of my peeps and her goons," as she defiantly hefted her voluptuous breast and squared her shoulders like a real soldier.

The whole room stood up and saluted her for protecting her turf the way she had. And 'B' threw his two cents' worth in as well. "You the dog, uh dogette shawtie, a bitch of a dog but you definitely the dog, uh doggette."

Rainbow touched her cheeks and nodded towards the other side of the club. "Let's catch a booth so we can kick it, yo."

As they made their way across the room, the rhythm of the club picked back up since there wasn't going to be a shake down. Bertha went back to serving drinks and the dancers got back into their thing.

After they got seated, 'B' addressed Rainbow. "Man, I told ya a couple of months ago that I'd started noticing groups of dreadlocks hanging around yo dope spots, but naw, you wouldn't pay me no mind as usual."

Rainbow massaged the corners of his mouth with his thumb and index finger before he squeezed his bottom lip. He lifted his head. "That's because up until now I've always figured there's enough business out here for anybody who wants a piece of the action, dreads included."

'B' arched a brow and shot back, "Yeah, well, it looks like some people want a lot more than just a piece." He snorted and cleared his throat. "To tell you the truth I was really hoping that y'all had a little more to go on."

Rainbow nodded. "Uh-huh, I feel ya on that, but I be kicking it with the dreads and I don't see them doing no small robberies like that. Matter of fact the way they be ousting niggas outta they spots is to up the quality and quantity. Mmh, that's just what I see."

'B' placed his glass on the bar with a thud. "So whatcha saying, dog, that it's some other bastards? Come clean, nigga."

Rainbow leaned back and stretched his arms along the back of the lounge seat. "What I'm saying is the girls that got took, ain't mentioned no dreads, man."

Sparkle raised his hands and spread his fingers out.

'B' growled, "Yeah, nigga, what? Raising your hand like you need permission to speak or something."

Sparkle shot him a bird., "You ain't acting like you wanna say it but we can't rule this nigga Don out of the picture. Hey, it ain't like he appreciates you dropping boulder rocks around the spots he wants to dominate. And straight up, the nigga don't particularly like that Mercedes was swept from under him like that, know what I'm saying." He gave both of them the evil eye. "Hell, probably ain't the only ho y'all done swiped from that fool either. You just don't know who had some of these hoes y'all be snatching up like bags of candy, yo."

Rainbow frowned and pinched his nose. "Damn, I hadn't even thought about it that way, but shit that's the rules of the game, cop and blow; every player knows that. Come to think of it, some hoes be spilling rumors that he had some bitch iced for talking about his business out in the open. And he has been spitting out some nasty bricks about losing that little Mercedes that he considered a diamond."

Rainbow's cell phone started vibrating on his hip. He raised his shirt to view the blinking light. Sparkle could see that it was Duke's code. *Damn, big boy must've really jetted down the way this time*, he thought. He felt Rainbow hunching his hip and slid over to let him out, wondering why he needed to talk to Duke in private.

Duke, a six-four, 300-pound hunk of street nigga, was the fourth member of their dude gang-turned-bank-robbing crew. They'd found themselves trapped in a big dope scam that had them in a position where they had to get the kingpin's digits or die. After that initial debt-clearing adventure, it became their main source of getting the big dough. After a couple of years of good licks, they'd gotten busted when 'B' had run into a fire hydrant a few blocks from Five Points during their escape. That first mistake had cost them five years in the joint. From that point, Duke had stayed strictly in the dope game. The rest of them had stayed in whatever game had made them the most money. Eventually, it led to each of them doing a couple of more bits apiece; most recently it had been Sparkle's latest venture in the lion's mouth.

While he was gone, they made plans to get their girls together to go on a boosting run through Alabama. "Yeah, dog, you gonna really like this little diamond Mercedes; she's funnier than a mug. She out there right now getting the ropes from Yolanda and Violet," Sparkle said.

'B' sat there wondering why he hadn't been told about or introduced to this Mercedes yet, especially since his main squeeze Yolanda was investing her time in the bitch's development. He frowned. "Whatcha just say?"

Sparkle repeated himself and 'B' frowned some more. "Aw, man, I just sent this new diamond with the prettiest smile a nigga done ever seen that I just scooped over to the crib to hook up with Yo. That's why I'm over here with Laurie and Pinky because I put a little seal on the deal by letting her groove with the Chrysler. How long they been out, man?"

Sparkle pinched his nose. "Couldn't be no more than a hour or so."

'B' started nibbling on his bottom lip as he considered what to do. Then he patted Sparkle on the shoulder. "Looka here, dog, I've got to make a few runs, so y'all keep me up on what y'all wanna do. You know I'm down with whatever way y'all want to handle it."

Sparkle gave him some dap before he left and sat back to wait on Rainbow. He was sure that he'd give him the ups on the Duke thang when he returned. Still he was more than just a little disturbed about all the secrecy.

CHAPTER TWO

The Game Heats Up

Aunt Rose bagged up the sugar babies, chewing gum and Little Debbie cakes for the cutie pie who stayed down the street on Jonesboro Road. When she waved good-bye and disappeared beyond the store window, Rose rushed to the door. She looked in both directions to make sure no one else was coming. She sighed and flipped the "closed" sign around and locked the door.

After turning off the light switch, she went to her small office in the back and closed that door too. She didn't want any late-comers disturbing her. She placed a call to Marietta and let the phone ring six times before hanging up in frustration, refusing to leave another message. *Where in the hell can that bastard be? He knows damn well we have to have those condos furnished before the week's out. Ain't no way he ain't got at least one of those messages I've left over the last few hours. Should've been called a bitch by now. That's what I get for relying on a bitch nigga. No way his ass ain't satisfied with that last package and nephew getting rid of most of it for him. What more could the nigga ask for? He act like he dealing with some old project bitch or something,* she thought grudgingly before dialing the next number.

Bertha's tweedy-bird voice brought a smile to her tension-creased face. "Hello, girl, how's things going? What, that little bitch still pulling those petty-ass stunts? She needs to cut that bullshit out, for real. Fuck her, I wouldn't even let that shit bother me if I was you. She ain't gonna do nothing but scream and holler in front of her squad. All those idle threats ain't about shit. Of course I'm sure of that, otherwise, I wouldn't tell you so. Is my nephew there?... Damn, he should've been back by now. Girl, don't tell me that he's still crying about that little ho. He really need to let that there go, for real, yo. ...Uh-huh, he just might be. Let me try over there then. I'll be through there later on. I'll see you then."

She hung up and called Don's cell number. He picked up right away. "Yo, this be Don, who this?" he said as he put another scoop of coke on the scale before placing it in a baggie.

"It's me, nigga, where the hell have you been?" she said while making neat stacks of the money she'd dumped on her desk earlier.

The tone in her voice made him a little uncomfortable but he had to concentrate on Al, who was zipping another baggie closed before placing it in one of the two large suitcases on the table. He switched the phone to his other hand and rested it between his shoulder and chin. "I been handling my business out here in Lithonia. Why, what's up?"

"So you with that nigga Al right now, huh?"

"Yeah, I be handling that; you know I be on point with my biz, auntie," he said, knowing Al was listening intently to every word.

Rose could tell that he didn't want to talk in Al's presence, so she decided to end the conversation. "Yeah, yeah, I figured that uh-huh, uh, don't worry about it. We'll talk later. I'm getting ready to leave the store in a minute. Is there anything you need me to handle for you before I go home?" She was hoping he'd feel the anxiousness in her voice.

He could feel that something was bugging her. "Naw, I can't think of nothing right off the bat. I shouldn't be here that much longer and then I'm heading for the club. I should be over there in about..." He paused to take a quick peek at his Rolex. "...a little over an hour or so. I tell you what; how about grabbing me some of that beef fried rice from that Chinese joint around the way? Oh yeah, and get them to throw some extra shrimp off in that bitch, too." She didn't respond right away so he started to repeat himself. "Hey, did you hear?"

She was about to tell him she would when she saw a head and a pair of hands pressed against the window. She couldn't see who it was, but whoever it was had to see the "closed" sign on the door. Her angry erupted immediately. "What the fuck?"

Don leaned away from the phone, puzzled. "Damn, auntie, why you cussing at me like that there?" All he could hear was her heavy breathing. "Aunt Rose, what?"

She squatted down, put down the phone, and crept along the floor in a crouch to the counter to get a better look. She peeked over the counter and saw two more figures pressed to the glass. Her nerves and anger were really shaken when she reached up beside the cash register and slid the cigar box off the counter. She swiped several beads of sweat from her forehead with the back of her hand. She reached into the box to get the snub-nosed .38 she always kept there for occasions like this one. She ran her fingers along the cold steel. The hunter in her had taken over. She belly-crawled to the other end of the counter, took a deep breath and sprung up aiming at the window. There was no one there now. She blinked a couple of times, shook her head and pinched between her eyes, wondering if she was tripping or what. She jumped nervously when she heard a car crank up. She immediately went back into the crouch and eased toward the door. When she pulled the closed sign slightly to the side, she saw a dark-colored sedan pulling away from the curb.

The first thing to come to her mind was that some of her dead ex-pimp's enemies from Miami had somehow tracked her down. She put her hand over her mouth measuring the gravity of such a thing happening. She suddenly remembered that she was talking to Don when she had spotted the intruders. She rushed back to the room and heard him yelling in a panicky voice. Wiping the sweat off her face, she picked up the phone. *There's no need to get him all excited, too.* "Damn, baby, I'm sorry, I thought I heard somebody rambling around in the back, but it was just a hungry mutt scavenging in the garbage."

"Whew, damn, woman, you had me ready to kill up a ton of bricks there for a minute. You aight then?" He wheezed a sigh of relief as he watched Al watching him.

"Uh-huh, yeah, I'm aight, those damn mutts. I told you to build a fence in the back. Maybe now you will some damn day. Aw, fuck the weak shit, I'm aight. That's fried rice with beef and shrimp, right?"

"So you heard me then?" He scratched his scalp.

"Yeah, I heard ya. See ya later." She hung up. She was tempted to see if she could find the car those muthafuckas had driven away in but she knew too much time had elapsed. That, along with the busy traffic on Jonesboro Road this time of night, would make it virtually impossible. She finished counting up the day's receipts and put them in the safe.

Don was staring at the phone when Al cleared his throat. "You aight, dude? Didn't look like you was enjoying that conversation too much there." He sniffled and folded his arms across his chest before he laid them across the table.

Don took a deep breath and muttered under his breath. "It taint nothing, dog; just some damn mutt in the garbage that had my auntie bugging for a moment there. She cool now."

"You say she all right then, right?" Al said with a false pretense of concern.

Don nodded. "Yeah, she aight. Come on, let's finish this up so I can get out there where she at. There's no telling what some of these perverts around this city will do to an old broad by herself." He scooped up some more of the coke and slid it on the scale.

"Yeah, let's do that." Al glanced at the clock on the far wall and realized that he had to make that run out to Henry County.

Don was still scooping away when he heard Mona's voice shouting through the door. "Come and get it, y'all." His mind was far away. He couldn't shake the feeling his aunt wasn't telling him everything. He started to scoop a little faster.

Al couldn't help wondering what was really bugging dude. Every since he had talked to him earlier, he felt that something wasn't right. Was it the pressure of the deadline for providing that furniture or was it something else that he couldn't put his finger on? "Be there in a minute, baby," he shouted loud enough for her to hear. He counted out the rest of Don's share of the coke and put it in one of the suitcases. He slid it across the table. "Here, man, this is the rest of your share. I'll finish wrapping up the rest of mine later. I can see that you are anxious to split."

Don nodded as he counted the bags Al was putting in the suitcase. Despite that they'd been dealing with each for a while now, he still didn't fully trust him.

Al spread his arms and gave him a questioning stare. Was he satisfied with the spilt or not? A quick nod from Don indicated that he was. Don picked it up and walked out of the door.

As he was closing the door, Al imagined bullets exploding inside his head. He blinked and tried to shake the thoughts. *Man, what is happening to me? All these murderous ideals running through my mind.* Was he enjoying this killing stuff too much or what?

The sound of Mona calling him again snapped him out of it. Moments later she opened the door frowning with her hands planted sternly on her hips. It was hard to keep from smiling as she stood there in a flowery print apron wrapped around her gorgeous figure. *Damn, maybe I can make a lady out of a whore after all*, he thought as he rose from the table and walked toward her.

"Put that stuff up for me," he grumbled and slapped her ass as he passed through the door.

"You can help me finish bagging it up after we crunch some of this grub. Oh yeah, and don't let me forget to call Cede, aight."

She rolled her eyes at his departing back, harrumphed and walked over to the table to handle the coke. As she was gathering everything, her eyes sparkled at all the money the coke represented. Her mind sparkled as well, on the thought of spreading her wet pussy and cumming all over Don's monster dick again. After handling the dope she joined him in the kitchen.

Al was in a sleepy haze after a night of passionate lovemaking when the phone started ringing. He covered his eyes from the morning dawn sipping through the curtains and picked it up to stop the irritating noise. He gritted at the sleeping Mona, who hadn't so much as fidget. He yawned and grumbled into the receiver. "Yeah, who this be? Damn, man, don'tcha think it's kinda early for this shit here? Okay, okay, godayum, how long will it take you to get over here? Shiiit, that's too soon, my nigga; make it an hour. Yeah, okay, see you then."

He tossed the cover over Mona's inert figure and got up to go to the bathroom. After taking care of his morning hygiene ritual, he came out wrapped in his robe and threw a towel on Mona's head. She moaned, cracked her eyes a bit and rolled her back to him.

"Girl, get your ass up and go make us some groceries," he growled as he pulled the cover from her head and tossed a wad of bills onto her face. She blinked a couple of times, forcing away the sleepy haze, gritted at his departing back and then at the money he had left all over her face and chest. Reluctantly, she sat up and stretched her arms yawning.

He got to the door and turned around and caught sight of her heaving breasts and the blanket sliding down one of her creamy thighs. He started rubbing his dick without even realizing he was doing it. But now wasn't the time to get up in that ass so he shook the sexy image from his mind and continued toward the kitchen to brew himself up a strong pot of coffee.

He was sipping on his fourth cup as he eyed Johnny B slap the wad of bills on the foosball machine in the game room. He was a little concerned about the agitated look on his face but chalked it up as early morning blues or the anxiousness of having to take care of business that early in the morning.

'B' was wondering why Sparkle nor Rainbow hadn't called him since they'd separated the previous night at the club. He'd finally gotten home girl's name right—Mariah—after a night of kicking it with her, Yolanda, Violet, Mercedes and Stacy. They had all gotten blitzed on blunts til dawn. Matter of fact he had made plans to hook back up with them after he'd taken care of his biz with Al. They'd pulled out of the La Quinta Inn in Lithonia with thoughts of getting back together in a couple of hours.

He'd been unsuccessful in catching his boy Duke, so he had to rely on his third connection, Al, whom he really didn't care dealing with because he charged so much more than his other folk. But he was on his dick and had to get shit rolling whichever way he could. So, dealing with Al and the extra ends he had to kick out caused him to have plenty of attitude.

Al could care less what he was going through as he tightened the sash of his silk blue robe and adjusted the glasses on his nose with the back of his thumb. "Do I need to count this, man," he grunted. He lifted the money off of the table.

'B' blinked a few times and sniffled. "Huh, naw, dog, you know that it's all there as usual."

Al eyed him over the rim of his glasses for a moment before he smiled wickedly. "Yeah, I know." He fanned the bills against his ear. Satisfied that dude wouldn't dare play any short money games with him, he nodded toward the bags of cocaine that were wrapped in red plastic Ziploc bags on the pool table. "You wanna try it out or what?"

'B' squinted, pinched and wiggled his nose before he picked up the bags and placed them inside an Adidas tan leather riding bag. "Naw, dog, we good. Besides, I'm over here all the time at your rigged-up poker game. If there's something wrong, I'm sure you'll make it right."

Al folded his big arms across his large chest. "I'd prefer you do it now, dog. It's a new batch of shit and I want to make sure that you are satisfied."

'B' tensed a little because he wasn't used to going through this routine. But to please Al and now himself as well, he scooped a pinch out of the bag, then dabbed it on his tongue before he snorted the remainder of the residue. He licked his lip. "Uh-huh, it's straight as usual, my nig."

Al nodded grimly and turned toward the mini-fridge. He removed a couple of Colt 45 cans, handed him one and took a long gulp himself. He eyed him intently for a few seconds and took another long gulp, then aaahed. "Say, man, a little bird told me that y'all having some problems at some of y'all spots. What's up with that there, dog? Do I need to be concerned about y'all or what?"

'B' cocked an eyebrow, twisted his neck and enjoyed the tingling sensation he received from the small crackling snaps. "Yeah, man, Rainbow was telling me about that last night. He thinks that your boy Black Don had something to do with it."

Al showed no reaction. *Damn, this nigga ain't got any idea I be dealing heavily with Don. Fuck him, might as well let sleeping dogs lie.*

There's no telling what I might have to do to this nigga or his boys, He took a short sip of his brew and rubbed the back of his neck. "Aw, man, that's kinda rough on you, ain't it? You know, with some of y'all hoes dancing off in his joint over there on Lee Street and all."

He considered drawing some of the attention off of Don but what the fuck; folk had to deal with their own problems. If those problems started to involve him, then he'd react accordingly. On the other hand, he didn't need any interference with his cocaine pipeline, which Don was a major part of. Especially now that the other deal was so close to being a reality.

'B' could sense that something was on his mind. He sighed heavily. "Yeah, uh-huh, it's rough, but why you say it like that?" His forehead was deeply wrinkled with curiosity.

Al ignored his expression and went to sit on one of the colorful bean bags scattered around the room and spread his legs wide apart. Once he got comfortable, he gave 'B' a "damn-you-actually-don't know look."

'B' hunched his shoulders. "Whatcha on it like that for, man? You got something to say, say it. Come on, dog, spit that shit out."

Al started rocking in the seat, crossed his arms and legs before he took a deep breath. "Man, ain't no need to be playing with ya, so I'm gonna give it to ya straight. You really mean to tell me that you didn't know that your little cousin Joker was hustling for that nigga Don?" *There, I let that shit out; now his ass has got to deal with it.*

He felt he'd said too much immediately and decided to leave him wondering. He didn't like getting in the middle of family but he'd already let the cat out the bag. So fuck it; let him deal with it whichever way he preferred. As he was about to step out of the room he glanced over his shoulder. "Hey, dog, let yourself."

'B' met him at the door, blocking his exit and ran a hand over his throat. "I uh, uh, didn't know nothing about that there, dog. Are you sure about that, playa?"

Al got pissed and growled. "Hell yeah, I'm sure, bro. Whatcha think, I'm some kinda joke or something? Joker's the one that scores; ah fuck, my bad. Whewwww, Joker's the one that goes to Miami and escorts the bitches back with the blow."

'B' leaned back against the door eyeing him suspiciously. He wondered why Al was revealing something like this to him. The thought of the cross or the double cross, or hell even the triple, crossed his mind. He noticed a sparkle in Al's eyes. It dawned on him that this devious, calculating, extra suave bastard was playing all the angles to his advantage. Regardless of how things turned out, this muthafucka would still win. That all-knowing gleam in his eyes told 'B' all he needed to know.

After a brief stare down, he patted Al on the shoulder. "You know what, partner; when it comes down to it, it's not really good to underestimate no one."

Al smiled. "Uh-huh, I know, but I don't think you'll let any nigga lead you astray. I know I ain't." He leaned back and wiped his mouth before continuing. "See you in the aftermath." 'B' walked back across the room in his pigeon-toed style and opened the door to the garage. He turned around with a crooked smile. "Yeah, in the aftermath, playa." He closed the door, walked to his ride and jumped behind the wheel of his New Yorker. He pulled out of the driveway and headed downtown.

✠ ✠ ✠

Beverly was feeling a little guilty when she turned onto the street the led to her nana's house. She couldn't shake the thoughts of hooking up with Sparkle out of her mind. She had to admit that she was more than just a little scared of that confrontation. Would he be the sweet gentle guy she'd know most of her life or would doing all that time have caused a bitterness in his heart that even she couldn't penetrate? Would she be able to convince him to give up the hustling life? Further still, would she be able to protect him and his boys forever? Sooner or later some pumped adversary was bound to dig into her past and reveal things she couldn't afford to let out. Skeletons in her closet, oh my.

She passed Mrs. Dobbs' yellow house and felt bad for not dropping by to visit the only woman other than her beloved nana that guided her along the right path during puberty. In the back of her mind she also wasn't ready for the possibility that Rainbow would be there. It would only add to the frustrating lust she felt for Sparkle.

She parked in front of the red brick house and got out of the car. She looked up and down the street reminiscing about all the good times she'd had chasing behind her three amigos, knowing that whenever she was around them, a new adventure was about to unfold. They were always into something or the other. Those niggas were crazy as all out but a good time was guaranteed nearly every time she hung out with them.

She started up the steps and froze when her eyes met those of her nana standing at the screen door. Her heart fluttered as it always had at the Lena Horne look-alike, when Christine Johnson flashed those pearlie whites on her. The eighty-two-year-old woman still had her original teeth and nary a wrinkle nor age spot on her still beautiful face. She was wringing her hands with a dishrag.

"CJ," as all the few friends still alive called her, pushed the door open and held her arms out wide to embrace her one and only grandchild. It was an embrace with a warmth that only two women who'd seen it all could feel.

"CJ," teary-eyed, held Bevy at arm's length. "Child, why are you so troubled? I can feel your anguish in my heart."

Beverly blinked and narrowed her eyes, amazed at how this woman could always sense what she was feeling without a word being passed between them. She took a deep breath, looked into those teary eyes, eyes that were identical to her own. "Mama, my boys are in trouble again and my hands are tied. I can't help them."

"CJ" grabbed her granddaughter's wrist and led her to the flowery print sofa. She grasped her shoulders to ease her down as they sat beside each other.

With a honey-coated voice that transcended all the years of Beverly's life, she said, "Girl, we both know that I ain't got that many years left on this earth. In all of my wildest dreams, all I want to see is for you to be happy above everything else. And you know something?"

Beverly blinked. "What?"

"Girl, I can see in your eyes that that boy Larry done come back into your life, ain't he?"

Beverly blinked again. *How could she possibly know that?*

"Let me finish, girl, before you go to looking all crazy and stuff. You my baby; I always know when something's bothering you. Wrong with ya, whatever. Shocking, huh! Shouldn't be. I've been feeling your woes since you was a little bitty thing, girl."

All Beverly could do was shake her head and sigh. She had to say something. "You know what, nana? I've neva been able to figure out how you do this but you hit it straight on the head. Larry, we all call him Sparkle now, has just gotten out of prison."

"Uh-huh," she moaned. "And?"

Beverly sat back and wiped her brow. "And I don't know what to do about it."

"Girl, that police chief thang got you all confused, ain't it?"

"Yes, ma'am."

"CJ" looked at her under-eyed and sniffled. She started rubbing the back of her ear and cranked her neck from side to side, smiling when the crackling sensation eased some of the tension. "Let me tell ya something. Hmm, let me see how I should put this. Oh yeah, I ain't about to tell you not to serve and protect the folk in Atlanta. Heck, this my home, too. But I am gonna tell you not to turn against the people that luv ya, that has always luvved ya. And I ain't neva told you this here before, but those boys are the reason you wearing that badge you so proud of. Ain't a doubt in my mind that either one of them would gladly give up their life for you, sweetie." Her eyes were sparkling.

Beverly leaned back and rolled her neck along the back of the couch. She knew her nana was right. Her boys would always be there for her. The question was, would she always be there for them? Deep in her heart she knew that she would under just about any circumstance. But would her dedication to her job prevent her from doing so if her back was against the wall. After all these years she'd never been confronted with that possibility, for all the things she'd done in the past was kept very secretive. Nobody knew but her and them.

"Come on, girl, snap out of it. You want some tea, soda or something?"

Beverly sat up and pressed imaginary wrinkles out of her skirt. "Sure, ma, you want some, too? I'll get it. No need for you to get up."

"Girl, please, I ain't crippled yet. Which do you want?" She stood up and headed for the fridge.

Beverly smiled at her enthusiasm to please. She leaned back considering her options.

Some thirty minutes later she was kissing her beloved nana on her rosy cheeks as they held each other in a loving embrace. She left and headed for her office downtown.

She was speeding down Peachtree at Five Points when she saw her childhood buddy Yolanda coming up the stairs from Underground Atlanta. Her closest friend was draped in her boosting gear. She shook her head at the outrageous getup and circled the block. When she swung back onto Peachtree, Yolanda was resting on the bench in front of the bus stop. She pulled to the curb and leaned out the window smiling. "Yo, what's up, girl?"

Yolanda's head jerked toward the familiar voice. She bowed her head when she recognized her girl. "What the hell it be, Bevy? Ain't seen yo ass in ages."

Beverly sucked on her teeth, then smacked her lips. "Girl, please, it ain't been but three weeks. Come on, get in. Where you headed?"

Yolanda waddled to the passenger side and eased into the car. Before she settled in the seat her head spun around in all directions, eyeing everything. She smiled. "Bitch, you sure you want to be seen with me in this shape?" She started rubbing her stomach.

"What the hell? For all anybody knows I could be taking yo ass to jail."

Yolanda harummphed. "Uh-huh, in the front seat?"

Beverly ran her eyes up and down her body and added, "Yeah, in the front seat."

Yolanda hunched her shoulders, coughed into her fist. "Okay, bad-ass police chief, you the one that's got to stay on point. Hell, drive on, sista girl."

"Again, where yo sneaky ass headed with all your goodies?"

Yolanda burst out laughing. "You a mess, girl. Damn shame the fucking police chief giving a fucking thief a ride to her dump. Hmmph, aw, what the hell, to the Montre's on Lee Street."

"Okay, strap in, girl; we got to obey the law."

"So why yo ass ain't strapped in then?"

Beverly batted her eyelashes shyly. "Girl, don't you see this shiny metal here? I'm the chief of police, that's why. But buckle yours just the same."

"Okay, okayeee, damn, still got to always call all the shots, don'tcha?"

"Yep, no doubt. And by the way, what's that nigga of yours been up to lately?"

"Hold up there, girl. Are we kicking sista girl shit or are you in cop mode?"

"Bitch, when have I ever been in cop mode with you, with y'all? Hell, if that was the case, yo ass would be in handcuffs beating against that glass back there calling me everything but the child of God and you know it."

Yolanda stretched her mouth down and scratched the side of her nose before she peeked at her shyly. "Okay, my bad. That black-ass nigga's still being "B." Hell, you know how that goes."

"Yeah, I do. I definitely know how that goes. Shit, his old ass need to really consider giving up that pimping shit." She burst out laughing. "Hell, he probably got to pop a lot of that Viagra shit just to get his old nasty-ass dick up."

Yolanda rolled her eyes and coughed. "Hey, girlfriend, believe this. His black muthafucking ass don't need no Viagra, Cialis or any of that stuff; old wrinkled-up hands and all."

"For real, girl?"

"For real." Yolanda whistled and stared out the window for a while before she ran her finger under her nose. "Okay, ho, why you ducking Sparkle? I know you know he been out the joint for a couple of weeks now."

Beverly stopped at the red light and pinched the bridge of her nose. "Shit, Yo, that nigga knows how to contact me and he ain't."

"And... so what's that got to do with you reaching out to him? You know how these niggas are with their pride and everything."

By then they had pulled in front of the club. Beverly sighed heavily and knuckled the corner of her eye. "To tell you the truth, Yo, I'm scared to death."

"Ain't had no dick in a while, huh?"

Beverly laughed. "Girl, you crazy."

"Well, have you or not? Bitch, you know that nigga got yo number. Hell, go get that nut off, girl. You know you want to."

"You right; now get yo thieving ass out of my car."

Yolanda punched her playfully on the shoulder and stepped out. When she pushed through the door, Beverly got a glimpse of Sparkle standing in the hallway with Rainbow. She saw Yolanda turning back to her. She sped off. She wasn't ready to face him yet.

She motored down DeKalb Avenue to her office. She parked in the underground space designated for her, folded her arms across the steering wheel and laid her head between them. She waited for her heart to stop thumping. Wow! Seeing him for that short span had turned her into jelly.

"Hey there, boss, why you all slumped over like that? Somebody die on you or something?" her secretary, Sarah, shouted through the window.

Beverly jerked erect, ran her hand down her face and her opened mouth before she blinked a couple of times. "Oh, hey, girl, just tired; that's all." She reared back on the seat. "What the fuck, Sarah, you take all that stuff home with you or something?" She frowned at the bundle of folders pressed against her chest.

Sarah's eyes bucked and she shook her head from side to side á la "Ugly Betty." "Got to keep you informed, sister girl. Got to keep you informed."

Beverly scratched behind her ear and smiled before she gathered her briefcase and kneed the door open. "Come on, girl, let's go get informed then. The whole city awaits." Side by side they headed for the elevator.

From the lower end of the parking lot, "RJ" grimaced as he watched the women gleefully prancing along. *Damn bitches holding me back from my rightful position in this damn city. Both of them bitches have to be doing something wrong. I can feel it in my bones. Just got to dig a little deeper to get something, anything on her. But fuck that for now. I need to get on that black bastard Al's ass to get that furniture so I can start opening these condos. Sumbitch always got an excuse. Got to put more pressure on his black ass. Maybe I should shake down his gambling hole. That'll stir into action for sure. Let him know I ain't playing games with him,* he thought angrily before he mumbled, "Damn, I can't do that. Oh yeah, I got it, I'll just shake that bitch of his up. She owes me, too."

The sight of that worrisome bitch Woo getting out of her car cracked his attention. She was steadily becoming a thorn in his side. A roadblock, a worthy adversary, he had to admit. She needed closer scrutiny. He would watch her. He wasn't about to let any of these bitches stand in his way. Steppingstones are what they were. One day he would be the mayor and then the governor and then...

❧ ❧ ❧

Mona put her small fist to her mouth for the fifth or sixth time stifling yawns in her still sleepy haze as she pushed the shopping cart down the aisles. *The nerve of that bastard to send a bitch to a fucking supermarket this early in the morning,* she thought as she sorted through the different varieties of meat. The gravelly voice that whispered in her ear brought back memories that she certainly could've done without. She closed her eyes, took a deep breath and turned to face RJ.

"Come on, sweetie, surely you haven't forgotten about me that quick. After all you'd probably still be in Fulton County Jail or worst if it wasn't for me, so could I get at least a fake smile or something?" He squeezed her ass and smiled at her flinching shoulders.

She shook off the icky feeling of his presence and mumbled, "No, I haven't forgotten you, RJ. How could I and even if I wanted to you, wouldn't let me, now would you?" She gnashed her teeth in a nasty snarl and rolled her eyes at him.

He pantomimed a shiver at the chill exuding from her eyes and his fake smile quickly flipped into an evil sneer as he spat, "Looka here, girlie, I ain't got time for your games so tell your boy to get that furniture for me like yesterday. Why his ass dragging me on this anyway?"

She couldn't respond immediately. She didn't have a clue what he was talking about, so she decided to play on his male ego. "Hey, man, I'm not even supposed to know about whatever the hell you talking about, all right?"

He leaned away as he considered if she was telling the truth. His eyes lowered to the floor and shifted back and forth trying to digest the probability of Al keeping a bitch that fine out of his biz to that extent.

Mona took his silence to mean that he was stumped. The bastard she'd spread her legs enough for him to let that little favor ride. But he had the nerve to step up to her with this shit anyhow. *Okay, muthafucka, you want to play a bitch out like this here.* She decided to dig into his ribs a little bit for the hell of it. "So, how do your majesty suggest I go about trying to get him to do whatever it is you want me to? Think about it for a second before you answer now. How do I get that stubborn-ass nigga to do something I don't even suppose to know about?"

She definitely had a point, but the pressure to get that furniture in those condos was causing his patience to run really thin. BJ wasn't about to admit he was as stumped as she was on how to go about it. Still it had to get done.

Hell, running the boo on this bitch is the only option I have left, he thought and decided to rely on some scare tactics. Make the bitch earn her new lease on the good life she was living. And bust her brain on how to deal with it. He didn't care what she had to do to outwit and avoid the wrath of Al about her getting into his business; that was her problem. All he wanted was the furniture, period.

With the thrill of her confusing dilemma warming his thoughts, he reached over and put a grip on the nerve of her shoulder blade and applied pressure, simply for the hell of it. He waited until she squinted from the pain before he snarled, "Jail bird-ass bitch, I don't give a damn how you get it done, or what your stinking ass has to do to get it done, just get it muthafucking done."

She opened her mouth to say something, but he applied more pressure. She tried to lean away from him, which only caused him to squeeze even harder and to lean in a little closer. Now she felt the spit flying out of his mouth to sprinkle the side of her face as fear started to compete with the pain.

The combination of vodka, garlic breath and cigarette smoke almost made her gag. She probably would've if the pain he was administering wasn't so unbearable. Her eyes actually started to water from the stench and pain when he growled into her ear, "Now, bitch, you've got two choices and I don't really give a flying fuck which one you choose because I'll end up busting a nut on either one of them."

Her forehead knitted in a knot with confusion and hatred.

He didn't give a fuck how she felt. He took his time to look around to make sure that no one was paying them attention before he spat, "One, I take your sorry, whoring ass back to jail right now; or two, I somehow slip up and let Al know that you've been spying on him from day one. Or your stanking ass come up with a way to get what I want done. Oh yeah, and don't forget that I still got ways to get with your baby sister if you give me any signs of bucking; you feel me, bitch. It's your choice, sweetie."

As suddenly as he had appeared, his conniving ass disappeared, strolling down the aisle and out of the door like he owned the motherfucking world. Mona bent over the cart until the tears stopped flowing and the pain subsided enough for her to stop grinding her teeth. Looking through the large plate glass window, she saw him get in his car and pull out of the lot. *Whew.*

To her relief the dirty low-life bastard was gone. In his place stood the butcher, who was eyeing her with a worried look etched on his face. "Are you aight, ma'am?"

She wiped the tears off her cheeks and said in a whiny voice, "Yes, yes, I'm okay, I was just having some cramps." Forcing a high-cheeked smile, she placed a hand on her stomach and pushed the cart down the aisle. She made sure to go to the farthest counter to get the best view of the entire parking lot, trying to spot him. Like a ghost he was gone. She took a deep breath and bowed her head into her hands and mumbled to herself, "What the hell do I do now?"

Her immediate thoughts were to get the hell out of town, but she didn't have enough money to do that. Plus, she couldn't leave her sister in all this bullshit. Then she thought about stealing Al's drugs and money, which brought a wicked smile to her face. That is until it dawned on her that she didn't know exactly where he kept his stash.

Mona's eyes brightened when she thought of his secret room. *That's probably where he's got a safe and everything.* But that idea quickly dissolved because she didn't know how to get down there. And even if she did, she wouldn't know where to look. Hell, she still didn't know how to get in it.

Even if she was able to accomplish those entirely impossible tasks, she still couldn't leave her sister at the mercy of that crazy-ass RJ or Al and all the different hoodlums he had working for him.

She had to come up with something, but what? Gradually a plan started to formulate in her mind. The more she thought about it, the brighter the smile spread across on her face. She spent the rest of her time browsing around the store half thinking of the groceries she had to buy and half plotting on the scheme running through her brain. One way or the other it was definitely on, for sho.

CHAPTER THREE

A Hustler's Dilemma

Al's car was gone when she returned. Mona wondered how long he'd be away as she placed the groceries in the pantry and ran up the stairs to start her search in the bedroom. After a disappointing half hour, she was about to give up when she thought of the game room. There had to be something there that would give her access to the secret room under the house. The thought of getting her hands on all that money and drugs had her pumped. Rejuvenated, she raced around the room for any clue she could find. Her burst of energy deflated quickly when she realized she didn't have any idea what she was looking for.

She was about to give up when she recalled the time she had accidently run up on the pool table sliding along the floor. Why hadn't she thought of it first? It had to be the pressure for the secret had to be there somewhere. She got on her knees and ran her hands along the bottom and then all along the edges. There had to be a lever, a button, a secret compartment.

Finally, her hand felt something. What could it be? Was it what she was hoping to find? Feeling close to the prize she got a warm feeling all over. Her skin suddenly started to crawl when she heard a car running over the gravel in the driveway. She couldn't get caught searching the room. From the car door slamming and rapidly advancing footsteps, she knew she didn't have enough time to get out.

Oh shit, what the fuck do I do now? she thought as nervous sweat started rolling down her armpits. Her heart thumped double-time when she heard the key being inserted in the lock. She dove under the table just before the door cracked open. Immediately, she realized she might've made a mistake with the probability that the secret room would be the first place he came.

On the other hand, he'd be showing her how to get there. Her hands started trembling when the mixture of anxiety and fear started overwhelming her. She pressed them between her thighs and prayed he'd check other parts of the house to make sure he was alone first. Not so, because no sooner had the words formulated in her mind, the door swung open and he headed her way.

She balled up in a fetal position, clenching her teeth tight to keep from screaming out. Her eyes bucked wide open with fear as she followed his long strides around the room, praying he'd go into the house. Her spirits were lifted when he started toward the steps that led into the living room. She was prepared to make a sprint for the garage door as soon as he disappeared.

Opening the door, Al called out her name once, twice, three times before he grumbled, "Damn, that bitch must be buying up the whole godayum store."

She got on her hands and knees, ready to get the hell out of there. Her breath caught in her chest when he turned away from the door and started back across the room. She sighed when he headed toward the jukebox. Her eyes brightened when she thought he was going to start some music. It would be a sure cover-up for any noise she might make to relieve her uncomfortable position. Suddenly, her heart began to thump again when the floor started vibrating under her. That same whirling sound she'd heard earlier, now sounded like a bomb going off in her ear. She covered her mouth with both hands to cover the scream she felt boiling up from her stomach. A scream that was sure to explode once he discovered her under the table. His knees started bending when his cell phone started ringing. He immediately walked back over to the wall and did something to stop the whirling just when the table had started to move.

She nearly fainted when he answered it. "Yeah, this be me; whatzup, dog? Damn, CeeDee, I was really expecting to have heard from you by now. Uh, so when you gonna be able to handle that thing for me? Shit, dog folk be pushing my buttons so that means that I got to push yours. You need two of those things, man. I sure hope your digits straight because I'm in a little bit of a bind myself. Okay, that's good, it ain't no problem then, no problem at all. Where you at or better still, how soon can you get over here?"

She balled her fist against her mouth. *Damn, I'm really stuck, for sho now.* This was where he conducted most of his dope biz.

"Tell you what, soldier, I need to get out of this house for a minute anyway. Where you say you at? The one near Wesley Chapel? Which room? Okay, I'll see ya in about twenty minutes or so. Hey, hold up a minute. Please tell me you got one of those sluts with some super head with you... Yeah, that's right, I need to release some fucking tension. Yeah, that'll work, in a few then. Bet, holla."

Whew. Mona almost pissed herself, when Al clicked off and walked over to the pool table and bent his knees like he was going to look underneath it this time. She couldn't control the tears rolling down her face. She sniffled, took a deep breath, shut her eyes tight and braced for the stomping she knew was sure to come.

She heard a panel being slid back into place and the soft sound of plastic being moved around. She opened her eyes. His legs were so close that she could see a distorted image of herself in the tip of his shoe. She felt that if she had breathed, he would've felt the air ruffling his pants. All he had to do was look under the table a few inches and he'd spot her.

Mona's eyes began rolling frantically when she heard the panel close. She lowered her head in relief. Then she felt something crawling on her ankle. Panicking, she looked down in time to see a large hairy spider go up her pants leg. Her worst phobia by far.

His feet started away. She buried her head and bit into the shag rug to keep from screaming. Her heart was thumping so hard it seemed like it was bumping into the carpet.

Al finally left the room and she gritted her teeth until she heard the car pull out of the driveway. She scrambled from under the table beating her pants leg like a madwoman, crying and screaming until the spider fell out motionless. She stomped it about ten times until she saw only a few smidgens of it in the rug. Shaken beyond her wildest nightmare, she braced her back against the pool table and rocked back and forth for several moments before she was able to stop trembling.

She took a deep breath, shivered one last time from the thought of that creepy, crawly, icky monster running up her skin and started to refocus on how she was going to get out of her predicament. She remembered him going by the jukebox to cause the pool table to move.

Shaking off the effect of her narrow escape, she stood straight up, ran over to the jukebox and ran her hands along the wall behind it. Her fingers felt a button and she pushed it. Her heart skipped a beat when the whirling sound filled the room. Her head snapped back to the pool table expecting it to be moving. It wasn't. *Damn, what now?* She removed her hand from the button and she felt a crack in the wall.

She tried to push the jukebox away from the wall but it was much too heavy for her to even budge. Still she had to give it everything she had and after a couple of grunted efforts, she felt it give way enough to reveal a hidden panel. *Jackpot*. She got light-headed with anticipation. Quickly pulling it open, her heart skipped another beat when she saw the wall safe he had left open in his haste to leave.

With her fingers trembling, she reached inside. Her heart deflated when she pulled out only four bags. She knew they only contained a half-ounce apiece from when she had helped him bag them earlier. There had to be more than that. She spotted a black metal box, which had to contain loads of money. Her heart deflated again when she realized there was another huge problem. It had a digital lock on it. She had no idea what the combination could be. She'd have to take it and figure a way to bust it open later.

Out of the corner of her eye, she saw a red light blinking from the bottom of the pool table. Now that she knew where the money was, she'd be able to snatch it up on her way out. She'd have to pack all of her stuff because there was no way she'd be able to return.

"Damn, when his ass coming back?" she muttered. For a brief second she stared at the floor lost in her thoughts before remembering the blinking light. She quickly crossed the floor and bent over to check out it out. It was only a blinking light. There had to be more to it so she ran her hand along the bottom of the table. Bingo, the shiny wood slid in. It was right under the glass enclosure that held the balls. Reaching her hand inside, she felt several cool bags of plastic. Her eyes brightened because she'd found bricks of kilos of dope. A meager two ounces would have been nowhere near enough to support her and her sister. And that small money box couldn't be his only loot, either. Hell, she might as well go for the whole enchilada. There had to be some big thousands stashed somewhere else.

Slowly the low whirling sound came back to her consciousness and she remembered the room under the floor. That's where the big stash had to be. She stood up and rushed back over to the jukebox. There it was; another button beside the first one she had pressed. Without a moment's hesitation, she pushed it and the whirling sound turned into a slightly louder humming. Her head snapped back to the pool table as it started to slide along the floor.

She got so happy that she dashed to the opening. She pulled up short when she could only see as far as the first couple of steps down. Even though she was scared to death of the consequences of being discovered, she had come too far to turn back. She slowly eased down the stairs, step by gingerly step.

Her heart nearly jumped out of her chest when the light suddenly flicked on when her foot hit the floor. She momentarily went blind from the sudden glare and stumbled back on the stairs. She arched her back from the pain of thudding her ass against the metal steps. She looked around wildly for a second or two and blinked at the three monitors stationed on the wall.

This sneaky bastard's been spying on everything. She looked at the two chairs in front of the screens. A flurry of butterflies fluttered in her stomach as she thought about what the monitors might contain. Her curiosity got the better of her as she sat down and began fidgeting with the roll of buttons on the arm.

Mona let out an involuntary shriek when the screens came to life, showing the various rooms in the house. Using a trial by error method, she figured out how to rewind the middle monitor, stopping at the scene of her little act with Stacy. She sped the film up until she saw she and Don facing each other. She sat there stunned as Don stood up and pulled out his horse dick and slowly started grinding it into her waiting mouth. She was so mesmerized that she didn't even remember sliding her hands into her pants. By the time that she got to the part where he was sliding all that dick to the edge of her pussy—doggy style and slowly, ever so slowly pushing it all into her trembling body—she was moaning through a nut.

Mona was actually reliving the feeling of all that monster male meat all the way up in her stomach. By the time the picture switched to Al and Don talking, she was sweating profusely. She pulled her sticky hand out of her pants. Her mouth flew wide open. She could not believe how much cum was all over her hand. She scooted back in the chair and looked down. The chair was glistening with her slippery juices. She grabbed the waist of her lacy panties and pulled them away from her sticky hairs. There was a puddle of woman cum saturating her crotch. She shivered at the sight of all that cum and the image of that horse dick sliding between her bouncy-ass cheeks.

She wiped her hand down her sweaty face, flinched at the odor of her heated pussy before she gathered her senses and looked at the clock above the monitors. Damn, she had been down there way too long. She had to get out of there before he came back. Looking down at the buttons, she couldn't figure out how to erase the film. Breathing heavily through her nose, she got up and got some tissue from the Kleenex box on the counter under the monitors, wiped the juices out of her crotch and then off of the chair.

She rewound the tape back to where she thought she had turned it on. She started back up the stairs knowing she had to get out of the house as soon as possible. There was no telling whether he had seen the scene. Or whether he'd it set up to witness her doing what she was doing.

She was halfway up the stairs when she looked back down and noticed a piece of paper laying beside the chair in which she'd been sitting. She didn't know if she had left it there. She hurried back down to get it. It had CeeDee's name, address and phone number on it. She sprinted back up the stairs. Rushing over to the jukebox, she quickly pressed the button, pushed it back against the wall and sprinted up the next flight of stairs to pack her clothes. She stepped to the closet and bent down to pick up her suitcase and froze. Slowly, she looked over her shoulder into Al's smiling face as he stepped out of the bathroom. Her heart sank into her stomach.

✠ ✠ ✠

Sparkle turned away from Rainbow in time to see Yolanda's head swerving back and forth. She had a look in her eyes that made him feel uncomfortable. He grabbed her by the elbow. "Damn, Yo, why you looking all fucked up? You act like you done seen a ghost or something."

He looked over her shoulder and saw the tail end of a car pulling away from the curb as the door was closing behind her. His intuition told him that something was amiss. He couldn't put his finger on it though.

Yolanda, being the strong woman that she was, couldn't understand why Beverly was so afraid to see Sparkle. *Damn, my girl is really messed up about seeing dude*, she thought as she turned to face him. "Hey, man, a bitch can't be feeling all fucked up with woman problems or something?"

She wasn't about to tell him that it was Beverly who had sped off. She'd let her deal with their situation when she felt up to it. After all, that's what friends were for.

Sparkle frowned and hunched his shoulders. *Woman.* He turned to Rainbow. "Yo, dog, why we hanging around this hole for anyways? Things be popping against us from every which way. We need to get out this bitch and find out who do all this fucked-up shit to you, to us."

Rainbow turned his mouth down as he frowned in concentration for a few seconds. "Yeah, dog, you right, let's roll."

They pushed past Yolanda without muttering a word.

She grunted, "Well, I'll be damned."

Rainbow sneered over his shoulder on the way out the door. "Hell, you'll be whatever, bitch." He slammed the door behind him, not giving her a chance to respond. They jumped in his car and sped down DeKalb Avenue. Things had to be answered. Somebody was gonna supply those answers.

Several hours later, they were leaving Princess's room at the Motel 6 when his cell phone buzzed at his side. Rainbow looked down at the blinking light and then at his boy. "Damn, man, that's Duke right there. I wonder what took him so long to call?"

"Hell, I don't know, man; whatcha gonna do, answer it or what?"

Rainbow debated for a moment and finally, he pressed the button. "Yeah, big fella, what's up? When? Where? Well, we're heading that way now. Okay, see ya in a few then." He hung up and stared out of the window.

Sparkle let him drive aimlessly for awhile before he spoke. "Okay, nigga, what he have to say?"

Rainbow didn't take his eyes off of the road as he continued to drive in silence. Finally, he pinched his nose. "Wants us to meet him at the Lounge, dog. For some fucked-up reason, he didn't want to talk about it over the phone. Shit don't sound too kosher to me; ya feel me, partner?"

Sparkle, knowing that they were in the middle of re-upping his crew, merely nodded. "So whatcha gonna do about Clara and Sissy?"

"Whatcha mean?" Rainbow replied, hunching his shoulders.

Sparkle ran his tongue across his lips. "I mean they just got robbed, my nigga. And beat up on top of that. You gonna leave them dealing in the same hole, partner?"

Stuck in his icy-chilled pimping role, he replied in a frosty tone, "Why the hell not? Them bitches are used to the rough shit that goes with this turf. Besides, that's where their customers come to score. Shit, partner, this ain't the first time some of my whores done got their asses kicked, know what I'm saying. Shit, that's why I allow them to stay in the clique. The hoes got heart, dog; the hoes got heart."

Knowing his boy's coldhearted attitude toward hoes that had fallen into his love trap, Sparkle hunched his shoulders, laid his head back on the rest and remained silent for the rest of the ride.

Duke's ride was nowhere to be seen when they pulled into the club's parking lot. But they did see three girls raising holy hell in 'B''s New Yorker. Sparkle leaned toward Rainbow's side of the car. "Man, who are those loud-ass hoes making all that racket in our boy's ride?"

Rainbow shook a cigarette out of the pack on the dashboard and lit it up before he answered through a haze of blue smoke and between long drags. "Bro, them bitches is Yolanda's sisters; your girl Violet's crazy-ass nieces."

Sparkle leaned back in the seat and folded his arms across his chest. "Man, you mean you telling me that Violet's got some crazy-ass nieces to boot? Come to think of it, that little red one, the one that looks like that honey Dawn Robinson who sings with En Vogue, was with her that night I met her at Dee's the day I got out. Uh-huh, that saucy little thing has got one jazzy-ass mouth, dog."

Rainbow tilted his head to the side. "Hmmphed, my nigga, all them hoes there has a jazzy-ass mouth. Shit must be deep in the genes or something, especially that dark-skinned one. Man, oh man, that bitch Nita Bug, my nigga, that ho there's got the nastiest mouth I've ever heard on a bitch. And you know that I done known my share of bitches, partner."

Sparkle turned his head back toward the arguing trio. "Damn, that ho must be really foul, for sure then."

"She is dog, she certainly is."

The girls walked away from the car and headed toward the club's entrance ahead of them, still raising holy hell.

As soon as they walked through the door, they spotted 'B' in a conversation with Big Bertha, Junior, Laurie and Pinkie. The three sisters strode right up to his table still spitting some dumb female nonsense.

'B' must've been into some serious kicking it because no sooner had they reached him, he gritted on them and slammed the beer mug on the table to get their attention. "What the fuck y'all hoes think this is? Bringing y'all asses to my table with all that clucking bullshit up in my ear like I need to hear that shit, for real."

The two redbones shut up, but Nita Bug, true to her nature, had to speak. "Nigga, we…" That's all she got out before 'B' dashed the mug of beer in her face, followed quickly by a backhand upside her head.

Nita Bug, the true warrior princess that she was, stumbled back a few feet, yelling, "Muthafucka, who the…" He cut her short when he stood up like he'd been shot out of a cannon and hit her with an elbow straight in the nose, grabbed her by the shoulders and slammed her head first into the side of the stage.

"See there, bitch, always running your stanky mouth when you know that nigga there, stupid."

Baybay, the older and thicker of the three, hollered at her baby sister in a much too gravelly voice for a girl. She was about to add something a little nastier before Rainbow came up from behind and slapped her upside the head, grabbed her by the back of her neck and yelled in her ear, "Biatch, that goes for your stank ass, too; shut the fuck up."

Baybay was not only the oldest; she was the most timid and got the message real quick, put on the chill and slunk over to a nearby table and sat down. She knew from past experience of being one of Rainbow's hoes that he would break her down real fast. She'd said enough. Nita Bug was definitely on her own as far as she was concerned.

Joyce, the cutest and smartest with the most sense and courage, went over to the stage to help Nita Bug up, who was dizzy and quiet as a church mouse. Warbling to her feet, she reached over the shoulder of one of the male patrons, picked up a napkin off the table and began dabbing at the blood pouring out of her nose.

Joyce grunted with the effort it took to lift and carry her groggy sister to the table with Baybay. When she was straightening up, she bumped into Sparkle's chin, causing him to bite his tongue.

He groaned and leaned back holding his mouth and mumbled, "Godayum, girl, shit, watch where the fuck you going, damnit." He touched his tongue gingerly with the tip of his finger several times to make sure it wasn't bleeding.

Joyce, who had bent forward from the impact, spat angrily, "Damn, man, why the fuck you standing right behind me for?" He rubbed the back of her head vigorously. She turned around and gritted on him something terrible. Those brilliant green eyes of hers froze him to the spot.

Sparkle arched his brow and grimaced, but before he could think of something nasty to retort, he heard Duke's booming voice roaring from the entrance. "Whatz up, y'all? Big Duke's in the muthafucking house."

He was smiling brightly as he twirled his huge hands wildly over his head. All three amigos could tell something was bothering him. By the time he reached the counter, his girl Cynt, hips swaying with rip the runway model swagger, came busting through the door clutching her ever-present gigantic purse. Damn thing was nearly bigger than her. She was a really cute little pixie who reminded most people of Jada Pinkett. Actually a lot of her friends called her "Little Jada" because of the resemblance and stature. She couldn't have weighed a hundred pounds soaking wet, with real bushy eyebrows and big dark brown eyes that looked even bigger behind a pair of round granny glasses that stayed perched midway down the bridge of her nose. What most people remembered most about her was her pouty red lips that always looked glossy and fit perfectly with her spunky attitude—one which made her the perfect little sparkplug to keep Big Duke grounded. And grounded was how she definitely kept his usually obnoxious ass.

She came up to the counter as Duke was sitting down and placed her multi-bejeweled hand on his shoulder. He looked at her dangling hand and frowned before he forced a weak smile and turned back to his boys. He took a deep breath and somehow lowered his big voice to a mere whisper as he started explaining how he'd gotten fucked around at the 617 Club on Auburn Avenue. His voice was so surprisingly low that all three of his boys were forced to lean so close that their foreheads were mashed against one another.

"Man, I know I had won at least seven or eight grand before this fight broke out between two of them niggas. One of them fools had claimed that he had barred the curve. Man, how in the fuck do you expect a nigga to respect a punk talking about he bar the curve? And then he started talking some dumb shit about he wanted his money back. Can you believe that shit there? Come on, man, we all know that if you can't keep the cheat off your ass in Georgia Skin, you be just a whipped muthafucka."

All his boys nodded in agreement. He continued with the boost of confidence. "Well, anyway, these niggas get in a scuffle and when everything settles down, my motherfucking money is gone."

The trio leaned back ready for whatever was coming next. Cynt stuck her face between them. "And he had a great big knot of money just like he said to y'all."

Big Duke smiled and patted her arm on his shoulder. "Anyway, to make a long story short."

"Please do." Rainbow couldn't hold back from jibbing.

Duke wrinkled his nose. "Fuck you, Bow; anyway me and one of the workers had some hard words. Man, I was ready to pull my shit on his ass and would've too if it wasn't for Cynt grabbing my arm. And that nigga Don sided against me. Even had Red Tony going along with that bullshit. And y'all know that I been looking out for that nigga for years." He leaned back in the seat and looked at them one by one. "I've got to get those muthafuckas back for that, yo."

Cynt moved his arm and sat down on his lap. "How you want to handle it, baby?" Everybody at the counter knew she was dead serious, for despite her small stature, she didn't hold back in the least when it came to protecting big dude.

Duke leaned back smiling proudly, feeling good about knowing his little soldierette was down for whatever. "Sweet stuff, I've been working on something all the way over here; trust that there."

He pinched his nose and looked undereyed at Sparkle. Sparkle knew he'd already come up with some really devious. He cranked his neck from side to side, pinched his own nose and looked undereyed right back at him.

When Duke started scratching his chin with his baby finger

and cocked one brow, they all knew they had to get ready for one helluva time. Some real drastic stuff was about to go down and all of them would have to be involved regardless of how dangerous it may get.

He stared directly at Sparkle. "Baby boy, you remember that time back in the white elephant that we got old man Moore to steal all the cards out of the commissary and Googie's slick ass helped us fix 'em up over the weekend and put them back in the store?"

The words had barely left his lips when Rainbow's face brightened up. "Oh, hell yeah, man, we kept the whole joint broke for the whole fucking summer. Niggas couldn't figure out what the fuck was going on."

'B' slammed his thighs so hard that it made everybody jump and he burst out laughing. "Uh-huh, shit, we'd still be living high off the hog off that lick there if we hadn't gotten out."

Sparkle jumped in, "Come to think of it, nigga, you never did give me the money for those fifty dozen billfolds I sent out in your name from that game we had on the yard for the Fourth of July. Let me see, that's like fifty dozen times fifteen dollars a dozen plus. What's it been now—ten, fifteen years, uh-huh, fifteen years of interest, it would come to."

He started counting his fingers. They all yelled, including the three girls, in unison, "Nigga, shut the fuck up."

Big Duke was smiling cheerfully right along with everybody else and then coughed into his fist. "Man, on the serious side, I feel like we can pull some of that same shit off on those niggas at the 617."

'B' looked around at all the girls who had gathered around listening to the conversation. That didn't fit well with him at all. He took a long gulp of his drink and cleared his throat. "Y'all hoes need to find something to do." When they didn't react quick enough for his satisfaction, he stood up and shouted, "Y'all bitches, all of y'all get the fuck to the muthafucking car right muthafucking now."

They sprinted out like the place was on fire. The last one, Cynt, who was still sitting on Duke's lap eyeing him shyly, started pouting and then left when he nodded for her to follow the rest. 'B' sat back down. But not before he stared down every patron in the joint until they turned away from his evil eyes.

Rainbow folded his arms across the counter and stared at Duke. "Man, you must really be pissed off about this shit. How in the fuck are we supposed to pull something like that off? We don't even know where them niggas buy their cards from."

Duke folded his arms across his big stomach. "I ain't said a damn thing about buying no cards."

Sparkle quickly put his two cents worth in. "Then how in the fuck?"

Duke cut him off, "We get into that damn safe in his office where he keeps them and his dope and his money and all kinds of shit."

"What?" Rainbow frowned.

"What?" Sparkle growled.

"What?" Johnny mumbled.

"We get into his..." Rainbow started and then bowed his head and ran his hand down the bridge of his nose before he frowned at big boy. "Man, we heard what you said, but how are we supposed to get in that big-ass safe, dude? Shit, as big as that bitch is, we'd need a fucking forklift."

Duke leaned forward over the counter and shook his head. "There you go again, underestimating the power of the scheming mind. And you call yourself a con man. Boys, Loretta would turn over in her grave if she was hearing this shit I'm hearing from y'all so-called players."

Rainbow rolled his eyes and picked up his drink and took a long slug.

Duke picked up 'B''s drink and drained it in one big gulp. Then he hollered for Bertha to give all of them a refill before he got up from the counter and headed for one of the tables in the back of the club. "Come on, y'all half-hustling-ass niggas," Duke said over his shoulder. He sat down and crossed his legs on the table and nodded for all of them to sit down.

He addressed Rainbow in a no-nonsense tone. "On the real now, Bow, you're the one that turned that bitch Mary Anne out years ago. Nigga, ain't no need for you to be looking all stunned and shit. You know damn well you remember her fine ass. The way you babied that ho, you had to know every time that bitch changed her cum-stained drawers."

That comment drew a few snickers from the other two as they nodded in agreement. Rainbow lifted his head and started massaging his neck. "Yeah, yeah, I did show that little whore some special favors but that shit was long ago when my ass was green to the game. Then again what does that have to do with this shit you about to get us into?"

Duke waved away his snooty reply to his pimping ability. "And that nigga Don hadn't even dreamed of being in the ATL way back then when you had that ho on the tracks."

'B' picked up Duke's drink and returned the favor of draining his. "Hey, dog, I've got to agree with my dog here; what the fuck do that have to do with what you want us to get into here? This a real serious move you talking about making, partner. The repercussions could be really rough; you feel me."

Duke took his legs off the table, threw up his hands in the air feigning discuss. "Come on, man, use your empty-ass head here for just a moment." He paused to tap the side of his own head.

"Can you think of any ho Rainbow has had that don't secretly still love his dirty ass?"

'B' pyramided his hands on the table, closed his eyes and buried his head into them contemplating for a few moments. Then he leaned back in the seat and folded his arms. "Now that you think about it, none; so what."

He looked at Rainbow, then at Sparkle before he addressed "B." "So our nigga here can get that ho to get the combination to the safe."

Rainbow leaned across the table astounded by what he had just heard. "Whoa, pardner, you know damn well that Red Tony ain't gonna go for that ho kicking it with me, especially with the history we got. Come on, dog, get real, will ya? And then for his ass to get ripped off like that; shit, he'd figure that shit out in no time at all."

Duke shot back immediately, "True that, playa, but he ain't got to know that you been with her."

Rainbow looked at him like he had lost his fucking mind. "So how we do that there?"

Duke waved for them to come closer and whispered, "That bitch Crystal, hell, maybe even Joyce. Yeah, the bitch a player, for real, yo. Anyway that bitch Crystal be eating that ho on the regular and I hear that Joyce has got the best head in the fucking girl-to-girl business. Hold up for a minute, yo. Hear me out; this some good shit here, dog. On top of that, Red goes for that kinda shit in the worst way. As long as it ain't another nigga, he don't give a flying fuck, know what I'm saying. So you get that bitch Crystal or Joyce, whichever one of them hoes you decide to use, to pull her to you. From there you use that old pimping magic you claim that don't ever get old." He leaned back in the seat with a shiteater grin plastered on his face and spread his arms triumphantly.

Sparkle finally joined in. "But even still, we can't let the bitch know what we're doing, player. Man, you talking about her putting her bread and butter on the line; hell, her jam, too."

Duke shook his head and laughed. "Baby boy, we gonna make it look like a botched burglary."

"Uh-huh, and you actually think she's gonna go for that. Come on, playa, you got to come better than that," Rainbow mumbled.

Duke acted like he hadn't heard a word. "And give her like twenty-five percent of the money we take out of the safe, that way she can't say a damn thing or she knows her ass will get snuffed." He cocked his head to the side and held his hands up for them to chill. "Shit, every bitch wants a nest egg her nigga don't know about."

Rainbow said. "Hold up, dog, didn't I just hear you say it's gonna look like a botched burglary, so we gonna give her twenty-five percent of what?"

Duke looked at him and rolled his eyes in disgust. "Man, what's up with you, your ears stuffed with year-old wax or what? I just said we gonna take the money out of the safe. She's gonna know how much was taken because those niggas are gonna bitch to holy hell about. So we give her twenty-five percent of that. Then again, if we don't give her that much, it ain't like you ain't never lied to a ho before. And it sho ain't like she gonna tell on herself."

Rainbow leaned back in the seat and stared down his nose at big boy for a moment and then his face broke out in a bright smile. He started to rub his hands together and nodded his head. "Aw, man, this shit is sounding better and better by the minute. So when you wanna start on this here?"

Duke turned his attention to "B." "Okay, 'B,' since you the one that got that bitch Crystal to start off dancing in the club in the first place, you can get her to pull Mary Anne." He paused to address Sparkle, too. "Or if it come down to dealing with Joyce, which I don't think will be that much of a problem, because the bitch loves money and the excitement that goes down with a real lick. Hold up, let me think about this for a second. Okay, I got it, get the bitch pulled to the Heart of Decatur hotel say by Friday and we can pull the lick on Sunday night. That's the only night when nobody's there; y'all feel me?"

Everybody nodded at the same time before 'B' got up from the table to look for Crystal.

Duke stood up smiling. "Okay, y'all already know what to get from the magic shop downtown, so I'm out of here. We'll keep each other abreast of how things are going."

Rainbow and Sparkle smiled at his departing back until he disappeared through the door before Sparkle spoke up. "This is gonna be a lot of fun; you know that, don'tcha?"

Rainbow slapped both hands on the table and stood up. "Yep," was all he said as he led the way out of the club.

CHAPTER FOUR

Even Good Girls Gotta Have It

everly propped against the pillow watching the morning news with Katie Couric, in her apartment in College Park. She'd lain awake most of the night wondering if her three amigos had anything to do with the robberies and shootings on I-20. Even though no one was caught, her grapevine of snitches rarely gave her unreliable information.

As badly as she wanted, she couldn't gather enough evidence to connect Don to those events. Maybe he was the culprit, maybe not. Either way she had to find out what was going on before her boys got whacked with it.

She sat on the edge of the bed, stretched her tired limbs and went into the bathroom to freshen up. Studying her image in the mirror, she felt like she was caught between a rock and a bigger rock. In order to keep the hit off of them, she knew she had to investigate these events all by herself, without any help from any of her colleagues or underlings. Talking about skeletons in the closet, boy, were hers ever rattling now. To involve anyone else would be taking too big of a chance of having her relationship with her amigos revealed. Her political enemies would have a field day if they had the slightest idea she was involved with them in any way. Consumed with these thoughts, she left the bathroom to go to her closet to pick through her wardrobe for something to wear.

She was admiring herself in bra and panties in the full-length mirror on the door, when her pussy started tingling. She imagined they were Sparkle's hands rubbing her crotch instead of her own. The more she thought of him, the further her hands slid into her panties. *Damn, why that man have to be a damn crook?* she thought as her nipples started to harden.

She was a little surprised when she eased her fingers between her pussy lips and it was gushy with her juices. She closed her eyes and imagined that his face was closing in on her. That his lips parted slightly to touch hers ever so gently. She had inserted two fingers into her pulsating womanhood, moaning and grinding her hips in rhythm with her thrusting fingers when the phone rang.

Its persistent jangling snapped her out of her lust-filled state of mind. She plucked some Kleenex out of the box on the dresser to wipe her fingers off before she picked the phone off of the lamp stand. "Ugh, nasty." She turned her nose up at the icky feeling.

Before she put the receiver to her ear, she felt a tingling along her spine. Her voice was full of tension when she answered. "Hello, Beverly Johnson speaking." She was immediately aware that the caller was either on a cell or in a phone booth because of the traffic noise in the background. She was about to repeat her greeting when the voice on the other end caused butterflies to flutter in her stomach. It was Sparkle. She sighed heavily without even realizing it.

"Hey there, girl, how ya doing?" His sexy tenor rang in her ear.

It took a few seconds to gather herself. Dayum, she hated the weak feeling she got in her knees whenever she heard his voice. *Why couldn't he just be a normal guy?* Then again, that was the part of him that attracted her so strongly.

"Damn, girl, you gonna answer or what?" he said when she took too long to reply.

She cleared her throat. "Yeah, I'm here, what's on your mind?"

"Just thought I'd holla atcha. It's been awhile, know what I'm saying." He had to shout over the traffic noise.

She smiled, knowing she was stalling, afraid he'd be able to detect the loud thumping of her heart. She held the phone to her breast so he wouldn't hear her heavy sigh trying to camouflage the intensity of feelings he'd caused. "Okay, now that I've finally got you on the phone, what do you know about all those robberies going on I-20?"

He leaned away from the phone, not believing she was coming at him like that. He cocked an eyebrow, took the time to catch his breath. "Whoa, sister girl, why you asking me something like that? I just wanted to holler atcha since I ain't seen you since I got out." He waited a full thirty seconds hoping she wasn't about to go into her super cop mode on him. When she didn't, he continued, "Okay, well, you know that I can't be talking about that kind of stuff over the phone anyway. So where do you want to meet then?"

Now it was her time to wait for him to respond. She was a lot less patient than he was and immediately repeated herself. "I said, where do you wanna meet?"

He had to think about that for a moment. In her position, he knew that she had to be very secretive about dealing with him. Finally, he coughed, then cleared his throat. "How about the Decatur MARTA station?"

"Too many people," she answered quickly.

"Damn, girl, you pick a place then." He could hear her heavy breathing over the line before she finally answered.

"I tell you what, give me a number where I can reach you and

I'll get a room at the La Quinta in Lithonia and call you. Don't you dare have me out there waiting on your ass all fucking morning."

"Whoa, you sure you want to do that?" He didn't try to hide his surprise.

She paused to contemplate his last remark. Strictly business, strictly business, she kept trying to tell herself. Or was it something else. She looked at the glitter in her eyes in the image in the mirror. Blinking several times, she shook her head as she tried to rid her mind of the possibilities. She finally mustered up the nerve to say, "Yes, I'm sure, give me the number. I'll call you within the hour."

She hung up immediately after he gave her the number, having little doubt he'd be there. If she didn't know anyone else, she knew him and he'd never lied to her.

She changed her underwear to some lacier, sexier flimsy stuff and dabbed on her best perfume. Not too much, enough to affect his senses up real close. Smiling to herself, she teased her hair and chose a soft pink blouse and dark velvet pants; the kind that clung to her bubbly ass. She called her secretary and let her know that she'd be a couple of hours late. Her smile continued to glow brightly as she got into her car and headed for the La Quinta.

After she hung up so abruptly, Sparkle looked over at Rainbow in the driver's seat. "Dog, she wants me to meet her at the La Quinta."

Rainbow rubbed his chin, eyeing him in his peripheral vision for a moment before he smiled. "Shit, looks like you've got to knock those boots there, my nigga."

Sparkle's expression turned to serious concern. "Bow, she asked me about the robberies, man."

"So?"

"So, are you forgetting she's a cop. The top cop, at that?"

Rainbow shook his head, not wanting to accept that his old buddy was actually leery about Bevy, the girl they'd practically raised from a little girl. He took a deep breath. "Hell naw, I'm not forgetting that she's a cop, but I'm also remembering the Bevy that I know, the Bevy that you know, the Bevy that could bust any of our asses every day of the week but has always let us know when the bull's eye is pointing right at us."

Sparkle cocked his head to the side and sighed. "Okay, okay, I feel ya. Anyway, I've got about an hour before she gets the room and calls me back. Whatcha wanna do 'til then?"

"Shit, man, we're gonna beat her to the hotel, that's what we are gonna do." He paused to light another cigarette off of the one shrinking in the corner of his mouth. "Besides, we got to cut this stuff up somewhere. Might as well get it done while you're digging up in her, man." He flipped his eyes to the Adidas saddle-bag they had gotten from 'B' earlier.

Sparkle flinched at the term he had used, referring his "digging" into Bevy, but hell, that was exactly what he'd be doing. He didn't really expect anything different from his boy; that's the way he was used to referring to women, regardless of who they were.

"So, in other words, you want to see her come and go. Get rid of her as soon as possible, huh. I thought you trusted her so much." Sparkle smiled shyly.

Rainbow laughed. "Yeah, I do and like you said yourself, she the top cop. Hey, what can I say? I'm still a cautious kind of fella." He stared out of the window. "Man, she's gonna reveal a lot more to you than she would me. She always has, you know. And that's because she's always been in love with your curly-haired ass, man. Tell me this, why you think she's never gotten married, dog? It surely ain't because she hasn't wanted to. She's been waiting on you, dude."

Sparkle cocked a brow and leaned against the door trying to come to grips with what his boy had said. He'd felt it for a long time, and he'd always hoped it was that way, but he didn't want to believe it. So to get his mind off of it he bent down and picked up the saddlebag. He dug inside to get one of the red Ziploc bags. Reaching into his jacket pocket, he took out a straight shooter and dipped it into the cocaine. After getting himself a real Scottie blast, he passed a refilled shooter over to Rainbow.

He leaned against the headrest and exhaled the smoke out slowly into the air. *Hmm! That shit felt good.* He waited until Rainbow had gotten a good one. "You right, dog, she's always kept us up on the heat and it surely couldn't hurt to find out all she knows. Shit, all her info comes from her troops and her snitches."

Rainbow shook his head because the blast had really rocked him, too. "That's what I'm saying, dog."

Sparkle took one more blast, pinched his nose. "Tell you what, soldier, I'm gonna get out and walk the last five or so blocks to clear my head a little bit, aight?"

Fifteen minutes later, Rainbow pulled over to a Sonic convenience store to let Sparkle out and then drove ahead to get a room at the hotel.

Sparkle bought a pack of Kool cigarettes, a Crunch bar and a sixteen-ounce Colt 45 and started walking down the sidewalk at a leisurely pace. When he got to within eyesight of the La Quinta, he saw a car stopped at the red light with the window down. Beverly was staring straight ahead and didn't notice him. He was tempted to shout out to her but held his tongue.

When she pulled into the parking lot, Sparkle started running. He ducked into a phone booth across the street to watch her. While she was in the office getting a room, he saw Rainbow step out of a room on the second floor and head down the tier. Aw aw, panic attack. *What do I do now?* he thought. This wasn't in the game plan at all.

He rushed out of the booth and ran to the opposite side of the registration office, barely avoiding her seeing him as she turned away from the sign-in clerk. He waited for her to leave the office before he stepped into the lobby and grabbed himself a couple of chocolate-covered donuts before he sprinted back out the door and raced to the other end of the building. He turned the corner just in time to catch Rainbow coming down the stairs.

Rainbow stopped in midstride when he saw the worried expression on his face. Sparkle waved him back up the stairs and ran to the edge of the building. He peeked around the corner and jerked back immediately when he saw Beverly walking toward them. Luckily, she had her head down rummaging inside her purse.

Whew, she hadn't seen him. He jerked his thumb at Rainbow again before he stepped around the corner munching on one of the donuts.

Beverly looked up to see him approaching. Her face broke into a wide smile when she looked into his eyes. She didn't say a word as she walked straight up to him and grabbed his hand and led him around to the other side of the building to a room on the corner.

While she was putting the key into the lock, he wiped his brow, relieved because of nearly getting busted right off the bat. Something told him to look up. Sure enough Rainbow was leaning over the balcony with a Cheshire cat smile on his face rubbing his hands together and licking his lips. Sparkle put his hand behind his back, waving Rainbow off and followed Beverly into the room.

She put her purse on the lamp stand between the two beds, then turned to face him with a frown on her face. "Why didn't you wait for my call?" She didn't wait for a response as she sat down, crossed her legs and folded her arms defensively across her chest. "Is it because you don't trust me? Whatcha think, I'm wired or something?" she snarled and opened her blouse to reveal a pink lacy bra and a pair of creamy chocolate 38 DD's.

Sparkle stood there watching her, wondering why she was being so open, so quick. He ran a hand down his face, sat down on the other bed, twisted his neck from side to side. He was enjoying the tension-releasing sensation before he turned his gaze to her luscious titties and then her dark penetrating eyes. A tingling hmmmph ran down his spine as it always did when she looked at him in that way.

Running his index finger under his nose a couple of times, he pinched it. "Kinda full of yourself, ain'tcha, girlie, like always."

She shifted her hips around the bed. "Is there a reason that I shouldn't be?"

He couldn't take his eyes off of hers as his lips slowly curled into a warm smile. He leaned forward to balance his arms on his knees and studied her intently for a few moments. He licked his lips before pursing and popping them. "If you were any other woman, I'd say, yeah, but you ain't any other woman so I say, hell yeah."

Her eyes narrowed without her really realizing that they had. He had certainly gotten her attention, that's for sure. She blinked her long lashes a few times and arched her brows. She got lost in his stare, as if she was hypnotized. Dayum, she hated the effect his eyes had on her, as a tingling shot all the way to her stomach; the bastard.

He didn't miss her reaction and spat game further. "Woman, you know that you've always been number one in my heart."

She reared back and gave him a nasty snake roll of her head before she retorted, "Nigga, it's sho hard to tell." She took a deep breath. "Baby, baby, baby, why you got to stay in this street-life bullshit? Ain't you suffered enough already because of it? I know that I have. Shit, I've been waiting all my life hoping and praying that you'd get out of it. You ever considered that a girl might want to have a house full of little Larrys for you?"

Ooooh, Rainbow was right; she real deep with this here. He knew he had her because there certainly wasn't no top cop in her right now.

She took a deep breath and placed a hand on his knee. She didn't feel close enough. So she reached over with both of her hands, embracing his face as her eyes started to mist up. "Because you're the only man I have ever loved, the only man that I could ever love, have ever wanted to love. Why can't I be more important to you than the streets?"

He held her hands and slowly lowered them into her lap. "Why can't I be more important to you than your badge?"

She slid her hands around his and laid them in his lap. She parted her lips to say something when she felt the heat; the hardness began to throb against hers.

His eyes squinted into slits as he watched her face, her nose flare. He could feel and see a woman in the throes of lust. No, not lust, love. He licked his lips as his eyes invited hers into his and then into his heart. She accepted the invitation more than willingly and brought her face closer to his; her eyes begging him to love her.

She certainly didn't have to do no begging; she didn't even have to ask for he was filled up with her as much as she was with him. Her lips parted slightly as her eyes started to close. Even though he wanted it, the touch of her lips caught him by surprise.

He wanted her to take the initiative for he didn't want her to have the slightest indication that he was taking advantage of her. He didn't have to wait long. His face started tingling all over when he felt her warm soft tongue probe into his lips. He released her hands. They remained resting on his ever-growing manhood. He started to massage her side. Her skin was so soft, so warm, so inviting. He moved his hands around her back and up to the nape of her neck. He opened his mouth, her tongue slide in further, very slowly until it reached his and started swirling around it. He reacted passionately to the contact as his tongue began to match the rotation of hers. Gently holding her head steady, he began to massage her tongue with his own.

She moaned softly. The warm sweet breath from her nose was like a caressing breeze on his skin as it rolled along his cheek. She turned her hand around on his lap and let out a trembling murmur as she wrapped it around his dick, even louder when it jerked up in reaction to her touch.

When he felt the precum oozing out of the head, he laid her down on the bed and started kissing her lightly on the neck, to her ear, licking it, twirling his tongue around and inside of it.

She squeezed, he moaned, she squeezed harder and rubbed her hand up and down his now pulsating shaft, stopped at the head, massaging it, gently at first, harder when he started grinding, hunching up. She couldn't wait any longer and slowly unzipped his pants and reached inside; first to roll her fingers in his silky pubic hairs. She gasped as she fisted the head, now drooling pre-cum on her palm. With her nose-flaring lust, she started sliding the head along his thigh, enjoying the manly grunt that escaped his lips.

He licked lovingly along her neck down to the top of her cleavage. She let out a grunt of her own and grasped the back of his neck to guide his tongue to her trembling nipples. He started alternating hot and cold air through her bra as he reached behind her to un-hook the straps that held those glorious globes in place. They came apart easily. He continued to tongue massage her nipples through the lacy material as he slid her blouse off of her shoulders and then the bra. She arched her back as he started devouring her naked perfumed breasts while he unsnapped her pants.

Her breath caught as he started working his tongue down to her navel. Her soft stomach became spasmatic with each flick. He inched her pants down while he feather-tongued inside her thighs. He stared intently into her face as he started at her ankles and tongue-bathed her softness back up to her crotch. She was moaning heavily now, eyes straining shut, mouth wide open.

Her panties were soaked as he lapped at her juices through the musky silk. Then he pulled them to the side and slid his tongue into her now gushing slit. Her soft trembling ass rose off the bed when he started slowly sucking on her clit. The moans turned into grunts as she lost all control. "Oh, Sparkle, Larry, oh, baby, ugh ugh, I can't stand it, I can't, oh oh ooooh yes. baby. Oh eat my pussy, yes, yes, that's it, that's it eat my, your ooooh ooooh ooooh uuggggh uuggghhh." She grabbed the sides of his head and started grinding her gushing pussy into his face.

As her climax began to subside, he reached under her to cup her ass cheeks and started intensely sucking on her clit, flicking it rapidly with his tongue. Her second nut was much quicker, more intense than the first as she screamed out loud, thighs trembling. "Ooooooh, oooooh, aaaah, aah, o baby, o baby, oh baby, so good, feels so good, so godayum good, so good, dayum, good, aaaaah, o shit, o shiiiiit."

He couldn't stand it any longer. With passion overwhelming him, he slid up her trembling, sweat-drenched body and shoved his entire pulsating dick into her with one plunge. She gasped from the suddenness of his attack on her swollen pussy. He raised one of her legs, as he stroked slowly into her, sliding his long dick along her clit with every deep, grunting dip.

She came again when he pulled her other leg up and sped up, in and out, in and out. She screamed out louder than ever. "O baby fuck the hell out of me, fuck me baby, ooh Sparkle, fuck the hell out of me. Oooh baby, I can't stop cumming. Harder, harder, baby, fuck me harder, that damn dick is so muthafucking hard, so muthafucking big yes, yes yesssssss."

He couldn't hold back anymore; her pussy was too hot, too good. "Oh, Bevy, oh, baby, here it comes. I'm gonna nut all up in this gooooooooood, ugh, uugggggh pussy, shiiiiiit."

She felt him coming. She pressed against his chest, pushing him off of her. Caught completely by surprise, his mouth gaped wide open, he couldn't make another sound as she grabbed his slippery cum-spurting dick in both of her small hands and stuffed it in her mouth to the hilt to let the rest of his nut squirt down her throat.

In shock he looked down to see the intense passion on her face as she continued to bob her head up and down until he was completely drained. Even then she didn't stop and kept slurping on the head, loving the taste of him, the intoxicating smell of their mixed sexes trapped in his hairs, the muskiness of his balls. Oh, how she loved this man.

Finally, it softened to the point of sliding out of her mouth and plopped with a squishy sound onto his stomach. She laid her head on his stomach, lightly flicking her tongue at it, totally exhausted, totally satisfied, rubbing his chest.

Breathing heavily, he reached down to rub her hair, the side of her face, then her shoulders and back. Damn, she smelled and felt so good, felt so soft. He sighed. "You know what, Bevy?"

She looked up at him, a wide smile on her face, then wiped her damp hair off of her forehead. "You enjoyed taking advantage of an innocent girl like me?"

He rose to his elbows, smiled down at her before he arched his eyebrows. "Innocent, innocent, who's innocent, me?"

She lifted her head off of his stomach, batted her long lashes a couple of times and retorted, "Me, of course." Suddenly, she took on a very serious tone, as the other reason why she had come to the hotel started to flood her mind. As her cop instincts took over, she felt the change go over him as well. She sat up on the edge of the bed, grabbed her clothes and started to put them on.

Then the thought hit her that he had never even taken all of his clothes off, well, at least not his pants. Damn, she had been so out of it that she couldn't even remember him taking off his shirt. The crotch of his pants was stained with a mixture of their juices. How disgusting, ugh. The intimacy she had been feeling faded completely and her thoughts changed into an even more serious mode. She was snapping the last buttons of her blouse when she stood up and went to lean against the dresser. "Like I asked you over the phone, what do you know about them robberies?"

He braced himself on his elbows and honed in on her just as seriously. "And I asked you, why you ask me some shit like that?"

She ran her tongue across her lips, placed a stubborn hand on her hips, the other on her pursed mouth studying him for a moment before she walked over to the bed and stood over him. He sat up, reached out to grasp her by the hips, holding her at arm's length, as he frowned up at her. "Bevy, you know that we are just as much in the dark about this as you are."

Her expression softened and she reached down to rub the side of his face, but he caught her hands and continued, "Sweetie, anybody, including me, hell, including you, is gonna try to stay on top of this here thing called survival."

Her face stayed soft. "Yeah, baby, I can feel you on that, but it ain't easy when you got to play by the rules, or at least do your best to." It was obvious that she was trying hard to keep the boss lady tone out of her voice.

"Well, I don't have any rules; neither do the niggas who are doing this, so whatcha think I'm gonna do?"

She seriously contemplated what he had said, realizing deep down in her heart that he was right, at least in his part of the world. But she still felt that she had to convince him otherwise. She squeezed her eyes tight and sighed deeply. "Larry, I can't protect you or y'all if my people run down on you. I can and I will warn you like I always have over the years, but if they catch you, there's nothing that I can do."

He leaned back, knuckled the corners of his eyes, clasped the back of his neck and stretched his head back before he took her hands. "That's just the chance I'll have to take." *Naw, she didn't go Larry on me, ah man, she ain't said that in years. This situation must really be bothering her if she went to the basics like that there*, he thought as his police antennae tingled a bit.

Seeing the seriousness in his face, she thought that she'd try some scare tactics. "Okay, fuck the bullshit, hard ass. If I witness you doing some life-threatening shit, I'll snap the cuffs on your stubborn ass my muthafucking self. There, is that plain enough for ya?"

He smiled up at her. The smile didn't reach his eyes though as he responded, "If I'm forced to save my ass and you happen to be around, I don't plan on leaving any witnesses. Is that plain enough for your stubborn ass?"

They looked at each other; their eyes bored into each other's soul and answered each other's question without saying a word. The love they shared and hid from the world would never allow them to harm one another.

She pulled herself out of the trance first, leaned down and kissed him on the forehead before she looked at her watch. "Dayum, you make a girl forget all about the time and everything. I got to get to my office. There's a whole city that I've got to protect from the likes of niggas like you. You gonna keep this room? I might just find myself needing an encore, know what I'm saying?"

He smiled and stood up to help her with her jacket. When she got both arms in the sleeves, he pinned them behind her back, pressed himself hard against her, nibbled on her ear and whispered, "One of these days you're going to give up that badge and be my wifey."

Loving the feel of his dick getting hard against her ass, she arched her back and moaned. "Nigga, I'll resign the very same day that I know." She paused to turn around to face him so that he could see the sincerity in her eyes. "That I know in my heart that you are through with the streets."

He kissed her gently between the eyes as he said huskily, "Bevy, if I thought you really would, I would."

She took one last heave against his chest and broke the embrace. She squinted intently at him for a few seconds before she turned away and stepped to the door. Before she stepped out, she smiled warmly. "Baby, no, Sparkle, Larry whatever, if you can really see my heart, you know that I will." She slowly closed the door shut.

As the sound of her heels faded out of earshot, Sparkle sat down on the bed to ponder her last statement. He knew that he was stuck with a very hard decision to make. Especially considering that he had been in love with her for as many years as he could remember living. Yet he loved the street life. He also had a special place in his heart for Violet, Rainbow, Johnny B and now little Mercedes, too. It definitely wouldn't be something he could push aside easily.

Now, that Mercedes, there was something about her that made

him favor her above all. He had asked himself several times over the short span of time that he'd had her what it was that had him so fascinated. Was it her delicate stature, or her innocent natural sexuality? Or the way she caught on to every hustle he turned her on to and mastered them all a lot quicker than he had done so himself? She was a natural, pure and simple. Aw man, that innocent sexuality of hers kept him hungry for her no matter what mood he was in. All he knew was that he could never get enough of her.

Could he give up the thrill of living life on the edge for one woman? Being truthful to himself he really didn't know. One thing that was becoming quite certain was that Black Don was becoming a very dangerous problem; one that had to be dealt with in the harshest of ways if it came to that.

After about ten minutes of solitude, he finally decided to go upstairs to get with Rainbow. When the door opened, it was to a grinning Rainbow, who trotted to the bathroom as soon as he let him in. He shouted over his shoulder, "Dayum, boy, you must've really rocked her world. My nigga, she was grinning from ear to ear when she stepped out of here."

Hell, he knew he had put his thang down right.

Rainbow was zipping up as he strolled back into the room farting and scratching his ass. "I done cut up all that stuff while you was doing your thang, so you ready to roll, or do you wanna hang around and get blasted first?"

Sparkle could think of nothing better to do after dealing with Beverly, so he sat on the bed. "My nigga, drop some of that shit right here," he said, pointing to the small lamp stand between the beds.

Rainbow gladly slid an eight ball onto the stand, filled up both of their shooters, passed him one of them and lit up the other one.

They sat there blooping in silence for the next couple of minutes before Rainbow finally spoke up. "How much does she know, dog?"

He wiped his face, stood up to take his jacket off before he sat back down and leaned his head against the headboard. "Man, she figures that we at least had something to do with it. She couldn't pinpoint nothing but that police nose of hers was working full time, dog."

Rainbow stood up and jacked his pants up. "'Tain't much we can do about what she thinks, dog. But check this out, we ain't about to let that nigga stop our flow. Damn, I can hardly wait for the weekend so we can start digging into those bastards' mint real decent-like."

The coke really had him pumped because he kept on rattling. "Aw, fuck that nigga for now. Let's go crash Al's poker game since we're out this way anyhow."

Sparkle leaned forward, pyramiding his arms on his knees and rested his chin on his hands. "Yeah, we can do that, but don't you think we need to lay some 'can't miss' shit on that nigga before he comes up with something that'll get us?"

Rainbow licked his lips and gave him a confident smiled. "Baby boy, I already got the twins on a mission to set that fool up for a trip to our little trap out there in the woods in Forest Park right after we get the scam started at the 617. My nigga, it's so sweet that his greedy ass gotta go for it."

Sparkle leaned back and eyed him up and down. "Damn, dog, why you ain't wired me up to that by now?"

"What difference does it make? Yo ass is gonna be there when the bitch nigga pisses and shits himself." Rainbow laughed and punched him on the shoulder.

Sparkle turned his mouth down nodding his consent. "Okay, wizard, so when do we do this?"

Damn, is he hearing anything I'm saying? He arched his brow. "The twins will keep me up with the progress and like I just said a moment ago, it'll go down after the scam at the skin house. Matter of fact they are about to get the job cranked as we speak."

Sparkle nodded. He should've known that his dog was on the case. All he had to worry about now was dodging Beverly's roving eyes. But damn, the girl had eyes and ears everywhere. Maybe after he'd gotten through this situation, he'd be able to concentrate on getting with her seriously. But, then what about his crew? "Hmmmph, what about them." He pondered as he sat and admired the scheming wickedness.

CHAPTER FIVE

Scamming the Scammer

"Hey, baby, how ya doing? Why you looking like that, you got into a spat with one of the cashiers at the supermarket or something?" Al asked Mona as he sat down on the bed and finished drying himself off.

Mona smiled meekly at his attempt at teasing her. Only moments before she had been sweating bullets, but now she was grateful he hadn't shown any sign of discovering her exploration into his private sanctuary. She could hardly believe that she had actually pulled it off with him already in the house. Therefore, it was a no-brainer that she roll right along with his mood.

"How'd you know that? Damn, you've got eyes everywhere, don'tcha?"

"Naw, sweetie, you were just looking a little frayed when I came out, that's all." He started scratching the back of his ear, a clear sign that she'd noticed him do when he had difficulty wording what he wanted to say.

She sighed when he took a deep breath and walked over to put his hand on her shoulder. His tone became serious. "There's something I need for you to do for me." She frowned. "Hey, before you start to looking all giddy and stuff, let me finish."

Mona nodded and studied his face intently, not knowing quite what to expect. Up until then all he had ever asked her to do was menial girly stuff. Her heart thumped when he said, "Ooookayeee,

I've got a job I need you to do for me. It ain't anything danger-ous—well, at least your part of it isn't—but there is a possibility for something to go wrong. So you've really got to have your wits with you." He swallowed nothing and continued, "Okay, check this out. CeeDee will be here shortly."

He paused to take a quick peek at his watch. "In about ten min-utes, I need for you to take a ride with him out to Henry County." He paused again, put his hand over his mouth and looked her up and down, studying her intently for any signs of rebellion. He saw none, good girl. "Put on some dark clothing, like that dark leather jumpsuit I got you the other week. Just in case."

She blinked innocently a couple of times, sighed deeply and ran her finger across her opened mouth. "Is it okay if I ask you what it is you want me to do?"

Al gave her his most convincing smile, sat down beside her, put his arm across her shoulder and started out in a low voice that rose as he explained. "Sweetie, I'm gonna be straight up with ya. There's a furniture warehouse out there in Henry County and CeeDee is going to steal one of the trailers. Ain't anything in it but really expensive stuff. What I need you to do is drive him down there and be his extra pair of eyes. Once he gets the trailer on the road, I want you to drive at least a mile or two in front of him to let him know about any police activity he may run into. Say like a roadblock or something." There were a lot of tension wrinkles creasing his forehead.

She sat there momentarily stunned, however, not for the reason he thought; the expression on his face read fear. But it was far from that because this was exactly what RJ had braced her for in the supermarket. Now it had dropped in her lap like a godsend. Hell yeah, she was stunned because she couldn't believe how lucky she was. Not only would she not have to push him to get what RJ wanted, she was about to be a part of the whole operation.

When she looked at Al, she sensed that he felt her fear or anxiousness or whatever it was he wanted to see and feel. She chose to let him think how he wished. It was right on point because his arrogant ass would feel more than obligated to offer something if he thought that she needed to be assured that everything would be okay.

He shifted around uncomfortably and pyramided his elbows on his knees with his fingers entwined and ran his tongue across his lips studying her. He squinted in concentration, trying to feel how she was taking the assignment because he didn't need her acting all scary. He had too much riding on this.

Damn, it's probably gonna take a little more than I thought. He considered other options. He had none. And with the pressure that RJ was putting on him, he had to come up with whatever the fuck it took, point blank. He knew that he had to give her only the basic information. The less she knew, the less she could tell if things did go wrong. Since he was limited on what he could tell her, thus curtailing his assurance, he decided to throw her a little better incentive. "Tell you what, sweetheart, you'll get ten percent of the total haul, the same as CeeDee is getting. Whatcha say about that there?"

He expected her to get more excited, but she didn't show any kind of reaction. Not good. And since he knew that his overall cut in the project would be in the six-figure range, he'd have to cement her interest; put her in a position where she had to commit.

"Tell you what, honey, since I believe that God blesses the child that has their own." He slapped his knees with enthusiasm, stood up and walked briskly over to the closet. With no hesitation whatsoever, Al pulled back a rack of clothes to reveal a wall safe, one bigger than the one downstairs.

Mona's heart jumped several beats, she had just found the golden goose. Now she and her sister would definitely have enough to disappear and go wherever they wanted to. Her eyes nearly jumped out of their sockets when he unlocked it, reached inside and pushed what had to be kilos of dope to the side and revealed stacks of dollars. She knew that the nigga had dough, but godayum.

After regaining her breath, she placed her hand across her chest, quickly checking herself and remembering that the entire house was being monitored. She sat on the bed and forced herself not to show how excited she really was. Suddenly, a tingling ran down her neck and all the way down her spine when she thought of what was already on the tapes downstairs under the game room. She had to force back the bile that started to stir in her stomach.

Damn, I almost forgot that I've got to get my ass out of here before he sees that shit. Her thoughts were tortured as he turned to her with two stacks of bills clutched in his hands. Her brows cocked with curiosity when he didn't even bother to close the safe, though he did push the clothes back into place.

The smile was creased deeply in his face as he casually walked back over to her and tossed both stacks into her lap. Stunned beyond belief, she forced herself to look down only once, not wanting to show she was overwhelmed. She willed herself to stay cool and gradually looked up at him.

Al's next words were stern. "When you and CeeDee get into Henry County, give him one of them stacks; they're ten grand apiece. Y'all will get the rest of it when the truck is delivered. He already knows where to go."

She still sat there without saying a word. *Damn, what more can this bitch want, fuck?* he thought angrily. Time was running out. With the way that cracker was putting all this pressure on him, this had to be done tonight or his ass was in deep shit. He sat down beside her and put his arm across her shoulder. "Hey, you're scared, aren't you?"

The tone in his voice was too kind and she knew he was hiding his true emotions. She had heard too much now, way too much and was quickly becoming a liability; hell, had already become a liability. She looked over at him and even though he was smiling, she could feel a cold undercurrent of danger. Along with that video she knew she was as good as dead if she didn't go along. What choice did she really have? None.

Mona swallowed nervously and nodded several times. "But, daddy, if I ride ahead of him, how could I be able to let him know if there's any trouble and how will I know where to go anyway?"

Al wanted to jump for joy. *Fucking mission accomplished, well, almost anyway*. He smiled. "Walkie-talkies, baby, I'll have one here as well, monitoring the both of you. And for security reasons I can't tell you where the drop-off is until y'all are on the way."

She nodded. Good enough as far as he was concerned. He slapped his thighs loudly, rubbed his knees a few times, anxious to get the show on the road. Sighing heavily, he got up and picked up the phone smiling brightly. Ten minutes later, CeeDee was ringing the doorbell.

Unbeknownst to any them, they had a very unwanted guest, Lt. Woo, parked several houses down the street watching as CeeDee entered the house. She had followed him out of curiosity when she had seen him leaving the Holiday Inn off of Wesley Chapel. She had been sitting in the Dairy Queen across the street to observe the in-and-out traffic because of the robberies she'd heard about recently.

Lt. Woo remembered CeeDee from the pool shakedown at the Red Roof Inn. He had been smart enough to dump his dope and other stuff into the pool when she had given him the chance. Smart of him then, dumb of him now. Not even checking to see if he was being followed. And since she had a few hours before she hooked up with her crew, she thought that she'd see what he was up to.

He was in the house for only a short time before emerging in the company of a pretty young woman. The woman seemed to be familiar but she couldn't put her finger on why. She let them drive a few blocks ahead before she pulled out to follow.

When she felt comfortable they hadn't noticed her, Lt. Woo picked up her mike from the middle console to call one of her boys to join her. "Whaddafuck," she shouted to herself when they turned on I-20 in the opposite direction of Decatur. She hung up the mike. This was something she hadn't expected. Her crooked cop vibes had kicked in and calling anyone now was out of the question. She was on her own; exactly how she preferred it.

With her curiosity growing more and more by the minute, she unconsciously slid her hand to her crotch. Her intuition told her that something exciting was about to happen.

Some twenty minutes later in the car up ahead, Mona's mind was running a thousand miles a minute when CeeDee told her to turn onto a dirt road and cut off the lights. She had no idea whatsoever where she was or where they were headed.

How in the hell this fool expect me to see where I'm driving without no lights? Shit, I can't even see my own hand, she thought as she took her foot off of the gas pedal. She rolled down the window and leaned forward. All she could see was the shadowy outline of the trees against the jet-black sky. No matter how much she strained her eyes, she still couldn't see a damn thing. Thank the Lord she hadn't lit up that blunt that Al had slipped her on the way out of the door. This shit here was spooky enough all by itself. God forbade if she was geeking, too.

"Ain't that much further, girly, riiiiggght here, CeeDee whispered in his country drawl as if somebody else was around to hear him if he had said it any louder. As far she was concerned they were in a no-man's land. He reached over to clasp her wrist on the steering wheel as she felt the branches scraping against her side of the car.

How the fuck could he tell I was going off the road in this pitch-black shit? She looked in his direction. She couldn't even see his big country ass. She sighed. "Damn, man, it's about time; jeez, talk about the fucking boondocks." she growled with disgust. Luckily, she couldn't see the expression on his face in the dark. If she had she would've probably jumped through the window.

He reached into the glove compartment and removed a small flashlight. "Let's make sure that we are on the same frequency," he muttered, then took two walkie-talkies from under the seat and synchronized them.

He handed her one and pressed the send button on the other one. "Breaker break 23, breaker break 23." He put it to his ear. For several moments all they heard was static and then Al's voice started coming through, loud and staticky in the still night.

"Well, shawtie, I guess it's on," CeeDee said with a smile as he slipped out of the car and disappeared among the trees.

No way she was gonna sit in that dark car all by herself. She counted to a hundred and got out to follow him. To her surprise she had only taken a few steps of being snagged and slapped by twigs and branches before she was able to see the long line of trucks in the back of a long warehouse dock. She lifted the binoculars hanging across her neck and hunted for CeeDee. Shortly afterward, she was frowning because she couldn't see him anywhere. *Damn, I wish he would've told me which truck. But hell, he probably didn't know where it would be himself.* She didn't even get the chance to finish that thought when the back lights of one of the trucks came on and it started backing up. "Oh shit, let me get my ass back to the car." She started backing into the bush.

"Goddamnit." She nearly screamed when she felt some upturned roots snag her foot. She lost her balance and fell into a briar patch. When she turned over to push herself up, she was assaulted by the sickening stench exuding from the ground. She gasped and put her hand over her mouth.

"Ugh." She grimaced when the rotten foliage and mud spread on her mouth and tongue. Her stomach heaved a couple of times but nothing came up. She unzipped her jumpsuit and took the tail of her T-shirt to wipe the mess from her mouth, having to spit several times to get the taste out.

Grimacing and grunting, she was finally able to get to her feet—but not without getting caught up several times by thorns and other stuff, where she had to snatch herself free. Mona realized that she had dropped her walkie-talkie. Cursing under her breath, she dreaded the idea of having to muddle in that mess to get it. Sighing heavily, she reluctantly got on her hands and knees to start groping in the icky mess.

After several disgusting moments of frantically feeling around, in what she could only wildly guess, she reached into her pocket to get her cigarette lighter. As soon as she flicked it on, she heard a faint crackling sound that sent shivers through her whole body. She froze in fear. All her attention was now focused on the sound and what could've possibly caused it.

Visions of wild stray dogs, rabid rabbits or even worse, a slimy snake, all crept into her thoughts as she looked wildly around herself. After a moment, all she could hear was the sound of crickets and what she hoped were other harmless night crawlers and the rustling of air through the foliage. Anxiously, she wiped her brow with her sleeve and took a deep breath to release the built-up tension in her chest. She flicked the lighter back on and started looking around again.

She was already on pins and needles and the flickering flame made it that much more eerie.

"Oh my God." She nearly screamed when the ground seemed to move, slithering. She fell back on her butt. *A fucking snake.* She was too scared to speak. Her eyes were bucked wide open with terror as she watched it crawl away. She trembled uncontrollably, when its path went right over the walkie-talkie. Chill bumps ran all along her shivering arms. Once the slimy bastard disappeared into the bush, she slowly reached down to pick up the walkie-talkie.

Ah fuck, he's probably way up the road by now. She cautiously stepped through the woods. She finally reached the car and had cut it on before she realized that she couldn't have the lights on. Reluctantly, she distinguished them and started forward until she felt the branches scraping the side of the car and remembered going off the road earlier. She slapped the side of her head and quickly shifted the car into reverse and slowly started backing up.

"Damn, woman, where the fuck are you, damn?" the staticky voice screamed over the airwaves, crashing the otherwise silent surroundings and caused her to jump nervously in the seat. She was concentrating so hard on backing up in the darkness, that she didn't even make an effort to answer him. She let him continue to squawk until she had cleared the path.

CeeDee had repeated himself three times, voice full of anxiety, by the time she finally acknowledged him. Wheezing with tension, she reached on the dashboard and retrieved the walkie-talkie. "I'm here, I'm here, man. Hold your godayum horses. I was busy backing out of that fucking cave you put me in, nigga. I couldn't stop, damnit, okay, oh fucking kayeeee. Fuck that, where you at?"

He let her know very harshly that he was waiting for her at the turnoff into the woods and that she had to hurry up. But she didn't even hear the last part because she was already gunning down the narrow dirt road before he had a chance to finish talking.

Within a minute, she was waving at him as she turned onto the interstate. All he could do was shake his head and crank the truck back up and follow her.

What he didn't notice was the car that pulled out of the woods after he had gotten about a half-mile down the road. Lt. Woo had parked in the woods when they had veered onto the dirt road. She couldn't even explain it, but her instincts had told her that they had reached their destination. With her suspicious nature running in overdrive, she had jumped out of the car and run down the dirt road after them. She had arrived in time to see the woman get out of the car to follow him into the woods. She had worked her way through the dense foliage as he was backing the rig away from the building.

Having seen enough she headed back to the car to wait for the girl to come out. In her haste to leave she stepped on a branch and froze because of the loud sound it made and the sudden intake of the woman's breath through the bushes. Knowing that she was only a few feet from the woman's location, she proceeded cautiously through the remaining woods to the dirt road.

Lt. Woo realized that she was heading in the wrong direction when she rammed her shin into their car. The woman scrounging about in the foliage muffled her loud humph. She quickly righted herself, spun around and headed the other way. She didn't even realize that she had been holding her breath until she had gotten back to the highway. She bent over to catch her breath and composure before she broke into a sprint for her car.

She was about to pull onto the interstate when she saw the headlights of the tractor-trailer in her rearview mirror. She was far enough away that she was able to pull off onto another dirt road and cut off her lights undetected by the driver. He pulled up on the side of the road, evidently waiting for the woman to join him, so she waited.

She remained crouched down in the seat, eyeing them through the rearview mirror, until both the car and the truck passed before she backed out of the woods and fell in behind them. She stayed a safe enough distance behind to be undetected and to keep the trailer's taillights in view. The woman had pulled far enough ahead to be running interference for him.

She followed them all the way to Forest Park's Farmers Market. This made all the sense in the world since there were no fewer than fifty other trailers there at all times. She parked on the side of one of the many warehouses and walked among the many rigs until she saw the car. From there she got on her hands and knees and crept under the remaining rigs until she got to the stolen one.

"Oh shit, whaddafuck we got here," she mumbled and frowned from shock when she got where she could see inside the cab. The driver was no other than the deputy chief, RJ, sitting in the cab going over the invoices. After minutes of what seemed like tense negotiations, RJ finally picked up his cell phone, then punched some numbers. "Okay, buddy boy, we got an inventory of…"

That's when one of the other trucks started cranking up, killing the rest of the conversation for her. She backed from under the rig and headed for the front so she could at least try to read their lips. But by the time she made it there and the noise of the other rig had moderated, there was another driver in the rig with RJ and they were preparing to pull out. She sprinted back to the other end of the truck in time to see the car rolling away. Lt. Woo took a deep breath, wheezed and sprinted for her own car, wondering which one she should follow. *Damn.*

CHAPTER SIX

The Freaks Come Out at Night

When Aunt Rose pulled up at the red light at the inter-section of Dunlap and Main Streets, she had a change of mind about going to open the store. She had just left the apartment at Dunlap II, one which no one, not even Don, knew about. Unlike the young hustlers of today, who lived in the same joints they trapped out of, she knew that she needed a hideaway all to herself. There was no telling when or if those gangsters in Miami would figure out her location.

Not only was stealing all those drugs and money from that pimp who had killed her pimp profitable, it was suicidal because dude had some far-reaching tentacles that had touched a lot of people she knew. The same day that she had walked away with all of dude's goodies was the same day she had signed her own death warrant. The only link of them hunting her down was her nephew Don, who at the time, was a petty hustler and green to the drug game.

Now that she thought back on it, bringing his truly naïve ass to Atlanta had been a stroke of genius. After all she couldn't have gotten on the streets and sold all that dope without drawing attention to herself even if she had the heart of a lioness. She'd given him a little at a time to let him prove himself, which he'd definitely accomplished. And now she was extremely proud of the way he had grown in the ranks of Atlanta's top players with her as the real brains behind the scene. There was one thing she could say about the youngun: He listened to and obeyed her every wish. Of course his rewards were plentiful.

Then there was the role she had played to get the greedy, old junkie of a boyfriend of two months to buy in to and let her run the convenience store in Jonesboro. Her acting skills of playing the needy naïve widow with money to burn deserved the kind of award one only earned in Hollywood.

The precious fool he turned out to be was much like the regular tricks she had kept on a string when she was high-stepping her donkey butt on the ho strip. And like those stupid tricks, he actually was crazy enough to think that she was in love with him.

She could still see the look of confidence on his scheming face the day she had come home with the money she claimed to have inherited from a dead uncle in South Carolina. He could've cared less where the money had come from as long as he saw himself in a bed of roses. Getting him to make that deal to buy the store from the old Jew couple was one of the easiest scams she'd ever pulled off. That fool even thought that it had been his idea. Men could be so naïve themselves sometimes, for he had forgotten all about the day a month earlier when she had slipped the owner a knot of bills to say that he was looking for a buyer. So if he was tripping off the speed ball she'd induced him to do that morning, any hustler worthy of the street wars he claimed to have conquered would've recognized that it was more than a mere happening.

He had been an even bigger fool when she convinced him that it would probably be better to put the ownership in her phony name since he was in and out of jail all the time. That damn fool had been so caught up in his own ego trip that he was actually smiling in the mirror at her, thinking she was playing a prank on him when with the sweetest smile, she glided the super-sharp barber's razor across his throat. Why not? He had served his purpose and usefulness, especially after he let her know that he had no known relatives. He wouldn't be missed by anyone, sealing his doom for sure.

She was still reliving those sadistic thoughts when she noticed that Main had turned to Lee Street. Her mind instantly turned to the reason she'd decided to come that way in the first place. She needed to talk to Bertha at the strip club that Don partially owned.

Now that was a real stroke of genius the way she had maneuvered Don from the petty hustler to first peddling dime rocks in the projects to co-ownership of the strip lounge and later, the 617 gambling spot on Auburn. She often wondered what those niggas Mack and Junior would really think if they knew that she was one of the shooters that night years ago. Or that she'd provided the police with the info that flushed the other gunmen, knowing that those gung-ho clowns would fight to the death. They did when Mack and Junior's buddies gunned them down before the police got there.

Except for that bitch-ass nigga Wyatt Earp who somehow managed to duck their permanent resting place overlooking the King Memorial. It still felt good to know that he had yet to figure out that she was the one that wired the drug squad to his having all the dope he had scored from her, as well as the whereabouts of several guns he had used in some unsolved murders. Was he ever the fool, like all the others who had served her purposes and had fallen on bad times and the graveyards.

Enough reminiscing; she needed to holler at her girl and she was never that fond of trusting the telephone. It was always better and safer to read someone face to face. Besides, she hadn't been with her girl in a few months now and really needed some of that female attention.

Ten minutes later, she entered the sparsely occupied club and since Bertha had her back to her washing some glasses, she headed straight for the office in the rear. She went to the mini bar in the far corner to fix herself a vodka and orange juice. After a few sips, she took a seat on the couch to go over mentally what she was going to say to Bertha. One of the things she admired most about her was that she was nobody's fool, so she had to pick her words carefully. After all, she had the same ex-street walker's mentality as she had.

Rose wrapped up her short think session and walked over to pull the picture of Hank Aaron's #715 homer to the side to get to the wall safe. Removing a blue metal box, she took it to the desk, took out several stacks of money and wrote Don a short note. She replaced the box in the safe and returned to the desk and called Bertha.

"Whatcha doing, girl?" she asked in a very sweet tone.

Bertha checked the caller ID and realizing that she was using the office phone, acted a little surprised anyway. "Is that you, Rose? Girl, you are full of surprises, aren't ya? I didn't even see you come in."

So how in the hell you know I'm her bitch? she thought with a momentary streak of anger before she decided to let it slide and said cheerfully, "Yeah, I know, can you come back here for a moment?"

Bertha held the phone away frowning for a second. "Okay, give me a few minutes." She hung before Rose could respond. Of course she had seen her come in through the mirror, but had figured she'd want some time to herself like she usually did when she made one of her unexpected visits.

When she stepped into the room, Rose gave her a brief smile before she walked over to the window to peek out of the blinds.

She stood there long enough for Bertha to start to feel a little uncomfortable in the middle of the room before she turned around and went back to the desk.

Rose flexed her shoulders, folded her arms across her chest and relaxed against the back of the chair admiring the heavyset red-bone. Bertha's cute cherubic face, humongous breasts, pert little nose and full, lavender-coated lips were well worth admiring. Rose often wondered if most people found it as hard as she did when it came to resisting her sexuality. Because of her size others had to be as amused when it came to matching Bertha's little girl voice with her body, which to her was an aphrodisiac all by itself.

The ever-conscious Bertha waited until she had unfolded her arms to rest them on the desk before she sat down in the chair facing her.

Rose waited while Bertha wiggled around in the chair to get comfortable before she reached into her purse to get a Virginia Slim cigarette. Staring at her intensely, she lit up and took a few drags before she finally spoke. "I need you to pump some info out of these dancers for me."

Bertha didn't like the beginning of the conversation because she didn't trust any of the girls as far as she could throw them. But her curiosity had been pumped so she sat there and waited patiently for her to fill in the blanks.

Rose felt she could trust her to some extent, not with every-thing. Hell, she couldn't think of anyone who had gotten on that level with her, but with the matter at hand, she was definitely the only one that she could. Suddenly she had the urge to get her buzz on. She took a key out of her bra to open the bottom drawer. Just before she twisted the lock, she looked at Bertha undereyed for a second before lowering her gaze to make sure that the clear tape she always placed there hadn't been disturbed. Reassured that it hadn't, she removed a shaving kit of brown suede and Ziploc baggies filled with reefer and cocaine. After receiving a brief nod from Bertha, she used a cigar leaf to wrap up a blunt with a mixture of the two drugs. She took two long tokes and passed it across the desk to Bertha, who took a few long ones herself and passed it back. They repeated that ritual until it got close to being a duck and then Rose, staring gently into her eyes, reached over to caress her hands.

With her eyes full of lust as the drug and sexual emporium hit her at the same time, Bertha slowly stood up and walked around the desk to stand directly in front of Rose.

Rose's drug-induced eyes looked up at her as the same lustful feelings started tingling through her body. She leaned her head forward to rest on her stomach. The heated aroma of her musky womanhood, drew her further down to Bertha's crotch like a magnet.

The feel of Rose's warm mouth triggered her into action and she started rubbing the back of her head as she pressed forward to meet that warmth. Bertha moaned softly to the sensation of her wet tongue soothing her skin through her clothing. Ever so slowly she began grinding her hips into Rose's face. Her moaning increased when she felt her soft hands start to edge her dress up her thighs. When the hem rose to the edge of her lacy panties, Bertha's stomach began to tremble.

Urged by her reaction, Rose started licking and kissing her crotch through the silky cloth. Bertha's thighs started trembling as well when she felt her juices oozing out of her tingling pussy. Suddenly, the phone started ringing, jarring her senses and both of them jumped. They stared into each other's eyes, neither wanting to give up the emotions they were feeling. Sighing heavily with disgust, Rose leaned back in the chair and nodded for her to pick it up. Bertha rolled her eyes back in her head, snatched the phone off the desk and said nastily into the receiver, "Yeah." Rose slapped her on the thigh, frowned and wagged her finger as she mouthed, "No-no-no."

Bertha pressed the receiver to her bosom, then took a deep breath with her eyes squeezed tightly shut until she was able to cool down. "Excuse me, who is this? No, neither one of them is here. No, not exactly, but most likely one of them should be here around seven or so. Okay, I'll let them know that you called. Bye."

She gently replaced the phone back in its cradle. Sensing that the mood had drastically changed, she straightened her skirt of imaginary wrinkles and went to sit on the couch.

After eyeing the frustrated look on her for a moment, Rose relit the blunt and said between drags, "Is that the time those two creepy muthafuckas usually come in?"

Bertha smiled at her outstretched hand and walked over to get the blunt. She squeezed it between her thumb and index finger, being careful not to let the hot ashes touch her manicured nails, and finished it off. "Most of the time, yeah." She harrumphed as she rolled it into a small ball and placed it in her mouth.

Rose sighed at the sight of her sexy tongue running across her lips and then took on a more serious tone. "What was the deal why that little bitch Mercedes left? I know that Don was showing her a lot of favoritism over the other girls but hell, she didn't seem like the type of bitch to let snooty bitches bother her, know what I'm saying?"

Bertha looked off as she stretched her arms to the point where her huge breasts jutted out enticingly. She started rubbing her neck before settling her gaze back at her. "Now you know that I used to let that little thing roll with me when I used to run packages for Don when he ran short of hoes to do it every now and then?"

Rose nodded and stared at her more intensely until she was forced to blink away the uncomfortable feeling.

"So I got to know her better than the others, anyway. I don't know how you going to take this, but she gave me every indication that she didn't like Don from the get-go."

As she expected that drew a frown and nasty grunt from Rose. Her eyes twitched at the corners wondering if Rose would snap or not. When she didn't she continued, "And to be straight up with you, she was just looking for somebody to cling on to to get away from him, if you ask me. And you did ask me, so there it is."

Rose's eyes swayed from side to side searching the floor for awhile before she finally nodded. "So the little sneaky-ass ho used my nephew. Is that what you're telling me? Because it certainly sounds like that in a fucking nutshell."

The sour look stayed glued to Rose's face after she stood up and walked over to the window. She stood there with her shoulders hunching up and down for several moments as she forced the anger out of her body. Finally she gave one heavy sigh and spoke over her shoulder. "And that don't seem sorta suspicious the way she did that shit, all of a sudden like that?"

When she didn't get an immediate reply, Rose turned around to face her with her nose flaring. Bertha stirred in the chair uncomfortably for a few seconds before she simply said, "No."

The corners of Rose's eyes twitched. "Well, it do to me." Without another word, she walked to the desk to relock the drugs in the drawer and strolled out of the room, slamming the door angrily behind her.

Bertha sat there shaking her head, stunned as the door shook from the rattling that echoed in the suddenly chilly room. "Damn, why her ass so upset about one little bitch? Hell, dozens of girls come and go out of this bitch all the muthafucking time," she muttered to herself as she left out and headed back to attend to her duties at the bar.

✠ ✠ ✠

Beverly was feeling womanly special after her rendezvous with Sparkle. And why not? She hadn't had any sex for months and on those few occasions, she came nowhere near the pleasure she got with him. After all these years he still had her number. Hell, a girl had to get some every now and then to keep feeling like she was a desirable woman.

The clicking of the police ticker tape, nor the humming of the printer, nor the ever-present din of noise in the squad room outside her office, was able to penetrate her revelry. But the aggravating banging on the door certainly was able to do so.

She squinted in anger at the rattling blinds before she frowned at the intruder of her solace. She blinked herself out of her mini trance to answer the door. "Yeah, who the fuck is it?"

Her grit faded instantly as her secretary entered the room. She smiled at Sarah, her middle-aged police lieutenant with graying temples. Her ever-present granny reading glasses were perched on her perky little nose, which she had to readjust when they slid down the bridge when she used her wide hips to bump the door open. She certainly fit the bill of the overworked aide-de-camp as she tried to balance an armload of folders against her bosom with one arm, while with the other one tried to keep a cup full of steaming hot coffee from slouching over the rim.

Damn, it seems like every time she comes in here, she's managing that miracle balancing act of hers, Beverly thought as Sarah mumbled something undetectably through the silver ink pen clenched between her ruby red lips.

Beverly shook her head with a smile as she tried to put everything down in one motion. She didn't quite make it as the black liquid practically jumped over the rim. Instinctively, Beverly stretched out her hand to try to prevent the spill from spreading all over her highly polished desktop. "Ow, ouch, damn, that stuff is hot, girl. Whatcha do, boil it or something?" she yelped as the hot liquid sprinkled her wrist and forearm. She quickly scooped up a handful of napkins out of the dispenser and began wiping up the mess.

"Sarah, how in the world could you bang on the door that hard and then try to put all that stuff down at one time anyway? Who dya think you are, Houdini? Damn, girl."

Sarah Barnes, rosy cheeks blushing under her gray eyes, peered undereyed at her boss as she pushed the glasses back up her nose with her baby finger. "I didn't. I do all the time with these big-ass hips of mine, but anyway Lt. Woo saw me approaching the door and called herself helping. Shit, if she called herself doing that, she could have at least taken the cup out of my hand, know what I'm saying? But so much for the hired help, huh?"

Smiling demurely, she attempted to straighten up the nonpresent wrinkles in her navy blue skirt. "Oh yeah, and by the way, she said that she'd be in here after she gets herself a cup of the house specialty here." She mugged up at the cup as she sipped and grimaced. "Why can't they change this stuff to Folgers or Maxwell House, or something resembling tasty."

"Sarah, it is Folgers." Beverly smiled.

Sarah wrinkled her nose and fluttered her eyelashes. "Hmph, could've fooled me. They need to get somebody else to make it then."

Beverly took a few sips from her Atlanta Falcons mug and smiled. "You could always bring yo own. Hell, maybe even get some of that cappuccino up in this joint. Then you may not have to go through that face-mugging thing you seem to enjoy doing so much." She friskily nodded her head.

Sarah, being in a little sassy mood of her own, took advantage of the one her boss was in and kept the good-natured conversation going. "Hmm, who been flocking in your nest there, honey? You sure in a peppy mood there, girlie." She smiled prissily.

Beverly blushed and stuck her tongue out with a devious smile. She knew that the frisky girl in her was trying to take over, so she started shuffling the papers on her desk. She squelched up her nose. "None of your business, Miss Nosey Ass."

Sarah wasn't about to let her off that easy and gave her a matronly smirk. "Hmmph, uh-huh, I knew I was right. You been doing the nasty, ain'tcha?"

Beverly's head jerked involuntarily for she couldn't believe that she was getting all up in her biz. On the other hand, if her inner glow was that evident, she must've really been feeling good. She gave her a hiccupped moan. "Aw, girl, shut your filthy mouth."

Their heads jerked to the door as Lt. Woo whooshed through like she was entering her own palace. Beverly's mini good mood snapped into a nasty grit at her boldness and she stood up and placed her hands on her hips defiantly.

Woo froze in her step and mouthed silently. "What?" She stood with her hands spread at her sides. "Wow, what's up? What did I do now?"

Maintaining her authoritative stance, Beverly gritted in a stern tone. "Lieutenant, how many times do I have to tell your disrespecting ass about coming in here like that? Damn, barging in like it's your office and shit."

"Aw, girl, please," Woo responded in her seldom-used Vietnamese-laced twang.

"I beg your pardon," Beverly growled as she leaned forward and placed her hands with the knuckles shining on the desk.

"Lighten up, boss lady. I got some good stuff to wiggle in ya ear." She waited wide-eyed for a response. When she didn't get one, she pursed her lips. "That is if you don't mind me reporting for duty, ma'am. Well, do you?"

Beverly covered her eyes and shook her head. *What a woman, whadda muthafucking woman this bitch here is,* she thought before she sat back down. "Okay, little lady, whatcha got? What gives?"

Woo's eyes blinked wildly with excitement as she snake-rolled her head and sat down in the chair opposite the one that Sarah was standing beside. "That's a little better. Uh, by the way, what are y'all girls in here talking about?" She squinted at Sarah, not even attempting to hide the disdain she felt for the older woman. "Surely didn't sound like no official police biz to me." Her twang had all but disappeared.

Sarah rolled her eyes at Woo, snorted and started ruffling through her paperwork before she cleared her throat. "What difference does it make what we were talking about? It ain't had a damn thing to do with you, Missy." She stood up and folded her arms across her chest and turned her mouth down when she spoke. "Go ahead, chief, get on with your business."

Beverly knew that it was time for her to intervene. "Ladies, ladies, I can see that y'all really enjoy each other's company. But shall we go ahead with your report, Woo? Or do I need to continue to referee this cat fight y'all insist on having?"

Woo rolled her eyes away from Sarah and smiled at Beverly. "No, bossa lady, no fight. I just want to keep you up on the activity on the hotel strip. I really think we are close to wrapping up the goods on one of the suppliers." She leaned back in the chair and wiped her mouth studying both women, wondering whether she should let them know about the deputy chief. But the look on Sarah's face sealed the no on that announcement.

Beverly leaned back in her own seat, all business now. "And please continue." She leaned forward to rest her chin on her hands that she had pyramided on her cluttered desk.

Woo shifted again in the seat, really cautious now as to how much she could or should say in front of them. Not feeling comfortable, she quickly decided to feed out only enough to let her know that she was still hard on the case. Besides, she felt that she had to dig a little deeper before she turned over what she knew of the deputy chief's obviously illegal activities. There was no telling what all that dirty bastard had his filthy hands in. Maybe what she saw at the Farmers Market was only the tip of the iceberg of a much bigger operation; and well worth investigating further before she let the big heads in on it. After all, he was still one of them, which meant that she had to walk very carefully or she'd wound up in some deep bullshit—shit so deep that she might not be able to dig herself out of it.

And if things proved to be a lot bigger, she surely wasn't beyond blackmailing him. What the fuck; he was a dirty cop. She squeezed her eyes that much more tighter. "I've, I mean, we've tracked the source as coming from a major supplier in Miami."

Sarah fidgeted in her seat and leaned forward, making sure to show the little bitch just as much disrespect as she had shown. She wrinkled her nose and ran her eyes up and down her body. She fought back the urge to reach across the table and slap her one good one upside her head, praying that the little bitch could see the hatred in her eyes. She chanced a peek at the chief and quickly looked away when their eyes met. The look on Beverly's face made her feel ashamed at the way she was allowing her personal dislike for the diminutive pest to affect her professional attitude.

It was hard but Sarah managed to swallow her anger and pride. Snorting out of self-disgust, she wrinkled her nose, then twisted around in the seat before she squared her shoulders and said in a gravelly tone, "Lt. Woo, we really do appreciate your keeping us informed with your progress." She paused to clear her throat and crossed her legs as she snuck another peek at Beverly. "We'll put it with the rest of the data we've collected so far." Satisfied with the bewildered look on Woo's face, she sat back and eyed the chief questionably and rolled them nastily from her adversary.

Woo squeezed her eyes into tight little slits as she conceded for the moment and reluctantly placed her paperwork on the desk. She leaned back in the seat and took a deep breath thinking, *What in the hell is up with this bitch?* She tried to get a handle on what Sarah was really feeling, especially since she had never agreed with anything she had ever said before. Blinking her eyes rapidly, she rolled them to the ceiling and pinched the bridge of her nose to help fight off the urge to reach out and slap the taste out of her smirking mouth. It was really hard but she managed to restrain herself.

Beverly covered her mouth with her eyes roaming from one to the other. The tension between them was evident. A smile crept to the corners of her mouth as she admired the way Sarah was forcing her feelings aside to display a sampling of professional manner. Since she would never pick sides the way they wanted her to, she cleared her throat to show she wasn't in the mood for any of their nonsense. It was also a wedge to shield the rift between the two wannabe combatants as she gathered her own thoughts for a response.

She shook her head trying to erase the comical image of a cat fight out of her mind and smiled demurely at each of them in turn. Pinching her nose as she dug a finger in her ear, she snorted several times to relieve the sudden itch there before she began to reshuffle the papers on her desk. After a couple of moments of icy silence, she stated in a stern voice, "Okay, ladies, now that we've taken the time to get the ants out of our panties, shall we go on?"

Woo blinked a few times as if she was coming out of a trance and started massaging her neck and collarbone. While Sarah squeezed the bridge of her nose and pulled on her earlobe. Beverly felt that her display of sternness was a worthy attention-getter, licked her lips and rubbed the corner of her partially opened mouth with her baby finger. "Lieutenant Woo, we are already aware of this so-called Miami connection." She squinted at the befuddled Woo. "So I think you should dig a little deeper before you bust up in my office like it's your private domain. And please excuse yourself now and investigate further. Thank you, you're dismissed."

Beverly placed her hands on her desk and stood up with them set firmly on her hips to indicate that the meeting was over. She ignored the smirk on Sarah's face.

Woo rose stiffly, rolled her eyes at Sarah, which certainly didn't go unnoticed and left the room.

"Ooooooh, that little bitch is gonna kung fu somebody's ass, for sure," Beverly said as she turned her attention back to Sarah. "Sarah, could you please stop gloating long enough to handle these for me?" She pushed a small stack of papers at her.

She managed to maintain a stoic look until Sarah left the office and then she picked up the phone. As she waited for the other end to pick up she couldn't help from feeling that Woo was holding back on her. Maybe it was because she didn't want to discuss her affairs in the presence of Sarah, or maybe there were other reasons. Whatever it was didn't sit too well with her. Would it become necessary to start looking at Woo as an adversary?

CHAPTER SEVEN

Snazzy Bitches on the Prowl

Rainbow and Sparkle were cruising along I-20 on their way to Al's poker game when they spotted Yolanda on the corner of Candler Road waiting to cross the intersection. She immediately broke out into a cheesy grin and started waving her arms frantically to get them to slow down.

Rainbow pulled onto the shoulder and cut an eye over at his boy and they both turned to watch her dodge through the fast-moving traffic to get to them. As she got nearer, Rainbow cocked a brow. "Hey, dog, I thought that bitch was supposed to be showing Mercedes and that new ho of B's the ropes with Violet?"

Sparkle hunched his shoulders and turned around to watch her through the rearview mirror. He wondered the same, but his main concern was about his girls since he hadn't heard anything from them in awhile. He started massaging his chin as he studied her while she reached for the door handle. He felt better when she didn't show any discomfort as she wiggled to get comfortable in the seat.

Rainbow turned around frowning at her over the top of his sunshades before he looked at Sparkle. "Cool with me if you ain't bugging about your woman, man; hell, so why should I?"

Acting like she hadn't heard a word, Yolanda leaned forward to press her elbows on the top of the seat and said cheerfully, "Where y'all niggas headed?"

"We were wondering the same thing about you, Miss Slick," Rainbow answered as he turned back around and steered into the speeding traffic.

"Yeah, girl, where's everybody?" Sparkle added.

Yolanda reached across the seat and pushed both of them on the side their heads playfully. "They up at Clara's room waiting for me to get back. I know y'all niggas got a blast for the head, so hit a bitch off with a little something-something." She put on an award-winning smile, placed her hand on Rainbow's shoulder and used the other hand to reach into his shirt pocket, which earned her a quick slap on the wrist.

They eyed each other from the corners of their eyes, both fully aware that 'B' had gone to score a nice piece of coke from Al. So why hadn't he given his so-called main squeeze any of that?

Sparkle responded first by turning his mouth, which drew her immediate attention. He felt rather than saw the contempt on her face as she slithered closer over to him. So close that he could feel her breath on his neck. She wasn't hesitant to spit. "Damn, bro, why you gotta be gritting like that there? Like I done said something wrong."

He leaned away, causing her to shift her head back before she held her hand in front of her face, blew her breath into it and sniffed. "What, nigga, my shit humming or something?"

He shook his head and smile at her witty ass. "Girl, you something else," he mumbled under his breath before he said in a louder voice, "Naw, shawtie, yo shit don't stink. I was just wondering why and how yo slick ass managed to leave Violet and them in a hotel room while you go scouting for some dope that should already be in the room with Clara since our boy just scored some shit a little while ago."

She leaned away from him like she was in total shock, definitely not wanting to believe that her nigga had done her like that. "Man, 'B' left us in the room over an hour ago and you saying that he had a fresh package. That son of a bitch ain't said a damn thing about it either. Fuck that, I ain't gonna be sitting around sucking on my thumb waiting on his ass. Hell, I got my own muthafucking money."

She pushed Rainbow on the shoulder before adding. "Hey, to tell y'all the truth, I was out here hunting down an eight ball or something before we hit the road again. Oh yeah, and those two new honeys are wild for a bitch. Must be both of their first time mixing a speedball with ganja. Hell, they back there geeking for a bitch."

She definitely caught Sparkle's attention and he turned around and squinted at her. "Why you say it like that, woman?"

She gave him a quick snake roll with a smirk on her face. "Shit, nigga, that little thang of yours is so hyped by all the shit me and Violet been pumping into her. Hell, let's just say that she's up there wilding out, ready to go and try to steal the muthafucking Hope Diamond. Dog, she even up there giving up lap dances and everything, she so pumped up."

Rainbow bellowed in laughter and punched Sparkle on the shoulder. "Looks like you done found you a winner in little mama there, dog."

He caught Yolanda's eye in the mirror before he tossed her a fifty block over his shoulder. "So when y'all going to get started on this stealing spree you talking about?"

Even though she was accustomed to using her wiles to get what she wanted from gangstas of all different kinds of lowlife living, she wasn't expecting him to throw her some dope like that. She smiled and looked around nervously at the ongoing traffic like he'd tossed her some top secret information, then she opened the small plastic Ziploc bag and chipped off a piece of the rock. She magically produced a shooter and put a piece to blaze and replied between harrumphs, "'B' called about a half hour ago to let us know that he'd pick us up in a bit. But we a bunch of bitches that know y'all niggas full of shit, so I decided that I was gonna hit the street and find us some stuff to do while we waited on his ass." She was never a big hitter, so after that first blast, she rolled the rest of the rock back into the baggie and placed it and the shooter back inside of her bra.

The two hustlers gave each other puzzled looks before Rainbow arched his brow and pulled into the exit lane. Suddenly, a thought hit him and he crossed over Wesley Chapel and reentered the interstate and headed back in the same direction. After a half-mile or so of heading that way, he noticed a smirk on Yolanda's face in the mirror. *This conniving-ass ho been working us from the get-go, knowing damn well that my boy here would be wanting to check up on his girls after what she had said. Uh-huh, her slick ass was figuring that she could get a free high and get back there without costing her jive ass one red penny, fucking bitch*, he thought as he saw the Red Roof sign in the distance. He cut an eye at his boy and knew instantly that he was thinking the same thing. All he could do was shake his head and honor the bitch's gaming skills.

The parking lot was full of cars as they stepped out and followed her swinging that big ass of hers like she was trying to entice whatever male eyes were in the vicinity. They smiled at each other as they fell in behind her like they were following the Pied Piper. No sooner had they entered the room when the little Asian spark-plug jumped up and wrapped her legs around Sparkle's waist.

Rainbow *pssted* and *harrumphed* at the excitement on his boy's face as the little bitch worked her magic on him.

Sparkle twirled her around like she was light as a feather.

"What's this I hear about you showing out up in here, sweetie?"

She smiled with glittering eyes. "Me happy to see you, daddy." She looked undereyed batting her long lashes at him and then started sulking with a sexy pout.

Rainbow had sat on the bed between Violet and Clara but when he saw the way Sparkle had melted under the little ho's charm, he got up and gave Sparkle a disgusting frown and headed for the bathroom. He couldn't believe his boy was going for that after watching how he'd handled women for all these years. He had to admit that the bitch was certainly due some praise because she was putting in some serious work on him. He closed the bathroom door knowing that he had to get in his boy's shit later on. No way was he going to let him be played like a trick, period.

After relieving himself, Rainbow stepped back into the room and immediately started gritting at them swapping straight shooters and gleaming at a XXX-rated porn flick on the TV. *Fucking freak*, he thought, checking out the wild-eyed group.

He was finally able to catch his boy's attention and waved for him to join him. When he didn't move right away he started jerking his head and threw his arms in the air mouthing. "Nigga, whaddafuck." He waited until he got within earshot and away from the girls to whisper. "Damn, soldier, what it take, a fucking grenade? I really need to holla atcha sucker ass for a few."

Sparkle slowed down when he saw the expression on his face. *What's his fucking problem?* He followed him into the bathroom. Without thinking he closed the door and plunged them into total darkness. He flipped on the switch and turned around only to jump back because they were so close that all they had to do was flinch their lips and they'd be kissing. Damn.

From the way Rainbow's brows were knitted tight, he knew this was a serious matter. But he couldn't figure out for the life of him what the problem was, so he opened his mouth to say something only to meet Rainbow's raised palm to cut him off. He backed away and sat on the bathtub.

Rainbow leaned back against the wall and started knuckling the corners of his eyes for a second or two before he sighed. "Nigga, how can you let that bitch play you like that?" he said with a hard grit.

Really confused now, Sparkle pinched his nose and pressed his back against the door. "Play me like what, dog, what the fuck are you talking about?"

Rainbow stared at him for a moment before he looked away and started massaging his neck and rotated his shoulders. Then he sighed heavily again. "Check this out, partner. How many times do I have to tell you don't be allowing no bitch to show all those type of outward emotions in front of your other girl?" He held up both hands when he saw he was about to reply before he was finished with what he wanted to get out. "What ten, twenty, a hundred muthafucking times?"

Sparkle made a face. He really wanted to say something like it not being that important but held his tongue because he sensed him in one of his hardcore pimping modes. He shifted his feet from side to side waiting for whatever was to come next. Then he realized that he was waiting for his reply, so he flexed his shoulders. "Yeah, uh-huh, about that many times, mmm–hmm, about a hundred fucking times is all."

He'd barely gotten the last word out when Rainbow leaned in closer and hissed. "You damn right about that fucking many." He paused to take another deep breath. "Do I really have to tell you why?"

Sparkle started rubbing his chin, looking like he was in deep thought before he sighed. "Because I don't want to give Violet or any other bitch I've hooked something that she can compare my actions to her with."

Rainbow coughed into his fist before he finally smiled. "Yeah, that too, but the way I see it, playa, is that the little bitch ain't paid nearly enough dues where she deserves no kind of favoritism and especially in front of an old player like Violet. Dude, old girl done earned her stripes with you and this ho is just starting, feel me?"

Sparkle frowned and folded his arms across his chest. "Favoritism, man, how am I showing her any kind of favoritism?"

Rainbow sat on the toilet and crossed his legs. "Let me ask you this? How long, naw, naw, let me put it this way. Have you ever let Violet hug and kiss on you openly in front of her and other folk? Nigga ain't no need to go scratching your fucking head and shit."

Sparkle looked to the side. "Never, man, she ain't never did it."

"Exactly, that's because she's been in the game long enough to know that a ho ain't supposed to do that shit there, period. So don't be letting shortie girl do it either. In other words playa make her earn her stripes and then you still don't allow her to do that shit in front of your crew partner. You feeling me on this?" He didn't give him the time to respond as he kept it going with, "So now what you got to do is put that little bitch on front street and let her know that she fucking special. So when we step out of this bitch, don't say a word to her. Go grab Violet and y'all split. Go back to y'all crib, fuck the brakes off her old ass, get higher than a muthafucka, whatever. And don't worry about shortie; I got her. Better still, I'll get Clara and Yolanda to preach to her about the do's and don'ts. Just gon' enjoy your time with Violet and me and 'B''ll get her on the boosting track where her ass belongs."

"Thought you was locked on going over to Al's to do your poker thang?"

"My nigga, later for that there; this biz here is a lot more important than slinging some cards. Hmm, by the time you catch back up with little Miss Slant Eyes, she'll be ready and eager for some heavy boosting tips and adventures with your old gal Violet. Besides, you already know you got a gold mine in your legend standing over there. So show her some respect for her station with you." He maneuvered his face to block out Mercedes' burning eyes and lowered his voice. "At the same time, you'll be having shortie know what she got to work at to be. Play ya cards, nigga. They right in your face, ya feel me?"

Sparkle blinked a couple of times, cleared his throat and said gruffly, "You mean pit them against each other without saying a word?"

"Exactly." Enough said, he got up and swaggered back toward the girls. Following suit, Sparkle walked straight past Mercedes, snapping his game into full effect in resistance to the warm sexy smile she was creaming him with as she wiggled on the edge of the bed. The smile disappeared when he ignored her and stood in front of Violet with a stoic face. "Where your keys at?"

Being the veteran she was, Violet didn't say a word. She reached into her bra and handed them to him. He took them and walked to the door, saying over his shoulder. "Let's roll."

Violet hunched her shoulders and got up to follow him. Mercedes pranced after them but quickly stopped in her tracks when he said on his way out the door, "Not you, shortie, I'll see you later." She frowned and sat back down on the bed, disappointed and puzzled.

As they were pulling out of the parking lot, he looked across the seat and smiled. "Call your boy in Buttermilk Bottom and tell him to fix us up a nice ball of the killer boy he be slanging."

She pulled her cell phone out and hit the digits. Some thirty minutes later, after they had copped the dope, they pulled into a

BP gas station a few blocks from her crib. While he was pumping the gas, they saw her niece Joyce coming out of the Long John Silver in the adjacent building with a box of food. She broke out into a brilliant smile. "What y'all two slick-ass old-timers up to?"

They very last thing I need right now is this shit-talking-ass ho showing up, he thought as Joyce plopped into the back seat while he was still pumping the gas.

"Whatcha think ya doing, bitch?" He frowned after he screwed the cap back on.

She rolled her eyes in disgust and spat sassily, "Shit, why I got to answer your ass? This here's my auntie car; ain't that right, Auntie V?" She emphasized "auntie" and it worked.

Sparkle caught the expression on Violet's face from the corner of his eye. Blood was a lot thicker than cum, he had to admit. It didn't mean he had to like it and he didn't. Nor did he try to hide his disgust for whatever good it did, which he quickly realized meant nothing.

He parked in the small parking lot and waited until Violet was heading for the door before he turned to growl at Joyce. She'd already gotten out and slammed the door. But not before making sure he saw the fire darts shooting from her eyes roaming up and down his body with her lips turned down in disgust. She knew she'd already gotten on his nerves but that wasn't enough, so she rolled her eyes. "You coming in too, playa?" he spat with such venom that it caused his blood to boil.

"Ugh, I'm gonna fix your little red, nasty-mouth ass one of these days, bitch," he muttered under his breath as he got out of the car.

He could barely control the laugh stirring in his gut when he saw her do the snake roll thing that snazzy bitches do when they really want to get you riled. "Whaddafuck you say, nigga?"

He felt no need to give her any more ammunition for she had

enough attitude. Even if he wanted to hit her with another sarcastic remark, she didn't give him the chance. She spun around and sashayed toward the door and slammed it behind her.

He had caught the sway of her slim hips, knowing she was throwing some extra pop to mess with him. 'Bitch, dirty-ass little red bitch, her ho ass trying to entice a nigga and that shit working, too." *She sho make a nigga wanna get all up her narrow little ass.* The thoughts tortured him and his libido as he rounded the car. He shook his head, trying to will himself not to let the little slut get to him like that, but those little sexy hips were fucking with him. "Naw, her little teasing ass don't go for a nigga like that," he muttered under his breath as he picked up the pace to catch them.

When she slammed the door, he grunted. "Uggggh, I'm gonna kill this ho before long." he growled as he kicked it back open, hoping to catch the back of her ankle or something.

No such luck, as they disappeared down the hall to Violet's room. Exasperated, he headed for the refrigerator to get something cool and wet to curtail his anger. That little red bitch definitely knew how to get under his skin.

After taking a few sips of the Cherry Coke, he walked leisurely to the bedroom, trying to play it cool. But he couldn't hold back from rapping hard on the door. The only response he got was a pair of muffled replies, which lit an instant fire under his skin, so he hit the door again and started rattling the doorknob. "Girl, open this damn door!" he shouted loudly. "Why you got the muthafucka locked anyways?"

Before he started to kick it in, he heard a shuffling of feet, and Joyce snatched open the door. She had an irritated look on her scowling face.

He couldn't stop from growling. "Bitch, who da fuck you think you gritting on like that there?"

His angry expression didn't faze her in the least as she wrinkled her nose and ran her fiery eyes up and down his body like he was some kind of insect or something. "Hmmph, *you*, nigga, knocking on the damn door like that, like you ain't got no sense or done lost your mind or something."

He gritted his teeth and growled, "You should've opened the door when I knocked on it the first time. You could've at least said something, damn. Why the fuck you got it locked anyhow? Ain't nobody here but us."

She turned her mouth down in a nasty sneer and stepped to the side. "Come on in, fool, ain't nobody doing nothing but getting a fucking hit, damn."

"Bitch, I know what y'all doing. I brought the shit, but your sassy ass wouldn't know that, would you?"

"Hoop, hoop, harrah, so you spent a little dough, Mr. Big Spender. Humph, is that what you want to hear, nigga?" she spat angrily before turning away. She headed to the bed where Violet was busy spreading the heroin into three piles on a small mirror. She followed by sprinkling nearly the same amount of coke on top of each pile.

He stood at the door shaking his head with his eyes narrowed lustfully admiring the way Joyce was putting that little extra sway to her hips. Her smirk made it quite evident that she knew he was watching. And he had to admit that for her to be such a petite woman, she certainly had some jelly roll in that ass of hers, very enticing.

I'm gonna deep dick dat dere bitch. Just let her keep on with that teasing-a-nigga shit. Uh-huh. Yep, gonna fix her ass up sumthing real good one of dese days. His mini sexual fantasy was abruptly interrupted by a grunt from Violet. Like any man with his hand caught in the cookie jar, he tried to look all innocent, but that was quickly given up when he saw the look in her eyes. A look that told him that he'd definitely been busted eyeing her niece's assets. And in case he thought that it was all on him she rolled her eyes at Joyce, too.

He pushed her display of jealousy to the side, sat on the edge of the bed and reached over to hug her around the neck smiling. "Whatz cooking, star?" He beamed.

She flinched away, rolled her eyes, grunted and shrugged her shoulders pouting.

"Aw, bitch, you can cut out the dumb shit, for real, yo." He grimaced and pushed her.

She gave him a snake roll which caused him to brace himself for one of her nasty retorts. But to his surprise she smiled, reached under the mattress to pull out a large blue and gold Crown Royal tie bag and dumped the contents on the bed. A bag of about an ounce of powder cocaine and three others with a ounce brick of ready rock tumbled onto the blanket. Her icky frown disappeared into a mild smile as she nodded towards Joyce, who was now leaning against the drawer. "Baby, look in that closet and get that shoe box wrapped in the red scarf."

A knowing smile dimpled Joyce's cheeks as she sprung up like a jack-in-the-box and sashayed to the closet. After first raising up on her tiptoes to look on the top shelf, she spotted the box in the corner on the floor and squatted to pick it up.

Sparkle sat there admiring the way her ass spread across her red spandex biker shorts. Then he flinched from the sharp elbow that Violet nudged sharply in his rib cage. He hated to admit it but honey had a donkey butt that demanded attention; one that couldn't be ignored easily.

"Ugh." He frowned from the blow and tried to look as innocent as he could manage. "What I do?"

"Nigga, you looking at her ass all googly-eyed and shit like I ain't even sitting here, that's what." She grimaced.

"I wasn't, I was just..." he started to say before her look silenced his oh so obvious lie.

"You was just, what? Aw, nigga, shut the fuck up. My God, a man can't help but to be a muthafucking dog, I swear."

He leaned away far enough to avoid any further blows. "Aw, girl, get real."

She reared back on the bed. "I am real. You was watching her ass, nigga."

He smirked before reaching over to pin her arms to her side, avoiding the swing he was sure would come at his head. Instead she pressed her lips together and rolled her eyes up to the ceiling. "Aw, fuck it, you ain't being nothing but a man. Come on, let's do this. Joyce, bring me that stuff on over here before dis nigga's eyes pop out of his muthafucking head."

Joyce placed the goods in front of Violet and whirled on him. "Muthafucka, I know damn well you wasn't."

He froze her with an outstretched palm. "Aw, bitch, please, you wish." He frowned in her direction like she was some kind of nasty vermin.

"Wish my ass, nigga, you are definitely too far up in yourself, that's for real, yo." She smacked her lips and looked down her nose at him.

Violet pushed her arm between them. "Aw, forget it. Come on, girl, let's handle this here before that phone starts to screeching and shit."

They got off one final grit toward each other before Joyce handed her the box and sat on the other side of the bed.

Violet took a deep breath, opened the box and took out a small digital scale and Ziploc bags of various colors and sizes. They commenced to cutting, weighing and bagging up fifties, twenties and dime rocks. Working at a steady pace and mumbling silently, it only took them about a half-hour to complete the task. Afterward, Sparkle reached under the bed and retrieved a black Adidas tote bag and removed a shaving kit and three sets of hypos and a cola cap. Violet quickly sprinkled the coke and heroin into the cap. He carefully measured and added water before stirring the mixture until all the powder had dissolved in the water. He could tell they were overanxious to see how he reacted to the potency of the speed ball first.

Damn dirty-ass hoes wanna see if my ass die first, he thought as he unlooped his belt to use as a tie to make his veins pop up. Violet knew he had the strongest resistance from the other times they had oiled. And scary-ass Joyce never had the nerve to hit herself.

He had started to jack the hypo for the third time when the big rush hit him. "Whew, dis here be dat shit, y'all," he mumbled as he snatched the needle out of his armpit and broke out into a sweat that quickly started to soak his shirt.

Joyce leaned forward over the bed with a quizzical look on her face wondering if the nigga was going to go out. No way she wanted to be around some stupid nigga who had overdosed. When he didn't fall over, she reached across the bed and shook his shoulder. "Owee, dat shit must sho nuff be the bomb, auntie. Look, Violet, this nigga's slobbering all over himself, hmm-hmmm."

When he didn't respond, she shook him again. "Nigga, you done broke out like you under a fucking shower. Damn, you sure you aight?"

He tried to wipe the sweat off of his forehead with the back of his hand and forearm. She was definitely right; it was like he was standing under a shower. He had all but forgotten about the hypo pressed between his fingers when she pulled it away and placed it on the mirror on the bed. He hardly noticed the blood that had started to stream down his arm when she began to dab at it with a face cloth before it could drip all over the bed. They hadn't noticed Violet's absence until she came rushing back with some ice wrapped in a rag and paper towels, then began wiping his forehead and neck.

When he came out of it, Joyce looked him up and down and spat sassily, "Shiiit, nigga, tain't no need to be looking stupid. Yo ass, aight. Fix me up some of that."

Sparkle blinked a few times to get himself together and cocked an eye at Violet, who nodded with her mouth twisted down. He wiped his mouth, then took a deep breath. "Bitch, give me a second. That shit there ain't no joke, yo."

"Sec my ass, nigga, come on, yo ass feeling good. I wanna feel that good, too." She practically screamed as she picked up one of the hypos, drew up some of the mixture, plucked it on the side and licked her lips in anticipation. He squinted at what she'd drawn up and thought, *I should let her loud-mouth ass do all of that there so she can shut her muthafucking mouth.* "Greedy-ass ho, you know damn well yo ass can't handle that much. I should go ahead and hit yo ass and watch you crawl all over the floor before your stupid ass dies. But I feel too good right now to have to clean the piss and shit that's gonna come out of your stanky ass."

He could've never faced Violet knowing he'd let it happen. Plus, he still had ideals of banging that ass. He took one last good nod and snatched the hypo out of her hand and squirted some of it back into the cap. She wasn't even paying attention, too busy tying his belt around her upper arm.

Ignoring the wide-eyed look on her face, he pressed the needle up against her vein. As the needle started sliding in, she noticed that the tube was only half of what she'd drawn up; less than a third of what he'd shot himself. Deep in her heart she knew that she couldn't stand it. She felt like he was trying to beat her for her shot. "What the fuck you call yourself doing, man?"

He looked at her and shook his head. "Bitch, shut the fuck up. I don't want your silly ass dying and throwing all up on me with your stupid ass."

"Aw, man, that's fucked up, yo." She frowned angrily.

"Aw, my ass." He gritted as he reached for her arm. She yanked it away like she was really pissed off.

Violet lost patience with both of them. "Y'all bastards wanna stop with the dumb shit so I can get me a fucking blast? Damn."

"Hell, baby, this bitch knows damn well that she can't handle dat," Sparkle said. "Hell, I'm fighting not to throw up my damn self."

Joyce, left holding the belt wrapped tightly around her forearm, balled her face up. "Who you calling a bitch, punk-ass nigga?"

"You bitch, because that's exactly how your low-tolerance ass be acting." He growled and hit her with a stare that shut her mouth. She pouted and stuck her arm out. For a pure redbone, her veins were really hard to see. She yelped from the sting of the needle prick. "Ow, muthafucka."

He wasn't hearing it. "Shut up, tender-ass bitch."

"I..." she tried to complain.

"Bitch, I said shut the fuck up and keep your bony-ass arm still."

Despite her angry grit, she complied. He had to stick her three times before he finally was able to register a hit, with her wincing like he was killing her the whole time. After jacking the plunger for the third time and seeing the beads of sweat pop out around her hairline, he said sarcastically, "Yo, jaw-jacking ass be acting like you all tough and shit. You ain't nothing but a soft wimp;

can't even take a little needle pinch without going through all that mushy girly stuff. Bitch, I swear."

The rush hit her so hard that she wasn't able to say a thing, couldn't even muster up a swallow. Sweat started pouring down her face. "Whew." She wheezed and moaned softly.

Sparkle leaned away and smiled. "Yeah, whew, aight, I told ya da shit was the bomb. And your sassy ass wanted the whole shot like you could carry it like that. You'd be kicking and rolling on the floor foaming out the mouth if I hadn't squirted some out."

He was really enjoying the I-told-you-so when he felt a slight nudge at his elbow and Violet's voice ringing in his ear. "Okay, baby boy, get me fixed up before dat crazy-ass ho start to puking all over the place."

Her flip remark must have triggered it. Joyce rose off of the bed with her hand covering her mouth and staggered toward the bathroom. She didn't quite make it to the toilet before the sound of her puking echoed throughout the room. He smiled and leaned sideways on his elbow, then shouted over the noise. "Dat's whatcha greedy ass get! I tried to tell yo hard-headed ass."

Violet held out the hypo for him to hit her with and he smiled when he noticed she had squirted some back in the cap. "That's right, baby. I knew you wasn't gonna be acting all stupid like sister girl in there heaving her guts out."

She smacked the pit of her arm and rubbed it up and down vigorously. "Take your time and make sure that you be careful with that needle. You nearly tore my skin off the last time." He drew a hit on the first try and injected the dope into her vein. As he started to jack for the second time, she grabbed his hand and jerked from his grip. She jumped up and rushed to the bathroom.

When she disappeared through the door, he heard two grunts. He rushed over and fell back laughing at the sight of Violet. She was hanging over the tub with her feet dangling over Joyce's legs, whose head was stuck down in the toilet bowl, Her body was still heaving and gagging.

He bent over holding his side for several seconds before he was finally able to speak. "See there, I told both of y'all greedy-ass hoes that shit was the bomb." A series of more gags and coughing answered him.

Before he could go help them, the phone started ringing. Sparkle rushed back into the room in time to catch it on the third ring.

"Whatzup, dog?"

"Who da fuck is this?" he started to say before he was cut off.

"My nigga, it's me. Whatcha doing?"

Sparkle's head was still ringing from the speedball rush, so he didn't recognize the voice immediately.

"It's Rainbow, fool, yo ass must've run into some bomb-ass dope or sumthing, huh?"

He sat up straighter on the bed. "Yeah, dog, I hear ya."

"Damn, you must've really hit a good one there. Ha ha ha, nigga can't even talk. Betcha mouth all twisted up and shit, huh? Make sure you save me some of that shit there, dog."

Sparkle wiped his brow with a damp rag and looked down at the rivulets of sweat rolling down his chest, steadily drenching his shirt. "Uh-huh, shit be good, dog, fo sho. So what up?"

"I betcha it is. Anyway, get yourself together. I'll take my time getting over there."

"Uh-huh."

"Uh-huh. Yo, dude, 'B' done split with the girls, says that he'll holla."

"When this happen?" Sparkle's voice slurred.

Recognizing that his boy was really fucked up from the hit, Rainbow took a deep breath. "Aw, man, tell you what, partner. I can tell yo ass did some really good shit. Who you score that shit from? Naw, fuck dat, it don't make a difference. Draw yourself up a good shot of girl by itself. That'll help knock some of the effect of that boy down a bit."

Sparkle continued to wipe at the sweat. "Okay, I'll do that. When you saying you coming? Whatcha got planned anyway?"

"Just got a call from our boy Duke. He's with Googie and they gonna hit the 617 tonight."

"Whaddafuck you say, man?" Sparkle grumbled and sat up.

"Said you got to get straight, man, 'cause we gonna hit that bitch tonight, playa." His voice had gotten really serious, real intense. "Just do like I told. We'll talk about it when I get over there."

"When?"

"Aw, man, you really are fucked up. Get it together, dog. I'll be over there in a half-hour or so."

"Aight. Aight, I'll see ya then," he replied between nods. He hung up and reared back on the bed, realizing that the heroin had definitely overridden the effects of the coke. Only one thing to do, hit some of the girl by itself. Out of the corner of his eye, he could see the girls emerging out of the bathroom.

He had to blink several times. He couldn't believe that those crazy hoes were dabbing themselves with toilet tissue. He shook his head. Maybe he was too high. Naw, it was true. Pieces of tissue were sticking all over their necks, jaws and arms. "Y'all some crazy-ass hoes. Y'all too damn wet, sticky and sweaty to be trying to dry off with some tissue. Come on now, that shit there is straight-up ridiculous."

Two sets of female darts shot spears at his head before Violet said, "Shit ain't funny, man, not funny worth a damn."

"Oh hell yeah it is, too. Y'all some clowns straight up." He kept laughing.

"Aw, fuck you, man." Joyce threw her two cents worth in, bumping his hip as she sat down mumbling incoherently before scooting away from the contact.

He faked an elbow at her and drew the coke into the hypo and started flexing his fist to get the vein to pop up. His eyes brightened when he spotted one right away and plunged in. "I told y'all the stuff was..." He couldn't finish because the rush forced him into silence.

Violet patted herself down before she looked at Joyce. "Honey, where dat cell phone? I know I had it when we was at the gas station. Whew, girl, I gotta stop doing this shit here, for real."

Joyce wiped her face, pinched her nose and started massaging her bottom lip trying to remember where it could be. Suddenly her eyes lit up. "Aw, damn, I think I left it in the car. Yep, that's where it's at."

Violet frowned and cocked her brow. "Well, go get it, girl. Ain't no telling who's been trying to call us."

When she left Violet turned to him, still picking tissue off of her face and neck. "Who was that on the phone?" When he didn't respond right away, she grabbed his chin, forcing him to look at her. "Damn, man, you deaf or something?"

He grimaced from the sharp pain of her nails digging into his flesh. But the rush from the coke storming through his body held his anger intact. It also gave him time to get himself together before answering her. "Oh, I heard you, girl, that was Rainbow."

She rolled her eyes and reached around him to pick up the hypo and began drawing up water to cleanse the blood residue for the next hit. "What the fuck he want? Didn't we just leave his ass at the hotel?" she mumbled, then had an afterthought. "Man, I ain't in the mood to be toting one of his dense-ass bitches around boosting and shit."

He shot up the coke. "Naw, baby, this ain't about no boosting. I think we're about to pull this sting off at the 617. You think that crazy-ass Joyce is up to playing lookout on the strip while we do our creep thing?"

Violet pulled out of her nod and muttered in a slurry voice, "Damn, I was sorta pumped up to hit a few holes to get off some of this stuff we done bagged up, to tell you the truth."

He frowned. "Star, we've been planning this here for a minute. It's time to pull this thing off, enough said."

Joyce came back into the room moaning. He could tell she'd overheard at least a piece of their conversation and was probably anticipating rolling out for a good score. After all she'd played a major part in getting the girl to get the combination to the safe.

To appease her eagerness he was about to tell her the plan to hit the club. He was rewarded with her game face. As worrisome as she was, he had to admit that honey was definitely all about getting paid and thrilled about pulling a stunt over on some top players.

It didn't feel like a half-hour had passed when he heard car doors slamming. It was time to get to stepping.

Rainbow dapped past him decked out in a dark brown suit. His initials were embroidered in shiny gold letters atop the shirt pocket. His brown leather umpire cap, pulled down low over his eyes and shining Stacy Adams gator boots, set the outfit afire.

Sparkle leaned against the wall admiring his boy. "Damn, nigga, I know damn well you ain't about to go *GQ* up in that bitch. On the real, playa, why you so fucking fly like we going on a high-fashioned picnic or a players ball or something?"

Rainbow strolled to the middle of the room and spun around in fashion show flair, twirling one of his signature ivory canes with a rams head knob on the top. Stepping behind him just as flashy was Cheryl and Sherry chatting away like a couple of high-class divas.

When Rainbow saw Joyce, his eyes lit up. To Sparkle's surprise she kicked the refrigerator door closed and walked right up to Rainbow with a cheesy smile and two cans of Miller beer. She handed him one, patted his cheek. "Come on, pretty muthafucka, that fly-ass entrance worked like a charm." She grabbed his hand and led him toward the bedroom.

Joyce stopped at the door and looked around at Sparkle. "Well, knucklehead, why you standing there looking all stupid and shit for?" she said sassily. "Come on."

The twins must have thought she was talking to them, too, so they followed. They'd taken only a few steps when Rainbow spun around and pinned them with an icy stare. They turned around and headed back to the living room and sat down on the couch.

"Bitches know better than to follow me out of command," he mumbled and then gave Joyce a nudge. He followed her into the room.

Sparkle overheard Rainbow saying, "You sure that bitch is totally scooped because we gonna need you to stay tight on her ass for another day or two in case she starts some shit. Might have to take her ass out, if she starts to sway, you feel me?"

Joyce, out of habit whenever she was on the verge of getting excited, started pulling on her ear lobe. "Nigga, please, ain't no way that bitch would play me like that. That damn pussy voodoo's on her for sure, man." She leaned forward, all up in Rainbow's grill, stabbing him in the chest with her sharp manicured fingers and frowned. "Oh, hell yeah, and I've been wanting to get back at that big black-ass nigga every since he slapped my sister Nita Bug in front of all those folk at the Decatur Festival. Hey, my pushing this magic pussy in her face must have worked because here's the combination to the safe right here." She reached into her bra and waved the folded piece of paper under his nose.

Rainbow gave her his best hundred-watt smile as he reached for the paper, only to have her snatch it out of reach. "Hold on a minute, playa." She batted her long lashes, face full of suspicion. "How I know your nasty-pimping ass ain't gonna try to go gorilla on me after y'all pull this here off?"

The words had barely rolled off of her tongue when he snapped his arm out with the speed of a cobra and put a vise grip of steely fingers around her narrow neck. She was in total shock, eyes bucked wide open in horror as he leaned forward and spat venom in her face, "Bitch, this is the only chance you get to question me, period, you got that?" His eyes were blazing to add to the death grip.

Oh, fuck, this sadistic muthafucka's really enjoying this shit. She felt the darkness overcoming her. Through the haze of bare consciousness, she heard him growl, "Don't you ever play games with me ever again, you feel me, slut-ass bitch?" He applied more pressure, yanking her closer to his satanic features.

She couldn't recall nodding, but she must have because she suddenly felt the pressure easing off. Through the thundering ringing she heard him say, "Good, now get your ass down there to the bottom. You on foot patrol, bitch." There was a slight pause before she faintly heard, "Stanky-ass ho, stay on point. If you fuck this up, I'm gonna bury your ass, for sho."

She staggered back and thumped her head against the door. Several minutes later she was still fighting the cobwebs when she felt a pair of hands pulling her along. She noticed the cemetery across from the King Memorial.

"Girl, you aight?" The buzz wasn't completely gone as the voice continued, "'Cause we ain't got but a little while to check things out."

Hell, I figured her ass already knew that nigga was crazy, Sparkle thought. "Hell, I thought she knew better, being a street bitch and all."

She swiped her hand down her face, jerking it away when she felt something icky on her palm. She took a quick double-take, then ogled at the mixture of blood and snot smeared from the base of her fingers to the hump on her wrist.

"Here, girl, use this tissue," she heard one of the twins say. The more her head cleared, the more she started to realize how deadly a situation she had gotten herself into.

CHAPTER EIGHT

Get Back Times So Sweet

I t was well past midnight when the phone finally rang. Rainbow, Sparkle and Violet all jerked nervously from the couch as the echoing noise dominated the air. They had spent the past few hours alternating blazing heroin, coke, reefer and combinations of all three while they watched television and played video games.

Violet, who had been answering most of the incoming calls and running the drug scoring missions, picked up on the second ring. She listened intently for a moment before handing the phone to Sparkle, who did his share of listening through a series of yeahs and head nods before he handed the phone to Rainbow.

"Bet, we rolling right now, soldier. See ya at the Krispy Kreme in about ten minutes." Rainbow unzipped his jacket, pulled out two Glocks, checked both of them before he handed one to Sparkle and then headed for the door.

They were lost in their own thoughts as they turned onto Ponce De Leon a couple of blocks from the donut shop. Sparkle started fidgeting, lit up a Kool cigarette and inhaled deeply. "Yo, dog, I know you all pumped up, too." He pinched his nose and sniffled. "Hey, man, why all the espionage bullshit? First, you don't let me know how deep Joyce is involved in this here and now you acting all secretive about handling this nigga Don. What's up, player?"

When they pulled up to the next red light, Rainbow snatched

the cigarette out of his mouth, then squared his shoulders. "Son, how long you been knowing me?"

Feeling no need to answer such a dumb question, Sparkle continued looking down the street. Rainbow was about to say something else when they saw Duke's black sedan parked in the donut shop's parking lot. Peeking through the misty window, they spotted Duke in the last booth sipping on a cup with Googie, their old gambling mentor from their prison days. Old fly-ass Googie. When they stepped inside, Sparkle's face broke out into a brilliant smile, one that matched Googie's. They strode to the back of the shop.

Sparkle spat at Duke out of the side of his mouth, "Aw, nigga, you could've told me about this one when you saw me on the track last week." He elbowed him in the side as he slid out of the booth. He squared his shoulder and started scissoring his arms in the air excited to see his old crew. He was dressed in black fatigues, the same as Duke. They embraced in a circle, pumping and rubbing each other on the back with exuberance. "Damn, y'all, it's been too long, niggas, too damn long." He beamed a gold- toothed smile as he held them at arm's length, showing no shame while admiring his two best students of the game.

Sparkle pinched his nose and bit down on his bottom lip. He stared at him in obvious awe, respect and love. "What can I say? You know what you are to me, playa."

Duke leaned back waiting for the display of emotions to subside before he teased, "Okay, enough of all that mushy girly stuff. We got to get a move out. We'll celebrate with a long orgy after we do this here."

They paused, looked him up and down and said in unison, "Fuck you, fat boy," followed by high-cheeked smiles as they slid into the booth.

Sparkle stared across the table at Rainbow, his eyes saying, *Thanks, you dirty muthafucka.*

Rainbow smirked and turned his attention to Duke. "The girls have been in place since early this evening fronting like they selling dope and keeping me up on everything that's moving and happening. Ain't nobody moved in or out of the joint for hours, so we set, dog." His smile brightened as he waved the paper with the combination on it in a big arc before slamming it on the table.

Duke picked up his glass and bumped it against each of their balled fists. "Man, I got to have this nigga. His jive ass sided with all of them snails against me after all those years of playing fair with him and in his joint." He paused to seriously eye Sparkle and Rainbow. "I know why y'all want this nigga, but Googie, why was you so quick to flow on this shit?"

Googie let him stew for a few before he shifted his lanky frame around in his seat, reached across the table to retrieve his glass of whatever it was he was drinking, took a couple of really loud sips, then took a deep breath. "Game is game, hustler. When you hipped me that my boys here was involved, I was automatically in. Besides, I happen to have a love affair with money like you and every other real nigga around this bitch. Oh yeah, and it'll be well worth it to see the expressions on these so-called boss niggas when they ass be getting scraped with a hard dick; no grease and they can't figure out what the hell is going on. That alone is enough to bust nut after nut, you feel me, playa?" He rubbed his bejeweled hands together with a gleam in his eyes. "What the fuck, these two niggas here be my prize protégés. I love all y'all niggas because y'all love living on the edge of this life just like me."

They all sat momentarily mesmerized with his spiel and nodded. Duke, the most impatient of the crew, spoke up. "'Nough said, old timer, let's roll."

They left the shop in Rainbow's ride, then turned right and stopped between street lights halfway down the block. Rainbow got out first and strolled innocently alone to Auburn Avenue. No one would really be paying him that much attention since he frequented the strip collecting ho trap. He spotted Cheryl immediately across the street leaning against the window of the Chinese place. He continued across Auburn and saw Sherry and Joyce on opposite corners scoring the scene. Good, the girls were on point. He motioned for Cheryl to join him where he pantomimed collecting digits as he lit up a cherry blend cigar. He puffed three times before putting it out on the bottom of his shoe. It was the signal to the others that it was on. They were set to make their move. Then he took his hat off and fanned it across his face three times. He waited until both girls down the street returned the same gesture before he headed back down the street where his boys had started toward him.

He got to the alley leading to the club and repeated the lighting signal and disappeared into the darkness. The rest of the crew entered the alley moments later, mumbling in whispers until they met him at the bottom of the stairs leading to the back door two stories up.

Googie lead the way up the stairs, stepping gingerly like a panther, followed by Sparkle, Rainbow, Duke and then Violet. Halfway up the first set of stairs they all froze when a loud squeaky noise erupted into the night air causing tingles to shoot up their spines. Sparkle waited until his knees stopped shaking before he turned halfway around and said in a trembling whisper, "Godayum, man, walk yo fat ass to the ends of the boards. You damn near had all of us jumping out of our skins, whaddafuck, nigga."

Duke pssted him off. "Shh, okay, scary-ass muthafucka, get your skinny ass on up there." He wheezed under his breath and nudged him up the stairs. They were nearly to the top when Googie shrieked. "Oh shit," and fell against the railing panting. The rest of them shrieked right along with him as a pair of glowing eyes sprinted by wailing.

Rainbow clutched his heart and cursed. "What the fuck, Googie? A cat, a fucking cat, you scary old bastard."

Googie swiped the sweat off his brow and sneered. "Nigga, yo ass sucked up like a bitch, too. Hell, all y'all niggas did. How the fuck was I supposed to know what the hell it was? I can barely see my own hand in this pitch dark, muthafucka."

Violet stepped past the mumbling men. "All y'all need to shut the fuck up. Dat shit shook yo ass like it did all the rest of us. Let's get this shit over with, y'all."

Rainbow ran his eyes up and down her body. "Hmmph, dat scary old lady up there jumping like he did is what spooked me and I won't scared, I was shocked. Girlfriend, I was shocked, big difference, shocked."

"Yeah okay, yo ass was shocked, whaddafuckever. Shocked, sure you was, then how come I can smell scary bitch coming off yo ass then?" Duke whispered as he eased by.

"Fuck y'all, fuck all y'all. Get yo ass to that window, dog, before sumthing else jump out of the shadows," Rainbow said, his voice much calmer than before.

Sparkle pulled a harness out of his jacket, tied a set of ropes around the stairs and bent under the railing and eased out to the window. He took out a glass cutter and cut a hole big enough for his hand to get through right above the latch.

He deftly flipped the latch, pushed the window up and crawled through, grunting loudly from scraping his shin along the ledge as he lowered himself to the floor. He quickly righted himself and stood up. There was a light breeze rolling against his chest. He shivered slightly before he realized that he was sweating like a dog, either from fear or the excitement or a combination of both. Exhilarated from the adrenaline rush of the first stage of a sting again, he shook off the tingling, unlatched three sets of locks and opened the door for the rest of them.

He heard a low guttural growl behind him. He was almost too scared to look around, but he did, right into the eyes and snarling mouth of a hairy beast. He turned back around to sprint for the door when he saw the dog spring at him. He opened his mouth to scream from those sharp fangs digging into his flesh when he suddenly heard *thump, thump, thump* before there was a loud crash. He turned around to see the beast whining and flopping its legs on the floor. *Damn, one of them fools done killed the dog.* He looked around to see the dart gun smoking in Rainbow's hand.

Rainbow held up his hand to say, "Hell, I didn't know, either. I was prepared for whatever, my nigga." He hunched his shoulders, stepped over the now prone dog and headed for the safe. Kneeling down in front of it, he pulled out a pen flashlight and fished out the combination. In a matter of seconds, he was stuffing boxes of cards, money and jewelry into a saddle bag draped over his shoulder. "Damn, man, I figured the niggas for at least fifty or so decks but hell, this here's closer to a couple of hundred."

"Huh!" Duke grumbled as he peered over his shoulder.

"Shit, it's like three, four, hell, maybe even five times as many as I was expecting. Fuck, we gonna need some more help with all these muthafuckas, man. Sparkle, call Lady and your nephew and tell them to meet us at the apartment over this way. Like ten minutes ago, whaddafuck." Rainbow handed some boxes of the cards to Googie.

As they were preparing to leave, Sparkle saw Duke putting together a torch set. He had been wondering what was in the saddle bag on his shoulder. He leaned over to whisper in Rainbow's ear, "What the fuck is big boy getting ready to do, yo?"

Rainbow frowned for a moment before he realized that he hadn't told him the deal. "Damn, my bad, I was thinking that I'd already let you know."

"Let me know what?" Sparkle responded angrily under his breath.

Rainbow rolled his eyes to the ceiling. "Please, man, ain't no time for that. Hell, I can't remember everything."

Sparkle sighed heavily. "Alright, but still what the fuck is he doing?"

He felt Googie's breath on his shoulder. "Yo, playa, we got to make it seem like a regular robbery, know what I'm saying?"

Sparkle stared off into space, scratched the side of his neck and mouthed. "Okay, man, I feel ya. Fuck it, let's roll, yo." It had finally dawned on him it was important to cover up having the combination. Boy, that dope really had his mind working at a snail's pace.

They slid out of the door, leaving Duke behind to do his thing, and headed for Rainbow's slum apartments four blocks away. When they reached the corner of Auburn, Rainbow flicked his lighter to let the girls they'd pulled off the lick and to stay on point until they got back.

Lady was waiting at the door when they arrived. Stacy followed about ten minutes late, eyes glistening with excitement when he saw all the decks of cards scattered on the bed and across the floor. He jumped directly into it.

Some two hours later they had completed the task of unsealing, marking, making slides and shake-outs, and resealing each deck.

Rainbow and Googie left to check on Duke and the girls and to put the cards back. They trashed the place to make it look like a robbery/burglary. They were pleased to see that big boy had managed to burn through the heavy steel safe. He was sweating like a pig leaning against the safe smoking a joint. He was so blitzed that he nearly jumped out of his skin when Rainbow shoved his shoulder to let him know that it was time to go.

When they gathered back at the apartments, they blazed rock, reefer and heroin for about an hour, celebrating a job well done. They went over the pattern of days when each of them would hit one of the skin games. Joyce was the first to split, having a date to freak Mary Anne and check her state of mind after she knew that the lick had been pulled off. Rainbow and Duke got ready to leave together after assuring the rest of them of a rendezvous later at the Red Roof Inn on Candler Road to continue the partying.

Sparkle was looking forward to getting a shot of good head to help release some of the tension.

He wanted to have a square alibi just in case, so he and Stacy decided they were going over to Al's spot to be seen at the poker game after the freak-off.

Having sealed up their plans they locked up the apartment and headed to their rides parked on the side street. The twins and Googie were to ride with Lady to wherever they were headed. As they were waving at each other from their perspective rides, the night was suddenly set ablaze with rapid gunfire. Damn, it hadn't been a perfect lick, after all. They scattered around and under the cars to avoid the onslaught.

With sweat flowing and bodies superhyped, they watched wide-eyed as several sets of feet shot by them and down the street with guns blazing behind them. They were being chased by two carloads of younguns spitting hot lead.

The gunfire was still echoing in their ears when they finally stood up after the guys and cars disappeared around the corner. Sparkle checked to make sure that everybody was okay. Googie was the first to speak. "Man, that was some scary-ass shit there. I thought our asses was busted, for sho. We better roll up out of here before the five-o show up."

Lights started coming on in the surrounding houses. Somebody was bound to throw a 9-1-1 down with all the racket. He didn't have to repeat it twice as they piled in the cars and sped away in different directions.

Rainbow, Sparkle, Duke and Googie got together the next day to split the initial take. The bigger share of the lick was going to come from the skin house now that it was flooded with their cards. While there they told the girls that another party was involved in case they got antsy. That way they'd be less likely to talk about it if they didn't know exactly who might be coming after them if they tried to cross them.

Joyce continued her lesbian affair with Mary Anne to keep a pulse on what the vics at the club were thinking. Rainbow, having handled her from back in the day, knew that she was one wily ho, but even wily hoes were scared of unknown adversaries.

They waited until the middle of the week for the robbery to wear off before they sent Cynt in to be the first to take advantage of the scam. After the whole crew had made a lick, they let Junior and Mack know about it. At first they were sorta pissed; after all they still had to deal with Black Don on a nearly daily basis. But they were also some greedy bastards and soon welcomed the chance to chop up some of Don's ends.

Rainbow occasionally intervened in Joyce and Mary Anne's secret meetings to bang the pussy and get an earful of how those niggas at the club were handling the aftermath. Things were running smoothly.

For a month they kept sending different teams to fill their pockets with the stern message not to exceed $10,000 in winnings. One night though Duke got really lucky when some out of town hustlers dropped in. He raked in six-digit money, the titles to a couple of fancy rides and hard-stepping hoes, who fell under Cynt's guidance.

Sparkle and Rainbow stopped by several times to play off the deck, winning big bucks. Playing off the deck was the best way to keep suspicions away because one wasn't actually in the game but caught side bets. You never touched the deck, stayed on the fringes of the game choosing anybody's card to bet on. Knowing the longest-playing cards was a straight-up mortal lock enabling you to trash talk other players into placing big bets and then bigger bets trying to recapture some of their loses.

Mary Anne proved to be a real trooper and eventually ended up back in Rainbow's stable. She never was told the whole story and was assigned to running the drugs out of the rundown apartments where they had fixed the decks up. She also worked cell phone orders, mostly in the suburbs.

CHAPTER NINE

Bang-Bang, Things Heat Up

The sexual tension was ecstatic with the musky aroma of the sweaty passionate bodies permeating the room. Sparkle sighed and rolled lazily off of Mercedes. It had been several weeks since they'd chilled off the scam. Most of the decks had probably been used up anyway. Money was flowing in good from the gambling, drug running and the boosting runs when Violet happily took Mercedes. In a weird sort of way, Sparkle was getting a little jealous of Violet acting like the mother hen sheltering the little princess under her wings. It was all good though because it certainly kept their pockets nice and fat with cheddar.

A comforting smile edged to the corners of his mouth when his eyes traveled to the oval ceiling mirror. He felt that familiar tingling start in his groin. *Damn, I can't get enough of this little bitch. I wonder if she done slipped some menstruation in my food or something. Damn, listen to me, all up in an old wives tale and shit.* He admired her glistening flesh. The rivulets of sweat rolling along her back to her luscious booty and creamy thighs reminded him of pearls. He blinked rapidly and groaned when he noticed a mixture of their juices lining the folds of her pink-lipped pussy.

"Whatcha say, baby?" she murmured, interrupting his hypnotizing lust and then cooed in a husky voice, "Oooooh baby, that fat-ass dick was the bomb, whew! I thought you was going to fuck me raw, for sho again." Her trembling climax finally subsided.

The sound of her sweet voice vibrating against his chest made his dick jump with a life of its own. He sighed with exhaustion. "Was it, girl? Whew! Girl, you really had me putting in some real work dere," he said between gasps of air. He rolled to his side and she moaned weakly when she felt his throbbing meat bouncing against her stomach. She reached down to grasp it and rolled her thigh on top of his. Her small fingers froze when she felt his body stiffen.

The hairs on the back of his neck pricked to attention. Was it his imagination or had he actually heard a sound like someone creeping through dry leaves? He heard the sound again and went into full alert.

Baby girl, still breathing heavily, began to speak. "Yeah, honey, daddy, we..." She froze in midsentence when he put his hand over her mouth. Her eyes budged in shock.

He whispered, "Shh, be quiet for a sec, girl, listen. You don't hear that?"

Her eyes twitched nervously back and forth and Mercedes tried to mumble a frightened reply into Sparkle's sweaty palm. He replaced his hand with a finger to her trembling lips and eased out of the bed butterball naked.

He crept to the window on the balls of his feet and eased the curtain back in time to see a shadowy figure edge around the corner of the house. He pressed his back against the wall.

Mercedes sat up in the bed with the sheet pulled up over her pert titties, nipples outlined through the dampened sheet. He waved his hands several times, signaling her to remain calm and mouthed that everything was gonna be okay. She showed no response, terrified.

He continued *shhing* her as he tiptoed to the closet. Tingling with anticipation, now as a hunter. Reaching into the multipocketed windbreaker jacket hanging on the back of the closet door, he silently removed a Glock millimeter pistol. Its weight energized his bravery genes as he quietly cocked it, placed it comfortably on his hip and crept to the bedroom door. He turned the doorknob gently. In commando mode now, he used a quick look-peek-jerk back maneuver around the doorsill.

Seeing no one, he placed his back against the wall and edged toward the kitchen where he felt the predators were headed. His senses were locked on radar as he entered the threshold of the kitchen. He had just turned his head to a slight sound behind him when the door was practically kicked off its hinges.

There was a loud thud as glass shattered and two dark-clad figures zipped through and spread to each side. He immediately raised his gun and spit fire at the splitting dangers. The return fire thundered back and he hit the floor, getting off several more shots of his own.

A dust cloud of plaster sprinkled his face, causing him to belly crawl backward into the hallway with the quickness. He peeked back around the corner and froze, as several rapidly fired shots zoomed over his head from behind. The thundering vibrations of the shot were still buzzing in his head when he heard a grunt, followed by a nervous yelp and the attackers sprinted out of the door.

Sparkle looked back and forth from his prone position. His squinted in the darkness as a silhouette emerged out of the shadows. He was too stunned to even raise his weapon, when a familiar voice whispered, "Yo, ace, you aight, dog?"

Sparkle released a heavy sigh and replied in a shaky voice, "Uh-huh, who dat? You, Rainbow?"

"Whodafuckcha think it is, fool?" Rainbow responded quickly. "Man, who in da hell you done pissed off now, dude?"

"Whew!! I'll be damned, I should be asking. Hell, I am asking;

this yo crib, man. Whoever them niggas was thought I was you, nigga," Sparkle spat as he sat up against the wall. "You got any idea who the hell dem niggas was? There, I'm asking you, man."

"Naw, partner, but we sho nuff gotta find out."

"That's for damn sure." Sparkle huffed and stood up.

Rainbow slowly eased out of the shadows, making sure to stay away from the window. He was still dressed in a black mono-grammed silk robe, matching his pajamas. He cleared his throat and said in a hoarse voice, "I think they've split, dog." He paused to take another look out the window. "I heard a couple of doors slamming and wheels screaming down the street."

"I think you hit one of them bastards," Sparkle whispered.

"Yeah, me, too, that's why they split. I know I heard one of them grunt," Rainbow spat as a smile finally came across his face.

"Oh yeah, one of them did. Matter of fact I'm gonna make a run outside to make sure every thangs safe. You check out things in here."

Sparkle nodded as he headed for the door. "Don'tcha wanna cover ya naked ass first?" Rainbow smirked as he blended back into the shadows.

Sparkle spun around, muttering over his shoulder as he headed back to the bedroom. "Ah, fuck you, man." Even through the darkness in the room, he could see that Mercedes still had the cover pulled up over her, frozen to the same spot. As he stopped in front of her, he heard her whisper softly, "Is everything aight? Those shots sounded like a damn cannon going off."

His first instincts were to cuddle her, but he kicked that emotion to the side and started pulling on his baggy blue jeans, Polo shirt and tan Timberland boots.

He put the gun in his waistband and covered it with his shirt. As he headed for the door, he looked at her frightened features and paused. He walked over and lifted her face to give her what he hoped was a reassuring smile. "Just lay back and chill. I've got to check outside to make sure but I'm pretty sure they've split."

He blinked in anticipation until she gave him a curt smile and walked halfway down the hall and turned back. When he got to the door, she sat up and scooted to the edge of the bed. Mercedes blinked demurely a couple of times before she sat on the chair and slipped on her red flowery print blouse. Then she stood and wiggled her hips from side to side as she pulled on a pair of faded blue jeans.

Sparkle sighed and his mind went all mushy. *Mmh mmh, baby girl's got one phat juicy juicy as those tight jeans fit around her like a second skin.* Her butt was so blessed you could set a cup on it without spilling a drop. It was the first thing he'd noticed at the strip club months ago when she was working the pole on the circular center stage. Didn't make no sense for her to have an ass that big and bouncy on such a little frame. He remembered how her large doe-like eyes had him thinking, *What's a girl like that doing in a place like this?* A pure aphrodisiac for sure. But the thing that made his dick ache and drool, was how she enjoyed dancing so much that he damn near thought they was actually fucking right there.

Her hypnotizing eyes were devouring his. He went all tingly when he saw the cum soaking through the crotch of her ultra-lacy outfit. Her face withered up as she undulated on the pole until she got a nut. He was certainly surprised when he felt his own nut squirting down his leg without even touching himself.

Pulling her had proven to be a real feather in his cap; not only did she keep him super-hyped for sex, she had blended right into all of their hustling scams.

"Y'all got any idea who dem dudes was?" Mercedes asked as her voice broke the trance of her curvaceous figure.

"Huh, what did you say?" Sparkle blinked as he walked over to her.

"Y'all got any idea who dem dudes was?" she repeated.

He frowned. "Naw, baby girl, but you can bet your sweet little ass that we're gonna find out, that's for damn sho."

She smile seductively, slithered off the bed and sashayed up to him and pressed her sweet softness against him. He tingled with a feeling of overprotection when she leaned her still sweat-dampened, curly head on his chest. He felt her trembling as she leaned back and caressed him with knowing eyes, and then pushed her pelvic bone against his swelling hardness.

She sighed. "You ain't gonna be away too long, are you?" Her warm breath breezed along his neck as she purred, "Because I'm not finished with you yet." Her eyes had a glassy glint in them.

Sparkle felt himself being drawn back into her magnetism, but he fought off the feeling. He started caressing her arms for a brief moment and gently pushed her away. Reluctantly, he stepped away, but not before he placed a gentle kiss on her forehead and whispered in her ear, "Just got to make sure whoever that was is gone," in a reassuring tone.

She had inched a little closer, smiling warmly into his eyes hoping to persuade him back to the bed when Rainbow yelled from the kitchen, "Yo, ace, come check this here out!"

It was extremely hard to break away from her intoxicating eyes, but he headed for the kitchen. "Yeah, partner, whatcha got?"

Rainbow, now minus the robe, was squatting at the kitchen door, staring intently at an object laying just inside the threshold. Something shiny was stuck in a dark puddle of what appeared to be blood. Since they dared not cut the lights on, neither of them could be sure. Sparkle reached up for the light switch but thought better of it. *Those creeping niggas might be on the rebound.* He knelt down beside his boy to get a better view. "Damn, looks like a bracelet, huh?"

Rainbow cocked a brow and peered at him. "Yeah, uh-huh."

As their eyes adjusted to the dark, they could see that it was indeed blood. There was a trail of it that dribbled over the sill and along the sparsely grassed dirt path beside the house, disappearing at the edge of the lawn. Rainbow traced the dribble around the corner of the house, figuring that it led all the way to the street. He squatted back down and took a ink pen out of his pocket of his pajamas and lifted the bracelet out of the puddle of blood. He held it up to the moonlight and under closer inspection could see the initial "J" engraved with gold letters etched inside the silver-plait woven jewelry.

Sparkle hunched his shoulders. "Got any idea who da fuck it belongs to?"

Rainbow tilted his head to the side, his expression bewildered. "Shit, dog, your guess is as good as mine."

Sparkle grumbled. "All bullshit aside, we got to get on this like yesterday."

Rainbow's eyes grew serious and he looked down the hall for a second before he stood up out of his crouch, grabbed Sparkle by the elbow and pulled him outside. He cleared his throat. "Hey dog, chill for a second. We haven't known these hoes dat long to be airing our biz out in the open like that." He nodded toward the house suspiciously.

Sparkle looked back toward the house and groaned, "Hey, whatcha trying to say, man?"

Rainbow cocked his ear to the door, his eyes squinting into a stare so cold that it would have chilled the blood of most regular niggas, especially those that didn't really know him. His chest heaved broadly and he menacing said, "Man, I done told you

over a hundred times, don't be trusting none of these hoes, man."
He poked him in the chest.

Knowing his boy was right, Sparkle nodded in understanding.
He reached into his pocket to extract a crumbled pack of Kools,
lit one up, took a long drag and exhaled slowly as he leaned against
the wall. Being more inquisitive than he was at calming his nerves,
he plucked it into the yard. "Okay, dog, I see whatcha saying. By
the way, who da fuck you got up in there anyways? Hell, how long
you been here? I thought I had the house to myself, for real yo."

Rainbow didn't respond immediately, but he cocked his head
to the side; a habit whenever he was puzzled about something.
Even after Sparkle repeated what he had said, he was still stuck
with the same blank expression on his face for about thirty seconds
before he finally turned to face him. "Huh, uhhhh, oh yeah, uh, I
got one of the twins up in there since you got to know." His mouth
turned down in disgust and he continued to stare off into space.

"Shit, man, which twin?" Sparkle said seriously.

Rainbow hunched his shoulders. "Hell, Spark, I don't know
them bitches apart when I'm all highed up and shit." He twisted
his neck in a circle like he was getting annoyed. "Man, what the
fuck difference does it make which one it is anyways?" The corners
of his eyes wrinkled in frustration.

Sparkle decided to ease off with the interrogation. "Naw, Bow,
you right, man. It don't make no difference, yo."

Rainbow finally smiled, punched him playfully on the shoulder
and then in his side. "Check it out, dog, fuck dese hoes. We got
to get on the trail of who dis here bracelet belongs to." His tone
turned more menacing with each word.

Sparkle twisted his head to the side and matched his stare for a
few seconds before he ran his hand down his face. After feeling
the tension of their stare-off abate, he took the bracelet off of the

pen, twisted it around several times, examining it more closely. "Man, the only 'J' I know is my baby sister's boyfriend, well, used to be old man. You think that nigga got the nerve to try something like this because I don't."

Rainbow turned his mouth down and stated matter-of-factly, "Dude, I think everybody got the nerve, except you, me and "B." He realized that he wasn't about to get a response and threw his hands in the air. "Where ya wanna start?"

Sparkle leaned back and twisted his neck in circles, moaning at the crinkling sounds that helped to ease some of the tension from his hyped-up body. Seeing that his boy was sorta struggling with his decision, he wrapped his arm around his shoulder as he led him back into the house. "Tell ya what, let's get dressed and take a ride downtown. Dem niggas on Auburn can't hold water. Hell, somebody's gotta have heard something about this bullshit."

✠ ✠ ✠

The air was shimmering in the parking lot of Turner Field. The occupant at the steering wheel in the purple-lensed aviator glasses wiped the sweat off his face with the damp dingy handkerchief he had only moments earlier wrung out. Sighing heavily, he looked undereyed across the seat at his partner and wheezed. "Damn, man, you sure they in there? Shit, we been out here way before the game started and I ain't seen no movement at all."

The passenger flicked the ashes off of the El Producto cigar out of the window, then waited until the deafening roar of the crowd eased down from the stadium across the way before he straightened up in the seat and sneered. "Man, it's damn sure hard trying to keep up with these fools. The part I can't figure out is why we can't just take their asses out and be done with it, you feel me." He didn't wait on a response and pulled his heavy pistol out of his waistband and aimed it at brick house across the street. The sadistic look on his face was quite menacing. "Like right muthafucking now, shit."

The driver eyed him up and down as he played with his bushy mustache. He was becoming leery of the psychotic emotions his partner was displaying. "Because folks said so. Face it, man, we Indians in this war, my man. That means that we sit back and do what the boss says, period."

"Why, man, we gotta kill them muthafuckas anyway, whadda-fuck."

"Chill out, dude, they must see a much bigger picture than you do; hell, than *we* do," the driver said grimly. *Why I got to get stuck with this sick knuckleheaded dumb-ass nigga anyways?* He took a deep breath and lowered the mini-binoculars so he could wipe another stream of the sweat off of his forehead.

The passenger grunted. "Fuck dat, I'm gonna…" He sneered as he reached for the doorknob and nudged the door open with his knee. With one leg stretched out of the car, he froze in mid-sentence when a menacing rod of cold steel pressed hard behind the back of his ear.

He heard a menancing voice behind him. "You gonna do what, muthafucka?"

The voice of death was so chilling that he damn near shit himself. That, along with the garlicky spittle splattering the side of his face, nauseated him to the point of spewing the entire contents of his body.

"Muthafucka, it don't matter what the fuck you think. If I even think about your stupid ass jeopardizing me, I'll…"

"Agggghhhh!" he screamed when the gun pressed deep into his ear bone.

✠ ✠ ✠

Beverly sipped the rest of her cappuccino as she lounged against her pillow watching the news with Katie Couric in her apartment in College Park. She had fought through a restless night of sleep wondering about the shooting in Jonesboro. Her gut instincts told her that her boys were involved with it in some way. Call it woman's intuition or whatever you wanted to. She knew that Johnny had some girls working out that way, but she couldn't recognize the picture that kept popping up on the screen. What the hell; her boy tossed women in and out of his web like plucking feathers off a chicken. On top of that, he hadn't answered his phone when she reached out to contact him. This caused her to worry that much more, for he usually got right back to her whenever she tried.

Even though there had been no suspects announced, she couldn't shake the feeling that Black Don was somehow connected to all the robberies and shootings. No matter how deep into her network of snitches she dug, she couldn't gather enough to tie him into the obvious drug area takeovers either.

Shaking those thoughts out of her mind, she got up and looked at herself in the full-length mirror on the bathroom door, feeling like she was definitely caught between a rock and a harder rock. She stared intently into the eyes of her image knowing she had to swallow the realization that she was on her own. No way that she could take the chance that someone could or would make the connection between her and her boys. Talking about skeletons in the closet, boy oh boy, did she ever have hers and they were sure rattling now. But as always she couldn't turn her back on her boys. Without a doubt her political enemies would have a field day if they had the slightest hint that it was her three amigos that used illegal funds to put her through college; studies that had led her into law enforcement. The rest is history. Hell, she could easily get suspended if they knew about her years on foot patrol when she practically guided the rise in the criminal lives of all three and the girls that worked so diligently for them.

Her mind was filled with these thoughts when she left the bathroom to go to her closet to pick through her wardrobe. There was a full-length mirror on that door as well. As she looked at her full figure, clad in yellow lacy bra and panties, she started to get a tingly feeling in her pussy as she thought about her recent booty call with Sparkle. She imagined that it was his hands that was rubbing her crotch instead of her own. The more she thought about it and him the further her hand slid into her panties.

Damn, why does that nigga have to be a damn crook? she thought as she felt her nipples getting hard. When she eased her fingers under the frilly fabric and into the folds of her pussy lips, she wasn't the least surprised that she was gushy. The aroma of her excited pussy caused her to close her eyes as she imagined his face closing in on her. His lips were slightly parted to touch hers ever so gently. Talking about deja vu.

She had felt her a nut building in her loins when the jangling of the telephone snapped her out of her lust-filled state of mind. Was this some kind of deja vu or what? Sighing heavily, she walked wobbly-legged to the nightstand and took some Kleenex out to wipe her fingers off before she picked up the phone. "Ugh nasty." There it was, damn nearly the same thing that had happened the last time.

The hairs on her neck started tingling before she even put the phone to her ear. She wasn't able to hold the tension from her voice. "Hello, Beverly Johnson speaking." Damn, the very same background of traffic noise. And as before when she started to repeat herself, the voice over the phone caused butterflies to flutter in her stomach. It was Sparkle.

"What's up, girl? How ya doing?"

She took a few seconds to gather herself. Dayum, she really despised the weak feelings she got in her knees whenever she heard his voice. Why couldn't he be a normal guy? Then again that was the part of him that attracted her so strongly.

"Damn, girl, you gonna answer me or what?"

"Yeah, I'm here. Whatcha got on your mind?"

"Needed to hear your voice, that's all."

"What, you called just to hear my voice?"

"Yeah, you got a problem with that?"

She smiled inwardly, knowing he had to have something other than that on his mind. He was stalling; she'd known him too long not to know that much. And as usual she took the lead. "Okay, since it's evident you want to play games again, were you involved in that shooting?"

"What shooting?"

"What shooting?"

"Yeah, what shooting, and why you asking me something like that, again?" He waited a full thirty seconds for her to continue in her super-cop mode but she remained mute. "Damn, and here I am trying to figure out how to get some more of that super pussy of yours. And again you come off on me all crazy and shit again."

"Ugh!!" she growled but she couldn't deny the fire he'd set off in her stuff with his nasty talk.

"Ugh?"

"Yeah, ugh, you one nasty man, you know that. Looka here, I've got to get to the station. Something has come up."

"Whew! Why you in...hello, hello, damn." She had hung up on

him. All he could do was hold the phone away from his face and stare at it.

"Hung up on your ass, huh?" Rainbow said from the other side of the table as he made a final shuffle before passing the deck for him to cut.

They were on their third game of Rummy 5000, idling away the time while waiting for Stacy to show up.

For the past couple of days they had traveled the hoods of DeKalb and Fulton counties in search of anybody who might've heard about a nigga being shot in the arm whose name started with a J. The forty-eight consecutive hours of non-sleep venturing had all been in vain.

When a car with a booming sound system pull into the driveway, they knew that it was him. Stacy rapped on the door several times before entering without waiting for a response. He swaggered in jacking up his sagging pants by the back pockets, skinning and grinning. He froze when he saw the serious look on their faces. Turning his mouth down into a full grit, he flipped one of the chairs around backward and sat down at the table with his arms folded behind his head. "Whatz up, man? Why y'all looking all glum and shit?"

Rainbow took one last drag on the blunt he had been pulling on and passed it to Stacy. "We've got a situation here that has gotten really serious, son, and we needed to know that you were aight, that's all."

Stacy scrunched his face up, stood up and flipped the chair back around, sat down again and started rubbing his chin. "Say what?"

Sparkle accepted the blunt from Stacy after he had taken a few draws. "There's some folk out here that might go after you to get to us." He leaned back and waited for the explosion he knew was about to come.

And true to form Stacy's overhyped ass went off. "Whodafuck ah ah, where da bitch at?"

Sparkle leaned forward, wiped his face and sneered. "Little nigga, chill the fuck down for a sec. The way we see it, that nigga Black Don is trying to stretch out his little empire some more."

The words had barely gotten out of his mouth before Stacy jumped back up. His nose was sprouting fire and he started pacing the floor, jaws clenching, flexing his fingers and growling; like he was ready to kill a brick. "Man, why yall ain't let me know about this before now? Dayum, unk, that's that's fucked up, yo."

Rainbow braced his hands on the table to get up but Sparkle held his hand up to stop him. He had this. He walked right in his path and stopped. Stacy tried to walk around him. It wasn't happening, as Sparkle put a hand on his shoulder and looked him straight in the eyes. "Come on, man, you know me."

Stacy waved his head from side to side. Sparkle paused and moved his head from side to side along with him until Stacy stopped moving. He added briskly, "You know me, right?"

Stacy blinked a couple of times before he pinched his nose and took a deep breath. "I'm gonna handle mine, unk, you know that's right." He tried to look away, knowing damn well that his uncle could see right through any bullshit. He certainly wasn't buying accepting the role of him being some type of pussy nigga.

Sparkle felt the fire was boiling in his gut, clasped his chin and made him face him. He narrowed his eyes, staring intently at Stacy. "Right, I said, right?"

Stacy turned away for a moment to regain his composure, took a deep breath, rotated his neck a few times and then he finally nodded okay.

Sparkle, feeling relieved he'd calmed him down some, continued. "Okay, now put your emotions to the side for a second and listen to me, good 'cause we done thought this thing through carefully. Ya wid me here?"

"Yeah, unk, I'm wid ya but…"

"Naw, partner, ain't no buts here. How many times I got to tell ya, ya can't hear what I'm saying if you thinking about what you're gonna say?"

Stacy took another deep breath. "Okay, okay, go ahead I'm listening."

Sparkle cleared his throat, gave a short cough. "Good, we need you to hang out with the girls til we get this nigga."

Stacy frowned. "You want me to play punk. Is that what it is? I ain't no punk, unk. Naw, fuck that shit there."

Rainbow had heard enough. "Naw, stud, it ain't about you playing punk or nothing like that. We know that you got a big heart; hell, the heart of a lion, for sho. That's why we need a thorough thug to be with the girls in case that bitch-ass nigga send his crew. Ya feel me?"

Stacy dipped into his pocket for his sunglasses, wiped his hand across his face before he put them on. "So y'all gangstas want me to ride shotgun for some hoes." He cleared his throat. "So I can stay out of the line of fire, right? Shit sounds like playing punk to me."

Rainbow shook his head and gave him one of his hundred-watt smiles and sniffled. "Hell naw, man, for one, I don't allow no punks around me period; and two, we need a strong soldier type of nigga, with some muthafucking heart to make sure that don't nothing happen to the girls. A nigga that ain't gonna run when it gets hot."

Knowing that they were mostly referring to Violet and Mercedes, Stacy yanked off his glasses, took a few steps back and cocked his head to the side. "What about your girls then? Who's gonna be with them?"

No sooner had the words left his mouth, when the door pushed open and a crew of five flashy honeys strode through the door. Led by Lady and Clara, all talking at the same time, they spread all around the room flopping tiredly on couches and chairs. Once settled they took guns from different parts of their bodies and placed them beside their hips.

Rainbow harrumphed and swept his arm around the room. "Answer your question? I think these bitches will be aight."

"Yeah, I guess so," Stacy said as he eyed the deadly looks in their eyes. He was to stunned to say anything else.

"Yeah, they'll be aight." Rainbow repeated as he thumped him with a backhand to the chest and followed it up with a quick wink.

Stacy accepted the slight blow with a leery smile. "Mmm-hmm, but what about Mercedes? That little bitch still be acting like she pissed at me for pulling that fake robbery on her."

Sparkle turned his mouth down. "She aight."

Stacy was doubtful. "She aight?"

Sparkle pushed him on the shoulder. "Yeah, and stop repeating everything I say, damnit."

Stacy laughed. "Aight, so what y'all gonna be doing while I'm…" He paused to cross his arms across his chest. "While I'm playing babysitter with these grown-ass women?"

Rainbow shook his head disgustingly. "Aw, youngun, can you please stop bitching so much? We're in the middle of setting a trap for this nigga that he ain't gonna be able to slither out of; rest assured of that there."

Stacy smirked. "Yeah, like y'all did out there in Jonesboro, huh?"

Rainbow's eyes shifted toward Sparkle. *Naw, he didn't let him know about that shit.* He turned full faced to him, ran his eyes up and down his body and hunched his shoulders.

Sparkle gave him a weak smile, licked his lips and opened his mouth to try to explain before swallowing his weak excuse and lowering his eyes to the floor.

Just in time to rescue him, Violet, Yolanda and Mercedes came strutting through the door like *Rip the Runway* models with their arms full of shopping bags. Grinning like Cheshire cats, they walked up to Sparkle. Violet lifted his face and kissed him on the chin. "Ugh, somebody needs to shave. Whatz up, sweetie? I got you a little something." She froze, mouth agape when she saw the look on his face. "Aw damn, what have I done now?"

He stared at her with unblinking eyes, took the bags out of her hands, placed them on the floor and motioned them to take a seat.

Yolanda set her bags beside the couch, sat down on the arm of the couch and crossed her legs. Mercedes set hers down as well, but stood there with her hands on her hips staring angrily and pouting at Stacy. "Whaddafuck he doing here?"

Stacy looked at Rainbow and Sparkle and hunched his shoulders with a "I told y'all so" expression on his face.

Sparkle cleared his throat loudly. Mercedes kept gritting on Stacy. He picked her up like she was light as a feather and placed her on the arm of the love seat. Not too rough but with enough force to let her know that he was dead serious. She got the message but that still didn't keep her from pouting. She blinked with blurry eyes but he wasn't having it. He wasn't in the mood nor did he have the time to put up with her female ego.

Once he'd stared her down into submission, he started pacing back and forth. "Okay, sweethearts, this is what's going on." Sparkle continued to pace but was forced to hold back a smile that threatened to crack his face with all eight girls' heads following him like they were watching a tennis match.

He flicked his arms at Rainbow for some help. Rainbow twist-ed his mouth to the side and looked away. He was trying to keep from laughing with the way that he kept clenching his jaws. *You on your own, dog,* Sparkle felt him saying with his eyes.

So he took a deep breath. "Stacy here is gonna hang with y'all for a while." He paused when he noticed their faces turn from one of curious puzzlement to straight-up anger. He didn't let that deter him though. "Ain't no need for y'all looking like that. Ya'll ladies belong to us so you might as well get those pouts off your faces. That's right, you, too, Yolanda. Not only that, y'all are our best friends too and we ain't about to leave y'all all by y'all selves, pure and simple as that. And that is until we handle some things we got to take care of." One by one they lowered their eyes.

Rainbow finally came to his aid and stood up beside him, bring-ing his pacing to a halt. "All y'all got to do for a couple of days or so, uh, maybe even a little longer, is go on cell phone calls. Four of y'all ride with Stacy here; four stay here, unless we need y'all for a role or two."

Violet, being the veteran hustler that she was, raised her hand like a schoolkid. "Hey, man, all due respect and all to Your Pimp-ship." She could hardly keep a straight face as she cut her eyes at his girls sitting around praising his very existence. "Okayeeee, and I feel ya on this, really I do, but I ain't about to hide in no shadows while my star nigga here is out there dodging bullets. This honey here don't roll like that, sorry." She leaned forward, resting her elbows across her knees and directed her attention at Sparkle. "Of all people you know damn well that I've got to be with you regardless."

Sparkle stood staring at her, feeling good that old gal was ready to ride and die with him, but he knew he needed her to run herd over the girls. He knew she was gonna take over anyway.

The look on his face let her know that she had struck a nerve, but the look in his eyes let her know that she wasn't going with him either. He ran an index finger under his nose. "Baby, I know how you feel and everything but I can't let ya roll on this one here."

She sighed her disappointment, but when she when she looked at Stacy and then the girls, she understood. "Okay, man, I feel where you're coming from."

Yolanda, who had been quiet the whole time, finally spoke. "Hey, I know that shit done damn near run its course, but does that mean that we can't go get the last of that free money at the skin house?"

Rainbow burst out laughing. "Naw, Yo, it don't mean that. Y'all just make sure that y'all stay together. Ya feel me?"

Sparkle could see Mercedes's devious little mind working overtime. She wouldn't oppose him in front of everybody, but there was no doubt she was anxious to get him alone to work some of her female magic. He'd have to disappoint her this time though, because he and Bow were going to get out of there before she got the chance to do so.

Rainbow patted Stacy on the shoulder and headed for the bedroom to get the saddle bag containing the coke they needed to cook up along with their guns and jackets. He came back in the room directing his attention toward Stacy again. "Yo, partner, now that we've got that settled, we really gotta roll. You cool, right?"

He didn't wait for a reply and tossed Sparkle one of the jackets and turned to Yolanda. "Where is your man, girl?"

Yolanda traced her index finger along her bottom lip, pursing them and popped them a couple of times. "Playa, your guess is as good as mine. I thought he was with y'all."

Sparkle and Rainbow frowned at each other, gave the girls one last grit and headed for the door. Those remaining sat around mumbling in groups for several moments before Stacy said, "Shit, ain't no need for us to sit around here looking all crazy and shit. Violet, break out those cards, girl. Anybody down for some Spades?" Oh hell, did that ever get them excited.

Several hours later, Violet was lounging on the couch with her legs crossed, relaxing between games, trying to concentrate on Erica Kane's umpteenth excuse for getting another divorce on *All My Children*. It wasn't an easy task because of the constant bickering coming from the loud-ass Spades game between Stacy, Mercedes, Yolanda and Lady. The other girls were lounging along with Violet watching the soaps and passing joints of speed ball. Everybody was trying to kill some time and ease the boredom.

Violet thought about going to Joyce's beauty shop to get some stuff done but she didn't know if she was still out working those Jamaican drug dealers in College Park. "Damn, that girl must like living on the edge. That's a really dangerous habit she's got of ripping folk off. One of these days…" she mumbled under her breath. She didn't want to think of the consequences of what might happen if baby girl ever got jammed doing that crazy stuff. She had to admit that girly was sho nuff good at her game. She worked that innocent image to perfection and those fools never even suspected that she was the one that got them.

The boys had been gone for quite awhile now and Violet was beginning to wonder why none of her regular customers hadn't called. She raised the corner of her blouse to make sure the batteries were charged on her cell phone. They were. Flipping her wrist she peeked at her ladies Omega watch, amongst the gold, silver and ivory bracelets adorning her arm, sighing in resignation to the boredom that was starting to get next to her. Her eyes shifted restlessly between the television, card game and toying with her jewelry. She started waggling her legs apart, bumping her knees together, thinking that something had to give before she went stir crazy worrying and bugging.

Out of the corner of his eye, Stacy watched her getting more and more agitated by the minute. Peeking at his diamond-studded Longines, he silently cursed the hour since they hadn't heard from his uncle or any customers.

"Damn, man, you on brain lock or something? Whatcha gonna do, use the card, dish it, pluck or whatever. You holding us up here," Mercedes squealed.

Clara, who was on a steady pout waiting for her turn to play, threw her two cents' worth in. "Yeah, dude, your mind must've gotten all froze up on that ganja gangsta weed you stole form yourself when you was play shitting in the bathroom a little while ago." She batted her long lashes to egg him on.

Stacy turned his attention away from Violet, removed the Swisher Sweet cigar from between his clenched teeth, snorted his disapproval of them rushing him and flipped a card on the table. "Hold y'all damn smelly thongs in place." He paused to snatch up the book they'd won. "Have any of y'all been paying attention to Violet lately? Damn, she antsy for a mug over there," he said in a whisper and nodded toward her on the couch. All four heads turned in the direction simultaneously.

Mercedes reached across the table to pat Yolanda's hand daintily and rubbed the corner of her open mouth with her baby finger, then rolled her eyes to the ceiling. "Uh-huh, looks like old Queenie there really needs something to do, don't she?"

Clara was ready to get anything started herself as she cleared her throat. "Yep, what y'all figure we should do about it?"

Stacy cranked his neck, started rotating and rubbing it, revelling in the tension-relieving kinks he felt go snap. "Yolanda, do that ring-back thang with the phone. I got us a plan."

"Uh-huh, mmph, one of ya schemes again, huh?" Mercedes sighed and rolled her eyes to the ceiling.

"Ah, kill the 'tude, Kung Fu shortie. Let's see what he's come up with. I'm tired of sitting around this bitch, too. Of course unless you wanna keep sitting here all night pitching pennies around the table," Clara snapped and poked her eyes out.

As expected, Mercedes's reaction befitted her impish attitude. She sat back in her chair with her arms folded across her chest and her lips set in a deep pout.

Stacy muttered under his breath, "Damn brat."

Her head snapped immediately in his direction. "I heard that you, you.."

He *pssted* her off and walked around the table on his way to the bathroom. He was about to twist the knob when the phone started to ring. *Damn, she quick*, he thought as he made a quick U-turn and dashed to pick up the phone. He made it just ahead of Violet.

She mugged up and down his body, making it hard not to laugh as he went into his pantomime. "Yeah, who this? Where you at? Damn, that's all you want. Shit, you expect me to come all the way out there for that?" He cocked a sneaky eye at Violet to see how she was reacting to his animated conversation. Her facial expression said she wasn't paying him any attention, but her eyes and the way her knees had stopped banging together let him know that she was honing in on the conversation.

He angled away from her to hide the smile that was threatening to show as he continued. "Okay, man, we'll be there in a few and yo ass had better have the exact cheddar, too. Don't bug about who I am, you want it or not? Okay, I'll hit you back when we're about to get there. Okay, in a bit, soldier."

He hung up, expelled a gust of hot air and stood with his hands on his hips. "Aight, ladies, who ready to ride with a nigga?"

Mercedes couldn't help digging in his ribs, if only for a little bit. "I know good and well you ain't talking about all of us going. Sho didn't sound like no helluva buy to me. I'll stay here."

Stacy realized right off the bat what her little ass was trying to do. *Uh-uh, baby girl, ain't gonna work.* He braced his shoulders, walked to her and reached down to pull her chin up to face him. "Looka here, china doll, Jap doll, Vietnamese doll, whatever the fuck you are, everybody in this crew was down with that robbery scam on your evil little ass. Hell, Rainbow and them tested each and every one of us, so you can quit with that personal pout." He stared her down until she lowered her gritty gaze. Then he sighed and turned to Violet. "Queen Bee, we got a buyer out there on Wesley Chapel. All he wants is a fifty slab. Whatcha wanna do?"

Violet ogled at him over the rim of her granny glasses perched on the tip of her nose. "What!! What I wanna do? Hell, I wanna get out of this damn house; that's what I want to do. Give me a second to throw something on." She sprung up from that couch like a hyped-up Slinky toy and nearly trotted to the bedroom. Snatching a jacket off the chair beside the bed and a package of ready rock out of the shoe box in the closet, she was ready to roll.

When she returned, they were whispering to themselves. The way that they stopped when she came back in caused her gaming antennae to shoot up. It dawned on her that some game was going on but she didn't give a fuck. She needed to do anything to keep her mind off her man, so she led the way out of the door. They felt the tension ease as they crowded into Violet's Mustang. It really felt good to get out of the house, as evident by the way the girls were clucking. Lady and Yolanda got into a argument of why Lady wouldn't show her any of her card-cheating scams. Clara bitched about how no one wanted to give her the ups on paper hanging. And Violet was schooling Stacy on the do's and don'ts of shoplifting. Their babbling went back and forth and around in circles all the way to Snap Finger Road.

They were all so caught up in their kicking it that no one noticed when the dark sedan pulled alongside of them on the narrow twisting thoroughfare. They didn't feel the presence of danger until after they were forced off the road. The terror didn't stop there as the little coupe bumped along for thirty yards in a ditch full of water until they crashed into a thick row of hedges. It jarred them to a nerve-jolting stop.

Miraculously, no one was seriously hurt; stunned and bruised for sure, but thankful to still be alive. Stacy was the first to shake off the shock. He kicked the door open and staggered up the ditch to the road in time to see the car speeding around a bend in the road and out of sight. He strained his eyes into the distance, but was only able to see part of the license. Even though still in a little bit of a shock, he was able to lock that portion into his memory.

He felt like he had seen the car somewhere before. For the life him he couldn't remember where.

He turned his attention to the girls and was relieved that at first glance, they all appeared to be okay. They looked a little bit woozy, which certainly had to be expected. He looked up and down the road for anybody that may be able to assist them and also to ensure that the car wasn't coming back to finish the job. Seeing neither, he opened the front passenger door and bent down to pick Violet's handbag off the floor. He leaned into the car and asked them if they were all okay.

It seemed like they all responded at the same time, as he tried to hone in on calling Sparkle to let him know what had happened. It rang about five times before he decided to redial, with the same results. He placed the phone back in the bag, puzzled, angry and swearing to almighty God that somebody was gonna pay for this. Oh, how somebody would pay.

After wearing thin with all the whining from the girls, who were still in shock, he began pacing back and forth along the road in an attempt to cool down. After a couple of trips he reached back into the car to get the cell phone again. Clicking in his sister Kim's number, he told her boyfriend, Jerome, Yolanda's son, about what had happened and where they were. He promised that he'd be there in a jiffy to get them out of the ditch. He sat down on the hood and wheezed. Boy, was somebody ever going to pay.

CHAPTER TEN

Dealing with Scoundrels

The persistent ringing of the bedside phone had roused Sparkle out of a deep sleep he had desperately needed. He reached over a snoring Violet to pick it up, sighing in relief that she and the rest of them had come out of the crash all right. He didn't want to split up with Rainbow but they both knew the girls needed additional protection now more than ever. They'd been roaming around the city uneventfully for damn near three days nonstop. As hyped up as he was to get to the bottom of who those predators were, even he had to admit that they needed some rest.

Cursing under his breath at the midnight disturbance, he answered the phone in a sleep-hazed growl as he rubbed the crust out of his eyes. "Yeah, who dis be?" He groveled as he peeked at the digital clock radio on the dresser. It read 3:15 a.m.

He squeezed his eyes shut, not wanting to believe that someone would be calling that time of the night. He was also very irritable from getting high on coke to stay awake and alert for those three days. He told himself for what had to be the thousandth time that he had to give up this lifestyle. When the caller didn't respond immediately, he asked in an even more agitated voice, "Godamnit, you gonna answer me or what? Fuck it, fuck you."

He removed the phone from his ear preparing to hang it up when a female voice purred, "Fuck, man, you got to answer the phone so damn nasty?" He couldn't pinpoint who the caller. He cleared his throat to say something exceptionally filthy but the voice said impatiently, "Nigga, is my Aunt Violet there because you acting stupid as hell."

Sparkle wanted to blast the bitch with a roll of expletives but he held them in and said irritably, "Is this Joyce?" He wished he could reach through the line to wring her scrawny neck.

"Yeah, it's me, who the fuck do it sound like, fool?" she spat sarcastically.

He wanted to slam the phone down as hard as he could, but held on to his composure. "Sorry, bitch, it's that you woke me up at three in the muthafucking morning and it's been one of those hard-ass days, so what's up?"

He could feel the tension ease out her voice as she replied sweetly, "Whatcha doing, Sparkle? I was sorta hoping that Auntie could come pick me up."

Her sudden change of attitude raised his antennae, because he'd never heard her sound so sweet. Despite his leeriness, he still put some concern in his voice anyway. "Violet's snoring like a bear. Where you at?" He wondered why she was calling so late.

Her voice got even sweeter. "At the Marriott."

"Taint no biggie, I'm up now. Give me a minute to get myself together. I'll be there in about ten, fifteen minutes or so. What room you in?" he said as he sat up in the bed and tried to stretch the tightness out of his neck.

He was totally taken by surprise when she answered in her normally sassy manner, "Not unless you got a rocket strapped to your narrow ass."

Boy, oh boy, did that bitch know how to dig into his last nerve. "Unless I got a rocket," he repeated with a snort.

"Yeah, nigga, strapped to your narrow ass, because I'm out here in Marietta."

Fighting the urge to slam the phone again, he grunted and then nearly shouted, "Godayum, woman, what the fuck you doing way out there this time of night?" He knew he'd struck a nerve right back at her sassy ass with that one. He felt her anger and held the phone away from his ear waiting for a loud verbal lashing.

He'd done right as she screamed, "Muthafucka, what damn difference does it make; you coming or what?"

He could almost feel his fingers squeezing tightly around her scrawny little neck and felt the urge to tell her so but he pushed that impulse to the back of his mind. He smiled at the thought of saying stuff that would make the big vein in her neck to pulse in anger. He wasn't about to leave her stranded all the way in Marietta, so he sighed heavily. "Okay, okay, you can stop pissing your thong. Give me fifteen minutes to get on the road and start counting, damn crazy-ass ho," he mumbled.

"Whaddafuck you mumbling for? I thought you said ten minutes?" she continued with her usual sassiness.

"Nothing, see ya in a few," he said and hung up while she was still smart-mouthing. As he was easing out of the bed, trying not to disturb Violet, who was still calling the hogs with her mouth wide open, he cursed himself for neglecting his body chasing that damned coke high. He grunted through the aches and pains in his back and knees as he struggled to a standing position. After stretching some of the kinks out, he put his clothes on and tiptoed out of the house.

Some ten blocks from the apartment he spotted an all-night BP station and remembered that he'd left his cigarettes on the nightstand. So he pulled over to pick up a pack and a six-pack of Heineken. When he walked in, the first person he saw was JJ, his baby sister's ex-boyfriend. He wondered why homeboy was way out in this part of the city this time of night; especially since he knew he now stayed in Lithonia with a geek monster, way on the other side of the county. Buddy looked like he'd been on a month-long coke binge. Damn, he was raggedy as all out, hair uncombed, big bags under his eyes, and clothes looking stank for a mug.

It didn't surprise Sparkle when he pocketed a pack of generic cigarettes off the counter when the teller turned his head. *Damn, buddy must be scraping the bottom for sure*, Sparkle thought as he watched him scoop up a couple of more packs and stuff them inside his raggedy coat. He looked up and saw him approaching the counter.

Sparkle recognized a look of fear and shock on his face when they made eye contact. But he shrugged it off as him being just as surprised to see him. He swallowed hard and greeted him in a croaky voice. "Hey, hey, Sparkle, what's going on, my nigga?"

Sparkle couldn't help thinking of how this down-and-out hustler used to be at the top of the drug game only a short while ago. Slick suits, Gucci loafers and designer outfits were his standard attire. It was the same dude that gave him his start when he'd gotten out of the joint. Looking at him now, made him think about what Googie had told him a long time ago: *Never outplay yourself where you become a product of your own product.*

"Ain't nothing better than clocking paper from your own paper," he replied, trying to keep the pity out of his voice. He playfully punched him on the shoulder.

JJ pinched his nose and shifted his eyes from side to side nervously, like he was expecting an unwelcome guest or something. Finally, he started to say something but suddenly jerked back toward the counter. Sparkle leaned back puzzled. He was about to ask him what was wrong when he felt someone brush against his back. Once a pickpocket himself, he instinctively spun around to his right with his elbow sticking out, prepared to strike a blow if necessary, and bumped into a tall, dark-skinned brother in a dingy trench coat. The brother grunted in pain and grabbed his left arm through his coat.

Sparkle turned around to face him, but he'd brushed by him and continued to the other end of the counter before he shot a quick peek backward and edged down the aisle.

Feeling both violated and disrespected, Sparkle started to say something to him when he noticed his coat bulging in the back. He automatically honored the boosting code and reluctantly allowed the moment to pass. Spinning back toward the counter, he pointed toward a pack of Kools before heading for the beer cooler. He was ready to exit the store and remembered he was about to ask JJ something. Popping his finger, he turned around to go back and talk to him when he saw him and the tall fella easing out of the other door. They quickly dissolved into early morning darkness.

He shrugged his shoulders and muttered, "Ah, what the fuck, that nigga's probably too busy bugging about where they're going to get rid of that stuff him and his buddy just stole, so they can get a early morning hit." He paid for his smokes and headed out of the door. When he pulled into the street, he saw them ducking into an alley. As he drove by, JJ was helping dude pull their haul out of his coat. If he hadn't been at a street light, he probably wouldn't have paid them that much attention. But it was evident that they were having a problem getting the stuff out. Dude let out a loud yelp. The light had turned green but for some reason Sparkle was stuck watching them as the guy started rubbing his wrist vigorously; the same arm he had bumped into earlier.

He shook his head at the pitiful sight of the fallen warrior. *That's the way life goes.* He realized that the light had turned. Luckily, he was the only one on the street at the time and not having to bear with the protesting horns of other drivers. Turning his attention back on the street, he continued on down Memorial Drive admiring the bright lights of the Atlanta skyline in the early morning dusk.

He made a left toward Buttermilk Bottom hoping to see Rainbow or some of the crew to get an update on their problems. After cruising past the ho strip and the MLK Memorial without seeing anyone, he made a left on Peachtree Street and headed for the ramp off Lucky to get on I-20 on the way to Marietta. That's when it dawned on him that the slim dude with JJ was favoring the same wrist that he thought Rainbow had hit on the ambush. He thought of hitting the next exit and going back to look for them. But knowing crack fiends the way that he did, they'd probably already found a crackhouse to get off in by the time it would've taken him to get back. Aw, what the hell; maybe he'd run up on them again; then again maybe not.

✠ ✠ ✠

The pin-striper's Stacy Adams boots echoed loudly off the tiled floor, pacing back and forth before the three well-dressed hoodlums seated around the dimly lit office. The menacing frown and snarl, which would've rivaled that of a starving panther, had brought all conversation to a halt. The smacking sound of three wads of money onto the sweaty left palm, fell into rhythm with the exotic music that boomed throughout the plastered walls. Visions of shapely strippers doing their nasty thang for the crowded room of horny patrons, added a sense of pain and pleasure through the minds of the young guns.

With that menacing snarl and eyes blazing venom, the prowler paused in front of each of them and blew a heavy fog of acrid smoke in each of their faces. The expression practically dared either of them to so much as blink; like troopers of the night, none of them did.

The prowler, tired of pacing, stopped in a wide-legged stance in front of the man in the leather chair nearest to the door. The young stud, attired in a shiny black suit, crossed and recrossed his legs, removed his white Kangol cap from his head, and ran his damp right hand over his neatly plaited corn rolls. Now with the uncomfortable gaze riveted directly on him, he blinked a lot more than he wanted to. It was embarrassing enough to show fear regardless of the situation and even more so in front of his gangsta running mates. His effort to maintain his version of a poker face failed miserably under the harsh glare. Without any warning the prowler suddenly slapped one of the wads of money into his lap. He automatically flinched thinking of what might follow; well aware of the prowler's violent tendencies, that at times seemed to be snatched right out of the blue for no apparent reason, other than being a nasty muthafucka for the hell of it.

He opened his mouth to speak, but couldn't get past the lump in his throat, when the prowler growled, "Stackadime, Stacka muthafuckingdime. Stack a muthafucking penny is more like it. Of all the people to let me down, you was the last I figured would go punk on me."

Stack uncrossed his legs and made a motion to get up, when the tip of a ivory cane jammed him in the chest and caused him to abruptly sit back down with his chest swelling sporadically. He started to clench his fist rapidly, fighting the urge to spring up, until he was frozen by the death mask that flashed before his eyes. For the first time in a while his heart skipped a bit when the prowler leaned so close to his face that he could actually feel the foul spittle sprinkling his forehead. His eyes glazed over when the prowler spat in a chilling death tone, "Go 'head, bitch nigga, go head, muthafucka. Get your pussy ass up so you can die."

Stack's shoulders flinched in anger, but as quickly deflated when he heard an almost muted click. He looked down at the stiletto blade that suddenly extended from the tip of the cane pressing a deadly dent into his chest.

The prowler leaned in even closer, so close he not only felt the heat of his breath but the spittle raining on his face and neck, mixing with the stinky sweat rolling into the vee of his open shirt.

"Young nigga, you ready to be a real killa or die; yo choice."

Doing his best to disregard the sweat and discomfort, Stack, refusing to be totally punked in front of his boys, braced his hands on his thighs, hunched his shoulders to try to draw up some of his steadily dwindling courage and said tersely, "I am a killa."

That drew a thundering thump to his chest again, as the prowler retorted, "Yeah, you are stud, but are you as ready to kill me as I am you?"

The deadly menace in those eyes caused the youngun to blink several times before he gave in and lowered his eyes to the floor.

Satisfied that the battle of wills was won, the prowler straightened up. "Uh-uh, that's what I thought."

Turning the anger toward the other two who were fidgeting nervously on the matching leather couch that was pressed against the desk followed quickly. With shoulders coiled like a cobra ready to strike, the words came out full of venom. "And you, Chopper and Percy, I thought I told y'all stupid muthafuckas to snatch up those two hoes at Rainbow's and bring them to me, but naw, y'all got to play it slick and try to get two crackheads to do your dirty work."

Chopper, who was dressed in a oversized black and brown checkered shirt, brown calf-length baggy shorts and tan Timberland boots, started scratching his nappy fro as he blinked nervously a couple of times and cleared his throat. "Damn, man, how the hell was we to know them niggas was gonna be there, playing rescue ranger and shit."

The words were barely out of his mouth when the prowler kicked him full force in the chest, stunning him so badly that all the air gushed out of his body. The punishment didn't stop there though as blow after deadly blow was pummeled into his ribcage. Balling into a knot, Chopper grunted in anguish with each crushing blow; ceasing only when full submission was evident from the youngster.

Rising menacingly the prowler turned his attention to the last of the trio, jamming the cane, that was still trembling with more pent-up energy, into his neck. Percy hadn't even bothered to budge during the onslaught on Chopper. But now with all that angry attention pointed at him, he sat up and twisted his neck, trying to ease some of the scary tension, anxiety and straight-up fear of the moment.

The prowler stood glaring at him for what seemed like an eternity, chest heaving in rage. With eyes blazing he stepped toward Percy as a voice whispered from the shadows, "Yo, how you expect them to do what you want if they all broke up from your one track-thinking ass?" The prowler watched the intruder emerge out of the shadows in their peripheral vision and spat.

"Joker, I know that you've been knowing these fools for a long time." He paused to slap the two remaining wads of money from palm to palm and then on a trembling thigh. "But something's got to be done for all these duckets I'm shelling out. I'll kill each and every one of these muthafuckas before I let them bitch me out."

Clearing his throat with a raspy cough, Joker looked the prowler directly in those evil eyes and sat on the corner of the desk. "Check this here out. I'm gonna go with these niggas this time to make sure it get done right."

He walked to the middle of the room rotating his gaze from one to the other. "We..." He pointed at each of them before slamming his fist into his own chest. "Are you gonna handle this, and handle it my muthafucking way, or one of us or all of y'all ain't gonna come back to remorse or celebrate." His eyes glazed over with deadly intent. "The after-party." He finished with a smile that would chill the dead. Hell, even the prowler raised an eyebrow and felt the chill coarse through his body.

Feeling a little more confident now that the job would be taken care of, the prowler strolled with exuberance to the desk and calmly set the last two wads on it. Not a word was said when Joker snatched both stacks up and put them in his pocket before waving at the trio. "Let's roll, niggas, time for y'all to earn this big boy cash now."

Percy was the first to react, thankful that he had been spared some of the wrath that had been dished out. He didn't hesitate and headed for the door.

Stackadime yelled at Chopper as he approached the couch to give him a hand. But the nigga was still balled up wagging back and forth to try to ease some of the pain in his ribs. Stack lifted him by the armpits. "Come on, dude, let's..."

But the prowler quickly cut him off with a stony stare and ice dripping from his tongue. "Leave that nigga to get up on his own like a real man."

Stack looked down at Chopper and shook his head, hunched his shoulders and turned away to follow Joker out the door.

The prowler leaned back in the chair with arms folded stiffly across their chest. "Bitch, you either struggle your sorry ass on up and walk up outta here on your own or get carried out and left wherever and whoever I get to dump your ass, permanently."

Knowing this fool meant every word, Chopper groaned and struggled to his feet on shaky legs, crouched over in pain, and stumbled his way out of the door.

The phone was picked up as soon as the door was closed. "Yeah, you ready to do that. Good, so meet me at the spot." He hung up smiling evilly.

✠ ✠ ✠

There was a eerie fog developing and it had Sparkle straining to see the road signs as he sped down I-20. The light drizzle that had started misting the windshield was certainly not a welcomed sight. *Damn, this must be some kind of an omen about me fucking with this janky-ass Joyce*, he thought as the exit sign came into view. As he sped down the ramp, he had to curse himself for not remembering the direction of the hotel. He knew that from that point the Marriott was only about a mile away, but because of the fog and rain, he could hardly see the Citgo sign across the street, much less being able to see that far. After a few anxious moments of contemplation as he waited for the light to turn green, he decided to take a chance and turn right.

After ten minutes or so and much more than several miles, he knew that he had made the wrong choice. Cursing to himself for taking that long to figure that out, he sighed heavily and checked his phone for the address. Once he located it, realizing he had made a mistake, he made tracks back in the other direction. His cheeks rose in a big smile when he was finally able to spot the Marriott sign, but faded quickly when it dawned on him that Joyce had forgotten to give him the room number. No sooner had he started cursing his luck and her, his phone began vibrating on his hip. He sighed a breath of relief when he pulled up the tail of his shirt and saw her code blinking brightly.

He smiled the prankster's smile and decided to let her stupid ass wait and sweat bullets for a while; at least until he got parked in the hotel's lot.

Ten minutes later, he shorted the blunt he had lit up after parking and headed for the lobby. The rain had picked up a touch, so he pulled the jacket's hood over his head and broke into a sprint. As soon as he stepped over the threshold, he figured that he was looking too suspicious because of the way the registrar was eyeing him. He removed the hood as he walked to the counter.

Breaking out into what he thought was a warm smile, he told the man behind the glassed-in desk that his wife had called him earlier that night but had forgotten to tell him her room number. After a short direct description of her, the guy let him know it was Room 22 on the upper tier. As a precautionary measure, he registered in Room 23. There was no telling what she may have gotten into, so he might as well play it safe.

Since he hadn't let her know that he was there yet, he went to the room and got off a couple of blasts before he decided go to her room. He was feeling rather nice when he gently knocked on the door. Joyce hadn't answered but he could see her shadow as it passed across the peephole. That really irked the hell out of him, so he began rapping on the door really hard praying that the loud nose would startle her jazzy-talking ass. He could see that her eye was glued to the hole so that loud bang really gave her a jolt.

He heard a low feminine grunt and hollered, "Silly-ass bitch, open the muthafucking door. I know damn well you could see who it is with your eye pressed to the damn peephole." He did his best to keep from laughing because he knew her ass had to be there geeking.

When Joycee snatched the door open with a nasty frown etched on her face, he knew that she was revving up to spit a jazzy comeback at him. So he was really shocked when she didn't but instead reached her arm out to push him to the side so she could look up and down the balcony. He could tell that she was nervous as hell by the way her eyes were bucked wide open and zooming back and forth.

There was no way that he could resist digging on her nerves. "Aw, scary-ass ho, I'm by myself. Godayum, get outta the way so I can get in the door."

She looked up at him with her eyes bucked wide open for a moment, then she tilted her head back and opened her mouth to say something but nothing came out. He frowned expecting her to say something fucked up as usual. Instead she spun around real sassy-like and stomped back into the room. She looked back at him over her shoulder before she sat down on the bed. Her green eyes slanted to slits, as her mouth turned down and she spat as nasty as ever, "Nigga, you gonna close the muthafucking door or what?"

Like most people who were geeking, she was snorting and gnawing on her tongue with a wild look on her face. *Damn, this bitch done run up on some really good shit from the way she acting.* He stared at her for a few seconds before he slammed the door as harshly as he could. "Well, thank you, Miss Twist Mouth, for thanking me for coming all the way out here for your sassy ass."

Rolling her eyes real bitchy like, she followed up with one of those real nasty and sassy snake rolls of her neck and spit venom at him. "Nigga, you make me sick with your lame ass." She ran her eyes up and down his body before she gave him another snake roll. "What... You think a bitch is supposed to jump at the sound of your voice; you and your fucked up attitude? Un-un, well, not dis here bitch, nigga."

He leaned against the door shaking his head in disgust and wonderment at her ungrateful ass. He was more than stunned by the way she was reacting. A little more than disappointed he thought, *Shit, it ain't like she was calling me from across the street.* In his own wired-up frustration he spat some venom of his own. "Crazy-ass woman, what in the hell is your problem?"

She harrumphed. "My problem, my problem?" Sparks were now flying from her geeked-out eyes. "What the fuck is your problem?"

That did it. *Bitch, you asked for it* blazed in his thoughts as he stepped menacingly toward her with his hands flinching into tight fists. He didn't enjoy slapping the spit out of a bitch's face, nor did he want to shout, but he had to let out the anger. "Yeah, you... You wacko-ass bitch, what's your godayum problem?"

The words had barely left his mouth, when she sprung up from the bed and spun around like she was some kind of voodoo priest-ess or something. Snarling and crouching like a cat ready to spring, she shouted back, "My problem, skinny-ass, wannabe gangsta-ass nigga, is that you be strolling up in here like you some big-ass grizzly bear."

He bent his head slightly, scratching behind his ear with one finger, stunned, but she wasn't finished. She looked him up and down like he was some little bug she could squash at will and snorted. "Hell, man, you ain't but five, uh, uh.. What five, two, three, whatever and weigh a buck fifty soakin' wet."

"What?" He reared back astonished at the nerve of this crazy-ass woman.

"Uh-huh, I said it, that's right." She placed her hands on her narrow hips defiantly. "Just because you got my auntie all strung out and shit. And a sister that tries, yeah, that's right, I said *tries* to keep that fake-ass, so-called curly fade jazzed up for ya..."

He cut her off because he couldn't see the reasoning behind this stupid conversation. "Bitch, are you for real? Yo ass really tripping now, for sho."

She reared back on one hip, stared at him undereyed with her mouth all mushed up. "Damn right, I'm for real, uh-huh and just because you got Violet all wobbly legged and stealing you all that fly gear, you got the nerve to actually think you are some GQ gorilla pimp or something." She looked him up and down once again, this time with a hissy harrumph. "But let me tell Mr. Boss wannabe playa, you ain't no goddamn GQ nothing."

He smirked for a second. But that little bit fired her up even more as her eyes slanted into even deadlier slits as more venom spurt forth. "And to think that Aunt Violet thinks you got sexy bedroom eyes. Shit's got to be old age getting to her or something."

For a reason that he couldn't fathom right off the bat, that really caught his attention and a jolt of lust ran down his spine. That look of defiance in her eyes had softened a tad, too. Pinching his nose, he pinned her with what he considered a sexy half-lidded gaze.

"Bedroom eyes, huh, is that what you think?"

She squinched up her nose and nodded. "Hmphh, nigga, please, I said that Aunt Violet thinks that dumb shit." She jerked her head back and narrowed her eyes like he was crazy. "And you can stop looking at me like that."

"Like what?" He mocked her and moved in closer. She backed up a few feet until her legs bumped into the bed and the venom stare weakened into innocent lust. He was close enough to see a shadow blush over her face. His animal instincts took over from there and he pulled her up against him real hard. She gasped and let out a breathless moan. She leaned back so she could look into his eyes from her barely five-foot frame.

She looked so tiny and vulnerable that he couldn't hold back any longer. He gently leaned down and lightly touched her trembling lips with his own. His eyebrows raised when he saw her eyes glaze over and cause a tingling shock to run up and down his entire body.

Not so tough now, are you, girlie, he thought until he gasped himself when his mouth was suddenly filled with a vibrant syrupy tongue that tasted like pure salty honey. He couldn't quite believe it himself when he felt his knees weaken as a heated stream of air caressed his face when her nostrils flared in heat.

Her nipples hardened and stabbed him in the chest like hot daggers, even through his clothes. His heart thumped hard in his chest when she moaned his name softly and began to gingerly hunch her pelvis into his groin. That moan quickened when he reached down and palmed her soft pliant ass cheeks, lifting and pulling her urgently inward. Her natural female aroma started to massage his nose and brain, causing him to grunt like a bull.

She moaned even louder when she heard his reaction and started swirling her tongue passionately around his. She seemed to cover every space in his mouth. He grunted louder himself when she started speed flicking the tip of her tongue along the roof of his mouth. Her tongue was moving so fast it felt like she was using a vibrator. The tickling sensation was buzzing in the back of his head from ear to ear.

She began thrusting her tongue flatly in and out of his mouth with the rhythm of her grinding hips, back and forth, round and round.

He grabbed the back of her head as his dick started throbbing against the heated softness of her thighs. He could feel the head getting slippery and slimy as precum began oozing out and soaking his drawers. He had to step up the pace to match her motions as she got faster and faster and more intense with each passing second.

His head started feeling airy with her rising passion, so he removed his mouth from hers and started kissing her along the neck. Damn, she smelled so good. Her mouth opened wide as her moans turned into groans that got louder and louder. She started fumbling to unbutton his shirt as his arms and hands began to roam all over her back.

When he started nibbling on her ear, her moaning increased even more and she forced him stumbling backward until he hit the wall. She spread her legs further apart until her pussy mound was positioned just right on his throbbing dick. His breath caught when she reached down, grabbed it and angled it down his own thigh so that she could slide up and down the length pressed against her clit. He grabbed her ass and spread the cheeks as far apart as they could go and pressed his fingers against her asshole. She greedily searched out his mouth again and started twirling her tongue wildly in and out in a fucking motion. From the sudden twitching of her hips and increased moaning, he could tell that she was on the verge of getting a nut. He was damn near there himself.

Knowing this, he picked her up and toted her over to the bed and threw her on it. She looked up at him in total surprise as he grabbed her on the inside of her knees and pushed her thighs as far back as his arms could stretch. The scent of her pussy hyped his urgings as he looked at her wet panties and began sliding his tongue over her pink lacy crotch. He immediately tasted the over-flow of her juices.

She couldn't hold back any longer as she screamed, "Oh my God, nigga, mmh." She moaned deeply as she reached down and pulled her thong to the side and he snaked his tongue into her now gushing hole. She grunted louder and tried to push her ass off of the bed. Her breath started coming in spaced gasps when he placed her clit between his lips and began massaging it. That did it. Her screams went out of control. "Oh Lord, my goodness, oh shit, nigga." She palmed the sides of his head and strained even more upward, back arched as he increased the pressure and speed-flicked his tongue all over her clit. "Oh baby... Oh, Sparkle, you're mak...ing me cooommmeeeee, making me nut all over your mouth... making me nut...oh shit, ooooooh, ooooooh, oh my God, Goddamighty, oh godayum, eat that pussy, man. Don't stop eat that pussy, nigga. Eat that aaaaaaaaaaaaaah."

He felt the cum oozing from her pussy; hell, more like a flood. Her legs began shaking so bad that he had to reinforce his grip on her thighs. All of a sudden, she started yelling, "Let me down, nigga. I gotta taste that fat digger. Come on, nigga, I need that hard muthafucka in my mouth now."

He loosened his grip on her legs. She pushed them the rest of the way down and crawled along his body and pulled his pants down so fast, that his dick made a loud smacking sound against his stomach, and pre-cum splashed a trail up to his navel.

Breathing like a savage she swallowed his entire length in one gulp. The pleasurable surprise of her deep throat effort made him breathless. He felt the back of her throat spasm as the head hit it. Before he realized it, she was lowering her cum-oozing pussy to his face and started humping on his extended tongue like a mad-woman. Her juices smeared all over his mouth and chin.

She slowed down some and began slurping up and down his dick forcefully, pausing as she got to the head, to twirl her tongue slowly round and round. He sensed that she was loving every motion and taste passionately. After a minute or so, she started applying more and more velvet pressure, with her head-bobbing rhythm matching her hip movements.

She started moaning toward another nut as his dick started throbbing and jerking deep in her throat. As if the more she sensed that he was getting ready, the more pressure and pleasure she put into devouring his dick. Her deepening passion had him at the brink of a toe-curling nut. She began moaning louder and louder, twirling her tongue crazily, slowly all around the head and then bobbing faster along the shaft. She slurped with more and more slimy pressure as he began feeling the stirring deep in his balls.

He began moaning in gasps and his hips started hunching to meet her bobbing head. Her legs started trembling and her moans went out of control. He could feel and taste another load of her juices oozing out of her soaked pussy. The reality of her getting another nut, when he knew that she felt him ready to cum, drove him over the edge. Glob after glob of cum began gushing into her throat. The pleasure was so intense that his hands and feet were curled into knots. She gagged a couple of times but still continued to apply more suction passionately, like she couldn't get enough and never wanted to stop.

As the last drops coated her tongue and throat, she lovingly moved her tongue sloppily over and over the head. When he looked between her thighs, she was licking and kissing his dick like she was worshipping it. The vision of utter lust and passion she displayed caused his already hard dick to start throbbing and drooling all over again. It was by far the best head he had ever experienced; had him wondering how he had gone so long without it. When he got so sensitive that he couldn't stand her devouring mouth any longer, he flipped her over and laid her over the edge of the bed, then banged that hot ass until they both collapsed from sweaty exhaustion.

When he stirred awake around noon, Jerry Springer's rowdy audience was ragging the guest on stage. He yawned, stretched the kinks out of his body, then turned and saw Joyce still snoring softly. Leaning her head on his arm, he watched her for about two minutes wondering how he was going to be able to stay out of that hot pussy of hers. It was certainly a problem he was ready to solve. Shit, her head and pussy were definitely in a class. *Hell, she's in another class all by herself.* Now he was stuck with the dilemma of trying to set up ways to get this one-of-a-kind sex without Violet knowing. Oh well, where there's a will… Figuring that she'd have to be hungry when she woke up, he decided to hit one of the nearby fast-food joints for some take-out breakfast. She damn sure deserved it.

She was still counting zees when he got back from a Waffle House some fifteen minutes later. So he started flicking water on her face until she woke up scratching her ass, yawning and knuckling the crust out of her eyes. He noticed that she had a slightly Asian look early in the morning. It gave him flashbacks to his Air Force days in Thailand when brothers were flooding that country with black Asians. That combination certainly produced the sexiest, most exotic children in the whole world.

When her eyelids fluttered once, twice, and she lazily opened them wide, his heart skipped a beat. To him she looked like a beautiful butterfly spreading its wings for the first time. She smiled at him with some pearly whites and for that moment, he felt a warmth meant especially for him.

Her eyes caught sight of the take-out boxes and he could nearly feel the heat rise in her cheeks. She started giggling like a little schoolgirl before she said in a husky early morning voice. "Mmm, there is something good in you, after all, huh?"

"Oh yeah," he replied as he lifted his chin and began rubbing the stubble on his jaws.

She looked away shyly and purred, "You probably think that I lured you way out here just for that there."

"Just for what?"

She pursed her lips and reached over to pop him on his thigh. "You know what."

He stepped back out of her reach for a second, before he ran a hand over his hair and sat down beside her. "Yeah, well, it had sorta crossed my mind a few times." He smiled.

She elbowed him playfully in the side and wiggled up into a sitting position. She looked down at her naked titties as if she had just realized that they were exposed. She folded her arms over them like she was embarrassed.

He let out a short snort. "Kinda too late for that, ain't it?"

She smiled back at him as she removed her arms. Then she took a deep breath. "Guess it is… But here is the real reason that I called."

She reached under the bed to remove a brown grocery bag, which was folded over several times. Biting down on her lower lip, exposing a deep dimple crease in her jaw, her eyes started sparkling as she overemphasized a dainty unfolding of the bag. She looked up at him innocently and removed four tightly sealed plastic bags and a blue bank deposit bag.

The blood rushed to his temples, when the realization of the contents hit him; not because of the dope and money but what the possible repercussions could be. He knew for sure that she had played somebody out of their goodies. The issue was she had now gotten him involved. He pinched the bridge of his nose, squeezed his eyes shut and shook his head from side to side, before he asked her with the most serious stare he could muster. "Girl, where, how? Who in the hell did you get that shit from?"

Her smile quickly disappeared, to be replaced by a look of fearful anxiety. She croaked, "Why you acting like that? I thought you'd be at least a little happy."

The look he gave her could've frozen hell over and she actually jumped when he shouted angrily, "Bitch, how in the hell do you figure that whoever you took this shit from ain't gonna fuck you up and whoever they think is down with you on this?" He studied her for a while to see if it had sunk in. "Hell, like me, girl. That's why your ass was looking all geeked, up and down the balcony when you answered the door last night."

She leaped up from the bed, nearly knocking him down, and placed her hands defiantly on her hips.

Aw-aw, here comes another snake roll. Why bitches be doing that dumb shit? he thought as he stumbled back. And sho nuff the roll came at him with eyes blazing fire as she hissed, "Godayum, I should've known that your sorry ass was gonna punk out on me."

He took a step forward with his shoulders hunched menacingly and spat back at her nastily, "Stupid-ass ho, don't you know those folks will torture, then bury your...your..."

He didn't get the chance to finish, before she transformed into Xena the Warrior Princess and pushed him on the bed with her claws clasped around his neck, straddling him. With her teeth pulled back in a nasty snarl, she pulled one of the claws back for a wild swing. But before the blow could reach his face, he grabbed her by the wrist and flipped her over. He got on top of her with the quickness and pressed his face directly in front of hers. "Don't say another muthafucking word," he shouted angrily.

The coldness of his eyes shocked her and she finally lay still. He'd certainly gotten her attention now. "Now whodafuck you stole this shit from?"

Her eyes misted over and a lump ran down her throat as she choked a reply. "I took it from some Jamaicans. Those funny-talking bastards were talking about ripping your boy Rainbow off."

He gave her a curious frown and sat back, disregarding the expulsion of air from her mouth when he pressed his full weight on her stomach. "I thought you told Violet they didn't want the trouble that would come from behind a move like that."

Her condescending look returned to one of defiance after she wiggled from under all his weight. He tried, but there was no way that he could hold back from smiling. This was more like the fiery Joyce that he was accustomed to and he definitely preferred that one over a fake crybaby.

Her voice transformed back into gangsta as well, as she grabbed his collar and pulled his face closer to hers. "Sweet-ass nigga, this is what I do and I'm good at it." She blew him a kiss and fluttered her eyes. "I saw, I played, I took, and then I called your sorry ass. Well, I actually called Violet because she's down with whatever and you, aw fuck it, I got you to come because I figured you'd be down and wouldn't give a fuck. Like you do when you scam folk."

"Yeah, but I don't scam folk that go on the hunt with machine pistols and machetes."

"Mmh, like those niggas you did time with in prison be joking with their homemade stickaniggas. Hell, if a bitch's game ain't tight enough to get away with it, she shouldn't be doing it. I'm a pro, nigga," she countered.

There wasn't too much he could say, so he shook his head. "You right about that."

"Damn right, I'm right about dat."

He smiled down at her. "You know what?"

That conniving look glittered in her eyes as she licked her lips enticingly. "What, you don't want any of it?"

He rolled off of her and lay on the bed, then looked up at the ceiling with his hands folded under his head. After a moment, he snorted, turned his head sideways to face her. "You something, oh yeah, you really something else."

She smiled at him. "Yep, I know." She sat up on the bed and started bouncing up and down like a little girl playfully pushing at his shoulder. "Shit, playa, whaddafuck; let's get blitzed up in this bitch. This here be some of that super-good, pink, golden-flake shit."

She had certainly gotten his attention then because that Peruvian golden flake was the best coke hands down. It had him puking his guts out from smoking it. She had said enough. They got busy. About three hours later of constant blooping, they finally hit I-20 on the way back to Decatur. They had just passed the East Lake exit when he looked over at Joyce fumbling in her oversized handbag.

"Ain't no way you gonna find whatever you looking for in all that junk." He smiled.

"Ah ha, for all you know." She grinned as she lifted a glass shooter up and waggled it in his face.

"Girl, I know damn well you ain't about to hit none of that shit right now. No telling who was pushing wheels on this road." He grimaced.

Joyce acted like she hadn't even heard him, as she reached under the seat and got the grocery bag. Digging inside she untapped one of the bricks of coke and stuffed the shooter. With the bag still in her lap, she lit the shooter, took a long toke and passed it to him.

"Ah what the fuck, why the hell not?" he muttered as he accepted the shooter and put it to blaze. When he handed it back to her, she absentmindedly grabbed it by the hot end.

"Oooow, muthafucka, shit!" she screamed as she snatched her hand away and dropped it in his seat. He raised up trying to swap it from under his ass, where it had rolled.

"Aaaaah, crazy-ass bitch, watch where you fucking going, man." She screamed again and reached over to grab the steering wheel, her face full of shock. Cocked sideways in the seat, he looked at the road in time to grab the steering wheel in a death grip and sway the car from crashing into speeding cars on the side and in front of him. As he swayed halfway onto the shoulder of the road, he felt a big bump and a loud bang as the car hiccupped and started fishtailing on him. He continued to struggle with the steering wheel and pumped the brakes like a madman until they lumbered to a halt.

He sighed heavily and dropped his arms to the seat before looking over at her. She had hung her head lazily over the grocery bag she had squeezed tightly to her body and wheezed. "Damn." That was all she could get out.

Shaking his head he grabbed the doorknob, kneed the door open and got out. Seeing that the car was tilting to her side, he circled the car. Damn, they had a flat tire. He walked to the trunk, opened it and grunted. "Damn," he spat again when he saw there wasn't a spare. He walked back to her side to get his cell phone out of the glove compartment. "Let me see, where the fuck we at? Hmmm, my nigga Duke is the nearest. Let me holla at his fat ass," he mumbled as he punched in his numbers. He kicked it with him through a bunch of bitching and cursing before he handed the phone back to Joyce.

CHAPTER ELEVEN
Hunters on the Prowl

Sitting in the driver's seat of his month-old Cadillac Escalade, Joker pulled out both of his Glocks from the double holsters crisscrossed on his chest. He quickly checked the rounds as he looked anxiously around the parking lot of the Red Roof Inn off Candler Road. He was wondering and hoping that his intended victims would have their guards down enough to make this job as easy as possible.

Chopper popping on that damn gum in the backseat was really starting to get on his nerves. He had closed the windows to keep it cool, and it made the popping sound even louder than usual. But was that really it, or was it the combination of fear and anxiety to go up against his own cousin Sparkle and Rainbow? They, along with Johnny Bee, had practically baby-sat him through his adolescent life of learning how to hustle and survive in the streets. Damn, what a dilemma. But his man was the reason he was driving his hot ride and living in the luxury condo out in Ben Hill. Boy, was he ever praying that they would listen to logic and reason, but deep in his heart he doubted it.

The sudden buzzing of his cell phone on his side, brought a welcome distraction to the boredom of the wait. He listened intently to the new orders he was given and clicked off with a grunt. "Aight, girlies, it's time to earn these big bucks," he addressed Stack, Percy and Chopper. They all started shifting around nervously in their seats. He pulled out of the parking lot and thought, *Finally.*

✠ ✠ ✠

Damn, it was a welcomed sight to see Duke's car pull up behind his. "Man, you best believe you called when you did, I was headed out the door," Duke said with a bright smile through the window as Sparkle approached.

Sparkle backhanded the sweat off of his brow and wheezed as he reached for the door handle and growled. "Well, don't just sit there on your fat ass. Get the spare, man."

Duke's head snapped back, surprised that his boy was taking his frustrations out on him. He gave him a body-length stare as he was easing his bulk out of the car. "Damn, bro, you at least could've said thank you, muthafucka, for showing up or something," he mumbled as he headed for the back of the car to pop the trunk. "Sorry, dog, you know I didn't really mean to come off on you like that."

Sparkle forced a smile and pat him on the back as he followed to help. "Oh yes the hell you did; you need to get yourself some manners there, buddy boy."

Joyce displayed a beaming smile before she turned her attention to Duke. With her elbows propped on the fender, she said, "Hey there, big dude, thanks for coming to get us out of this mess; a mess thanks to knucklehead over there."

Sparkle pantomimed a mug of frustration and gritted. "Me knucklehead, you the one that dropped...?"

Big Duke certainly didn't have no time for their petty arguing as he interrupted them and pulled the spare out of his trunk. He looked at Sparkle as he rolled it along the pavement. "Listen to the girl. She's telling you some good, ugh, ugh, ugh," he grunted as a barrage of bullets lifted him off of his feet and slammed him into the back of Violet's car.

Joyce let out a blood-curdling scream when she saw the blood splashing from his thighs and shoulders. "Oh my..."

Sparkle tackled her and rolled with her cradled to his body under Duke's ride, knocking the wind out of her as he did so. He looked up in time to see several arms jerking back into a shiny black SUV as it roared down the interstate and out of sight. "Stay here," he said to Joyce as she rolled out from under the car. When he got to his knees, he looked down to see Joyce following him.

"Girl, I told..."

She cut him off with the quickness. "Fuck dat there, what, who the fuck was that? Aw, man..." She cut her own self off as she sprinted over to Duke. Sparkle immediately followed her with his eyes scanning the area for any other gunmen. Seeing none, he helped her grab Duke's arms and pull him to a sitting position up against the rear bumper. Duke was grimacing in pain from their efforts.

"Where you hit at, man? Don't worry, we can get you to Grady Hospital in a short..." Sparkle said as he stood up and made a step toward the car to get his cell phone.

But Duke halted him in his tracks. "Naw, dog."

A bewildered Sparkle stared at him like he was losing his mind. "Naw!!" he repeated in shock.

Duke shook his head. "Naw, dog, I'll be aight and the cops will get me to the hospital. Uggggh... That ain't what's bugging me because if they had hit something vital, I wouldn't be able to talk to you right now."

"Man, you delirious; I'm going to call Grady," Joyce spoke over him as she stepped past Sparkle.

"No, wait a minute, girl," Duke grunted as he grabbed his bleeding shoulder.

"What?" She looked at him like she was missing something.

"I've got a shit load of powder under my seat. Y'all have got to disappear with it before the five-o show up." He moaned as his voice started showing signs of weakening. It was evident that he was getting weaker from the lost blood.

Joyce took one last look at him and headed for the front of Violet's car.

Sparkle snatched his head back as she walked away not wanting to believe that she could possibly be that cold to leave his boy for the police to gather up. Duke grimaced again in pain and Sparkle leaned down toward him. "Man, you got to muster up some strength from somewhere because we can't leave you out here like this."

"Come on, man, he's right, ain't no need for all of us to get a dope case to go along with explaining this shit here," Joyce yelled at him as she sprinted for Duke's ride with the grocery bag folded in her arms. "Get the keys, nigga."

Sparkle was still frowning at her, astonished when he felt Duke tugging at his arm. He looked down to see the keys dangling in his other hand.

"She's got the right idea, dog. You know damn well the five-o is gonna search the ride, especially with my ass getting all shot up out here on the interstate, so go man, get the hell out of here, now."

"You heard the man, Sparkle. We got to roll, man!" Joyce shouted from the passenger window, her voice filled with desperate fear and anxiousness.

Sparkle didn't want to leave his boy, but from the look on his and her face he knew that he had to. He sighed, gripped his boy by the shoulder really hard and headed for the car. There was really nothing to say nor was there any time to be wasting. He pulled onto the highway eyeing Violet's car in the rearview mirror until it disappeared as he headed down toward the Flat Shoals exit ramp.

Sparkle took several turns down different streets and then headed back toward Candler Road. He turned into the road that led to Candler East Apartments and looked across the seat at Joyce, who was still clutching the grocery bag to her body. She was staring off into space with a blank look on her face. After they had parked in the lot that led to his sister Debra's apartment, they finally looked at each other and said, "Damn" in unison.

✠ ✠ ✠

The persistent rapping on the frosty glass window of Beverly's office door on the sixth floor of the Atlanta Police Headquarters on Pryor Street, interrupted the discussion she was having with her longtime friend and secretary, Sarah.

They had been going over the list of police deployment for the upcoming Fulton/DeKalb County Festival. For the first time the extravaganza was being held in Inner City Park on Peachtree Street downtown. With the likes of T.I., Ludacris, Young Jeezy, Keyshia Cole, Soldier Boy and a variety of other up-and-coming rappers performing, a young rowdy crowd was certainly expected.

With the blinds drawn that she had recently installed to keep any and every one from staring at her every move, she nodded toward Sarah to open the door. Being in a pretty good mood, Sarah smiled and sprung up with a pep to her step as she went to open the door. That smile dissolved like an Alka-Seltzer when she ran smack dab into the smug expression of Lt. Woo. The solemn look on Woo's face caused both Sarah and Beverly to momentarily forget all about the festival.

Woo tooted her nose up and rolled her eyes, ignoring whatever Sarah was about to say and stepped to Beverly's desk. She waited for her boss, who had stood up when she entered, to sit back down before she took a seat in the cushioned high-back chair in front of her desk. "Sorta hate to disturb you, chief, but I just got a report, from a reliable source that some real serious drug take-over activities are about to go off along the motel strip on I-20."

Before Beverly could reply, the buzzer on her desk started shrieking wildly, instantly drawing all of their attention to the urgent message unfolding on her desk. Sarah made a move toward the machine but Beverly held up her hand to stop her and snatched the ticker tape that was spewing out of it.

Her expression turned into one of bleak concern as she read the message. But she quickly regained her composure, folded the message and patted it down on her desk. Wiping some non-existant sweat from her brow, she eyed Sarah. "Remind me to have you look into this, okay." She continued to tap on the message. Sarah nodded in reply.

Beverly turned her attention back to Woo. "Now what were you saying?" She had already been told by Woo the latest on the duo drug operation of the Black Cats and Red Dogs. So why was she in here practically repeating what she already had said? Maybe she was there to get her to reveal something, but she wasn't about to do anything like that, not with her anyhow. Especially since that was the area where her three amigos plied a lot of their trade. She was especially concerned now, because normally they did their thing under the radar, holding violence to a minimum.

Woo squared her shoulders as she prepared to respond. "I think we need to beef up the patrols along the interstate because the violence has escalated to drive-by shootings. And in an area where there is a constant flow of pedestrian occupation."

Eyeing the message again she asked, "Where at in particular do you suggest we do this?" Woo toyed with the corner of her mouth. "I'd say, ah, between East Lake and Wesley Chapel."

Beverly blinked as a red flag flashed in the back of her mind.

The recent rash of robberies and shootings, in which she had little doubt and less evidence, was initiated by Black Don, who she assumed was trying to gorilla his drug and gambling ventures into Decatur. No way were her boys going to lie down and let him have it, period. She definitely wanted to keep the area under a microscope. Lt. Woo, whose particular informant had been 100 percent reliable, sat in front of the chief's desk waiting for specific instructions on how to handle the situation. She was really suspicious because of the bad vibes she was getting from the chief concerning this particular case. *Something ain't connecting properly with this bitch. I wonder what it is. I'm gonna find out, that's for sure.* She managed to hold her gut instincts in check and waited.

Beverly excused Sarah from the office and stood up to walk to the window that overlooked the State Capitol Building. She looked down into the parking lot. She was forced to do a double-take when she saw the deputy chief hand a briefcase into the window of a dark-colored SUV.

Why is he looking around all suspicious? Hell, why am I even thinking like that? Damn, was her own self-made paranoia getting to her that much? She was rubbing the corner of her mouth with her baby finger when Woo cleared her throat behind her.

She turned around abruptly, feeling that she had to be extra careful addressing Woo, whom she felt was already suspicious enough. She blinked several times as she gathered her thoughts and walked back to the table. "I want you to get with the Black Cats' squad leader to post stakeouts at all the hot spots we discussed earlier. Keep a direct line open to me to keep me abreast of anything that goes down. Oh yeah, I'll be letting the DeKalb chief know about it. Aaah, you're excused."

Woo nodded and got up to leave. When she placed her had on the doorknob, Beverly cleared her throat and pinned her with a serious expression. "Oh, and Lt. Woo, tell Big Bertha that I saw her mother at the Lenox Square mall."

She looked shocked for a brief moment but didn't say anything as she opened the door and left. The look of surprise on Woo's face was enough for the chief. It was also enough to keep her wondering how much Woo really knew. Those thoughts occupied her mind all the way down to the squad room, where her crew was waiting around playing chess and cards. She had given them a brief warning of precaution as they headed out of the building destined for Decatur. Woo also was contemplating which of her crew was the chief's informant. During the same time, Beverly was sitting in her office wondering how Woo had known about the I-20 incident before it had come over the ticker.

✠ ✠ ✠

Aunt Rose checked the two young thugs in her rearview mirror, as she headed to her other hideaway at Dunlap Apartments in East Point. There was no way she was going to let these wild bastards know where she actually laid her head. Shit, Don didn't even know about the spot she had down the street in Dunlap Two. They had been silent ever since she had picked them up at the Waffle House on Wesley Chapel. She had been on her way to open the store when she received the call from Don.

She hadn't thought much of the traffic jam that resulted in the arrival of an ambulance and a convoy of police cars. But she had certainly taken notice when Chopper and Stack seemed to slouch into their seats when she zoomed by the scene heading in the opposite direction.

As she weaved in and out of the slow-moving traffic, she silently cursed her nephew for causing all the heat because some slicksters were able to pull a gambling scam on him. As far as she was concerned, that's what he and the old man got for trusting that stupid ho with the combination to the safe.

Well, one thing was for sure, they wouldn't have to worry about her little snake-bit ass anymore. She smiled to herself as she wondered if the bitch would make for some good fertilizer for the reefer plants she was buried under out there in the woods in Henry County.

She took a deep breath of satisfaction as she recalled the euphoria she had felt during those hours of torturing her traitorous ass to get all that information before overdosing her on some pure cocaine. Helping Don dig that shallow grave was some real labor though, even if she spent most of the time supervising his big ass. Oh well, some things just had to be done.

She shook away those thoughts and cocked a weary eye at the younguns. "Y'all boys want to get something to eat out of this Hardee's here? I could whip y'all some eggs and bacon, but y'all niggas probably want to gobble up something right now."

Chopper licked his lips greedily while he rubbed his stomach, which was growling something terrible. He looked across the seat at Stack, who was staring blankly out of the window. Man, he hated when Stack had that look on his face, like he was mad that he had to share the air with the rest of the world. It usually meant that something crazy was about to go down. But to heck with him, he was hungry for a mug.

He smiled at the back of Aunt Rose's head. "Damn, Miss Rose, I'd love to chow down on some of your Southern fried cooking, but a couple of them sausage and egg biscuits can't get in my stomach fast enough, know what I'm saying?"

Rose gave him her sweet old lady smile and backhanded the sweat off of her forehead. "Whew!! Do I know what you saying?

Hell yeah, I know what you saying. Hell, I'm glad you said that there because I ain't really in the mood to be hanging over no hot-ass stove right in now either."

She flipped her eyes away from him in the mirror and pulled into the Hardee's parking lot on the corner of Dunlap and Main. It was hard to hold back the smile as she watched Chopper rush to beat her to the door. She had walked around the back of the car, then headed to the front entrance when she noticed that Stack hadn't gotten out of the car with them. She knew that the bastard was hungry because she'd heard his stomach growling along with the other one. Turning around in a huff, she went back and yanked the door open, leaned in the car and put her face directly in front of his. She definitely didn't have the time to be baby-sitting no grown-ass nigga, so she reverted to her sweet old lady persona. "Son, ya might as well bring yourself in because ain't nobody gonna be playing waitress for ya."

He looked at her, like he was breaking out of a trance and said in a low voice, "Okay, y'all go ahead and order me whatever y'all getting. I'll be in there by the time y'all sit down."

Rose stared at him as if he had lost his mind, deciding whether to cuss his ass out or show a little more patience. She chose the latter since they didn't really know her real role in Don's operation other than that of a sweet old lady. "Youngun, I can see you're bugging about something, so you can just sit out here. We'll make it take-out." She forced a smile and went into the restaurant. While she was waiting in line she called Don.

He was on his way over to do some dealing with Al. "Yo Auntie, is this you?" he screamed over the traffic noise.

She leaned away from the phone. *Who else do this fool think would be using my phone? I know damn well that he checked the caller ID before he even picked up. Then again maybe his careless ass didn't.* She wanted to scream but there was no need to take it out on him because that boy Stack had gotten her irritate. She blinked away that little attitude and said softly, "Yeah, baby, it's me."

"You pick up my boys yet?"

"Uh-huh, we're about to order some breakfast at the Hardee's down the street from the apartments on Dunlap."

"That's good, that's good, you gonna leave them out there or what?" Don answered like he was covering the phone.

She covered the phone herself for a moment because she noticed Chopper trying to eavesdrop on her conversation. So she leaned forward to whisper in his ear for him to get three orders of whatever he was craving and moved away from the line of customers. *Little nosey-ass brat all up in a bitch's business.* When she felt that she was far enough away from the crowd, she resumed her conversation with Don. "Yeah, I'm gonna leave them there because I got to go open the store. Whatcha want me to tell them?"

"Tell them that I'll be over there in a hour or so," Don mumbled.

"That's all?"

"Yeah, they'll be aight until I get over there."

"Aight, I'll see ya later on tonight then. Bye, baby." She hung up not waiting for him to reply. Catching the look on Chopper's face when the cashier put the orders on the counter, she could tell that the nigga was broke. She stepped up her pace to the front of the line and paid for the goods. She took them on to the crib. She waited until they had eaten half of their meals and gotten settled before she told them what Don had said. Neither of them showed too much of a reaction. Her intuition told her that they were holding something back. She was right.

Stack slid his bag to the side and stared at Chopper. Chopper eyed him up and down and hunched his shoulders as he spread his arms wide apart. "What? Why you gritting on me like that, man?"

Stack sprung up and slapped the table so hard that it knocked Rose's drink into her lap. "Man, you sitting there like it's aight."

Chopper leaned back in his seat puzzled. "What you talking about, man?"

That look on his face made Stack even more frustrated as he leaned forward, arms spread wide on the table and yelled, "Come on, dude, don't fucking sit there and act like you ain't noticed that Joker didn't give you your money! This nigga Don has to know about that shit, too."

Not only had this young punk spilled the drink on her without so much as "excuse me," but he was shitting on her baby, too. Oh, hell naw. Rose sprung up from the table, like a jack-in-the-box and stretched her arm across the table.

Stack froze, mouth gaped in astonishment, when he felt the tip of the stiletto, which magically appeared from thin air, pressed against his Adam's apple. He damn near shit himself when he looked into the eyes of the madwoman. He had never even imagined her in that way and quickly lowered his eyes in submission.

When she felt his courage evaporate, there was no need to say anything. She looked through him for a moment, before the blade disappeared back into her sleeve. Without her expression changing one iota, she picked up her purse off of the table and walked out of the door.

Chopper, who had sat there stunned, staring wide-eyed during the whole thing, swallowed a difficult lump down his trembling throat. "Damn, man, I know you wasn't expecting no shit like that," he said hoarsely. "I know that you felt that killer heat from that old bitch because I sure enough did. Whew!"

Stack thudded heavily back into his chair, crossed his arms and looked over Chopper's head blankly at nothing.

Chopper continued, "What da fuck? I felt like she could've drove that thing in your neck and walked out of the door the same way she just did, not feeling a damn thing. Shiiittt," he mumbled with a biscuit poised at his mouth, the same way it was when Stack first slapped down on the table. "Hell, Stack, there's a lot more to sweet Auntie Rose than she's let on."

Stack licked his parched lips and wheezed. "Uh-huh, you damn right there is. Shit, I can see now why Don's bad ass be acting all humble and shit when she's around him. Old bitch is a she-devil."

Chopper turned down his mouth, hunched his shoulders and walked into the living room. He picked up the Nintendo control from off the top of the television. Clicking on to some Mike Tyson, he stared at Stack, who gave him a "what-the-hell" look and joined him. They needed to kill time while they waited on Don.

Meanwhile, as Rose neared the corner of Main Street, she changed her mind about going to the store. Instead of making a right that would've taken her to Jonesboro, she made the left and headed toward Atlanta. Maybe Bertha could help her figure out what the hell was going on. Her gut feeling kept telling her that something was wrong.

Roughly ten minutes later as she was passing the MARTA station across from the lounge, she thought she saw Bertha running across the intersection to the Krispy Kreme shop. The rumblings in her stomach helped to make up her mind to follow her. She'd left the half-eaten bag of goodies on the table when she'd blown her cool with that youngun. That and the womanly weakness for a good Danish had her parking in front of the shop. She pulled up in time to see Bertha walking to a booth in the rear of the shop.

From the moment she stepped out of the car, she could see that something was bothering her girl. As she approached her booth, she noticed the puffiness around her eyes. It seemed like Bertha had been crying. Hell, she was still crying. Rose picked up a couple of napkins from the counter and held them up to her face when she reached the table. Bertha looked up and was certainly surprised to see Rose and smiled. "Thank you, girl, I didn't see you come in." She accepted the offering and dabbed at her eyes.

Rose sat across from her, reached into her box and got a lemon-filled croissant. The creamy filling oozed out of the side of her mouth as she made a crazy face and gnawed into the tasty treat. As expected that drew a smile from Bertha. "Girl, you nuts, you know that?" Rose dabbed at her mouth with one of the napkins, smacked her lips and reached across the table to grasp Bertha's hand. "Now tell me about it."

Bertha sniffled, sighed heavily and moaned, "Rose, I just got a call that baby brother got shot out there on I-20 a while ago."

"What, why, girl?" she managed to express with sincerity written all over her face. *Oh shit, that was her brother. Damn, I didn't even know that she had a brother.*

Bertha shook her head and purred, "I don't know but they got him at Grady's pulling bullets outta his big ass."

"You don't know how bad he hurt, girl? Want me to go over there with you?"

"Naw, but thanks, girl. I'm waiting on one of his boys to come get me now."

Rose was about to say something else encouraging when she spotted that bitch Lt. Woo leaning against a car in the mall parking lot across the street. The way she was standing there, it surely looked like she was waiting for someone. She then saw one of the dancers from the club sprinting toward her. They talked for a brief moment before getting into Woo's car and pulling into the street. *So that's how that little bitch been getting all the ups at the club?* she thought when she heard Bertha speak. "Whatcha say, honey? My mind was somewhere else." *I got to find out what that bitch is up to.*

"I said, Johnny should be here any minute now," Bertha repeated while she continued to dab at her eyes.

Rose had found out what she wanted to know without even asking Bertha. She wanted to console her girl a little while longer but now she had to get behind Woo before she got too far away. "Looka here, sweetie, if there's anything you need, let me know, okay? I gotta go check on some things at the store. You gonna be aight?" she said in as sincere a tone as she could muster. She barely heard Bertha's reply because she was fast-stepping out of the door to get to her car.

Damn, she was acting sorta strange. "What the hell; my sorrows are my sorrows. I can't expect everybody to get into misery's boat with me," Bertha muttered and bit into a pastry.

Rose managed to get to the corner of Lee Street in time to see Woo's car disappear around the curved road. She made a quick right and pushed the pedal to the floor. As she came out of the bend, she saw Woo's car two traffic lights in front of her. She blinked with excitement as she closed the distance between them. Then the damned phone started ringing. Her first impulse was not to answer it, but she saw Don's number on the caller ID. "Yo, what's up, baby?" She really didn't want to be disturbed.

"Just thought I'd let you know that I was on my way. I should be there in about ten, fifteen minutes or so," he said as he zipped the last ounce of rock in a sandwich bag.

"Okay, you know where I'll be." She locked the phone under her chin so she could downshift for the upcoming light.

"So you at Al's, right?"

He pulled the phone away and frowned at it. "Yeah, I thought you knew that." He could feel that something was bugging her, but he didn't want to discuss it in front of Al.

Since she was in a awkward situation, she decided to end the conversation. "Yeah, yeah, I did. Uh, baby, this traffic out here is bad as hell. I'll call ya when I get to the store."

He was about to hang up anyway because Al had started to look a little irritated, so he got ready to clip off when he thought of something. "Hey."

"Yeah?" She was getting irritated, too.

"How about grabbing me some of that beef fried rice from that Chinese joint. You know the one that I like. Oh, yeah, and get them to throw some shrimps off in that bad boy, too."

She didn't respond immediately and he found himself fighting a tingling moment of panic, so with a slight squeak in his voice, he started to repeat. "Hey, did you hear..."

Rose had opened her mouth to respond when she saw Woo's car make a sudden left turn on Second Street. She made a swerve around the few cars ahead of her and pushed the pedal to the floor, speeding right through a red light. The cars at the intersection had already started across and she barely avoided being hit by them. The concentration of the near collisions caused a momentary lapse of her pursuit and she bypassed the street Woo had turned down. She made a quick U-turn through a gas station, but by the time she arrived to the street, the traffic was too crowded for her to enter. She didn't hesitate to jump out of the car and sprint to the corner, but by then Woo's car was out of sight.

Frustrated she went back to her car and laid her head on the headrest. Only then did she notice the voice screaming on the phone. She had laid it on the other seat when she'd left the car. Now she remembered that she had been talking to Don. She wiped the sweat on her forehead with the back of her hand. "Damn, baby, I'm sorry. Some fool ran a red light and nearly crashed into me. The muthafucka didn't even honk his horn or nothing."

"Okay, cool down. You aight, though? Damn, woman, you had

me worried to death for a minute there," he said with a heavy sigh as he watched Al watching him.

"Uh-huh, I'm aight, the bastard...aw fuck it. You said fried rice, beef and shrimp right, gotcha."

"So you heard me then?" He pinched his nose.

"Yeah, I heard ya. See ya later." Rose hung up and considered if she should ride down Second Avenue to see if she could spot the scheming little bitch. But she knew that it was useless with all the traffic and distance between them by now. Her eyes squinted with curiosity as she finally was able to get back on the street. She headed for the store in Jonesboro.

On the other side of town, Don was sitting and staring at the phone, feeling that his auntie wasn't being totally truthful with him when he heard Al clear his throat across the table.

"Hey, you aight, man? For a minute there you was really looking kind of fucked up." Al crossed his arms on the table eyeing him suspiciously.

"Taint nuthen, dog; my auntie was tripping, had me tripping right along with her but everything's cool."

"So she aight?"

That's what I just told you nigga, he thought. "Yeah, she aight." He started placing the last bags into his saddle bag.

"That's good, that's good," Al replied. Then he looked at the clock on the far wall and realized he had to check in with JR. It was way past the time to finish furnishing those condos with that furniture he'd had hijacked. Surely the money should've started rolling by now. He prayed that greedy bastard wasn't playing games with him.

Don was tightening the straps on the bag, when Mona stuck her head into the room and let them know that the food was ready. No matter how hard he tried he couldn't shake the feeling that Rose wasn't telling him what was happening.

Al read how he was acting the wrong way. Lately, he started feeling that something wasn't right. He could feel it in his bones. He wondered if it had anything to do with the missing section of tape he'd noticed the last time that he viewed it. There must have been some way that he had accidentally erased a portion of it, but he certainly couldn't recall doing that and nobody else knew about it. Or did they? Maybe it was the pressure from the big move he knew was getting ready to go down or just plain old paranoia caused by a combination of things.

He shook himself out of the mini trance he had fallen into. "Be there in a second, sweetie." Al turned to Don. "You chowing down with us, partner? There's certainly enough to go around."

"Naw, dude, my aunt's getting me some Chinese food." He headed for the door.

As he watched him leave, Al imagined blowing the back of his head off. "Damn, that's the second time that I've thought that. Man, what's happening to me? I'm really starting to enjoy this psychopathic shit," he mumbled to himself. The sound of Mona's voice calling out to him again drew his attention away from Don and his ugly thoughts. "I'm on my way now."

He looked up and saw her standing in the kitchen doorway with her hands on her hips. When he walked past, she rolled her eyes. And since the curtains had been left opened, she was able to see Don getting into his car. Her mind started sparkling at the thought of welcoming him back between her legs with that pussy-shocking, gigantic dick of his. "I've got to figure out a way to get some more of that." She hadn't even realized that she was rubbing her pussy until Al called for her. "Coming, big daddy," she purred with a shiver as she sniffed at her finger and thought of how much Don could make her pussy flow.

CHAPTER TWELVE

Enjoying the Spoils

Violet was squirming on the cushion to keep her butt off of the concrete of the stoop when she saw Duke's ride turn into the parking lot of the apartments. A smile crept to the corners of her mouth as she wondered how good the package he wanted tested would be. He wasn't a user, so he really valued her opinion. And she usually enjoyed the bombs he'd come up with. What addict wouldn't love a free high that would knock them for a loop?

She knew that he'd expect her to have all her gear ready so she stood up, picked up her pillow and headed for the door. Her head jerked back in shock when Sparkle and Joyce got out of the car. *What the fuck, where the hell is my car?* She hugged the pillow to her stomach and arched her brow as they approached.

Sparkle carried the grocery bag in one hand and Duke's saddle bag in the other. He had a downtrodden expression on his face as he nodded for her to go inside. With her mouth turned down, she waited until both of them had walked past her, with neither of them saying a word, before she followed.

An exhausted Sparkle walked straight to the couch, dropped both bags on the floor between his feet and flopped heavily on the cushion with a loud and long *aaaah*. Joyce, also exhausted, walked to the refrigerator, yanked the door open and grabbed a couple of Colt 45s. She tossed him one, which thudded off his chest onto the floor. She used the other one to wipe around her face and she flopped down in the love seat across from him.

Violet used the heel of her shoe to kick the door closed. She marched right in front of them, dropped the cushion on the floor and wrapped her right arm around her waist to use it as a prop for her left arm. She cupped her mouth, shifting her eyes between the two of them. She was too awestruck to really think clear. "And?"

Fifteen minutes and the rest of the six-pack of beer later, Sparkle and Joyce explained the past few hours to Violet; all except their sexual episode, of course. By the time they finished, the only thing she was thinking about was the cocaine's money value and getting high. She knew that Duke would use his wits as far as the car and the police were concerned.

All was kosher as they ended up in the bedroom laughing about all kinds of dumb shit that had happened in the past few days. They were well into their second eight ball when Sparkle got a call from Rainbow.

The urgency in his boy's voice put him on the edge. It was unlike him to act so nervous about anything; even going back to when they were in the same unit in the war. His mind drifted back to the days of those deadly excursions into the jungle to gather up all the dead soldiers. They were always high on whatever they could get their hands on; whether it be cocaine, heroin, reefer, acid, liquor, beer or any combination of them. Hell, it was whatever it took to help them deal with the possibility of the enemy springing out of the trees, bushes or straight out of the ground with guns blazing serious lead.

He still suffered through the occasional nightmare and waking up in a cold sweat with images of soldiers' whole bodies getting blown away from stepping on mines or being bombed to death from grenades strapped around little children walking into a crowd. Every now and then, those nightmares would dissolve into street battles over drug turf right there at home. There was only one constant and that was waking up in those cold sweats.

The tone in Rainbow's voice had him revisiting those recurrences, especially with what had just happened to Duke. Which also reminded him that he had to call Grady to check out big boy's condition. He had to walk down the street to the pay phone because of the possibility of the police monitoring calls.

A verbal cat fight between Violet and Joyce snapped him out of his revelry. He couldn't help but to smile as they argued about which side of town they were going to first with the kilos of coke that Joyce had ripped off of the Jamaicans.

However, the two dilemmas facing him were far more difficult. He was suffering from the dual anxieties of riding with his boys, thus, having to deal with Beverly and her crew of police monsters along with Don's army and the possible violence that occurred. He also was trying to figure out a way to bust Joyce's head and pussy as often as he could without Violet finding out. Whew!

Might as well watch old girl work her magic, he thought as he laid his head back on the bed post with his hands crossed behind his head, forming a somewhat comfortable cradle. With the coke caressing his brain, everything became entertainment. So he went into chill mode to enjoy the show.

Violet leaned a shoulder against the headboard with a look of determination cemented on her face. She went into her spiel. "Girl, I'm telling you for the hundredth time that it's better to roll with the suburbs with dis cher." She flipped a bag of rocks from one hand to the other. "Where we can dump a load at one house at a time? I'm telling you, girl, that my white folk out there be calling all their friends and everything. And they be smoking up the same stuff they done just scored with you. Godayum, what the fuck more can you ask for?" She stood up and threw her hands exuberantly in the air and then flexed her arms across her body to emphasize the easy job. "Mo money, mo money, mo money, fer sho." She ended with a flair of spreading her arms out while rotating her head around the room.

Not to be outdone so easily, Joyce reared back and hit her with a snake roll on every other word. "And I'm telling you about all my buddies out there in East Point and College Park. We can pull just as much money over der." She ended with a series of finger pops in high-arching circles.

Sparkle knew better but he was unable to resist throwing in his two cents' worth. "Why don't y'all hussies just go y'all separate ways and get it over with?"

As he had expected, they simultaneously whirled on him and Violet yelled, "Nigga, stay your ass out of this."

Joyce added sarcastically, "Damn, a bitch can't even do a damn thang unless dis heah bastard gotta have something to say."

He flinched, a little pissed for a second, until he realized that she was keeping up with the normal bullshit between them to throw off what had happened at the hotel. Even though he quickly realized what she was doing, the little bitch had a way of scraping on his last nerve. He couldn't help but to give her something back. "At least you got the bitch part right," he mumbled.

"Whatcha mumbling for, nigga?" Joyce gritted.

"You heard me, ho."

"Whatever." Joyce skirted him a palms up to freeze whatever comeback he had on that and turned to Violet. He decided to keep his mouth out of it. The longer they argued, the worse things would be but he wanted them out of there before his boy Rainbow arrived. They continued to argue back and forth. So he adjusted his tactics, with the hope that he made good sense to them.

He wanted to show Violet her due respect. "Yo, V, check this out, sweetheart. Uh, and you too, Joyce." He paused to make sure that he had their full attention. "Okay now, because I've worked both areas y'all talking about, I got the feeling that with this new package, there are going to be bumps in the road. I feel that since y'all are introducing a new kind of coke..." He picked one of the packages up and hefted it in his hands. "And we know they ain't had nothing this good before, hell, taint no telling how dey gonna react behind dis here. That's why it'll be better to start with the more civilized folk out dere in the burbs."

He saw out of the corner of his eye that Joyce was about to interrupt him, so he threw a palm in the front of her face to chill her. "Not that you won't make some generous ends at the Point and the Park but the monies a lot easier in the burbs. Especially if y'all start out there in Lithonia; ain't nothing but comfortable money out dat way. And most important of all, is that whoever these hunters are that's gonna be after our asses, they won't be out there on the prowl. Y'all feel me?"

He could tell by the tension-relieving deflation of Joyce's shoulders, that the last part of his statement had really caught her attention. She propped a finger up to her nose and sniffled before she replied, "Okay, okay." She opened with a dainty wave of her hand. "I see whatcha saying." She peeked a look at Violet, who had stubbornly crossed her arms across her chest. "But sometime during the night, or at least tomorrow, we gonna holla at my crew or leave a number or something."

Smiling her approval, Violet got up off of the bed and started gathering the three ounces they had cut up into dimes, twenties, and fifty blocks. Without a word she strutted out of the room.

Joyce had been stuffing a huge piece of rock into her shooter while Sparkle was talking "Godayum, Auntie, chill yo ass for a sec. I know you saw me packing this bitch!" Joyce yelled.

Violet kept on walking as she yelled over her shoulder. "Bitch, you best to burn that shit on the way because I'm out of here."

Realizing that she was dead serious, Joyce barely got a short puff in before she snatched up her purse and sprinted out the door behind her.

Sparkle sighed a breath of relief as they departed. After a few more blasts, he decided to take a quick shower before Rainbow got there. He wasn't sure when he would get another chance. There was no telling what tonight or the next couple of days, for that matter, would lead to. He also was still counting his blessings because Violet hadn't pulled one of her dick-sniffing acts on him. He could still feel and smell the scent of Joyce's body mesmerizing his nose. Thank God for her greedy ass seeing all that coke.

Damn, that cold water was revitalizing. He was drying off when the doorbell rang. He gave a snorted grunt because he knew that Violet had locked the security gate again. Funny how she never wanted it locked while she was there. Like a nigga want to stop whatever he was doing to walk all the way down the steps to open the door.

He knew it was his boy though, so he sped to the intercom beside the bed and shouted out that he'd be down there in sec. He grunted and smiled when he heard him mutter some fucked-up shit as he headed back to the bathroom to finish drying off and to put on his robe. When he finally made it to the door, he was greeted with an impatient grit. He didn't let it phase him though as he turned around and went back into the apartment.

"Damn, nigga, you knew that I was on the way. You're supposed to be ready to roll."

From the tone of his voice, Sparkle could tell that he was irritated. But there was nothing else to say; put his clothes on and get his piece ready for whatever action that was called for. He knew that Rainbow wanted to run his mouth to release some of the tension that had been building up for the past weeks. Especially now that his boy Duke had gotten all shot up. That went right along with Beverly's revelations of thinking that Don was behind it all.

Rainbow was pacing back and forth in front of the television while Sparkle was putting on his clothes. "Dog, how in the hell did that black muthafucka find out about the scam man?" Sparkle looked up while he was sliding into his boots. "Yo, man, how you know all this shit is about that there? Are you sure about that? Stuff was happening before we did the 617 thang."

Rainbow stopped pacing and peered at him over the rims of his shades. "Man, it has to be that and besides, ain't nobody seen that ho Mary Anne for days. Shit, there's even a rumor going around that he done had her done in."

That caught Sparkle by surprise. Maybe he wasn't in the loop as he thought he was or cared to be; he hadn't heard about it. Surely Joyce would've mentioned something like that. Then again she was probably too deep in her scam to hear about it. He rubbed the stubble on his chin. "You for real, dude?"

"Hell, yeah, I'm for real. What other reason would I be telling you for?"

Sparkle used the palm of his hand to rub his eyelids while his weary mind worked on the latest revelation. The violence was certainly getting too close for comfort. The steadily building tension led to his breathing a heavy sigh. "Okay, dog, where you want to take it from here?"

Rainbow snatched off his shades and looked off into space for a moment, before he sat down on the edge of the bed. "Man, give me a blast of that shit, then we gonna ride to collect some digits while I let this plan in my mind come all the way together."

Aw shit, here we go with that all-of-a-sudden commando shit again. Sparkle turned his mouth down nodding in agreement and walked over to the closet. He bent down and lifted the floorboard to get to the shoe box that held his personal stash. Sitting beside his boy on the bed, he removed the Ziploc bag that had been recently filled with some of the coke he'd gotten from Joyce and flipped it to him.

Rainbow reached into his shirt to get his white gold spoon with the Mercedes-Benz symbol and took a couple of tokes. While he was drifting off to Scottyville, Sparkle was busy rocking up a fifty slab in a test tube. He didn't even wait for it to dry before he was blasting away as well.

"Hmm, dog, dis here be some new shit, ain't it?" Rainbow harrumphed.

"Yeah, man, it's some stuff Joyce took off some Jamaicans over there in College Park or East Point one," Sparkle replied after taking a hit.

Rainbow stood up and started dusting some imaginary lent off of his raw silk pants and started picking in his ear. "Damn, man, I knew I should've trapped her red ass a long time ago."

Sparkle shook his head, knowing that he had to be tripping on the coke really hard. He knew first-hand that he'd been trying to put his mack game down on Joyce every since he'd first seen her. He'd never gotten anywhere. He wondered what Rainbow would say if he let him know how fantastic that bitch was. He decided to let him jabber on, not really paying him any attention while he finished getting dressed.

Afterward, they checked and rechecked their guns to make sure that they were in good working condition. Their gut instincts were telling them that it was getting real close to killing time; if not tonight, then really soon.

As they were heading out of the door, Sparkle looked over his shoulder. "Okay, what first, go pick up 'B' or go for the green?"

Rainbow pinched his nose and sniffled. "Ah, man, I knew there was something I was meaning to tell you. 'B''s out there in the N.O. hustling at the Mardi Gras. He called me about an hour ago and told me to meet him at Hartsfield tomorrow at noon."

Sparkle leaned back sideways and gritted on him. "Why you take so long to tell me that?"

Rainbow spread his hands out. "Hell, man, was you not listening to me or what? I just said…"

"I heard what you said," Sparkle cut him off.

"Well, then, oh yeah, little Mercedes is rolling with Lady and Clara. Damn, let me call them before we jet," Rainbow replied as he shouldered by him on the way to the car.

As Sparkle watched his back, for the first time in a lot of years, he felt the sting of negative vibes of fear and doubt coming off his boy. He took a deep breath and gave a silent prayer for the things to come. A bad omen, a bad omen indeed.

CHAPTER THIRTEEN

The Hunters and the Hunted

After a paranoia-filled night of smoking blunt, speed balling, playing cards, other table top games and taking turn peeking out of the hotel blinds, they gathered the girls right before dawn to move them to the La Quinta in Lithonia. Settling them into a pair of suites in the middle of the second floor turned out to be quite a circus. Imagine eight streetwise female slicksters, each taking secret stabs trying to convince them to take them along. Not one of them wanted to be stuck in no connecting room with a bunch of paranoid clucking hens.

Rainbow and Sparkle were able to untangle themselves from their tentacles around ten-thirty. They wanted to have at least a half-hour or so to do a little recon at the airport before 'B' arrived. Sparkle was on his second strawberry milkshake at the ice cream parlor, when he spotted 'B' and Miriam strolling down the terminal's aisle about fifty yards away. He directed his gaze to encompass the entire surroundings to see if anyone was trailing the pair. Or paying him any overdue attention. When they got close enough to make eye contact, Sparkle shifted his eyes toward the Hertz parking lot.

'B' and Miriam walked outside and immediately spotted Rainbow waving to them from a car in the second row of rentals. He reached into the back to pull up the latches as the pair crossed in front of the car. 'B' reached across the seat with his palm up and Rainbow gave him a fisted dap.

'B' snatched his hand back. "Naw, nigga, give me the trunk keys. What am I supposed to do with these here bags, dog?"

"Shit, looks like enough room back there to me, partner," Rainbow said as he turned from him.

"What?" 'B' and Miriam yelled in unison.

"Just kidding, dog, just kidding." He smiled as he tossed the keys over his shoulder.

"Ow!" Miriam shouted when the keys clunked off of her forehead.

"Damn, my bad, come on, dude, I'll help you with those bags." Rainbow twisted his mouth up and hunched his shoulder as he was getting out of the car before she could say anything.

Rainbow waited until 'B' had opened the trunk before he put a fist to his mouth to stifle a laugh while putting his other fist out for some dap. 'B' grunted and waved him off as he bent over to put the bags in the trunk. When he straightened up, there was a smile on his face and they embraced, pounding each other on the back.

'B' held him by the shoulders at arm's length, blinked a few times before he pinched his nose, then snorted. "What it be, playa, you sounded really stressed over the phone or was it all the static coming over the line? Damn, those Orleans folk be getting some kind of hyped up in the French Quarter. Shit, you can barely hear yourself think. Man, you'd think that after Katrina, things would be a little toned down. Shiiit, those country muthafuckas were all the way live; hell, even more than before." He shook his head as he recalled all the ruckus.

Rainbow nodded solemnly. "Yeah, they do, don't they?"

That expression on his face caused 'B' to get serious real quick.

"Uh-huh, so clear me up on this shit, man." His dark skin turned blue-black with anger.

"Thought I'd wait until Sparkle joined us." He paused to look around the raised trunk at Sparkle, who was still sitting in silence, making sure they hadn't been followed.

"Fuck it, man, dat nigga Don is still shooting hot lead at us. They hit up Big Duke on I-20 the other day." He slammed the trunk and walked back to the driver's side. On the way he caught eye contact with Sparkle and dapped himself across the chest three times. As he was bending down to get in the car, he heard 'B' mumbling something. He sat down and turned to face him. "What's that you said, dog?"

'B' was massaging the corners of his mouth as he stared at the back of his head for a moment. "Boy, I can hardly wait to get my hands on Joker. I'm gonna leave my whole ankle in that little nigga's black ass."

"Why you coming off on our little player like that for, partner?" Rainbow asked as he lit up a Kool cigarette and eyed him in the mirror.

His head was bowed and he was rubbing his forehead before he looked up to the roof. "My nigga..." He took a deep breath. "Our little player's been running dope from Miami for that nigga Don. Uh-huh, he's been doing that shit behind our back for damn near a year and there ain't no telling what else he's got his young stupid ass doing."

Damn, come to think about it, I ain't seen Joker since he got out of the youth center. Hmm, heard that youngun done got himself a condo and big car, no fucking wonder, he thought as he contemplated the consequences of his protégé siding with the enemy. Not good, not good at all.

Before they could go any farther, Sparkle opened the front passenger door and sat down. He turned around to wave at Miriam and throw dap at 'B.' He turned around to settle down in his seat, but he couldn't get comfortable because he felt some bad vibes tingling in the air.

"Damn, what's the dilly, yo?" he questioned as he looked back and forth between the three of them.

Rainbow started to speak but 'B' threw up his hand. "My nigga, Joker's been down with that punk-ass nigga Don. Which means that Stack and his little gangsta-ass crew is probably down with him, too."

Rainbow interrupted, "Yo, wait a second here. You didn't say nothing about Stack and those other younguns." His mind went back to all the times the younguns were at his crib gambling and sucking game out of him. Damn.

'B' cocked his head to the side and threw a palm into his face. "Dat's because you didn't give me a chance to finish what I was telling you."

Rainbow reached back and pushed his hand down. "Okay, partner, you got the floor. Go ahead and finish then."

Sparkle didn't give him the chance to respond as he jumped back in. "Hold the fuck up. Stop the godayum presses. So how come you just telling us this?"

'B' bucked his eyes. "Because I just found out while I was in Orleans. Hold up, I take that back. I found out about Joker before I went to Orleans. Hey, man, straight up, I was like too fucked up to bring it to y'all without checking things out first. I did a little checking around while I was there. That's when I found out about those other young muthafuckas."

Rainbow and Sparkle looked at each other with doubting expressions. Neither of them knew what to do, so they turned their attention to Miriam.

She was lying back chilling and listening to them air their bullshit. But now the spotlight was on her. "Whaddahell y'all want me to say?"

Sparkle turned around to look at her and thought, *Damn, she has a remarkable resemblance to that girl Eve, minus the blonde hair, but definitely the same pouty lips and chilling demeanor.*

She batted those sexy eyes and wiggled her little booty in the seat real dainty-like and said in a raspy voice, "Dat nigga Stack, he's like way out dere with the nose job on my sister, but she's all up into that nigga Al. Anywho, he likes to tell her everything, trying to show her he's gangsta and shit."

Rainbow, not in the mood to be hearing about no family dramas, hissed out loud, "Where those niggas at?"

"How the hell am I supposed to know? I'm here with y'all niggas," she hissed right back at him.

"You just said..." He froze when he saw the look on her face in the mirror. He started feeling stupid for even throwing that at her and slumped down in the seat a little before he slung his arm over the steering wheel and shook his head. "I guess that's the part we got to figure out for ourselves, huh." He looked up and she was nodding at him in the mirror.

Sparkle brought an abrupt end to their one-on-one when he turned around and slapped 'B' on the shoulder. "Hey, soldier, it sho took your ass long enough to holla at us."

"Hey, fuck dat, I'm here now, ain't I?" 'B' said with a frown, but immediately followed that up with a smile.

"Sho ya right, partner, sho ya right." Sparkle nodded several times and then turned back to Rainbow. "You hip him about what happened in Jonesboro?"

"Not yet, but I was getting ready to." Rainbow cocked an eye to the mirror to see 'B''s reaction.

'B' leaned forward and propped his elbows on the back of Rainbow's seat. "Let's see, I'm figuring y'all niggas done been on the hunt. So why couldn't y'all wait for me to get back? Damn, Bow, you knew y'all had done this while you was talking to me. What's the deal on that, dude?"

"Ain't no big deal. You wasn't here so why bug you with it?"

'B' stared at the back of his head, his jaws clenching in anger. "Dog, that's fucked up. So now which of you two so-called partners of mine are going to tell me why?" he hissed at both of them in turn.

Neither of them even bothered to turn around to face him, choosing to avert the harsh stare they knew he was giving them. They started scratching their jaws and the sides of their necks. That really hit a nerve with 'B.' It was the same way they used to act when they tried to leave him out of the rough-and-tumble stuff ever since they were kids. 'B' was really starting to get pissed off now. To camouflage his frustration, he sat back and turned his face to the window, fogging it up from the steam flaring out of his nose.

Recalling the way he always acted whenever they seemed to be shutting him out, Rainbow and Sparkle eyed each other sideways until a smile started edging to the edge of their mouths. Turning their heads away from 'B''s line of vision, they started coughing to try to hide the laughter that began snorting through their noses.

The familiar sound caused 'B' to jerk away from the window with his face all balled up. Sparkle sneaked a peek in his direction, doing his best to hold it in. But the fire shooting out of 'B''s eyes triggered a sprinkle of spittle to spew out of his mouth before he could cover it. Laughter erupted from deep in his stomach.

It splashed all over Rainbow's neck and the side of his face. He swiped at the sprinkling onslaught and jerked his head back, thumping really hard against the window.

"Ow, whaddafuck, godayum, man, cover your muthafucking mouth, shit!" he screamed in disgust.

"Good, get his ass, Sparkle; serves his red ass right." 'B' slapped his knee and laughed. "Leaving me outta shit and then got the nerve to laugh about it."

Sparkle leaned back from the window holding his hand over his eye and turned a hard grit toward 'B' but he couldn't hold it, so he faked an elbow at his face that was hanging over the seat. After a moment of ribbing each other, Rainbow pulled out of the parking lot. His tone had turned serious. "All bullshit aside, we got to go ahead and take this nigga out, once and for all."

Sparkle cleared his throat and motioned toward Miriam. "What about honey here? That nigga don't know her, so we can wire her up. And when she get under that nigga, we can take his ass out at a love nest. His freaky ass sho won't be looking for that there."

Rainbow didn't give her a chance to respond. "Uh-huh, that just might work. Plus, we can get Joyce to play the tag team with her. She's real good at getting a nigga to trust her. Fer sho, one of them can get him to take them to one of those outta-the-way hotels so we can wax his ass."

Sparkle laughed. "Yep, and while they're working him, they may be able to find out who all's rolling with Joker, too. I got a funny feeling that they all had something to do with that hit on Duke."

'B' joined in, "Miriam, baby, this here's gonna be some hot and deadly games you're about to pull off. I know you got the heart, but are you ready to throw down on this?"

Miriam blinked her long lashes and started running her baby finger along her collarbone for a moment before she pinched her nose and snorted. "Gangsta 'B,' you told me that you was going to make me a lioness." 'B' frowned and slanted his eyes toward his boys. He knew they were snickering with the lioness bullshit but he decided not to interrupt her. She kept it flowing. "Well, baby, I'm ready to use my claws. That nigga done dogged some of my buddies at that club of his, so his ass has got to go, straight up. When y'all ready to do this?"

Rainbow uncovered his mouth and cocked a eyebrow at Sparkle, who cocked his right back at him and then turned to 'B,' who was beaming like a Cheshire cat. All of them were a little surprised at Miriam's thuggish display. "You go, girl," they said in unison.

'B' smiled at her like a proud daddy and patted her on the thigh before addressing his boys. "What y'all say about bugging his office at the lounge?"

"Hell yeah, his and Big Junior's at the 617, too," Rainbow added quickly.

Sparkle spat immediately as well, "Man, fuck the 617. Let's just burn that bitch down, since he want to get revenge and shit. That way his ass'll be stuck at the lounge most of the time. Uh-huh, we can really keep tabs on him better at one spot."

"Sounds like a plan to me. Let's do it." Rainbow gritted as he pulled into the traffic heading out of the airport.

Rainbow and Sparkle immediately jumped on their cells to hook up with the girls. While 'B' was lying back in the seat eyeing the skyline, he tried to figure out a way to punish his little cousin Joker without his boys taking it overboard. After all, blood was thicker than water. As he watched his boys rattling on the phones, he shook his head feeling sort of weird about how thin that bloodline really was—at what limit they would take their revenge or whether there was a limit.

✠ ✠ ✠

Rose had a lot of things on her mind when she pulled into the parking lot of the club. Not only had she not heard from Don in a couple of days, but those two younguns were still stuck up in the apartment. Every time that she went over there to get her chill on, those bastards were either playing video games and bitching about how long Don was keeping them there; and generally leaving the place in a mess. She was at her wit's end cleaning up behind two grown-ass men. She dreaded the thought of going over there, but somebody had to do it.

Kicking it with Bertha was some good therapy. That's why she was there now. She needed a good friend's ear to bend and listen to her bitch about life.

The beaming smile on Bertha's face hit her like a ray of sunshine as soon as she stepped through the door. Any other time she would've gone straight to the office in the back, not wanting to be noticed by the patrons of the club.

As she approached the bar, Bertha held up a glass, tilted it toward her and started fanning herself with a drink menu. "What can I pour you up, sweetie? You look like you could certainly use a stiff one." She beamed as she placed the glass on the counter real ladylike.

Rose propped her elbow on the counter and rested her chin on the back of her hand, as her eyes rolled to the ceiling contemplating her options. She licked and popped her lips. "You got any pimp juice up under those panties that you could pour me up right quick?" She bit down on her bottom lip and squinted her eyes up real sexy. "Naw, home girl, go ahead and pour me up one of them Heinekens. Uh, it's on the house, right?"

Bertha wiggled her head around real silly-like. "Duh, of course on the house. Shit, it's your house." She snickered. "I might as well let you know now that Max and Junior are back there in the office."

The expression on her face changed with the quickness. "Damn,

I sure ain't in the mood to be hearing their bitching and crying about Don this and Don that. Girl, hurry up and pour up. Aw, fuck it, give me the bottle."

Bertha reached under the counter and into the cooler to get the beer. As she was snapping the top off, the telephone started ringing. They stared at each other for a moment before Bertha sighed and picked it up. "Yeah, this here Bertha," she said into the mouthpiece. Then a grimace of concern etched its way across her face and she snatched her tinted shades off and said breathlessly, "What!!!" She lowered her forehead into her hand and started massaging her temples. "Where have they taken him? Okay, I'll be there as soon as I can." Sighing deeply, she ended the conversation as a single tear rolled down her cheek as she stared at nothing, stunned.

Rose felt a tingling start at the base of her neck as she watched Bertha's chest rise in discomfort. Her eyes blinked with uncertainty while a feeling of dread bumped at her heart. She struggled to find her voice, mouth agape, mind spinning, female intuition causing stars to spiral before her eyes, knowing something bad had happened. She closed her eyes, squeezing so tight that her corners ached, trying to will away the thoughts running through her mind. Finally she thumbed the dampness off of her eyelashes and found her voice. "What happened?" She wheezed as she tried to control her composure.

Bertha lowered her eyes, not really wanting to witness her reaction and mumbled, "He got beat up really bad out near the Farmers Market. Some kids saw him crawling out of the woods. He's on his way to Grady's now." The rest of whatever she said sounded like a lot of mumbo-jumbo, as a combination of fear and anger consumed her thoughts as she headed for the door.

✠ ✠ ✠

Al fought back the impulse to slap the emergency room attendant for not giving him the information he sought. The attendant took a step back when he saw the thick veins pop out of his neck and lowered his hand to his beeper to signal for security. Al noticed the motion and checked himself. There was no need to draw unwanted attention. So he forced a smile that caused the attendant to take his hand away from the beeper. He walked away eyeing him over his shoulder toward the elevator. Al pinched his nose and snorted as he maintained his smile until he disappeared.

As the door was closing, he started looking up and down the corridor, trying to spot somebody else in authority who could help him find out where his boy was. The whole time he wondered who could have done this. But he was really more concerned about his portion of the coke package that he was supposed to be bringing him.

This was the first time that he had used some of the money that he owed RJ to re-up with. What really made him feel extra fucked up, was that his gut instincts had told him not to chance it. But his greed had taken over, figuring he could double up on his profit and be able to invest more into their venture. He'd already provided the furniture through the hijacked truck. Man, if they could pull off this project of high-priced furnished condos, there was no telling how much money they could reap in doing this all around DeKalb and Fulton counties.

If nothing else, he had to find out where the coke was. Even he couldn't afford to lose that many bricks of raw. Especially when using other folks' money to get it, damn. After all those years of grinding in the red light district, he finally had a connection that could get him fully legit. The chance to get in with the big boys.

And most of it was based on his word; how much they knew he could be trusted to come through when he said that he could.

He was really spaced out in his near panicking thoughts when he heard the sound of a familiar voice from the elevators. He recognized Bertha's voice immediately and started toward her, totally ignoring the protest from the attendant who had reappeared. He even let out a short laugh when the doors started closing.

"What room he in?" he asked when he turned to face her. She didn't say anything as she punched the button for the fifth floor, as he was reaching to grab her arm. As the elevator started upward, he repeated the question, more harshly this time.

Bertha looked down at the hand gripping her arm with disdain. She certainly wasn't used to people manhandling her and wasn't about to start now. She jerked her arm away and said with a grudge, "Man, I don't know what kind of women you're used to being around, and handling, but I ain't one of them."

The grit on her face let him know that she meant what she said. Even though a stroke of anger glazed across his eyes, he didn't want to draw any more attention to himself. He laid off the gorilla tactics. For now anyway, he'd deal with her smart-mouthed ass later; that was for sure. He turned away from her and started tapping his foot to help control the rage that was boiling up in his gut. Bertha frowned for the entire ride up and *tssked* at him when she got out of the elevator, then headed down the corridor without saying another word.

He growled under his breath as his eyes followed her to the last room. At least she had left the door ajar. That cooled him down a tad. When he entered the room, she was nowhere in sight. *Bitch must've gone to the bathroom or something*, he thought right before the toilet flushed. He looked from the bathroom to the other side of the room where he saw Rose standing at the window, staring into the horizon. He'd started toward her when his peripheral vision was drawn to the figure lying in the bed. Damn, the figure was kind of small, much too small to be Don. He was in a bit of a daze as he walked to the bed and then cocked his head toward Rose with a puzzled look on his face.

"Who in the hell is that, Rose?" he asked after he pulled the cover back and saw the face.

Rose hadn't heard him come in. She looked at him over her shoulder and squinted her eyes, momentarily astonished by his question.

"Whatcha mean who is that? You mean to tell me..." She caught herself before she could finish. Her eyes squinted when it dawned on her that there was a possibility that Al didn't even know JJ. "Damn, I assumed it was Don myself from the way Bertha reacted to that phone call." Al probably wasn't even aware that JJ had been paid to try that sneak attack on Rainbow. She wondered where that nigga Percy was, his buddy on that lick.

Why am I even thinking about that punk? Quickly shaking that thought away, her mind drifted to how she knew that she was under the radar as far as Don's business went with this nigga. She preferred to keep it that way.

"Excuse me, but you don't know this dude?" she inquired as she pointed to the bed.

He cocked a brow at her. "Of course I know JJ. I didn't recognize him at first but to tell you the truth, I thought you was talking about Don when you called. I wouldn't have..." He paused to take a deep breath. "Hell, I wouldn't have rushed all the way over here for that nigga there. He ain't nothing but a burned-out crackhead." He turned away and muttered something to himself. She tilted her back and asked him what he had said.

He snorted before he turned back around. "I said I was thinking that Don had gotten fucked up and had fucked my money up and how I'd hate to fuck him up about my ends," he said disgustedly as he spun away from her and left the room.

Luckily, he had left when he did, because he hadn't seen the stiletto that had slid into her hand. He had closed the door too fast on his exit. The stiletto had disappeared as quickly when Bertha came out of the bathroom and went to sit on the bed.

Rose watched her for a second and walked over to place a comforting hand on her shoulder. "Don't worry about it, girlfriend. We'll get to the bottom of this before long. That Al's one cold-hearted bastard."

Bertha could only nod her head as the tears started rolling down her cheeks. *Damn, that's both of her brothers getting fucked up in that short a time*, Rose thought as she stood up and got ready to leave. She stroked Bertha's head gently. "You sure you're going to be all right, because I've got to handle some things." She waited for her to nod that she'd be okay before she walked out of the room.

Rose intended to catch the elevator but it was taking too long, so she fast-stepped to the exit door and sprinted down the stairs. She really wanted to catch Al without anybody around to teach that nigga a lesson. Who did he think he was threatening to harm her baby? She'd show his ass what he could and couldn't do. By the time she got to the emergency room door, she saw his car leaving the parking area. She proceeded to her car plotting on how she was going to get him. She jumped into her car and sped out of the parking lot. As she pulled onto the street and headed for Peachtree, she began smiling as a plan started formulating in her mind.

✠ ✠ ✠

The traffic was bumper to bumper along I-20 as Turner Field came into view. Rainbow checked on his boy 'B' in the mirror. He was gnawing at what was left of his fingernails. Actually he was chewing on the meat under the skin that was under the skin. He had the bad habit of doing that whenever he was nervous about something—a habit that aggravated the hell out of Rainbow. "Damn, dude, when are you going to realize that you ain't had no nails on those rough-ass claws for centuries?" Rainbow said with a sneer.

'B' ignored his ribbing and turned his finger around, trying to find any piece of skin hanging loose. There was none but he kept nibbling away anyhow.

"Come on, man, stop dat shit." Rainbow shivered in disgust.

'B''s eyes brightened mischievously knowing he was bugging the hell out of him. "Nigga, if you had been paying attention to what you was doing, you would've seen that you could've gotten off this busy bitch way back yonder."

"Yeah, but I didn't, because I was trying to think about the best way to work that nigga Don into a position where we can handle his ass," Rainbow snapped back at him.

A smiling 'B' tapped Sparkle on the shoulder. "You hear that fool? Now he got some ESP shit going on."

Sparkle rubbed a finger under his nose, gave a short snort of a laugh and cocked an eye across the seat at Rainbow. "Uh-huh, check him out, the great Hodinbow, magician at large." He turned his attention to "B." "Ain't that a bitch? Looks like he ready to do some hocus pocus on that nigga right now, but we need to just whack this fool any way we can."

'B' groaned, stuck his head out of the window and stretched his neck to see if he could see a crack in the traffic flow.

"That's the same thing I been telling this curly-head pretty boy all along," Sparkle added as he dipped his glass shooter into the bag of coke for the fourth time since they had left the Checker Club skin game in Ben Hill.

Not really giving a fuck how their silly asses were thinking, Rainbow caught 'B''s eye in the mirror and then looked over at Sparkle, shook his head and retorted, "Because I don't wanna be hollering at y'all from down the tier on death row a year from now. You know, wondering how we could've done it without a hundred witnesses. That is if y'all two overhyped niggas don't mind."

"Yeah, well, I tell ya what I mind. I mind that those girls are taking so long to pin that nigga down at a spot we can take his punk ass out. Makes me think that nigga flipping game on them hoes." Sparkle clearly was not trying to hide his frustration.

'B' snorted and shoved Rainbow's shoulder. "Listen to this nigga, dog, sounds like he got some player hating going on here, all jealous and shit. Yo reckon that's because Joyce said that nigga's shit be hanging to his knees got anything to do with it?"

Sparkled started to turn around to go off on him, but Rainbow jerked the steering wheel sharply to the right, causing him to lose his balance and slam into the door. He proceeded to veer to the right emergency lane and accelerated down the road despite the loud honking horn of several cars in protest. It included a police cruiser that was jammed between a SUV and a mobile home. And to add insult to ignorance, 'B' and Sparkle waved at the astonished officer, whose head swirled all around anxiously when they zoomed by.

'B' got all excited and started jumping around in the back seat as he screamed, "Dat's what I'm talking about, nigga! Sho some gangsta with yo sorry law-abiding ass."

"Aw, fuck you, man, I'm tired of hearing your bitching," Rainbow yelled back at him as he jetted to the East Lake Meadows exit and streaked to Memorial Drive and then on to Candler Road. As they neared the intersection, Sparkle told him to pull over at the BP gas station. Rainbow waited until he had pulled in front of one of the pumps before he turned to face him while he was about to open the door. "Man, why you want to pull up here all of a sudden?"

"Ain't that the twins' Nissan over there at Joyce's and 'ems beauty shop?" Sparkle grunted as his eyes strained across the street.

Rainbow cocked his head to the side and strained at the car he was talking about before he nodded in agreement. "I believe that is their whip. Uh-huh, yeaah, that's they shit with them teddy bears in the back window."

"Thought they was supposed to be pulling that nigga Don for the ambush," 'B' said as he leaned over the seat to get a better look himself.

"Hell, I thought they were, too. Then again they may be working together with that ho Joyce and they just touching bases. Then again they may be getting they wigs hooked up; you know how those women are about their hair, man," Rainbow shot back and started rubbing his chin as he concentrated on the possibilities. He sat up straight in the seat and rolled his shoulders. He reached for the door handle. "In that case, we really need to holla at 'em because I don't like no bitch working beyond my instructions without letting me know about it." He raised his knee to shove the door open, but Sparkle reached across the seat to grab his shoulder.

With his pimping in question, Rainbow jerked his shoulder away and frowned at the hand. "Man, what's the matter with you? I know you ain't about to tell me how to handle no ho. It ain't like they going to come over here to us if they don't know we here."

Sparkle shoved his shoulder back on the seat again. "Just hold your ass still for a second there, man." He nodded toward the small grocery store parking lot on the other corner. "Ain't that that nigga Percy?"

'B' had placed his elbows on the back of Rainbow's seat as he strained to see across the street. "Uh-huh, dat's dat punk aight, but check that shit out. What the fuck he got those little binoculars to spy on his own sisters for? And who's that skinny muthafucka wid him?"

Sparkle pinched his nose and said gruffly, "That's what caught my attention. Hold on, wait a fucking minute here. That's the skinny nigga who was with JJ that night I was telling you about. You remember when I was looking for you in Buttermilk Bottom? Come on, dog, you got to remember that. Help me out here, will ya?" He started snapping his fingers as he searched his memory.

Rainbow frowned in the direction of the shop, his expression clearly full of puzzlement, as he tried to recall what Sparkle was talking about. Not a clue registered.

Sparkle eyed him impatiently for a moment. "Come on, dog, you got to remember that night when I told you I had seen JJ boosting at the little country store on Memorial. The one with the old kerosene pump on the porch. He was acting all strange and shit and when they went outside, I could tell that the nigga was favoring his left arm. Yep, the same one you shot that night at the crib."

Rainbow rubbed his brow and stared blankly toward the car they were talking about, trying hard to place the guy's face. "Dat's the dude?" he asked as the veins started swelling in his neck and he leaned closer to the window and squinted. "You sure, dog?"

"Hell yeah, I'm sure because he was favoring that same arm after he bumped into me that night. Just like he doing now. Uh-huh, probably still got it wrapped up and everything."

As if right on cue, the dude reached up to adjust the sun visor and sure enough his arm was still bandaged. Suddenly overcome with rage, Rainbow opened the door and was nearly out of the car when Sparkle lunged across the seat and grabbed his arm. Rainbow wasn't having it and jerked his arm out of his grasp and started around the car. He came to an abrupt halt when 'B' kicked the door open.

Rainbow grunted and grabbed his knee. He heaved heavily and gritted at 'B' for a sec before he straightened up. His eyes were blazing fire across the street. His thoughts raced back to recall the two dark-clad niggas kicking the door off the hinges with their guns spitting death in the pitch-black kitchen. And one of them yelping out in pain after he fired in their direction. He looked down at Sparkle, who was still laid out across the seat from when he had tried to stop him from getting out of the car. He was looking up with a pleading look on his face. Rainbow sighed deeply and came close to sitting on his face when he got back in the car.

Sparkle scrambled out of his way and sat back up and frowned. Rainbow pinched his brow and reached across Sparkle's lap to open the glove compartment and remove the gold bracelet with the 'JJ' engraved in it. He turned in the seat to face 'B,' squared his shoulders and turned to Sparkle waving the bracelet around. He started nodding with his mouth twisted down. "Dat's that nigga, yo. Man, fuck some patience on this one here. I've got to have that bitch nigga right now." His voice had zoomed back to a fever pitch.

Sparkle waved his hand frantically across his face and yelled over, "Hold up, man; think about it for a minute. Now that we know who's down with the cross, all we got to do is follow them niggas and see who's all down with them."

'B' spoke up from the backseat. "Makes sense to me, hero."

Rainbow looked back at him and then over to Sparkle before he settled back breathing hard through his nose and gripped the steering wheel until his knuckles ached.

With his brow arched with caution, he reached over and started massaging his collarbone. "Dog, I feel your tension. I'm tense, too, but we got to see if this stuff goes deeper than Don. Neither of us bothered to think about that before, know what I mean?"

Rainbow held his head back and squeezed his eyes before he reluctantly nodded in agreement. 'B' placed a hand on his shoulder. "Tell ya what, partner, y'all check out them niggas' reaction when I walk past them on the way to the salon. They know we're partners and if them niggas start to yakking and acting nervous, we'll know they on some kind of assignment, you feel me? They may even get nervous enough to lead us to whoever sent them."

Rainbow glared at the hand clamped down on his shoulder. "Man, them niggas could just be waiting to score or something. Regardless, how in the hell is that supposed to prove any damn thing? He knows that was me and Sparkle at the crib that night."

'B' responded quickly, "True dat, but Percy knows that we roll together and be down like that."

Sparkle added, "Uh-huh, that's right, partner, that three amigo thing Bevy be calling us." Rainbow fidgeted around in the seat, then shook his head from side to side, before he took a deep breath. He was still steaming but he finally nodded and started rubbing a hand across his mouth and chin.

'B' and Sparkle eyed each knowing that he had made up his mind. "Okay, I see what y'all saying, but 'B' go around the block and cut through that alley so you can cross right in front of them. That way they won't be expecting us to be checking them out from over this way."

'B' didn't waste another word and reached down to his ankle

and took a .32 automatic out of its holster and slid it in his waist-band. He puffed his shirt out to conceal it before he opened the door. He turned his mouth down as he nodded to both of them and eased out and headed down Candler Road.

They concentrated hard on the pair across the street to make sure that they didn't pay 'B''s departure any attention. As far as they could tell, they didn't. In a little over a minute, they saw 'B' as he crossed the street and walked in front of the car. Percy and the other guy reacted immediately and started fidgeting in their seats. It was easy to tell that their conversation really piqued as they motioned toward him as he headed for the salon. Percy leaned forward peering through the binoculars with intense pur-pose, not wanting to miss a thing. When 'B' entered the beauty shop, his head started shifting from side to side, probably trying to catch the twins' reaction. Then he passed the binoculars to the other guy, lifted a cell phone and started punching numbers. Rainbow and Sparkle smiled openly at his animated antics as he talked with his head swiveling rapidly back and forth down the street like he was expecting some intruders or something. When he nodded his head several times and put the phone away, they had the answer they were looking for.

Responding swiftly Rainbow called the salon and asked for Joyce. She was mumbling something as she took the phone from the other hairdresser. "Yo, redbone, this here's Rainbow. Yeah, sweetie, I'm doing okay. Check this out, after I hang up ease... No, no, wait about a minute and go tell Johnny Bee to pull out of there with the twins and go to room 316 at the La Quinta in Lithonia. Yeah, in about a minute. I'll call you back after they leave. You betcha, I'll pick you up so you can blow a few rocks with us. Bitch, don't worry about who's with me. You'll see soon enough. Yeah, good girl, I'll holla."

After he flipped the phone closed, he smiled over at Sparkle.

"Now all we got to do is follow them fools." The wait wasn't long at all for the action to start. As soon as 'B' and the twins exited the salon and headed down Candler Road, Rainbow revved the car up, ready to follow Percy, when the other guy suddenly jumped out of the car and ran across the street to the Wong Chan Chinese joint on the corner. He joined two guys at one of the tables and started talking to them really fast.

The pair, both wearing dark toboggans and big sunshades, left the joint, jumped into a black sedan and immediately turned down Candler in pursuit of the twins' Nissan. Rainbow and Sparkle sat curious as all hell as they watched the guy run back across the street and shout something at Percy as he was getting back in the car. Percy was pulling into the street before he got the chance to close the door and sped down Memorial Drive toward Atlanta.

They looked at each other for a moment before Rainbow pulled out to the intersection. "Damn, man, which of these fools do we follow?"

Sparkle looked up Candler and then down Memorial as the two cars sped away. Scratching his head and rubbing his hand up and down his face, he finally said, "Uh, uh, Bow, I think we better follow Percy here because we already know where the other two are headed."

Rainbow hit the right turn, before the light even turned green and pressed on the gas. "Yeah, dog, that there makes sense. Here, call 'B' and let him know what's up and to keep an eye on those two following them." After a few blocks, it dawned on Sparkle that Rainbow had told Joyce that they'd pick her up. He looked over his shoulder toward the salon, as they were going around the curve in the road. "Damn!!"

"What's the matter now?" Rainbow cocked a brow at him. "Man, we told Joyce that we'd pick her up."

Rainbow slapped down on the steering wheel. "Fuck, I sure did, hell. She'll just have to wait on there, dog."

"Yeah, you right; it's just that, aw, what the fuck, the bitch's got the best head in the muthafucking world and I sure don't want her cutting me off of that there."

"What! You let a bitch rule you with the little head?" Rainbow eyed him with a sneer on his face.

"The head ain't that little, man."

"Whatever, dude." He gave him a quick *tssk*.

"Okay, I feel your square ass, but we got to track these niggas here. Aw, damn, man, go ahead and call her and let her know that we'll be there to get her in a few."

Sparkle smiled and picked up the phone to call the salon. "Yo, Mary, let me holla at Joyce. Yeah, baby, it's me. Yeah, I'm with him now. Hold up there, girl, you ain't got to holla, geez." He pulled the phone away from his ear to escape the octave rampage on the other end. Then he looked over to Rainbow and mouthed "fuck you" while he waited for the rampage to end. He was finally able to get with a word in. "Yeah, I... Yeah, he did, but you know that I got you, babe. We got caught up in some heavy shit. We'll be by to get you in a few, though. Okay, now that's better, dat's my girl." He held the phone to his chest and let out a long whew.

Rainbow shook his head and smiled, which quickly turned into a frown when Sparkle's face balled up and he gritted. "What, when? Ah damn, where they at now?" Sparkle lowered his head and started massaging the bridge of his nose. "Okay, when she call back, tell her to call us. We'll be heading that way in a bit. Later, sweetie."

Rainbow sniffled and squinted his eyes in anticipation. "What was that?"

Sparkle stretched and rotated his neck. "Miriam's about to meet our boy. This may be it, dog."

"Where, when?" Rainbow said in a very anxious tone as he stared at Percy's car a half-block ahead of them.

"She'll call us when she get the chance, I guess."

After hearing that, he figured that he didn't need Percy to lead them anywhere now. "Aw, man, fuck dat," Rainbow screamed and pressed on the gas pedal. "We can go ahead and do them niggas right now," he growled as the veins in his neck pulsed in anger.

Sparkle was quick to slam him across the chest with the back of his hand. "Slow your roll there, partner. Them fools can still lead us to da niggas who sent them after us."

Rainbow raised his foot off of the pedal and started rocking back and forth with his legs waggling wildly as he tried to get a grip on his rage. He finally wheezed. "Aight, aight. I'm cool, I'm cool, whew! Man, fix me up a blast, will ya?"

Sparkle wasted no time complying to his wish and started hooking him up a big chunk of rock on the shooter.

"That's better, dog; we gonna get them, dog, for sho. You damn right, whoosh, whoosh. We're gonna get them. Call the hotel. See what the girls are doing," Rainbow spewed between tokes.

Sparkle nodded and made the call, but no one answered.

"I wonder were these fools are headed?" Rainbow muttered as they followed them across the Atlanta city limits sign and veered to Decatur Street until they got to Buttermilk Bottom and on to Grady's parking lot.

"Man, this shit is getting weirder by the minute. Whatcha wanna do?" Sparkle asked as they parked a couple of rows from them.

"I'll keep an eye on the ride. You follow them and make sure they don't spotcha," Rainbow said while he watched the pair go into the emergency room entrance.

Sparkle jumped out of the car and followed them, slowing down at the entrance door to watch them get on the elevator. He certainly didn't want to lose them now, so he stepped up his pace so that he could see what floor they were going to. He stared at the blinking lights until they stopped at the fifth floor and jumped into the neighboring car and quickly pressed the button. The door opened and he edged his head slowly around the sill and saw them at the nurses' station. Percy's head started to turn his way and he jerked back. He pressed the close button but held the door until he heard their steps coming back his way. The tension started tingling down his neck and he leaned against the wall, as the pair walked by crisply. Counting to ten, he reopened the door and poked his head out, in time to see them go into the last room on the corridor.

Sparkle eased out of the elevator and walked as nonchalantly as he could down the hall. He got to the door and looked back down the hall to make sure that no one was paying him any attention. Then he leaned his head to the door and listened intently for several moments before he cracked the door to peek in. He heard three voices mingled together, but he couldn't quite make out what they were saying. Suddenly, he heard footsteps heading toward him and eased the door shut and headed back down the corridor. Luckily, he was a short distance away from the restroom. He ducked into it to prevent them from seeing him as he heard the door to the room opening. He stood beside one of the stalls until he heard their shoes click by. He tiptoed to the door and cracked it open.

They were getting back on the elevator. Sparkle left the restroom and high-stepped it back down the corridor. Ever so carefully he cracked the door, took a quick peek in and then back down the hall before he entered the room.

In the dim light he saw that there were at least three beds, each one separated by a partition. He started creeping on the balls of his feet to each one. When he reached the last one, he could see the silhouette of two people standing over a figure lying in the bed. He had eased to the edge of the partition to get a better look, when he heard one of them say something about going to the bathroom.

Oh shit, he thought in near panic mode and looked around for somewhere to hide. He quickly moved to the other side of the bed and hit the floor and rolled under the bed. He shivered a bout of tension away and stared at a pair of women's feet as they walked past.

"Damn!!" Sparkle muttered under his breath. When he heard the bathroom door shut, he made a break to get out of there. No sooner had he slid from under the bed, he heard the main door open again. With the quickness he rolled back under.

The unmistakable sound of a man's footsteps caused him to try to ball up in an even tighter ball. He sweated through the conversation between the guy and the woman until dude left. His footsteps were followed quickly by those of the woman. The other woman came out of the bathroom and the two women had a brief conversation before one of them left the room. All three voices sounded familiar to him, but in his geeked-up state of mind, he couldn't pinpoint who they were. Along with the loudness of the television, the machines whirling and the announcements over the intercom, he was only able to catch bits and pieces of what they talked about.

After the second set of feet left out of the door, Sparkle eased from under the bed and tiptoed back to the edge of the partition.

He held his breath as he tried to listen to whoever was left over there. Only the labored breathing of whoever was in the bed, so he chanced a quick peek around the partition. What he saw caused a frown to immediately edge across his face. He was sort of surprised to see Bertha sitting on the edge of the bed. But what really hit him was the figure of JJ lying in the bed bandaged from head to toe. His leg was propped up on a hanger, with a cast running halfway up his thigh. Damn, buddy was fucked up.

Sparkle stood there in shock, but only for a brief moment as he thought of Rainbow waiting downstairs, most likely desperately itching to follow Percy and his boy. He had to get back down there. Soft-stepping to the door, he eased it open and practically ran for the elevator. All three cars were in use, with the nearest one on the fourth floor. Without a moment's hesitation, he sprinted down the corridor, past the nurses' station, drawing looks of surprise, frowns and shouts from its occupants, and hit the emergency exit door in full stride.

He descended rapidly down the stairs, covering three steps at a time, his right hand sliding along the railing. As he got to the second-floor landing he saw, too late, a "wet floor" sign and tried to slow down, but his momentum carried him into the slippery floor. Before he even realized it, his feet shot from under him. He spiraled crazily, his back and head ramming into the wall, then caroming down the stairs, bouncing and rolling down and finally thumping hard into the first-floor wall. He ended up balled awkwardly in a fetal position.

"Ugghhnn!!" Sparkle moaned as the pain caused stars to circle his head. Dazed for sure, he pushed himself up off of the floor and staggered to the door. He couldn't hold back the tears that started running down his cheeks as he alternated rubbing his shoulder and left kneecap. He grunted his way through the door into an emergency room crowded with patients. To his surprise, hardly anyone paid him much attention as he walked stiff-legged out of the door.

With his eyes squinched up in pain, he took a quick double-take at an older lady that looked vaguely familiar, shook his head and started speed-stepping through the parking lot. He hunched his shoulders to his lack of memory because he couldn't place where he had seen her before. *Fuck it, it'll come back to me sooner or later*, he thought as he quickly turned his attention to the whereabouts of Rainbow. The car was nowhere in sight. "Damn, I must've taken too long up there or something."

He grimaced as he started limping toward Auburn Avenue. Halfway through the lot, the sound of screeching tires caused his heart to skip a beat. He whirled around toward the sound and instinctively dove between two cars, pulling his gun out of his waistband before he even hit the pavement. He quickly rolled into a squatting position ready to fire. The pain from his fall was completely forgotten.

"Damn, nigga, you tripping hard for a mug," Rainbow shouted through the passenger window. "Come on, dude, those fools turned left on DeKalb. Getcha ass up before they get too far away."

Sparkle stretched his neck over the hood of the nearest car, eyeing him angrily. "Whaddafuck you leave the spot for?"

"Fuck dat, move now, talk later!" Rainbow yelled back at him.

Sparkle groaned loudly as he staggered to his feet and limped to the car. He eased into the seat gingerly, but before he could close the door, Rainbow mashed the pedal to the floor and sped off down the lot. A completely shocked Sparkle was caught leaning halfway out of the door. He barely got the word "muthafucka" out before he slammed on the brake, causing the door to bump Sparkle across the seat crashing into his shoulder.

"Whaddafuck, nigga!" Sparkle screamed as his right leg kicked under the dashboard.

Rainbow elbowed him back to the passenger side and pressed the accelerator, swerving in a wide arc onto the street as he sped toward Auburn, cursing under his breath. He ran through three straight red lights in pursuit of Percy's car, which was still out of sight. He continued with the pedal to the floor until he finally was able to spot them as they passed the East Lake MARTA station. Only then did he slow down and began railing them at least two lights away. Neither of the occupants of the other car seemed to notice that they were being followed—at least they gave no indication from any movement of their silhouettes through the back window.

With his concentration locked on their prey, Rainbow didn't know that Sparkle had lit up a rock until the acrid fumes assaulted his nostrils.

"Hit and pass, nigga, hit and pass," he said out of the side of his mouth.

Sparkle exhaled slowly, closing his eyes so that he could put more concentration into the full effect of the exhilarating smoke. The euphoria enveloped his entire body as he sighed. "Aaaaaahhh, did I ever need that there." He tried to tune out the anxiousness in Rainbow's voice.

Rainbow knew all too well the tension-releasing feeling his boy was enjoying. Hell, he needed that feeling right then, so he leaned closer to him and hissed, "Hit and pass, bro. Damn, you make a nigga have to shout and shit."

Sparkle blinked rapidly with his eyes budging as he cocked his head sideways toward Rainbow, whose mouth seemed to be moving in slow motion and his words echoed throughout the car. It had to be the excitement of the chase or something because he didn't recall this dope ever having such a mind-blowing effect on him.

It suddenly dawned on him that he had never gotten the chance to test the coke he'd gotten from Duke when he got shot. He had to give his buddy credit; this stuff was a real head banger.

Rainbow, backhanding a stinging slap against his thigh, immediately brought him back to the here and now. He gingerly placed the glass shooter in his outstretched hand. "Aw, godayum, man, you put the hot end in my hand," he yelled as the shooter hit the dashboard and rolled under his seat. He shook his hand vigorously, grimacing and frowning at his boy, who had crouched against the door with his knee and forearm raised to cover himself from the hot glass missile in case it shot in his direction.

"Man, keep your eyes on the road, for God's sake," Sparkle yelled as he felt that he was going through some déjà vu like when he was with Joyce.

Rainbow rolled his eyes at him. "Man, could you please stop hanging on that damn door and get the thing from under the seat. I sho can't drive and get it, too."

Sparkle rolled his eyes at his boy and wheezed as he began to unfold his body so that he could bend down and put his head under the seat. It didn't take long at all for him to spot the shooter rolling back and forth on the carpet between Rainbow's legs. He cursed out loud and got on his knees between his legs and stretched his arm out for it.

Rainbow looked down at his upturned face and put his hand over his mouth to try to stifle the laugh boiling up from his stomach. It didn't work as he burst out with spittle flowing freely over Sparkle's eyes and face. He shot his hand to his mouth immediately. "Sorry, dude."

"Sorry, my ass," Sparkle yelped and pressed his face harder into the seat. Damn, he was directly in front of Rainbow's crotch. He began to jerk his head back when he felt the shooter on his fingertips. He stretched his fingers out, but it rolled out of his reach again. Feeling as shitty as he could possible feel with his boy's dick print pressing against his forehead, he wiggled his fingers out and finally got a hold of it.

"Damn, dude, you pushing my foot on the pedal," Rainbow grumbled at the same time that he saw a police car pull up beside them. A streak of panic ran along his spine as beads of sweat immediately started to form on his forehead.

With a heavy sigh, Sparkle braced his hand on the floor for leverage to raise himself up. But the pang in his neck from Rainbow shoving him down into his crotch to keep the police from seeing him made him feel momentarily paralyzed.

"What the fuck you doing, man?" he muffled near his crotch.

Rainbow pressed down harder. "Shh, be quiet, my nig, five-o is right beside us," he hissed out of the side of his mouth as he tried to maintain a picture of composure for the officer who was momentarily gritting on him. Even though he was greeting him with a nod of his head, he also had a stern look on his face. It seemed like an eternity before the light finally changed and the cruiser sped on ahead of them.

"Okay, man, dey gone. Damn, that there was close, soldier, too damn close." He wheezed while he wiped the sweat off his brow. Sparkle, using Rainbow's thighs for a brace, pushed himself up as roughly as he possibly could, frowning stiffly at his boy as he handed him the shooter. "Here, nigga, you damn near broke my neck, man. Oh yeah, and you can wash those musty-ass nuts of yours like yesterday, muthafucka." He spit out the window several times. Ugh, damn, that there was really rough on a nigga's nose, fer sho.

Rainbow eyed him up and down as he smirked. "What in the fuck you doing smelling them, nigga?"

"Aw, fuck you, man," Sparkle spat as he was wiping the thought off of his mind.

"Naw, on the real, dog, I'm sorry about that. But that five-o would've pulled us over for sure if you would've come up looking all geeked up and shit."

Knowing that he was right, Sparkle still waved him off and stared straight ahead trying to spot Percy's ride or the cops. Neither were in sight. Rainbow's cell phone started ringing. It was Miriam. He nodded a couple of times and hung up. Then he looked at Sparkle with a gleam in his eye. "We got this nigga finally, partner."

"For sho, man?" Sparkle muttered in response.

"Uh-huh, he's in room 25 at the Heart of Decatur Hotel waiting for her to get back from the Dairy Queen on the corner." He reached into his waistband and tossed Sparkle his piece. "Checkmate on that bitch, dog. His ass can't get away this time, the horny bastard. She managed to get a key to room twenty-four. We're going to stop at 'D' Queen to get it. When I get everything ready in twenty-four, I'll give the signal to knock on twenty-five three times. That'll keep him from concentrating on hearing me opening the suite door. Pht, pht, pht, and we roll."

Sparkle found it hard to keep the smile off of his face as they pulled into the Dairy Queen lot. Rainbow came out in record time, along with Miriam, who got into the car and reached the key out to him. He didn't even realize that he was holding his breath. The anticipation of finally getting rid of this nigga Don had him hyped up for sure.

"Here, baby girl, we about to do this fool, so don't be pulling out all scared and shit if you hear some gunfire." He got out of the car and handed Miriam the car keys. He turned from her and saw Rainbow going under the hotel's arch. He sighed away some of the tension and adjusted his baseball cap before he headed that way. He had made only a few steps when he suddenly jerked his head back toward the street and he saw Al's car zoom by. He turned right on Candler Road and bumped across the railroad track and down the hill out of sight.

What the hell is he doing way out this way? Sparkle thought, shaking his head in bewilderment. As he was about to turn the corner to pass under the arch, a familiar car passed by him, but he couldn't see who the driver was through the tinted windows. By the time it dawned on him to look back to check out the license plate, the car had spun around the corner and definitely too far away from him to be able to read it clearly.

Sparkle turned back around and passed under the arch in time to see Rainbow going toward room 24. He picked up his pace, hurried into the adjacent room, rushed to the adjoining door and knocked rapidly three times. He counted to ten and knocked again. Confused because he didn't hear a gunshot, he automatically figured that his boy must've run into some kind of obstruction. He pulled out his own pistol, pressed it against his thigh and opened the door, ready to fire. As the door creaked open he stood there stunned to see Rainbow standing over Don's inert form. His obviously dead body was lying on the floor under the TV set.

"Man, I ain't heard no kind of shot; you must have a silencer or something," he asked Rainbow.

"Naw, dog, this bitch was like that when I came in the door. Looks like somebody beat us to his ass."

"Damn, that's fucked up, yo," Sparkle replied in obvious disappointment.

"Why? His ass dead, ain't he? Saved us a bullet or two," Rainbow said as he headed to the door. "Come on, let's get out of this hole before some maid or maintenance dude gets to roaming."

Peeking out of the door, Rainbow sighed when there was no one in sight and he motioned with his head as he neared the fence. They jumped it and sprinted up the incline to the train tracks where Miriam was waiting with Rainbow's car on Decatur Street. "Gon' down Candler to I-20. Let's see if we can corner those niggas that followed 'B' so we can pump some information out of their asses. They should be close to the La Quinta by now, so push it, girl," he whispered the instructions to her. She pulled out immediately.

As they were pulling away, he looked down the incline and saw the same lady he had seen at the hospital's parking lot walking to the end of the hotel rooms 24 and 25. He couldn't quite make out the face, neither could he shake the feeling that he had seen her somewhere before. He was sure that wherever it was, there was some kind of danger involved.

CHAPTER FOURTEEN

Nitty-Gritty Time

ose was beyond being stunned when she opened the door to room 24 and saw her beloved nephew lying on the floor. She couldn't afford to be caught there with no dead body, regardless of who it was, so she eased out of the room and headed back to her car. Later, as she was driving down Main Street in East Point, she was to stunned to even think straight.

She was in such a daze that she couldn't recall walking over to his inert body to check his pulse, but she must have from all of the blood that was smeared on her blouse. She couldn't recall holding him to her bosom or the tears that flowed down her cheeks. But her eyes were still puffy. She looked into the mirror and pulled it down to see the blood all over her face. She looked further to see it all over her arms and hands.

She drove around aimlessly for what seemed like hours and hours, with no destination ever entering her thoughts. She had no idea where she was when she finally came out of her zombie-like state. She knew that she was hungry because of the rumbling in her stomach but she didn't have a appetite. *Now how in the hell was that possible?* she thought when she noticed a Waffle House and pulled into the parking lot. As she stepped out of the car, she saw that the dreary night was turning into a dreary day.

She mustered the strength to make an order, but all she ended up doing was sip on the coffee. She noticed that several customers were looking at her strangely, so she went into the bathroom to get away from their staring eyes. Looking into the big mirror, she saw that she was indeed covered with blood.

Her mind quickly snapped back to reality and she began washing the blood off of herself. She managed to get a lot of it rinsed off. From there her calculating mind kicked in. Her thoughts turned to Al and the shit he was talking at the hospital. A smile slowly crept to her lips; he was already a dead man. The only thing left was figuring out the best way to do it. But first things first. She had to get to the store, her safe haven whenever things got tough. To the few people that knew of her and Don's relationship, she would act the grieving aunt, so that when she took Al out, no one would suspect an act of revenge. But there would be revenge; there was no doubt about it.

She left the Waffle House trying to recognize where she was. After driving through several lights, she saw the Farmers Market warehouse. She was in Forest Park, only a half-hour or so from the store and her house. When she got on Jonesboro Road, she noticed an open pasture and pulled onto the shoulder. She saw what she was looking for almost immediately. Picking it up she went back to the car and steered back onto the highway. After traveling for about a half-mile, she put the daisy on the steering wheel and started plucking petals.

"He suffers, he suffer not, he suffers, he suffers not," she repeated to herself until all the petals were gone. She nodded her head, smiling, knowing now how she was going to do it.

✠ ✠ ✠

Lt. Woo walked around the pool at the Motel 6, with the same superior strut she always did when she was on one of her many drug raids. The grim intimidating sneer on her face was genuine as she turned her mouth down at the fools who had gotten caught up in the net. On the other hand, she was extremely proud as she shook the hands and patted the backs of her well-trained drug squad members. A wave of euphoria coursed through her body as she secretly thanked her many informants for supplying her with the correct data to orchestrate the successful raid. As she always did, she gave the users and pushers time to get rid of whatever illegal substances they may have had on their persons. Smiling mischievously at the wet and shivering mob, she wondered how many of them would be silly enough to try to hold on to some. There were always a few who figured they could get away. It was rare that one did, though.

These scare tactics had proven to be a good deterrent in slowing down the drug traffic on I-20 in the past. The ordeal had a way of chasing some of the people, especially the users, to the various rehab centers in the Metro area; as well as causing the pushers to ply their trade elsewhere.

Since the jails were already too overcrowded, it wasn't feasible to take all the violators in, so the scare tactics usually worked out pretty well as an alternative. Still there was always a handful of diehards, who tried to hold on to their product. Hell, if they were that stupid or desperate, they deserved to be locked up.

After watching those few fools get shoved into the police van, she left instructions with her top subordinates and left the scene, leaving them to wrap things up. As she pulled onto the entrance ramp to I-20, she picked up her cell phone and placed a call to one of her favorite snitches to make plans for a rendezvous.

As she neared Candler Road, she got a sudden urge for something sweet and decided to get a box of donuts from the Dunkin Donuts across the street from the South DeKalb Mall. As she pulled into the parking lot, she was surprised to see the police chief seating at the counter. *Might as well give her my briefing now*, she decided as she got out of her car and entered the shop. With a bright smile, she took a seat on the stool beside her.

The chief greeted her with a questionable one of her own and invited her to join her at one of the booths to enjoy a cup of coffee and snack as they chatted. Before they could even get the conversation started, some boisterous customers entered the shop. As they looked at the group, irritated at their disrespectful entrance, they heard a resounding boom in the background.

"Sounds like somebody's car must be backfiring out there or something," Beverly said as she sipped from her steaming cup of brew.

"Probably so, ah, what I wanted to…" Woo started to say when the sound repeated, this time longer than the first, much too loud and long to be a car backfiring.

Their reactions were simultaneous, when they realized that it was a rapid succession of gunfire. As one, they exploded from their seats, knocking coffee cups and donuts off of the table, as they sprinted for the door with their guns drawn. With determined looks on their faces, the rambunctious group scrambled wildly in all directions at the sight of the firearms.

As Beverly followed the smaller, quicker Woo in a full run in the direction of the gunfire, all of her gut instincts told her that her boys were involved.

✠ ✠ ✠

Several minutes earlier, Rainbow and Sparkle had entered the room that 'B' had gotten for them at the La Quinta. They had just dropped Miriam off in room 316 where the girls shared a suite connected to 317. Checking the parking lot when they got there, they saw no sign of the car that had followed them. Naturally, they wondered about that and what 'B' could have done to get rid of them. Fuck it, they'd deal with it later.

They went to the hotel lobby to pick up some chocolate-covered donuts and coffee at the snack bar in before they went to the room. One of 'B''s scantily clad hoes greeted them at the door and waved to the beds. Then she and another half-naked pixie giggled and scampered to the bathroom.

Lying on the bed, looking all tired and satisfied after an obvious round of ménage à trois with the two vixens, was 'B' who was smiling like a Cheshire cat. Not even trying to hide his disgust, Rainbow flopped on the bed on 'B''s legs. He let out a painful grunt as he sat up awkwardly and pushed him off of his legs.

Leaning to the side, still pinning his feet, Rainbow smiled. "Godayum, dog, here me and Sparkle are going through some life-and-death shit and here you are doing...doing, whatever the fuck you were doing."

Sparkle thought that he'd egg him on a little more and sat on the bed, too, bumping his ass against his shoulder as he did so.

"Yeah, fool, what happened to those guys that were following you and the girls?" 'B' grunted loudly, shot an elbow to Sparkle's back side and tried to kick Rainbow through the covers. "Man, get the fuck off my feet. That shit hurts. You know how bad my dogs are."

Rainbow laughed and scooted away from his kicking feet. "Aw, man, shut the hell up and getcha sorry ass up." Then his expression turned quite solemn. He started rubbing the sides of his face. "By the way, that nigga Don's dead."

'B''s brow balled up in astonishment. "Whatcha mean he dead, like *dead* dead?"

"Hell yeah, like *dead* dead, like graveyard dead," Rainbow said as he looked at him like he was brain-dead.

'B' wiggled his way from under the cover and scooted to the

edge of the bed. "Damn, that's fucked up. I mean it's not fucked up like fucked up because that punk had to go, for sho, but fucked up that y'all got to worry about if y'all got away with it or not."

Sparkle shook his head first. "Naw, partner, we didn't kill him. The nigga was dead when we got there."

Rainbow stood up. "Yeah, man, evidently someone else wanted his ass as bad as we did. Uh-huh, and I saw that nigga Al's car rolling out of there before I made my move to go inside. And that ain't all."

"Damn, there's more?"

"Yep, there's more. Another car that I know I've seen around the way several times rode out like they were following him."

"Hmmph."

"And there's more."

"Well, godayum, man, how much more can there be? Shit."

"And this old lady I keep seeing was heading for the room as we were scooting out of there."

"Damn."

"Yeah, damn."

Rainbow yanked the cover up and threw it over his head. "So what about those fools who were following you?"

"Huh!!" 'B' replied as he stared blankly at the wall.

"Huh, come on, man, you heard me."

'B' started rubbing his eyes with his gnawed-up knuckles. "Oh yeah, uh, when we pulled into DeKalb County Jail's parking lot, those fools just kept on driving by. I guess they didn't want to be seen nowhere near the big house."

Rainbow and Sparkle smiled at each other before Rainbow started scratching the top of his head and sighed. "Anyway, we still got business to take care of and you laying around getting your nasty, little-ass dick sucked and soaked."

'B' turned his mouth down as his eyes shifted around under half-closed lids like he was ready to do some rapid-fire comeback. As usual, he didn't disappoint, being that he still thought he had mack-of-the-year qualities, even though he was old as sin.

He pulled his dick out, still dripping after-cum and shook it. "Red-ass, wannabe, gangsta-ass nigga, ain't a damn thang small or nasty about this magic stick here. Ask those bitches over yonder if this mutha here can still work miracles in their mouths, pussies or wherever else I slang this bitch here."

Both of them jumped back cursing as the slime spewed back and forth. Sparkle picked up a towel laying on the back of the chair and tossed it over his head. "Come on, crazy-ass, has-been pimp, wipe ya ass and get dressed. We ain't got all night to be bullshitting around."

'B"s attention was suddenly drawn to the giggling sound coming out of a crack in the bathroom door. The change in his expression from angry buddy to gorilla pimp was scary as hell, even to his lifetime partners. He snatched the towel off of his head and growled, "Y'all bitches had better get y'all cum-bucket asses out here and get me some damn clothes."

Before the last word was even out of his mouth, both girls sprinted into the room giggling and acting all girlie as they started scrambling through the assorted outfits on hangers beside the basin. Now that they were busy doing their duty, his features softened and he turned his attention back to his boys. "Okay, so how we gonna handle this thing now?"

Rainbow, who was admiring himself in the dresser's mirror, patted his hair and ran a finger over his tongue. "I figured we'd roll by the hotels and pick up the dope the girls left hidden. And then hit the club to check on Mack and Junior to give them a rundown so that they can get themselves together because the five-o's gonna definitely harass them investigating Don's demise."

"Sounds like a plan to me," Sparkle added as he watched 'B' as he steadily growled at the girls while he got dressed.

Damn, 'B' has got to be one of the evilest men in the whole world. Nigga keeps a permanent grit on his face, especially in front of these whores. Sparkle shook his head at the constant verbal assault. He looked over at Rainbow, who was still stuck on admiring himself in the mirror. He couldn't hold back on the sarcasm. "Nigga, how many times have you seen that bitch looking back atcha? Come on, dog, get outta the glass before the damn thing cracks."

Rainbow tilted his head back slightly. "I'd rather look at me than any of y'all ugly muthafuckas." They continued to throw mental barbs at each other until 'B' was fitted, armed and ready to roll. They stopped at the other room for a brief moment to give the girls a rundown before they piled into 'B''s New Yorker and hit I-20.

Minutes later, after leaving the Holiday Inn and Motel 6 on Wesley Chapel, they were rolling toward the Red Roof Inn. For a reason that he couldn't understand, Sparkle started getting a tingling sensation at the nape of his neck. He quickly chalked it up to the usual déjà vu he experienced every time he passed this way, recalling that first day out of the joint when he had watched that drug raid. There was something about that place that never set right with him. He tapped 'B' on the shoulder as they turned off of Candler into the driveway that led to the inn. "Yo, dog, let me out here at the Citgo. I'm gonna pick us up some cigarettes and a couple of bottles of Ole E. Y'all ain't got to wait on me. I'll walk on up to the room."

As Sparkle was standing at the counter to pay for his items, he could've sworn that he saw Lt. Woo going into the donut spot across the lot. He shrugged at the likelihood of it being her because all Asian chicks seemed to look alike to him. Perhaps he was being jittery because of all the recent events and circumstances that had them all hyped up.

He paid at the register, then exited the store from the door opposite of the donut shop. It was likely because subconsciously visions of Woo were playing in his head. He walked down the dark, tree-lined walkway behind the United Bank and leaped over the short concrete wall that encircled the bank.

Beyond the wall, there was a sharp inclined embankment that made it difficult to keep his footing. He kept his head down to try to avoid the many broken branches that cluttered the small terrain. As Sparkle made his way, he slipped a couple of times as he fought to maintain his balance. He paused to examine his hands for cuts and bruises and looked over the wall when he heard and then saw 'B' and Rainbow as they were getting out of the car.

He opened his mouth to shout out to them but froze when he saw three ominous figures getting out of an SUV. He squinted his eyes to get a clearer look, as a tingling sensation of pending danger began to pound along the back of his neck.

The flickering shadows caused by the dimly lit moon rays, fighting through the wind-blown leaves of the surrounding foliage of trees, made the scene appear surreal. Their movements were herky-jerky, like they were moving in slow motion.

At first glance it seemed like one of them was holding a cane or thick fishing rod, but his heart told him better; his instincts sharpening. So he followed his instincts, that had saved him so many times in the past, and bent down to car hood level after he crawled over the wall. He started creeping along the cars. In case his eyes and mind weren't playing tricks on him, he laid the bag beside one of the cars and pulled out his gun. When he carefully chambered a round, the sound seemed to be so loud that it caused him to cringe, but it was only in his own mind. It didn't appear that 'B' or Rainbow was aware of any of it by the way they headed toward the hotel without even turning around. The trio of stalkers split up and started creeping between different cars silently. His adrenaline rush went into overdrive when the stalkers picked up speed and then one of them called out to his boys.

When they had first picked up speed, Sparkle raised his gun over the hood of the car and had actually started to squeeze the trigger, when they slowed down. Because they had yet to raise their own weapons, he waited anxiously as 'B' and Rainbow turned around to the sound of the voices calling out to them.

Even in the dim lighting, he could read the shocked look on their faces as they spun to face the menacing sound. Sparkle blinked a couple of times in shock himself when he recognized the voice of the guy who had called out to them. The familiarity of the voice was probably the only thing that kept his boys from open-ing up fire themselves. 'B' choked out in a hoarse voice, "Joker, what the fuck you doing, man?"

He was followed immediately by Rainbow's sneering grit. "Baby boy, I know damn well that you ain't behind this shit."

Stackadime and Chopper joined Joker's side with their guns hanging loosely but anxiously at their hips. Stack bit down on his lower lip and smiled before he spat, "Looka here, soldier, y'all know what the deal is." He cocked the sawed-off, double-barrel shotgun to emphasize his deadly intent. "Y'all ripped off my main man and the only deal is that you give up your spots to reimburse the Black Don or you die, right here, right now. It's as simple as that, dog."

Rainbow, showing no signs of fear, ignored Stack totally and directed his full attention toward Joker. "Baby boy, we've been looking out for your ass since snot was bubbling out of your nose. You've got to be bullshitting me on this one here, for sure."

No sooner had the last syllable rolled off of his tongue than Stack fired a shot, re-cocked and fired another shot at their feet, digging up globs of pavement. The resounding boom was so loud and sudden that it even stunned Sparkle and shockwaves ran down his spine.

But he knew his boy Rainbow, and true to form, he didn't even flinch; instead, he pushed 'B' to the side, drew his piece and started blazing lead at the trio. His first shot caught a startled Chopper in the shoulder, actually through the shoulder, as blood and cloth splashed from his back. The force of the impact caused him to ram, with a loud thud, into the nearest car. The second shot hit him in the stomach and he clutched his midsection as he bounced off of the car, grunting to the pavement.

In the same moment Rainbow had opened fire on them, Sparkle drilled a couple of rounds into Stack's back and legs, lifting him off of the ground. He flopped down into an awkward position like a pretzel.

Joker seemed to get hit from both angles almost simultaneously as he spun one way and then the other like a top. Miraculously, he didn't go down at first, as he staggered around with a shocked look on his face at being caught in a deadly crossfire.

When he looked down at his wounds and then back up under-eyed at Sparkle, his face had suddenly changed to the whimpering little kid that they had pampered as a snotty-nosed runt. Sparkle froze and lowered his piece. The battle appeared to be over before it had even started. He took a step closer to help the little Joker he remembered. Before he realized it, he had tripped and fallen on an unseen object on the pavement. Grimacing as he rubbed his knee after the gritty contact, Sparkle looked up to see Joker's deadly firearm aiming at his head. He was no longer the little Joker that his mind had momentarily deceived him with. Instead, there were the cold eyes of a killer—his killer. He blinked his eyes and prepared to welcome death. Everything seemed to be moving in slow motion, from the blinking in Joker's eyes, to the snarl that had formed on his lips, to his finger slowly pressing on the trigger. There was a loud boom and he closed his eyes and mind to the inevitable. But for some reason he didn't feel any pain. Was this the way that heaven or hell welcomed him? Then Sparkle blinked a couple of times before his eyes set on the horrifying sight of Joker still standing there, but with a hole in his forehead, before he tumbled to the ground.

When Sparkle got up off of the pavement and crawled over to kneel over the fallen Joker, he saw both of his buddies scampering for the staircase to avoid the still pouring of hot lead that was ricocheting off of metal and concrete. Somehow Chopper had regained his composure and was alternating shots at him and his boys.

As he dove for cover, he saw out of the corner of his eyes, two figures running toward the fray, guns blazing. His first thoughts were that their hunters had back-up. But then he remembered the Asian girl going in the donut shop and thinking that she made him think of Lt. Woo. But now he recognized her as indeed being the evil little bitch.

Sparkle's heart skipped another beat when he recognized Beverly as the other threat that was rapidly approaching. His thought immediately shot to the conversation they had discussed in the hotel room. But this time it was a lot more than a conversation between lovers. This time it was a reality, she was a cop and he was a bandit caught red-handed in the act. He had to get those thoughts out of his mind with the quickness because both women were coming at them with guns blazing and shouting in no-nonsense explicit terms.

In his mind and heart he knew that he couldn't fire at Beverly. They went too far back for that. Yet on the other hand, he knew that he wasn't about to go to nobodies jail, either. So he did the next best thing. He screamed, "Five-o, five-o." He got to his feet and crouched behind the car nearest to the building. Then he looked over to his boys and tried to whisper, "Yo, man, it's Beverly and that crazy-ass Woo. We got to get out of here."

He knew that they had heard him because their eyes budged out, obviously feeling the same dilemma that he had when he recognized her. He heard them curse as they both stared through the gaps in the stairs and saw what he saw.

Quick to respond, Rainbow shouted, "Yo, dog, 1012, 1012!!!!" It was their personal signal to fire warning shots in the air before hightailing it. Immediately all three of them laid a round of fire over the heads of the fast-closing policewomen. When they dodged for cover behind the parked cars, Rainbow and 'B' turned with the swiftness and sprinted around the corner of the hotel. Sparkle knew that they would hit the wooded embankment and scale their way to I-20 toward the woods behind the nightclub, on their way to his sister Debra's house in Candler East Apartments.

After firing another round in their general direction, Sparkle set off running in a low crouch through the other cars. Destination: the other end of the hotel. When he started his escape, he made eye contact with Stack, who was leaning against one of the cars holding his leg and arching his back. There was a mixture of fear and panic written all over his face. He also noticed that Stack's gun was way out of his reach, so he paused just enough to smile at him. "That's the way it goes, youngun." He chanced one more look over the cars for the women's pursuit. "You chose the wrong side, kid, but don't worry. I'll read or hear about that nigga of yours Don from the DeKalb County Jail, see ya."

The only thing that Stack could do was grimace in his discomfort and stretch his fingers unsuccessfully for his piece. To make matters worse, Sparkle kicked the gun up under the car, winked at him and continued with his crouched exit away from the scene. He knew that he couldn't reach the gun in time to do him any harm. But in the back of his mind, he was sorta hoping that the fool did get to it and have a shootout with Bevy and Woo and get his stupid ass killed. That way he wouldn't have to worry about him possibly snitching on them.

"Aw fuck," he screamed when he got to the next to last car before the corner of the building and more shots came in his direction. *Damn, I should have put that fool down, shit*, he thought as he dove to the pavement and rolled to the far side of the car. Sparkle looked over the edge of the hood and saw Chopper leaning against a car firing at him. He opened up on him. His aim proved to be good but he could tell by the way that his body jerked, that it wasn't his bullets that impacted his now lifeless form first.

A bullet was fast but there was no way that it was that fast as his body was lifted backward into the air before it fell to the pavement. It could only mean that one of the policewomen had blazed him first. With that brand-new terror entering his mind, he broke into a full sprint to the corner. He barely made it as the boom came a mere fraction of a second before a sprinkling of concrete from the side of the building dusted the side of his neck. Man, did that ever put some more pep in his stride and he sprinted to the edge of the embankment. He looked to his left and saw Rainbow and 'B' struggling to get to the top about a half a football field away.

He jumped over the ditch, slipped on the muddy edge and dove into the bushes. Boy, did those guerilla tactics from military training ever come in handy, as he belly-crawled and maneuvered his way up the steep incline. After nearly a minute, that seemed more like minutes, of getting slapped and snagged all over his body by the twigs, bushes and whatever else was assaulting his face, arms and legs, he finally made it up the slippery embankment to I-20. With sweat, blood and mud seemingly everywhere, he struggled to the railing and had lifted his aching leg to straddle it when his heart took another tumble. His weary eyes didn't want to believe it, but there they were. Flashing lights of the police, rapidly approaching from both directions on I-20 and Candler Road, had him diving back into the bushes. He laid low until all of the cars had turned toward the direction of the hotel.

Feeling a lot more comfortable, he struggled back out of the bushes and hobbled across the interstate. It didn't surprise him that he ran into an identical batch of foliage behind the club. He dreaded going through the same type of deep woods again, only this time it was going downhill. But he didn't have a choice. So he sighed heavily and started the downward trek.

Since he could see the huge club sign high above the tree line, he knew that he had to veer wide to the right to avoid the long parking lot, that was most likely full with eyewitnesses. With the excitement of the chase bumping hard in his chest, he stopped several times on the way down to gather his bearings and equilibrium. He constantly was tortured by snagging vines, thorns and branches, occasionally getting tripped and one time sliding head-first into some bushes but he finally made it to the East Lake apartments. He was now in familiar territory, but that certainly didn't mean that he could get wide open. So he kept low as he crept along the rolls of razor wire fence. He reached a gap in the fence that had been previous clipped with what looked like wire cutters.

He quickly scaled to the top. When he reached for the top rail, his hand slipped away and along with it was a piece of rag that, on closer inspection, he saw was a piece of 'B''s shirt. He smiled at the thought of the old geezer getting snagged and struggling to pull away, cursing like a sailor.

He muscled himself over the top and was about to descend down the other side when he saw a line full of clothes between adjacent buildings. A light bulb flashed through his tired brain and he crept over and grabbed a windbreaker and a pair of jeans close to his size. He scampered to the other end of the building and pulled the jeans on top of the ones he was wearing and slipped into the jacket.

Sparkle walked along, removing pieces of briars and twigs out of his hair that had joined him along the way through the woods. He slowed down to check himself out in the reflection of one of the cars parked under a street lamp. Satisfied with his altered appearance and knowing that he was out of the vicinity of the hotel, his stride took on a more calm gait. It wasn't long before he was able to see the winding road that led to his sister Debra's apartment.

As his adrenaline rush from all of the excitement finally started to slow down, he considered dropping by Dee's crib for a half-hour or so for some of her good sex and relaxation. As he got closer to the apartment complex, the more he thought about it and the better he started to feel. Even the hazy night started to look more serene. Hell yeah, that's exactly what he was going to do. He picked up his pace thinking of her nice, warm, freaky body waiting there for his enjoyment.

When Sparkle got to the spot that he had chosen to cut over toward her crib, a DeKalb County police cruiser turned down the drive. His adrenaline shot right back up in a rush of panic that tingled along his body. His first instinct was to make a break for it, but he was too tired and too far away from the apartment.

So he sucked up his last bit of courage and maintained his casual pace.

He was nervous for a bitch with sweat starting to roll down his chest as the bright beam of the cops' spotlight hit him square in the face. He threw up his arm as a shield from the glare and said in a calm voice, "How you doing, officers?"

When no reply came from the car, he knew that their gazes were locked in on him as they waited to see if he would show any signs of panic. When he didn't, he could hear one of them sigh heavily before he said, "You see anybody running through here in the last minute or so?"

From his many past encounters with the blue crew, he knew that it was best to appear a little surprised and dumb. So he put on the proper expression and said straightforward, "No, sir, I didn't see anybody." He looked back down the street and played the naive citizen. It must have worked because they took the spotlight off of him and proceeded down the street. He breathed a heavy sigh of relief and then caught a glimpse of two figures leaning around the corner of the building next to Debra's apartment.

He slowly turned his head to check on the silhouettes in the cop car. Neither appeared to be facing in his direction, so he headed for her crib. As he stepped onto the walkway, he heard Rainbow's voice squeak out of the shadows. "What them cops say, man?"

Sparkle didn't even pause, as he placed a foot on the steps. "They looking for our asses, but I must've thrown them off pretty damn good because I ain't in the back of that rolling cage."

'B' stepped from around the corner and joined him at the steps, mumbling painfully. "Godayum Joker, ain't that a bitch? Who-dafuck woulda thought dat nigga would cross me, hell, us?"

Sparkle tried to blink the weariness out of his eyes and looked over his shoulder at 'B.' "Evidently youngun got sucked in by

Don some kinda way." He leaned against the wall as he pressed the doorbell.

Rainbow involuntarily jumped at the sound of the seemingly loud chime. He was still breathing hard from exertion as he said between gasps, "Man, fuck that nigga, Joker. Those fools couldn't have known that Don was dead or they wouldn't have done what they did. But anyway you look at it, we looked out for his little ass long before he even knew about some damn Don. And he ended up choosing that nigga against us, so like I said, fuck Joker. May his tricking ass rest in fucking peace."

Sparkle was about to respond when the door cracked open enough for Debra to stick her roller-filled head out to blast them. "Whaddafuck y'all niggas want? We all are in the bed around..."

Debra's mouth stuck in a wide "O" when she heard 'B' mutter, "Sshiiiiit," as he and Rainbow dove immediately to the pavement as the spotlight of the police cruiser hit the wall. She gasped in astonishment as they tried to press their bodies into the cement.

Debra threw her hands up to block the glare of the bright light out of her eyes. Sparkle gently pushed her back inside and closed the door. He leaned his back against the door and crossed his fingers across his heart like he was warding off a vampire before he mugged up. "Aw, girl, go do something about that crust in ya eyes. Uggggh, and please don't forget that slimy stuff running down to your chin while you at it."

She backed up a couple of steps, rubbing the back of her wrist along the side of her mouth, cinching the sash of her robe as she gritted hard at her brother. "Nigga, please, ain't nobody ask y'all crooks to ring my doorbell." She turned away and headed for the bathroom. She had only taken a few steps when she stopped, flexed her shoulders and cocked her head to the side. She looked back as 'B' and Rainbow came belly-crawling across the door sill.

Her eyebrows seemed to spit fire as she sneered. "Is that sirens? Oh hell yeah, those sirens, whaddafuck? Oooooh my God, y'all stupid fools done got in some shit, and bring y'all dirty asses right to my doorstep, I swear." She looked them up and down with pure disdain. "Mmm-hmm, briars and shit sticking all over y'all getting into some dumb-ass shit."

They looked down at themselves and started picking stuff off.

"Ooooooh, and y'all gonna just drop it all over my rug and shit." She didn't give them a chance to reply as she looked at them undereyed and pointed to the patio.

Again, as a group, they put their hands to their ears and then spread their arms out wide, with their faces balled up. She tilted her head back, rubbed her eyelids as her jaw swelled up like a balloon before she blew out a long stream of frustration and moaned, "Okay, okay, in the bathroom then with y'all no-good asses, shiiiiit."

As they lowered their heads walking past her, Debra sighed heavily, shook her head and walked to the back room at the end of the hall and mumbled, "And clean up behind yourselves, too." She slammed her bedroom door with authority.

Trailing his boys, Rainbow looked at Sparkle with a confused look on his face. "How did you... Where you get those clothes from? Ah, fuck it." He grimaced and pushed 'B' out of the way. Debra came out of the back moments later and gave them a look that could've frozen hell over. "Now what the fuck is up, man?"

Rainbow stepped out of the bathroom first, wiping his dampened head with a towel. "Aw, come on, Booboo, we done been through enough as it is."

She whirled on him like a scene from *The Exorcist*, eyes blazing as she harrumphed loudly and gave them a reply of indistinguishable nasty words before she wrapped her arms around herself and stormed back into the bathroom.

"Whew!!" Sparkle said to them before he shouted down the hall, "We need a ride downtown!"

She shouted back through the closed door. "Fuck y'all!"

All he could do was smile at her sassy attitude. But he knew her, and regardless of whatever, his baby sis would be cursing them out while she was putting her clothes on, if for no other reason but to get them out of her hair. And it would last all the way downtown.

While they waited for her to get ready, 'B' and Sparkle grabbed the miniature backgammon set off of the vanity chest and got involved in a heated match. Rainbow, with his superhyped-up ass, spent the time pacing the floor, looking back and forth between the bedroom and peeking through the patio curtains, checking out for the police car that was still cruising along the main thoroughfare of the complex.

All of a sudden, 'B' jumped up and walked over to the couch. He stood there for a moment staring at the wall before he punched the top of the couch and snarled, "Damn, I just thought about it. Man, I left two ounces under the fucking seat in my roller."

Sparkle made a pyramid with his arms and rested his chin on the back of his hands. "Baby boy, I was watching when those two policewomen came running up on the..."

'B' didn't give him the chance to finish. "Is that supposed to make me feel better, because they were women?" He stopped to take a deep breath. "Shit, a cop is a fucking cop regardless, man."

Sparkle shifted around in his seat to face him. "Dude, chill ya ass down for a second, will ya? Damn, one of the women was Beverly, fool."

"Yeah, uh-huh, and I heard ya when I was under the stairs," he retorted harshly.

Before Sparkle could reply, Debra came storming out of the

bedroom struggling to put her arm in the sleeve of her jacket. Her cheeks were puffed out to the max. Whenever she got like that, Sparkle knew better than to say anything to her. But 'B' was too caught up in his own thoughts to notice her attitude.

Big mistake, Sparkle smiled as Debra in her still boiling rage, stopped right in front of him, with her hands placed firmly on her hips. When he didn't even look down at her, she really went off on him. Kicking him on his foot, she spat, "Black-ass nigga, you got a nerve to be showing up here waking me up with an attitude. After all, y'all fools done come all up in my crib, this time of night, and with the five-o on y'all tail."

To her surprise he bowed his head down with the saddest look she had ever seen on him. His expression must've really defused her anger, at least a little bit anyway, as the tension eased out of her face. With her face balled up with concern, she asked. "Damn, man, it be that rough, huh?"

When he didn't respond, she turned her attention to Sparkle. "Whaddafuck done happened, man?"

Sparkle looked away from the seriousness in her eyes and started picking at his nose before he answered that his little cousin Joker had just been killed.

"What?"

"What?"

"What?" all three of them asked at once. Sparkle looked shocked for a second, then turned back to them. "Whatcha mean, what? I thought one of y'all had shot him in the head. Ah, man, that means that it must've been either Woo or Bevy, damn."

Things had happened so fast that he wasn't really sure what had happened. That really took the air out of 'B' and he flopped down onto the couch and lowered his head into his hands. "Damn!!" It was all he could get out.

Debra put her hand on Sparkle's shoulder, trying to console him. "Aw, man, I'm sorry about that, dude." She turned to Rainbow. "Oooh, Woo and Beverly, y'all playing with some real heavyweights now. Are y'all sure that she didn't see any of y'all, 'cause if she did, I know that she's gonna be paying all of y'all stupid muthafuckas a visit and real soon, too."

She went into the kitchen and retrieved her pocketbook off the top of the refrigerator. "Hey, y'all, I sorta hate to be putting the rush on y'all and shit. Let me stop lying. I want y'all hot asses out of here like yesterday. So where are y'all going 'cause I ain't got all night to be messing around with y'all asses, for sho. And it better not be too far away. I can't be leaving these kids in the house all by themselves for too long, either."

She looked back down the hall one last time and then went to the door and opened it. "And y'all can close that damn door, too, Miss Ebony, with your nosey self." They all heard the door shut followed by a pattering of little feet before they headed out of the door.

On their way to the parking lot, Sparkle said to Debra, "Sis, we got to get to the club, but first we got to go to the La Quinta to get Rainbow's ride."

She rolled her eyes at him over the hood of the car and snorted. "To the La Quinta then, because I ain't about to go to nobody's club." About a half-hour later, they were waving at Debra as she shot them a finger on her way out of the hotel's parking lot. They jumped in Rainbow's ride without even going up to the girls' rooms. Soon afterward, as they were passing the Red Roof Inn, they saw several police cars and ambulances flashing lights. They didn't see a coroner's van but they knew that one had to be there.

As they were discussing what to do, 'B' shouted the loudest. "Man, we need to get back to that car to get that coke, for real yo."

Rainbow replied in a aggravated tone, "Dude, will you please stop bugging about that stuff in your car? For one, there ain't no way we can afford to go down there, period. Police all over that bitch, nigga. Come on, use your fucking head for once. And secondly, I don't think that Bevy will even let them know that's your ride anyways."

'B' huffed but he knew deep down in his heart that Rainbow was probably right. Still he had to have his say. "Man, I see whatcha saying and all, but there ain't no telling what those fools are gonna be crying when those handcuffs get tightened up on their asses."

CHAPTER FIFTEEN

Chasing the Hunters

Rainbow forked down his last piece of French toast at the Waffle House before he decided to put an end to the argument. Sparkle and 'B' had been going at it nonstop for the past half-hour and he was fed up. "Looka here, fellas, I've been listening to y'all for quite a while now and not once have y'all mentioned this nigga Al." He growled as he sipped his coffee.

Sparkle was quick to reply. "Come to think of it, he might have done that nigga Don. What other reason would he be at the Heart of Decatur, know what I'm saying?"

'B' threw in his little bit. "I agree with ya, dog, one-hundred percent. I ain't said nothing to y'all before because I didn't want y'all to go tripping on me and shit. But the bitch straight up told me about his dealings with Joker. Hell, I didn't want to accept that shit but it's evident that things were a lot worse than I thought."

"What, nigga, you telling me that you already knew about this shit? Damn, dog, that's fucked up there. You should've been hipped us to that, playa. But fuck it, I say that we pay that fool a visit while we out this way. Man, he's gotta know something," Rainbow spat full of anger, then stood up and headed for the door. Before he could place his hand on the knob, his phone started buzzing on his hip. He lifted the tail of his shirt and sighed. "Ah, shit, fellas, there she blows." He grimaced as he looked over his shoulder at them before he picked it up. He listened for nearly a minute before he finally answered. "Damn, Bevy, you're really all up in a nigga business, ain'tcha?" There was a long pause. "Yeah, uh-huh, I realize that..." Another long pause. "Naw, they ain't with me. I just told you they ain't with me. Looka here, sweetheart, let me go check on a few thangs and I'll get back atcha." He clicked off without waiting for a response.

Fully aware of the gravity of their conversation, Sparkle felt the need to chill on whatever, so he fixed up a hit, took a long toke and passed it to Rainbow, who followed suit and passed it to "B." After a few rounds, he caught Rainbow's eyes. "What's the top cop talking about, dog?"

"Yeah, dude, did she say anything concerning us and that situation or my ride?" 'B' added anxiously.

Rainbow stared at both of them real hard before he let out a heavy sigh. "Yeah, man, she knows that it was your car and that it was us out there. But don't go getting all excited and worked up because she also assured me that nobody else did and your car is still in the same spot." He took a moment to wipe the back of his hand across his mouth. "Now, here's the fucked-up news. She figured that it had to have something to do with us going after Don, so she sent a crew of cops over to the lounge to bust his ass, for any muthafucking thing. And last but not least, we definitely don't have to worry about any of them younguns screaming on us in handcuffs; they all dead."

Suddenly, Rainbow pulled onto the shoulder of the road, got out of the car and started pacing rapidly back and forth.

Damn, bro sho nuff acting funny for a bitch. Godayum, what's with all this here pacing? Sparkle thought as he got out of the car and sat on the hood. Neither he nor 'B' said anything and traded the shooter while they waited for him to walk the steam off. After a few minutes, Rainbow's phone sounded off on his hip. He lifted his shirt tail to see Violet's number flashing up at him, so he snatched it up and threw it at Sparkle. He continued pacing, mumbling under his breath.

Sparkle scooped it out of the air and sighed. "Yeah, what's up, baby? Naw, we didn't have time to re-up. Shit's been happening. Damn, I thought y'all had plenty of stuff. Okay, hold on a minute; let me ask him." He lowered the phone to his hip. "Yo, Bow, you wanna stop by the crib so I can pick up the girls some more stuff? They out there tripping, yo."

Rainbow paused for a second and looked at him like he was crazy. "Man, y'all can do whatever y'all wanna do but I'm going to make that fool Al tell me what the fuck's going on; hell something, hell anything." He snarled and got back in the car.

Sparkle also jumped back in, followed quickly by "B." He continued his conversation with Violet. "Looks like it's gonna be a while, sweetie. What's Mercedes doing? Is she winning? Damn, figures. Check this out, we about to hit Al's poker game while we waiting to hear from these folks. Y'all get one of y'all customers to run you to the crib. Okay, let everybody know that we aight."

A short time later, they pulled into Al's driveway. Rainbow jumped out of the car before it even had a good chance to stop and practically ran to ring the doorbell. Several frustrating attempts later, he stormed over to the garage door. He immediatcly saw that the door was ajar and waved for the two of them to follow him.

For a poker game to be going on, it was awfully quiet; it was darn right eerie. As Rainbow put his hand on the doorknob to go into the game room, Sparkle noticed what seemed to be a line of light in the floor around the pool table.

He quickened his pace to catch up with Rainbow and grabbed

him by the elbow as he nodded for him and 'B' to follow him. They went to inspect the line of light and Sparkle got on his knees to peer through the crack. "Hey, man, it looks like some stairs down there."

'B' got on his knees to have a look, too. "Man, I can see some chairs down there. This dude's got some kind of secret room down there. Hmm, I wonder how he gets down there?"

Sparkle stood up and started walking around the room thinking out loud. "There's probably a panel in this room somewhere."

"That's what I was talking about, fool," 'B' snarled as he stood up and started looking around the walls. The sound of the door opening caused all of them to jump nervously in the direction.

"I thought I heard somebody down here," Mona said. "I thought you had gone, sweetie. Wait a minute. I thought y'all was Al." Mona started down the stairs. "What are y'all doing down here?"

'B,' who had paused after looking behind one of the pictures on the wall, took a double-take at Mona. In the dim light she seemed to look very familiar. He couldn't put his finger on it. He walked over to her. "We came by to get in Al's poker game. We rang the doorbell, but when nobody answered, we came through the garage because the door was opened."

"I was in the shower jamming on some Ciara. Still, what are y'all doing searching around the room like this here?" she responded.

'B' squinted at her for a second before he waved her over to the pool table and pointed to the line of light. She knew immediately what they were looking for, so she walked past 'B' directly to the music box. She pulled it away from the wall to reveal the button that opened the false floor.

The three of them turned to the whirling sound and watched in awe as the pool table started to slide back. They waited for her to lead the way down the steps. She didn't get halfway down before she let out a scream that ran shivers down their spines.

Rainbow quickly pulled her gently to the side. "Damn, whadd-afuck?" He continued on down the steps.

Sitting in one of the seats facing the monitors, head cocked to the side with a smile stretched across his face, sat Al, dead as a doorknob.

The trio wasted little time leading her back up the stairs and into the game room.

After several minutes of boohooing, Mona mustered up enough composure to speak. "I heard him down here talking to some woman, but all of y'all know how he don't like a bitch all up in his biz. Besides, I wasn't supposed to even know about this room, so I stayed upstairs and took a shower. After I was finished washing up, I heard y'all down here and figured, like y'all had figured, that he was starting up a game, too. That's why I came on down because he be expecting me to make folk comfortable and to answer the door as the other players arrive." She went back to her sobbing.

"Looka here, sweetie, we'd love to hang around and do the consoling thang with you, but we know that you got to be calling the five-o and explain this here," Rainbow said. "So we gonna bounce and get out of your way. If you need anything later, holla."

He stepped away from Mona and raised his hands to the ceiling. "And girlie, please don't be mentioning us to no five-o, okay," Rainbow said as he nodded for them to get up out of there.

She nodded her understanding and slowly got to her feet to walk them to the door. She watched through the curtains as they backed out of the driveway and drove down the street. She blinked her watery tears away, sighed heavily and set out to go through the whole house to look for whatever cash, jewelry and drugs she could find. Afterward, she would call her sister to let her know that it was time to hit another city. Shit had gotten way too hot in this one here.

During her search, she kept shaking her head at the way that

'B' was looking at her. She knew what he was thinking because he had recently pulled her sister into his stable; he didn't realize that she was her sister. As far as Al went, she'd leave that up to the neighbors to report his demise after the stench of death got overbearing, giving her way more than enough time to be wherever she decided to go. One thing was for sure, though. There was no way that she was going to welcome the police back into her life. The nigga was dead, oh well.

✠ ✠ ✠

After departing the death scene, the fellas went back to the La Quinta to pick up the girls. There was no need to leave them in this vicinity knowing that the fuzz would be out in force. With the feeling that their major adversaries had been disposed of, it was safe to take them back to the track to get that paper. The overjoyed women felt as if they were getting released from prison and reacted as such; whooping and hollering like a bunch of schoolgirls.

Rainbow had only about a eight ball worth of coke left, but they all enjoyed it like it was the last one that they'd ever get. Shortly afterward, Rainbow split with his girls and Sparkle did as well with Violet and Mercedes. 'B' decided to take Yolanda and Miriam to the Holiday Inn off Wesley Chapel. All was good again in the hood.

Sparkle and the girls had gotten about halfway to the apartment on Memorial Drive when Violet's phone started buzzing. She answered it and immediately handed it to him. It was Rainbow. "Yo, bro, since it gonna be hot around this bitch for a minute, y'all wanna hit a party out there in Henry County?" When Sparkle didn't respond, he heard Rainbow take a deep breath. "Look at it this way, partner; after all that laying up, the girls are in the mood to do some partying. Hell, and we might as well make some cheddar off of some of them white folk out that way, you feel me? Plus. that would be the last place that Bevy's crew would be looking for us."

When Sparkle still remained quiet, he threw him one final spiel. "Nigga. brang yo ass on over here, because we might as well get out of DeKalb and Fulton and let this shit cool down some."

Sparkle looked at both girls through the mirror and finally replied, "Okay, man, we're on our way over there now. See y'all in a few."

Rainbow was sitting on the stoop when they pulled into the back yard and parked parallel to the garage. Sparkle had a devious sneaky smile on his face as he got out of the car. "I hope you got some rubbers around this joint because Violet says there are a lot white freaks that love to get nasty after they've blooped a few."

Rainbow stood up and spoke over his shoulder as he led them into the house. "Man, I hope you brought some of that killer blow because I ain't got but a ball left over here."

Sparkle spotted the smirk on his face and began to wonder what it was all about. "My nig, you could've told me that on the phone. You know damn well we ain't been by the crib yet."

Rainbow stopped in the kitchen and turned around. He arched his brow. "Well, it looks like you got to go get some then, right?"

"And what's wrong with you getting some from over there in the Bottom?" Rainbow gave him a condescending look as he spoke to the girls. "Y'all girls, come on, we're going to do us a little of this here boy while my nigga goes to get that."

The look on their faces, especially Violet's, let him know that he had hit on the right spot. Rainbow reached around him to grab Violet's and Mercedes's hands and led them into the living room. Mercedes had a real tender look on her face but she followed them willingly.

"This nigga," Sparkle mumbled under his breath as he heaved his shoulders, frowned at their departing backs and left the house to get the car. Fifteen minutes later, he pulled into the parking lot of their apartment. He was grumbling as he headed for the door, when he heard a car door open and shut. Instinctively he picked up his pace to the door. Damn, the security door was locked. Sparkle immediately snatched his Glock out of his back, expecting the sound of guns to be blasting his way. He spun around ready to go to war, when he heard a familiar voice shout out to him in a commanding tone. It had taken him only a moment to recognize the voice of his childhood sweetheart. Try as he might, it was difficult not to smile as she walked up to him. She was in one of her usual disguises for whenever she ventured into the hood: an oversized jacket, baggy pants, a baseball cap cocked acey-deucy and large aviator glasses. If it hadn't been for her voice, he would've easily thought that she was one of those wannabe hard-as-nails, young, hip-hop honeys.

She wanted to make sure that she had direct eye contact with him so she tilted the glasses down her nose, to make sure that he saw her intensity. "Whatcha ready to run for there, partner? Yo ass be guilty of something; feeling real nervous and shit, huh?"

She leaned back with her hands on her hips, eyes narrowed curiously as he lifted the back of his shirttail to ease the gun back in its customary place. She didn't give up a blink or any other sign of fear, which didn't faze him in the least; her being who she was, a straight-up gangster boo and all. He ran the knuckle of his index finger over the corner of his eye as he looked over at the car she had gotten out of; a paranoia move, for sho, but he really didn't expect to see anyone. It wasn't her style.

Reacting to his reaction, she looked back at the car herself, sorta like reading his mind, before she propped a high-ankled boot on the first step and leaned forward with intensity bristling from her shoulders.

Her icy stare nearly caused a shiver to escape, but he wasn't about to show her that kind of weakness. He leaned on the door sill as chill as he could be and waited for her to throw her lecture at him. When she harrumphed loudly, clearing her throat, Sparkle held his hand up to stop her, turned around to open the security gate and held it open for her to go enter. He opened the door to the apartment and left it open for her to follow. He headed directly for the refrigerator, took out two Heineken brews, then tossed her one over his shoulder, which she snatched out of the air with one hand and popped the tab. He smiled at quick reacting agility and said over his shoulder, "So what's up, sweetheart, or should I say, Chief, with that tone of command in your voice?" He snatched a bag of pretzels out of the cabinet and went to sit on the arm of the sofa.

She stood beside the fridge shaking her head while she watched him open the bag and toss a few pretzels into his mouth. She stared at him for several seconds before she sashayed over to stand over him. Her brows arched menacingly. "You can tell Johnny Bee that it may be best to let his ride lay in the parking lot for a few days. There's a full-scaled stack out at all the hotels on the strip, and especially the Red Roof where this killing shit went down." She stepped back to watch him intensely for a moment. But when he didn't show any reaction she crossed the room to sit in the love seat in front of him. "Sparkle, Sparkle, Sparkle, when are you going to get out of this life before it's too late? You certainly can't mean to do it forever and I definitely can't ignore all this bullshit y'all niggas be doing forever, either."

Sparkle pinched his nose, lowered his head, took a deep breath, made a smacking sound with his lips and stared at her until she finally blinked and turned her eyes away. Then he licked his lips. "Bevy, when are you going to stop trying to get me to show you my hand when I ain't even been dealt any cards yet?"

She sat there staring at him for a few seconds before she pursed her lips and blew hard and shook her head. Then she started counting her fingers. "One, two, three."

His brow balled up, full of curiosity, as he cocked his head to the side and ran his hand up and down his neck, really puzzled as to why she was reacting the way she was. He straightened up smiling and passed her the bag of pretzels and gulped down the rest of his brew. "What the fuck you doing that there for?"

She responded by snatching the bag out of his hand and throwing a couple in her mouth without saying a word, only gritting.

He blinked involuntarily a few times and twisted his neck in circles. "Ooooh, why are you starting out with all this hostility there, girl? This here ain't like you."

She quickly threw a couple more pretzels into her mouth and took a long swig of the beer. "You still think that this is a game, don't you?" she snarled.

"Hell, girl, from the way you acting right in now, so do you," he answered with an impish smile that dug into her restraint. Feeling her frustration nearing its boiling point, she suddenly stood and smashed the bag into his chest. With her face balled up in anger, she began to pace around the room to give herself time to cool off a little. After only a few steps, she noticed a row of pictures of Martin Luther King Jr. at several historical events along the wall.

The moment of nostalgia took her back for a second as she stopped at one particular picture and started rubbing her fingers on it. It was one with King, Coretta, Abernathy, Andrew Young, Jesse Jackson, and Joe and Violet Hankerson standing in front of Morehouse College. By their youthful appearances, the picture had to be taking back in the early sixties or late fifties. Probably during the years when they had just gotten out of college or not long afterward. The kind of black and white photos that most people had forgotten about years ago. Then she started staring at a more recent photo of Sparkle, Violet and her son, JoJo, in front of the Ebenezer Baptist Church. She studied it for a while before she finally muttered over her shoulder, "So you and Violet's been a couple for a while, huh?"

He could see the obvious pain on her face and it bothered him. "Yeah, ole girl took me under her wings when I got out of the joint. Why you ask?" He got up and stood behind her as she continued to roam through the gallery of flicks. As much as she kept up with their activities, he knew damn well that she had to know about his relationship with Violet. Maybe it was something that she didn't want to accept.

She peeked at him over her shoulder and rolled her eyes. "So that's how you got to be so well dressed so quick? And don't be looking at me like that there. And yeah, I've been keeping up with your ass since you got out. I'm the chief, remember?" she completed without even turning around.

He was really surprised as he arched his brow and tilted his head. "Damn, you still on to every thing that I do, ain'tcha?"

She ran her baby finger along her throat as she replied. "Uh-huh, that's right. Man, I saw you get off the bus at the Greyhound station," she lied. There was no way that he could be sure if it was the truth.. She really enjoyed that look of surprise on his face.

She turned to face him with a bright smile on her face and poked a stiff finger in his jaw, digging into his dimple. He really hated when she'd done that years ago when they were young, and he hated it just as much now.

She ignored the grit on his face and dug her finger in a little deeper to aggravate him like it always did. "Still got those holes in your face, don'tcha?" She shook her head smiling. "And I still get weak in the knees every time you smile and I see them. Most people got two; why you got just one?" She snorted a laugh through her nose and her expression turned serious. "Looks like I'll always have a schoolgirl crush on your sorry ass. It's sho bad that we took the opposite paths in life. Hell, I still think you could have made one helluva lawyer or teacher."

Sparkle harrumphed loudly and started scratching his neck as he smiled devilishly at her. "Yeah, well, that might have been nice, but you know firsthand how I feel about those authoritative roles. It ain't me, Bevy, what else can I say?"

She snorted and smirked. "Do I ever."

He ran his finger under his nose and harrumphed again. "Uh-huh, but you know what? I've never told you this before, but I'm so very proud of you, Bevy. And I often wonder what your police buddies would say or act or think if they had any idea of how you got your start. I know that must keep a lot of pressure on you. Shit has got to be rough, girlie."

Her gaze lowered to the floor as she stared off into some empty space, getting lost in the possibilities of actually getting discovered. After a few moments, she shivered involuntarily at the thought of having to explain that shit. She quickly gathered herself. "Mmphed, yeah, y'all boys really went through a lot for me and I appreciate that with my life." She shook her head and smiled. "But on the other hand, y'all niggas be putting y'all share of gray hairs all over my head." She took a deep breath. "By the way, when are y'all gonna start doing the right thing; if it ain't too much for me to ask?"

He put his hand on her shoulder and squeezed gently. "Girl. we did the right thing twenty some years ago." He bent down and kissed her on the forehead. "Yep, shit, how many niggas can say that they helped to make the top cop in Atlanta?"

Beverly Johnson, the top cop, lowered her head and nodded several times with her lips turned down. "Y'all niggas better remember to stay away from those hotels for a while. I'm serious, baby, that shit is gonna be hot for a while for sure, you feel me?" She got up and headed for the door.

Sparkle's eyes squinted up at her departing backside while he nodded a couple times. Then he sat back and stretched his neck in circles. "Tell me something?"

She paused at the door and looked over her shoulder. "Yeah?"

He leaned forward to rest his elbows on his knees before he stared at her seriously. "Did Rainbow put you up to this?"

She smiled sweetly and turned all the way around to face him. "No, I put him up to it. So what in the world am I gonna do with y'all three niggas? Y'all a full mess; you know that, don't you?"

He lifted his chin with a wide smile and nearly shouted. "Love us until the end, I guess."

"You wish."

"Yeah, I do."

She sighed heavily and closed the door.

CHAPTER SIXTEEN

The Sh— Hits the Fan

Mona had finally found all of the goodies, after hours of ransacking the whole house. She had to give it to his old dead ass; he was a real slick one indeed. The last place she would've thought about was the back of the jukebox. She smiled at the saddle bag filled with money and bricks of coke. The only thing left to do was to gather her few personal belongings that were scattered around the house and then locate her sister so they could split this whole scene.

Boy, oh boy, was she ever pumped as she flipped the bag straps across her shoulders and headed up the stairs. For one haunting moment she could've sworn that she had seen someone at the window of the garage door. She jerked nervously toward the imaginary ghost but there was no one there. She chalked it up as nervous energy. After all there was a dead man in the basement, which a couple of dirty-ass street niggas knew about along with her, and there was no way that she was gonna trust those mutha-fuckas not to throw all the weight on her to save their own asses. Straight up, she had to get her ass out of there with this saddle bag full of dope and money. Fuck that dead-ass nigga and those slick-ass niggas. Each nigga and bitch for themselves. Having thought it all out, she ran around packing everything of value to her in a suitcase. Afterward she took one more survey of the house and headed for the garage. She flipped the car's ignition and froze. Damn, she had to wipe her fingerprints off of everything she could imagine that she had touched in the house. The only ones that could connect her to the obvious murder scene were crooks themselves, and they weren't about to say anything with the fear of having themselves checked on. So she made sure that she hit everything from light switches to cooking utensils.

Finally she was ready to roll. Dusk had set in, which made her feel better about going unnoticed by the nosey goody-two shoes that lived in the neighborhood. *Aw hell, a couple of more minutes and a good blast will do me some good.* She started fixing herself up a Scottie-chasing blast.

After calming down from the euphoria, Mona gathered the last of her belongings and headed for the car. She turned the key in the ignition and was about to shift into reverse, when from the corner of her eye she saw a gleam of light through a crack in the door coming from the game room. At first she thought that she was geeking from the hit. She sat up as far as she could, her head nearly touching the roof of the car. She wasn't geeking; that was for sure.

Damn, I could've sworn I had closed that, she thought as she opened the door and muttered to herself, "I really must be tri..." She froze in her step when she got to the top of the short steps and saw the floor under the pool table start to widen.

Fear hit her like a jackhammer. "Oh shit, this nigga ain't dead." It nearly paralyzed her mind and she rushed over to grab a hold of the table to try to keep it from opening. But she couldn't stop it, as her feet started sliding along the floor.

"Aaarrrgggh!" She started screaming when she saw the shadow of someone coming up the stairs. "Oh my God, oh my God." Fear had her shivering so hard that she peed on herself when a man's head came into view. She let go of the table and ran for the car, but fumbled the keys to the floor when she tried to put them in the ignition.

Crying hysterically now, she reached to the floor to pick them up. After two or three frantic times, she finally managed to get a grasp of them. Her hands trembled as the car started, but when she lifted her head to back up, there was a man's face at the window. Her screams really went out of whack as she put her hands to her head and went off. "Please don't kill me. I'm sorry, baby. Please don't kill me, please don't."

There was a hard rapping on the window, which made her start to scream even more until it registered on her that her name was being yelled over and over again. Trembling uncontrollably, she looked at the window, blinked several times before she finally mouthed, "RJ."

He motioned for her to roll the window down, which she was reluctant to do at first. But then she took a deep breath and tried to push the button. But her hand was shaking too much, so she gripped her wrist to hold it still enough. After several tries, she was finally able to push the button.

"Hey, chill out for a minute there, girlie. I know exactly what you are thinking. Hell, I would have been scared to death myself," he said with a gentle smile as he reached inside the door and pulled the handle. With the same smile plastered on his face, he held out his hand to help her get out. When she hesitated, his smile intensified. "Come on, girl, you've got to help me figure out who did this."

She blinked away some of the initial fear and reached out for his hand to allow him to help her get out. She sat against the hood and folded her arms across her chest and considered telling him about the guys being there, but her mind spiraled with that revelation. Hell, she didn't trust the cracker any further than she could toss him, so she definitely didn't think those dudes wanted his dirty ass in their business like that. He took her silence as a sign of the fear that apparently still had a grip on her.

"Calm down, sweetie; take your time." He sat beside her and grabbed one of her hands and patted it reassuringly.

The more she thought about it, the more she felt that she had to get the heat off of herself. And besides, he hadn't even made any mention of calling his police buddies about the body, meaning that there was probably a lot more to the situation than he cared to mention. Telling him anything to keep from going to jail; hell, enough to be able to get away from him right now, would do. So she talked and he listened intently to the description of the conversation and the car they'd left in. He knew immediately who she was talking about but he didn't let her know that. For a brief moment, he considered killing her because she knew too much about his business. But he changed his mind when she revealed her plans to leave Atlanta. Seeing the suitcases in the backseat helped to make him believe that she was telling the truth. So he helped her back into the car with an assurance that he'd devise a believable story to tell his colleagues. He smiled brightly as Mona backed into the street and drove away.

After he was certain that she had left, he went back into Al's private sanctuary and finished the search he had started before he'd heard her getting ready to leave. He made a thorough search through all of Al's paperwork for the next hour until he had gathered all the information that could possibly connect him to Al.

When he was satisfied that he'd located it all, he went back into the garage and found a container of gasoline. He trailed the liquid around all of the downstairs rooms, lit flames in the basement and left. It was time to make the person whom he felt was responsible for messing up his plans to pay.

✠ ✠ ✠

Lt. Woo thought that she was still dreaming when she heard the irritating buzzing sound, which shook her out of her nightmare. The sound seemed to go on and on until she felt the weight of her bed partner disappear from her side. She blinked once, twice, three times as she struggled to shake the cobwebs out of her hazy mind. Ever so slowly the blurriness cleared up.

She reached her hand up to rub the laziness from her eyelids. Sighing heavily, she rubbed her tongue across her lips. "Ugghh," she groaned at the taste of overworked pussy coating her face and tongue, that went along with her morning breath.

She suddenly remembered the wild sex and drugs that had lasted practically the whole night. Going beyond the aftertaste, she smiled recalling all the orgasms she had experienced and delivered. She felt her sex mate stir. Then she froze and watched her get out of the bed through her partially closed eyelids. The little bitch picked up the cell phone off of the nightstand and headed for the bathroom. Her inquisitive antenna was now on full alert as she honed in on the reasons why she was being so secretive.

When she heard the door begin to open, Woo pressed her lids shut and pretended to be asleep. She watched intently as Crysty tiptoed around the room gathering her things. She could barely control her anger when the conniving little bitch picked up her cell phone and car keys. Woo fidgeted under the covers, about ready to spring up and choke the life out of her. Crysty shook her head several times and squinted her eyes at Woo's prone figure before she laid the car keys back down and left the room. It was just in time because Woo was about to spring up and do her thing on her ass. As soon as the door closed, Woo was up in a flash, slipping into her clothes like she was on some Wonder Woman stuff and cracked the door to peek out. When she didn't see her anywhere on the balcony, she eased out of the room in search of her. She spotted her on the phone in the lobby as she was coming down the stairs, probably calling a cab or whoever she had been talking to earlier. She stayed in the shadows as she worked her way to her car and slid down in the seat to wait for whatever transportation she was expecting. *I wonder why she's in such a hurry because she could've made the call or calls she needed to while she was in the bathroom,* Woo thought as she considered calling her crew. She quickly changed her mind because it might be better that she see what Crysty was really up to first.

She could've been going back to the club and didn't want to wake her. Then again, why would she have to sneak away to do that, to even consider taking her car? Nom the bitch was up to something she didn't want her to know about, and she was gonna find out what it was. While she lay crouched down in the seat, waiting for whoever was picking her up, Woo placed a call to one of her reliable informants and got an update on some of the activities she had been keeping up with. No sooner had the phone started ringing on the other end than a dark sedan pulled up in front of the office. Crysty ran out and jumped in. She let them get a two-light head-start before she set out behind them.

✠ ✠ ✠

Rose had rung up her last order of the day when she felt a headache coming on. She went to the door, flipped the "closed" sign around and went to the backroom to lay down for a moment. She had barely closed her eyes on the couch when the phone started ringing. It was her girl Bertha. They weren't too far into the conversation when it became apparent that she was aching for some female attention. It had been quite some time since she'd had any of the big girl's loving, so she told her that she'd be around to the club after she closed the store.

She hung up, went to the bathroom and took herself a cold shower to help relieve some of the stress that had consumed her ever since she had found her nephew dead. After revitalizing herself, she contemplated going to the house for a while before she headed to see her girl. She wanted a blast really bad and since she no longer had any coke at the store, she decided to do just that. She figured she might as well enjoy herself as much as possible. It took her only a few minutes to check all the doors before she was ready to leave.

When she pulled away from the store, she didn't see the car that was parked down the street pull out behind her. With all the thoughts that were running through her mind, it never occurred to her that someone would be following her. She wasted little time once she got there going to her stash in the backyard. Normally she would have taken the time to separate the bags into eight balls. But she was in sort of a rush, and it was lucky that she hadn't. Unbeknown to her, as soon as she closed the door after going back inside, the stalker was turning the corner checking his weapon and missing her by mere seconds. He jiggled the doorknob, cursing in frustration when it didn't budge. His frustration quickly turned into exuberance when the bedroom window opened on the first pull.

His adrenaline rush was at its peak with his prey only steps away. He nudged the bedroom door slowly, not wanting to make any sound to alert his victim. He held his gun chest high, ready to pull the trigger when disappointment hit hard again as he heard the front door slam. His immediate response was to run across the room, only to run into the sound of another door closing.

He pulled the door open to the empty feeling of the car backing out of the driveway and quickly pulling down the street. He jerked his gun up to pour lead, but quickly realized that it would be a stupid move to open fire in the quiet neighborhood. He sprinted down the street as the car was turning out of sight around the corner. Quickly reaching his car a half-block away, he was soon in hot pursuit of Rose's fast-fading taillights.

✠ ✠ ✠

Boy, all Sparkle could think about was getting Rainbow back for setting him up with Beverly like that. A wicked smile inched to the corners of his mouth as a plan for revenge began to formulate in his mind. Even though he was certainly more than a little peeved with his boy, he was still grateful for the insight she had given him. It was sure something his paranoid-ass buddy 'B' would be thankful to hear about.

Shaking those thoughts out of his mind for the moment, Sparkle went into the bedroom closet and removed a shoe box buried in the corner. He took the box to the dresser and removed two of the ounces of powder cocaine he had gotten from Duke when he had gotten shot up on I-20. Replacing the shoebox in its hiding place, he took the packages into the kitchen and started cooking the coke in the microwave, using plastic ice trays.

Some twenty minutes later, after he had cooked up the whole batch, he was placing the rocks in plastic bags. He thought about how his boy Duke was doing since he had been transferred to DeKalb General Hospital. He made a mental note to remind Rainbow and 'B' that they really needed to pay big boy a visit. After all, the shots hadn't hit any vital organs, so he shouldn't be there that much longer.

Sparkle had just finished pulling the last tray out of the microwave when the telephone started ringing. He zipped across the living room to answer it on the third ring. He was pleasantly surprised to hear Mercedes's sweet, sexy voice on the line. He really didn't care too much for what she said though, as she was delivering a message from Rainbow about why he was taking so long to get back over there. His first thoughts were to get him on the phone to chastise him for the stunt with Beverly. But he decided to rein in his emotions and let Mercedes know that he would be on his way shortly. It didn't take him long to get ready to roll out.

When Sparkle walked in the door, there was a loud, boisterous Spades game in progress, which quickly came to an immediate stop. All the girls bum-rushed him, trying to be the first to get a blast before they headed out to the country.

He tossed Mercedes one of the bag of rocks he had cooked up and headed for the kitchen where he heard Rainbow's and Violet's voices making deals for when they got out there. He really wanted to get in Rainbow's shit right then and there, but that wouldn't have been a good idea in Violet's presence, which the dirty muthafucka probably knew from the smile on his lips.

Sparkle got in his line of vision and mouthed angrily, "I'm gonna get you, dog. I'm gonna getcha."

Rainbow eyed Violet out of the corner of his eye and mouthed silently, "Yeah, nigga, whatever." He then said out loud, "You ready to do this here, partner? How much ya bring?"

Without so much as acknowledging him, Sparkle threw the package to Violet as he said over his shoulder, "Whenever y'all ready to roll, partner."

He rolled his eyes in his direction and headed for the bathroom. By the time that he came out several minutes later, everybody had taken a blast and were ready to go. They were on their way to the third customer when Violet laid her hand on Sparkle's lap and smiled devishly. "This is the house where the freaks are, so y'all two niggas ain't gotta be looking all crazy when they start to want to suck on some dick and pussy. Because it's definitely about to get off the hook in this here bitch, for sho."

Lady, who was in the backseat toying around with Carla, Princess and Mercedes, started laughing as she rubbed her crotch. "Sheeiiit!! I ain't got no problem with a little snow bunny head. Those freaky muthafuckas know how to get low and nasty for a bitch, humph."

She was quickly followed by a chorus. "Hell, I ain't neither." Everybody started laughing and getting pumped up for the upcoming freak show. A little over a half-hour later, the house was rocking full of folk getting geeked to the gill. Folk started doing stripteases all up in folks' grills. One juicy redhead had started throwing her fat crotch in Sparkle's face when his phone rang. It was Bertha and she let him know that Max and Junior had made a deal with one their favorite customers but couldn't locate the supplier.

Figuring that it would be rather nice to be able to hand Duke a big wad of dough when they went to see him at the hospital, Sparkle told her that he'd call her back when he was on the way. He hung up and looked around the room for Rainbow to tell him what was up, but he didn't see him among the horde of naked bodies twisting around in all sorts of positions. *Man, where's this fool?* he thought as he began his search into both bedrooms and bathrooms. No Rainbow. Then he lifted his cell phone and started to punch in his number, when in his peripheral vision, he saw some movement outside of the patio doors. He wasn't surprised to see one of the white women bent over eating out of the outstretched legs of Mercedes, while Rainbow was long-stroking her fine creamy ass doggy-style.

He slid the door open and cleared his throat to get their attention. When they didn't respond, he said gruffly, "Yo, dog, we got to make a run downtown, like yesterday."

Rainbow continued stroking the woman into a series of muffled orgasms as he looked over to him. "Give me another minute here, my nigga. This one will be out of it by then." His face started transforming into an orgasmic grit of its own.

Sparkle shook his head and started to close the door, but then he said as if it was an afterthought, "Baby girl, go ahead and get dressed; you rolling with us." He closed the door and went to find Violet, gave her the rest of the coke and let her know what he was going to do. Some fifteen minutes later, they had reached I-20 and he gave Rainbow the whole rundown of what was happening. True, he didn't necessarily need him to help him take Max and Junior the four ounces, which was half of the quarter kilo that they wanted. Still, it was a little satisfying to disturb the pleasures he was having. And truth be told, he really didn't feel that comfortable traveling downtown all by himself, with all the recent events still running hot.

Mercedes rode quietly in the backseat. It really didn't matter where they were going or what they were doing. She was glad to finally be able to get some time with her man. When they got to the house, they immediately started rocking up the coke into ounce blocks. There were only six left and there was no way that they were going to depart with the last of what they had.

Max and Junior were really grateful when they handed them the four ounces in the back office of the club. While they took care of that business, Mercedes spent her time gathering the latest gossip from some of her former striptease buddies.

After concluding their business they were really surprised to see Mona when they came out of the office. She was sitting in one of the booths with her lookalike baby sister, Crysty. Seems like she wasn't about to hang around no dead body, either. As they walked by them, Sparkle overheard one of them say something about Hartsfield Airport between giggles. While Crysty appeared to be gleaming with joy, Mona looked as if she was forcing her glee. It was quite understandable as far as he was concerned.

As they left the club, Sparkle's attention was drawn to someone flickering a lighter inside of a car in the club's parking lot. He nudged Rainbow in the side to get his attention and nodded toward the car. "Yo, dog, what the fuck is this bitch Woo doing here? I don't see no signs of her crew. Whatcha think? We should go tell Max and Junior that this ho's doing the stakeout thing."

Before Rainbow could respond, the sound of several gunshots rang out in the night air.

"What the fuck?" Sparkle said before he pulled Mercedes close to his body to protect her. Another set of shots rang out and then they heard Woo crank up her car and back out of the parking lot. Only then did Sparkle recognize the car she was driving. It was the same one he had seen leaving the Heart of Decatur hotel just before they had discovered Don's body.

Could it be possible? Damn, the bitch was a cop and a worrisome-ass one at that. Then again what did that really mean because half the bastards on the force were crooked ass muthafuckas. Another set of tires screeched out of the MARTA parking lot across the street. A large dark car sped onto the street, swerving in a fishtail onto Lee Street and zoomed down the street.

When Woo's car jetted after it, Sparkle's curiosity went into overdrive. "Come on, dog, something ain't adding up here. Let's follow them and see what's up."

Rainbow didn't hesitate for he needed some answers, too. He pulled Mercedes right along with him to the car. As they were zooming by the MARTA lot, they saw a man staggering against the lamp pole before he tumbled to the ground.

"Hey, did that look like...?" Rainbow started to say.

"Yeah, the fucking deputy chief. Man, what the fuck's going on here?" Sparkle finished as he strained his eyes to keep Woo's taillights in sight as she wheeled around a bend in the street.

⨭ ⨭ ⨭

Aunt Rose didn't really start feeling suspicious until she had stopped by the Hardee's restaurant on Dunlap Avenue. She was standing in the line waiting for her order when the hairs on the back of her neck started to tingle. From there her street instincts took over and helped her to control her composure as she accepted her change from the cashier and headed for the bathroom. While inside, she counted to twenty and cracked the door enough to see a suspicious character across the street at the Chinese joint. He was in a dark coupe and jerked his head away when she tried to make eye contact after leaving the bathroom. She leaned further in his direction to get a better look, and he responded by acting as if he was getting something out of the glove compartment.

He had ducked down rather quickly, but not quick enough. *Damn, is that& naw& Now why would he be way out here, unless...,* she thought as her anger started to rise. She could've sworn that she'd seen him peeking over the edge of the door when she'd left the restaurant.

Her antenna was at full alert as she watched him in her rearview mirror when she turned onto and drove down Main Street. Her adrenaline pumped up immediately when his head jerked up and he was instantly on her tail before she had even got two blocks away. Still, to be absolutely certain, she made a right on Second Street and stopped at the first available service station to get gas. She stayed at the pump until she saw the car pass and jumped back in hers and headed back to Main. Now that she knew that he was definitely following her, she started thinking about going to some dark and crowded area with plenty obstructions, where she could confront him. After passing up several possibilities, she decided that the Lee Street MARTA station would be the perfect place.

As she was turning into the gated fence, she noticed Lt. Woo standing outside her car in the club's parking lot. That really piqued her curiosity, pushing her antennae up that much further why it seemed that nearly every time that she came by the club, that the little bitch was somewhere around. Was that little slut sniffing at the same pussy that she was? She'd have to get in her shit real soon if that was the case. But right now she had to handle this fool following her. *Whaddafuck's up with all these cops?* she thought as she pulled in between a couple of SUVs and settled in to wait on her pursuer.

A few moments later, she saw his car pass by and then back up and enter the parking lot. This fool had now become the prey as she checked her wristband blade holder to make sure that it was working right. She quickly scanned the area for any witnesses. There were none, so she took a deep breath and eased out of the car, making sure that she made enough noise for him to hear.

With her senses on full alert, she tiptoed to the other side of the car trying to camouflage her exact position. She was poised for attack as she faced the direction where she figured he had stopped his car. Therefore she was taken totally by surprise when she reacted to a rattling sound to her left, only to have her feet taken from under her by his unseen hands. Dazed from her head and back being slammed solidly against the vehicle parked next to her, and then the unforgiving pavement, she was barely aware of the cold steel of his gun pressed into her neck. Much too late it registered on her wobbly mind that he had yanked her by the hair and slammed her into the SUV. "Bitch, do you realize how much money you have caused me?" he spat angrily in her ear as he gripped her neck in an iron grip.

Flinching and gasping from fear and shock she could only mumble, "What are you talking about? How did I cause you any money?" The foul spittle from his obviously drunken mouth caused her to recoil away from the stench as he continued. "Bitch, don't play games with me. Your stupid ass killed my man Al. That shit fucked up my digits big time and now your stanky ass has got to pay for getting in my godayum business."

He emphasized how pissed he was by yanking harder on her neck. She groaned as the darkness of unconsciousness started to cloud over her senses. He yanked hard one more time and pulled the trigger. Only the bullet didn't go into her neck as he had planned. He grunted in pure shock as his gun hand instinctively jerked upward when he felt a sharp pain in his neck. Followed immediately by another burning sensation in his rib cage. He folded over, mouth gaped in shock, while her stiletto craved a deadly path across his stomach. Blinking into a void of nothingness, he fell to the pavement as the blackness began to take over. But not all of his consciousness was lost as he struggled to his feet and got off several shots as her car was backing away. He staggered after her, getting off some more shots in pursuit, until he ran out of energy and ebbing life flow. With the dizzying spiral of death surrounding him, he leaned against a lamp pole as her taillights faded into the night. Blinking to oblivion, he slid down the pole, seeing nothing at all when his head clunked off of the pavement.

✠ ✠ ✠

Lt. Woo paused momentarily at the entrance to the parking lot to see that it was the deputy chief fading to his death. She now knew that she was in hot pursuit of a cop killer. She knew that she had seen the car several times, but at the moment, she couldn't remember where. That was okay, though, she'd know soon enough. She picked up her mike to call for assistance, when her hand suddenly froze before she pressed the button. She had seen the same car at too many drug scenes she had stacked out, as well as at the club, for it to be a coincidence. She'd see where it was headed before she decided on whether to call her crew. After all, she already knew that RJ was involved in the hijacking ring, so there was no telling what else that he and the person she was following were engaged in.

She followed the car into East Point and when the car made a right turn on Dunlap Avenue, she got a good look at the driver behind the wheel with the aid of the lamp pole. It was the old lady that she had seen frequenting the club and several drug hot spots, but she hadn't really paid her that much attention up until now. The bitch had killed RJ. Why? She'd have to get the ups on her whenever she reached her destination, which had to be nearby since she had slowed her pace.

She drove past as the car parked and the lady got out and headed down the sidewalk. She quickly parked in the adjacent lot and ran to the corner of the other apartment building. She realized that she was moving too fast and tried to slow her momentum. She was forced to grab onto the wall when her feet slid from under her, taking her beyond the edge. She groaned in agony as her backside rolled onto a scattering of jagged rocks and pinecones on the ground. She covered her mouth to keep from crying out loud as she looked down the roll of apartments, hoping that the sound didn't attract the attention of her prey. Momentarily stunned, she gave a silent pray as the old lady didn't show any recognition of discovering her, and entered the apartment several doors down. *Now what? Do I call for backup now or come up with a plan to get in the apartment?* Woo thought.

"Damn," she cursed under her breath when a set of headlights washed across her back and forced her to roll behind some bushes aligned beside the walls. There was no need to let anyone see her.

After the car had passed, she started to creep along the wall until she got to the door she had gone in. She could see a silhouette of the lady through the shades at the kitchen window and she started looking around thinking of a way to get in. It didn't take her long to figure that one out as she smiled when she saw an upstairs window opened. She took a deep breath and set to the task.

✠ ✠ ✠

"Hey, baby, this ain't too much tales in the hood for you, is it?" Sparkle smiled at Mercedes, who was sitting between him and Rainbow as they followed Woo. She gave him a curt smile in return. Luckily there were several other cars on the street where they couldn't easily be detected. After all, the little bitch was a sort of a super snoop, so it wouldn't be that difficult for her to spot a tail. So to play it safe, he stayed a couple of cars behind; but not far enough where he couldn't recognize the car they were following.

"Hey, dog, this little bitch sure is acting funny. Damn, there ain't no way that she could have missed the deputy chief dying beside that pole. If we saw it, she had to see it, too," Rainbow said as he checked his piece. From the way things looked, they weren't on the trail of some small fry.

"Ain't that the old lady who was tracing that nigga Al out of the hospital? Shit, dog, she looks a lot like that old lady that came out of Don's house that night, too." Rainbow relived the frustrations that night had caused.

"Who are these people? I'm getting a little nervous, sweetie." Mercedes finally spoke up in a scary tone.

Sparkle pulled her closer to him, trying to offer her a blanket of security. *Damn, why'd I have to bring her along anyway? Aaw, fuck it, she here now,* he thought as they watched Woo slip down as she got to the corner of the building.

Rainbow parked the car in front of a house that seemed to be abandoned, not far down the street. They told Mercedes to stay in the car as they got out and eased back to the apartments. They peeked around the corner of the building, but there was no sign of Woo or the old lady. Rainbow nodded for Sparkle to go to the other side while he covered the front entrance.

They met up at the end of the building. Sparkle started rubbing his hand across his mouth as he said, "Hey, man, I only saw one way for her to disappear like that."

"Whatcha mean, man?"

Sparkle shook his head and started massaging his brow before he spoke. "There's only one window open back there, but I don't see no way she could've gotten to it unless she did some Spiderman shit and scaled the fucking wall."

Rainbow cocked his head to the side, his face also full of puzzlement. "Come on, let's just knock on the door and if it's the old lady, we'll pressure her to reveal whatever the fuck's going on."

"And if she don't?" Sparkle asked.

"Fuck it, man, we take her ass out; you can bet your own ass that she knee deep in this here shit." They eased up to the door and to both of their surprises, it was still ajar. As Rainbow was about to push it open, they heard sounds of a struggle coming from upstairs inside the house. He eased it open and turned around to *ssh* Sparkle, then stepped inside.

There was no one in the living room. Like the sound of the struggle, they heard a soft moan come from upstairs. Walking on their tiptoes they started easing up the stairs. There were no lights on, which made it feel that much more eerie and dangerous. The door to the bedroom on the left was cracked and they could see a figure lying on the floor beside the bed. As they approached the prone figure, Sparkle saw a hand shoot out and hit Rainbow in the temple. He fell down like a rag doll. Sparkle jumped back and to the side as a foot grazed his ribcage. He raised his weapon to fire at the shadow silhouetted against the curtains. As he fired, he could have sworn that he saw the figure jerk back from the impact. But there was no way he could be sure because his lights were put out by a stinging blow to the back of his head.

✠ ✠ ✠

Sparkle moaned loudly when he came to with his head throbbing from the blow he had taken. He shook his head, trying to rid himself of the cobwebs that gripped his mind. Finally able to shake away the weariness, he saw Rainbow tied and gagged a few feet away.

"Hey, they seem to be waking up," he heard a sweet familiar voice say as he watched Rainbow's eyes fluttering. There was a look of pure defiance written all over his face as he watched Woo walk over to him and kneel down in his face and snatch the gag out of his mouth. "Bitch, what the hell's the matter with you?" Rainbow spat after he worked the cramps out of his jaws.

"You don't remember me, do you?" she snarled angrily.

"Of course I remember your crazy ass. You done kicked in enough of my girls' rooms; how in the hell I can't know you," he snarled back at her before she slapped spit out of his mouth. He struggled against the ties bonding his arms behind his back; all to no avail.

She leaned even closer into his face and grabbed his jaws in a death grip, which had his eyes about to pop out of his head. She spat in his face, "Muthafucka, you don't remember the woman you raped back in the war with your army buddies?"

Rainbow looked her straight in the eyes. "Bitch, I ain't never raped no fucking body."

"No, but you certainly didn't stop your buddies, either, which makes it just as fucking bad, as far as I'm concerned."

"What the fuck do that have to..." His words were choked in his throat as the recognition etched across his face.

"Wait a minute. There was only a little...oh shit, it can't be."

"But it is, muthafucka, that's right. I'm that little girl and my mother died that night. But you wouldn't know that, would you? Because your sorry ass left us there." Her eyes widened as her voice raised several octaves. "Just left us there, you, you, you bastard."

"That's right, our mother died that night. She was dead while my sister pulled me out of her dying womb," another voice added from the shadows.

Rainbow and Sparkle stared at each other in total shock as Mercedes stepped out of the shadows into the glow of the moonlight. They stared at each other as they shared the same thought. Rainbow was the first to speak through his swollen lips. "So that's how you knew every move we made?"

Woo stood up and started pacing before them. "That's right, my baby sister here really had y'all fooled, didn't she? Betcha thought she really loved you, huh, Mr. Sparkle? Ha, ha, ha."

"So you was behind all the robberies and killings?" Sparkle said astonished.

She hunched her shoulders. "Uh-huh, those boys were getting in the way of my revenge; they had to go."

"You mean that you sent that nigga JJ after us? Damn, you the one that fucked that fool up, too, ain'tcha?" Rainbow snarled.

Woo's wicked smile said it all. "Some people will do anything to stay out of jail, and for a high, wouldn't you say?"

"So why kill her?" He nodded toward the prone body beside the bed.

"Aunt Rose, the ho from Miami? Hell, to tell you the truth, I think she might have gotten in a few deaths of her own; the wicked muthafucka that she is. Besides, that bitch was living on borrowed time anyway and she knew too damn much. But enough, boys, it was nice hunting. Now it's time for some nice killing. I've waited a long time for this here," Woo snarled as she snapped the guitar string so loud that it popped an echo before she wrapped it around Rainbow's neck.

There was a sadistic smile on her face as she started to pull the lines tight. Rainbow twisted and struggled, but to no avail, as his eyes started to budge out of his head. Her smile changed drastically when the loud report of gunfire blazed through the night. Woo's grip automatically relaxed when the bullet spiraled through her neck and she tumbled to the floor. The sound was instantly echoed by the explosion of glass shattering when Mercedes dove through the window.

"Y'all aight?" The wonderful sound of Beverly's voice was that of an angel as she sprinted to the window to see Mercedes disappearing down the dark alley behind the building. She quickly checked the pulse of the unconscious Rainbow before she untied him and helped him to his feet. "It's a good thing that I decided to follow you after I left Violet's apartment." She stood up and headed for Sparkle. "But what ho from Miami was she talking about?"

Rainbow and Sparkle looked toward the bed and then back at each other in shock.

Hell, Aunt Rose was no longer there; she'd disappeared.

About the Author

L.E. Newell was born in Atlanta, Georgia. He is the author of *Durty South Grind*.

Visit the author on Facebook.

Reader Discussion Guide

1. Are you curious or perhaps confused about who's behind Rainbow's and Sparkle's troubles?

2. What is your opinion about Beverly's dedication to these hustlers?

3. Could, or would you be, under similar circumstances?

4. Do you think Lt. Woo's overzealous intent to destroy the clique is in the line of duty "to serve and protect" or beyond?

5. In the vein of the ever increasing prison recidivism rate, how do you feel about Sparkle's choice—to go straight or come to the aide of his lifelong friends?

6. How do you feel about how easily Violet accepted Mercedes under her legendary wings?

7. Is she doing it to control the girl as a protégé, or as a means to measure her status with her man, or as a way to control him and her?

8. How long would you be able to accept denial after denial trying to be a law-abiding citizen, knowing that your felony record is a major roadblock; compared to a life of money, romance, drugs and countless luxuries that you've been accustomed to for years?

9. What do you think of Mercedes' role and devotion to the gang? Is she sincere, optimistic, greedy or maybe even revengeful?

10. Who do you think is the controlling force behind the young hoodlums and why?

11. What do you think of RJ? Is he a bigot? An overambitious crook with a badge? Or a silver spoon-born optimistic?

12. Do you see Al as gangster gone wild, a love-blinded fool, or a psychopath?

13. What do you think of Beverly's persona, as far as measuring up to what fits a person of police chief status?

14. Imagine the answers to these questions being a jigsaw puzzle to your own life—one that you actually survived. In the end this is what I chose to do: "Tell ya about it." Hopefully, one of these younguns out there wanting to live the life will read this and see *"That it ain't worth it."*

Durty South Grind

BY L.E. NEWELL
AVAILABLE FROM STREBOR BOOKS

CHAPTER ONE
Breaking the Chains

It was another humid day in the summer of 2006 in the rural woods of southern Georgia. The sun was finally starting to break through the daily density of fog at the Valdosta State Prison. The sounds of the stirring of the inmate population inside the life-choking, razor-wired fences found Sparkle awakening to the final day of his bit and hopefully the beginning of a new life in the outside world.

The irritating clanging of chimes over the PA system was really starting to irritate him. He rolled over and squeezed the hard plastic-covered pillow as tightly as he could over his head to block out the persistent noise. He tried squeezing his eyes tight but that didn't work, either. Finally, he realized that more sleep was out of the question and sat up in the bed. It had been well over a year since he'd given up eating early in the morning. He had begun feeling nauseated and occasionally had thrown up after devouring that godforbidden slop. Getting to the chow hall certainly wasn't a priority for him.

A sharp rapping on the door was followed by the voice of his chain gang running mate, Skeet, yelling at the top of his lungs. "Yo, Sparkle, get yo ass up, man!" This did away with whatever rest was left.

Sparkle fell back on the bed, turned over on his stomach and pulled the wool cover over his head, shouting in a grumbling tone, "What?"

Skeet rapped harder. "Hey, man, come on; get yo ass up, nigga. We got some thangs to kick around afore you raise up outta here."

Sparkle, still in a sleepy haze, thought, *Aw man, I'm getting outta this dungeon today. Man, let me get up outta this here rack.* He had a big smile spread across his face. He peeked over his forearm and focused on the door's frosty sheet of Plexiglas where Skeet was still yelling, "Come on, man, get up and splash some water on that ugly-ass mug and get the funk outta your mouth." He was cheesing hard through the pane. Sparkle could only see his teeth and big bulbous nose. Even though he was looking directly at him, he continued rapping and yelling, "Come on, bitch, get yo ass up. It's time for you to roll outta this dungeon."

"Ugh," Sparkle grunted and frowned from the nasty film of morning mouth coating his tongue. Smacking his lips, he sighed and yanked the cover off his head and glanced menacingly at the door.

He sat up and rubbed the crusty sleep out of the corner of his eyes with the palms of his hands. Breaking out into a big smile, he began rubbing his knees and reached under the plastic mattress for his crumbled pack of Kools. After taking his time lighting up, he took an extra long toke and started waving Skeet away from the door. "Yeah, yeah, I'm up, man. Why dontcha go get that fat butt boy of yours up." He stretched and yawned. "I'll be with ya'll in a few."

Skeet rapped his gnarled knuckles on the pane one last time. "About time, nigga; I'll be out at the basketball court. And don't have me out there all morning waiting on your jive ass, either." He gave him a staunch salute before disappearing.

"Yeah, yeah." Sparkle pressed his fist to his mouth and stifled a yawn. He stood to stretch his five-foot-ten, coffee-brown frame, twisted the kinks out of his neck and staggered to the wash basin to handle his hygiene.

With Skeet's footsteps fading, his thoughts flowed to the image of a sweet, young filly hunching up under him, giving up husky sighs and pussy aroma from his hard grinding fuck. He smiled at his dull image in the metal mirror and splashed cold water on his face. He brushed his teeth, picked out his mini fro and started putting on his prison whites for the last time.

Several minutes later, he checked the creases in his pants as he exited his room. He strolled down the catwalk toward the winding stairs. As he reached the steps he heard an all-too-familiar voice grumbling in a country drawl.

He immediately felt that old tingling of hatred run up and down his spine. He knew it wouldn't do any good to ignore it, so he slowly angled his head sideways to acknowledge the voice.

Old "Chew Tobacco" Jones was grinning at him, displaying a row of brown, crooked teeth. The big burly country hick, his distinctively foul body odor disturbing the air, placed a swollen hand on the railing. He tapped his ever-present nightstick along the wall as he approached in a rolling gait.

In a skunky wisp of air, he said, "Damn, boy, you trying to ignore me or sumthang?" He stepped a few feet closer before continuing with a nasty sneer. "You best to keep yaself oudda trouble now."

Sparkle pinched his nose and spoke, holding his breath between clenched teeth. "What's up, Stank Breath Chew Tobacco?"

The CO's face turned beet red as he frowned and growled, "Whaddafuck you say, nigga boy?"

Sparkle pinned him with cold-killer eyes and blasted his funky ass. "Cracker-ass, redneck bitch, who gave your dumb hillbilly ass permission to speak to me?" He paused and rubbed his nose again, letting it sink in. "Get the fuck outta my face." He turned away to stifle the laugh that was boiling up from his gut. A look of total shock spread across Jones's face.

A red-faced, neck-throbbing Jones grabbed his throat as if he were about to choke on his wad. His neck got puffy red as he opened his mouth to say something but nothing came out. He shifted his head back and forth, checking to see if anybody was watching this boy belittling him. Then he gritted, showing all of his tobacco-stained brownish teeth. He pulled back his nightstick to strike before Sparkle leaned in closer to him and hissed, "Yeah, stanky muthafucka, do it and let's go see the magistrate."

The hillbilly opened his mouth again to speak but Sparkle cut him off. "Yeah, bastard, I said it. I'm a free man today and if you hit me with that damn thing, your ass is gonna do some time. Yep, some muthafuckin' time in here with these killa niggas that you been fucking over all these years."

With the stick frozen in midair, he squinted his hate-filled eyes, heaved and lowered the stick. "You black bastard, you better hope that your sorry ass don't ever come back this here way again. Your ass will be mine."

"Bitch-ass cracker, your funky ass better pray that I never see your ugly mug on the other side of these fences." Sparkle's deadly look sent a shiver down the CO's spine. He backed away with trembling lips.

Sparkle cocked his head to the side and scratched his chin, and then took a deep breath to keep from laughing. Turning abruptly away he started walking down the stairs. He could feel the fire snorting out of Jones's nose, along with the hate darting from his eyes, burning a hole in his back.

He didn't give a fuck how Jones felt with all the fucked-up shit he used to do. Brushing the confrontation out of his mind, Sparkle continued out the door. Immediately, he spotted his boy Skeet and his kid Lil' Jack in an animated conversation. They were seated on a bench beside the basketball court. As he strolled toward them, they broke out in wide smiles.

Skeet nodded toward the sidewalk and the pair walked up ahead of him. Sparkle got dap and backslaps from dudes congratulating him for surviving his bit and wishing him well on his return to the bricks. He eventually passed all of the well-wishers and walked between Skeet and Lil' Jack, placing an arm around each of their shoulders.

Lil' Jack smiled up at him and said in a squeaky voice, "Damn, big bro, you finally gonna get the chance to be a hood star again, huh?"

Sparkle blinked several times as he returned the smile. He'd always been amazed at how much Jack smiled like a girl. Hell, he was shaped like one, too. He used to joke with him all the time about him being a mistake of nature. For a moment Sparkle thought of what a helluva pimp Jack would make on the ho stroll on Auburn Avenue. He'd personally pumped enough game into his head to pull it off, too. A lot of dudes around the joint didn't realize how coldhearted the little fella was.

Because of his friendship with Skeet, they had become really close. Even though Jack was a near replica of the sexy diva Toni Braxton, he'd always treated him human without any of the homosexual bullshit involved. Sparkle figured he really appreciated it; he never acted feminine when they were alone. Often Skeet had him boy-sitting whenever he was at work in the gym or out hustling drugs and parlaying tickets.

He rubbed Jack's curly head. "Little bro, I'm going out there to do the straight-and-narrow thing." He winked.

"That's good man; that's good." Jack nodded.

When they got halfway down the long curved sidewalk, Jack spotted one of his sissy friends. He patted Sparkle daintily on the shoulder. "Hey, I know that ya'll two probably got some things ya'll wanna kick around before you leave. I'm going to holla at Miss Queenie over yonder, so take care of yourself, handsome." He twisted his little hips in the direction of his partner.

When they got out of earshot of the throng of niggas hanging out in front of the mess hall, Skeet nudged him in the side. "Ya know dat thangs are gonna be rough out der, my nigga; ya sure you gonna be able to handle that for me?"

Sparkle could tell that Skeet had doubts about him coming through with the drugs they had discussed over the past few months. "Homefolks, all you got to do is let me know that you done sent that package request to your sister and I'll be on that thang right away." He put his arm around his shoulder. "Make sure that you keep these niggas outcha business, so we both can get paid."

Skeet cocked his head to the side with his sneaky smile. "Yeah, man, we got this plan down tight and I sho nuff gotta keep these nosey-ass snitches outta my shit." He paused to scratch behind his ear. "Man, I hate to make you feel like I'm doubting you and shit. But you know how damn near everybody who gets out be claiming dey gonna do des and gonna do dat. And folk never hear nothing from them; go straight ghost on a nigga."

Sparkle stopped about ten yards from the entrance to the main control office and pulled him by the wrist. He stared straight into his eyes. "Yo, peeps, you remember that day when you cracked that fool upside the head? He was set to steal on me about that slum-ass reefer he was trying to gorilla down my throat?"

Skeet lowered his head and started massaging the bridge of his nose, listening intently.

"Well, baby boy, that alone is enough to keep my mind on the struggles you gotta go through in this crazy house. So you can count on me, dog. Word is bond, like it's always been with us."

"Yeah, I feel you, man." He continued to look down in shame for doubting his main man.

The captain who ran the control room came out the door. "Say, man, they been hollering for you on the walkie-talkies for about a half-hour now. 'S up, you ain't ready to go home or something?"

"Hell yeah, I'm on my way now, Captain." He turned away from him and embraced his buddy one more time. "My nig, I gotcha. Have your sister holla at a nigga when she get the paperwork," Sparkle whispered.

Skeet grinned like a black Cheshire cat. "It's on the way as we speak. Hell, that there's a wrap; make sure you take care of yourself out there."

"Shit, dog, that's automatic. You stay strong up in this hellhole."

"No choice, partner; no choice."

Sparkle rubbed his chin as he squinted at his boy and then looked around the compound for the last time. "Man, I sho' ain't gonna miss this place here."

"Yeah, man, I feel you on that there." Skeet nodded, following his gaze.

Sparkle lifted his chin and gave Skeet one more brotherly hug. He headed into the control center, toward freedom.

☩ ☩ ☩

A couple of hundred miles to the north, an individual was tossing and turning in their sleep, struggling with the constant nightmare that punished and punished, year after year.

The hot balmy breeze did little to stop the sweat from stinging the child's eyes. The heat was unbearable. The countless number of mosquitoes nibbling on little arms, legs and neck couldn't be swatted away, no matter how often and hard they swung. They kept biting and biting, growing bigger and bigger as the child's blood flooded its stinger mouth, like a hypodermic needle pumping a junkie's vein. The child got woozier as its life flow oozed down its arms.

The foggy faces of lust-crazed men poofed into view and leaned closer to the terror-filled eyes, which quickly began fading in and out of focus. Ever so close, yet out of reach. A white one with stubby hairs rubbing harshly against the child's burning skin, followed by a black one that ogled as slobber ran out of the corners of his mouth. His head angled from side to side like a lunatic; a brown one, then a yellow blurring in and out of vision.

The faces continued to swirl madly around as the mosquitoes got bigger, jaws snapping and gnawing on the child's ever swelling arms. Suddenly all the different colored backs appeared altogether in a hideous mass, sweating and stinking as they came into focus, going up and down, followed by a blood-curdling scream.

The individual's eyes shot open, a body consuming fear was causing the air to come in rapid gasps, hands rubbing vigorously all over the body that was drenched in flowing sweat, desperately trying to wipe away the icky feeling of total despair. He sat up in the unfamiliar surroundings, wondering how he had gotten there, brushing away oily hair that was plastered to the sticky forehead, before burying his head into his hands, scared to death as to why this kept happening. Tears from decades of suffering rolled down swollen cheeks, puffed with pain, wondering if the nightmares would ever stop; nightmares that were constantly increasing in frequency and intensity. Damn, something had to be done to make them stop. There was only one way to make them go away. And it would definitely come to pass. Please come to pass before insanity took over.

CHAPTER TWO
A New Beginning

The noonday sun cast eerie shadows on the freshly painted wall when Beverly Johnson picked up the persistently ringing telephone. Atlanta's newly appointed police chief listened intently to the familiar voice on the other end of the phone.

Only moments earlier her mood had been really upbeat as she had given the city designers the final instructions on remodeling her office. At least now it had a little bit of a woman's touch, with flowers and beautiful paintings to remove all of the masculine overkill.

Subconsciously, she looked at the reflection on the blank screen of her laptop. The image of a proud black woman brought a bright smile to her eyes; the first ever appointed as the head of the department of public safety in a major American city. And why not, this was the same city where Martin Luther King Jr. had begun knocking down all those racial barriers so many years ago.

She sighed and blew air upward that ruffled the ever-present bangs that rested on her brows. She pinched the bridge of her rather pointy nose and hung up the phone, pondering over the message that had brought a mixture of both joy and disturbance.

"Damn," she muttered and started punching keys to verify what she had heard. As usual the particular source proved to be reliable. With contrasting emotions buzzing loudly in her mind, she pushed away from her desk and walked to the window overlooking Peachtree Street and the downtown Atlanta skyline. It was the only city that she had ever really known. A city that she loved and had been entrusted to keep safe.

She closed her eyes, wondering whether this was the start of a dream come true or the continuation of a never-ending nightmare. What was she to do? How long could she continue to live a lie? Folding her arms across her ample bosom, she looked to the clouds, thinking of all the people that believed in her. What would they do, especially her political enemies, if the truth about her past ever really came to light?

She sucked on her teeth with the confidence that had gotten her to the status she now enjoyed. After a moment of meditation, she ran her manicured hands across her forehead and knuckled the corners of her eyes, pressing imaginary wrinkles. She spoke much louder than she thought. "We'll just have to make sure that nobody finds out."

"Never find out what, bossa lady?" a voice stuttering with an oriental accent called from the doorway.

A shiver of fear of being discovered ran down Beverly's spine as she jerked around. Quickly regaining her composure, she spat venom. "Lieutenant Woo, how many times have I told you to knock?" She paused to place her hands on her hips. "Knock and wait for me to tell you that it's okay to come in."

The petite Vietnamese officer, the feared leader of the dreaded Black Cat drug enforcement team, squinted her cheeks and smiled. "Bossa lady, you aight? You ain't never told me that." She hunched her shoulders meekly and eased through the door.

She had only taken a few steps and opened her mouth to speak further, but Beverly cut her off. She advanced aggressively toward her and growled, "Lieutenant Woo, I still did not tell you that it was okay to enter."

Woo's eyes widened and she raised her hands in a defensive posture as she backed up. "Do you want me to go back out and knock first?"

Beverly rubbed her forehead as she stared down at the floor for a brief moment before she spoke over her shoulder and turned around to walk back to her desk. "Naw, come on in and this had better be good."

Lieutenant Woo stepped forward timidly toward the chief's large desk and placed papers on it. "Is it okay for me to sit down?" After receiving a curt nod from the chief, she eased into the chair and patted the papers. "I need authorization to hook up with the Red Dogs over in Decatur to straighten up those hotels along the county borders."

Beverly's eyes squinted in concentration as she placed a hand over her mouth and leaned back in the seat. After watching Woo swallow a lump down her throat, she nodded for her to continue. Woo hunched her narrow shoulders and leaned forward. "That's it, bossa lady; I want to clean up the whole strip on I-20. From Little Vietnam to Lithonia. What else is there to say?"

Beverly pyramided her hands across the bridge of her nose, cocked her head to the side and stood. "Okay, go do your thing."

When she didn't get an immediate reply from the diminutive lieutenant, she sat back down and started shuffling some of the paperwork that was piled on her desk.

Woo sat puzzled for a few seconds and then pushed the papers further across the desk. "Thanks, but aren't you forgetting to sign the papers?"

Beverly didn't take the time to look up and waved her dismissal.

Woo blinked a couple of times and mumbled, "But…"

"But what?" Beverly said sternly.

"Are you going to authorize these or not?"

"I just did and I'm sure that you're going to do an excellent job." She paused to lean back in her chair and stared back at her. "Oh yeah, and the next time that you come in my office, I'd really appreciate it if you would knock and then wait until you are welcomed in. Understood?"

Woo gathered up her papers. "Understood." She slowly got up to leave. When she arrived at the door and started to turn around to speak, the chief's hand was pointing toward the door. The expression told her that it would be useless to say any more, so she sighed heavily and left.

When she closed the door, Beverly stared at it for a minute, wondering why she had come to her office. Especially when she knew that her staff handled that sort of thing. Was she trying to get closer to her since she was now the chief instead of one of her colleagues? Hell, she couldn't really blame her for that. Or maybe she was being a little too paranoid because of the call. *Check yourself, old girl, ain't no need to start getting all unraveled now*, she thought and then dug into her black purse to retrieve her cell phone. She punched in some numbers.

"Might as well make sure that the playing field is all clear," she hummed to herself as the phone rang. "Hello, you know who this is. There are some things I want you to look into."

✠ ✠ ✠

A half-hour after entering the control room, Sparkle rolled down the window to catch the breeze in the old prison van. He watched the rural Georgia countryside en route to the bus station. Old gray-haired Sergeant Jones gave him a bucktoothed smile. "Yo family's going to be waiting on you at the bus station in Atlanta? That's where you're going, ain't it?"

Sparkle was way too deep in his own thoughts to be paying him much attention. Sarge cleared his throat and repeated himself. Sparkle blinked. "Sorry about that, Sarge; my mind was way out there. Ah yeah, they'll be there when the bus shows up. I think my sister said the bus would hit town around noontime."

"That's good, man, that ya family be sticking wid ya and all." The van shrieked to an abrupt stop and Sarge took the time to light a cigarette. The sudden stop caught Sparkle by surprise and forced him to brace against the dashboard. He was about to shout a number of obscenities before he looked up and saw an old country convenience store.

Sarge let out a stream of blue smoke in his direction. "Dat dere's da bus depot; you near about there now, home, I mean." Sparkle shot a frown at him, wondering why he had stopped so far away. Sarge didn't acknowledge the frown as he reached across Sparkle's body to open the glove compartment. Having no idea what this hillbilly was up to, Sparkle leaned back in the seat. Sarge smiled at his reaction. "What's wrong with you, partner?" he snorted in response. He pulled out a flask and took a big gulp of some rot-gut home brew. He aahed and belched loudly, and then to Sparkle's surprise, offered him a taste.

Sparkle gathered himself together. "Thanks, Sarge, but no thanks. I'd rather keep my head on straight now."

Sarge harrumphed, took another big swig, aaahed again and

wiped his mouth with the back of his knuckled hand. "Just thought I'd offer. You were one of the few guys back yonder that acted like he had some sense."

Sparkle forced a smile at the so-called compliment. At the same time he was thinking, *This droopy-jawed muthafucka's gotta be out of his godayum mind if he thinks I'm gonna drink sumthang after his... uh, uh, damn what's that mutt's name...dam...Uh-huh, the one that used to slobber all over everything. Oh yeah, that fucking Hooch, Turner and Hooch, that big nasty drooling mutt with Tom Hanks...Oh hell to the naw.*

"Whatcha thinking about, son? I say sumthang funny?" Sarge grimaced, puzzled why Sparkle couldn't appreciate his good-natured gesture. *Hell, how many boys do he think could even get an offer to share a drink wid me*, he thought as he harrumphed and took another big swig.

Sparkle shuddered slightly; struck between insult and common sense, he chose the latter. "Naw, Sarge, I was sorta getting away from any mind-blowing stuff, if you feel me." He paused to nod at the flask. "And from the smell of dat there and the way you aahing and shit, I really don't think I could handle it."

As he expected, that drew a smile out of Sarge, so he continued, "Now if you wanna score me one of them root beer sodas out of that machine over yonder, I will gladly touch glasses with ya."

The wrinkles eased out of Sarge's brow as he chuckled. "Aw, fella, you right, what's wrong with me?" He tapped the side of his head with the flask. "And here I'ma C.O. and offerin' you some rot-gut home brew."

Sparkle smiled innocently, hunched his shoulders and spread his hands out.

Sarge smiled back. "T'ain't much correcting in that, huh?"

"No offense, but it sho ain't."

Sarge nodded. "None taken. Come on, let's get you on home."

Sarge escorted him to the counter where a gray-haired, leather-skinned, chew-tobacco gal cashed his twenty-five-dollar state check. Sarge handed him his bus ticket to Atlanta. "Take care of yourself, son. Don't let me see ya this way again."

Sparkle saluted him as he drove off in a cloud of dust. He turned to the lady, who was whittling on a piece of wood. He bought a cherry Slurpie and went to sit at a rickety wood table with a red-and-white checkered cloth. After a five-minute wait, he looked over at her. She was still whittling away, eyeing him nonchalantly. He nodded toward her and then pinched his nose. "You don't mind if I wait on the bus out on the porch, do you?"

She grumbled what he took for a yes and headed toward the door. Opening it, he turned back to her. "How long is the bus gonna be?" She held up all ten fingers without muttering a word. Taking that to mean around ten minutes or ten o'clock, he went outside and sat in a wooden rocking chair on the other side of the soda machine. He started rolling a joint out of the ounce of reefer he'd hidden in his socks earlier.

He had a pretty good buzz by the time the bus pulled up in front of the store a half-hour later. Since the bus was nearly empty, he eased his way to the backseat and stretched out. He began day-dreaming about the things he had to do in the forthcoming days.

Before he'd even realized, he had dozed off. The next thing he knew he was being shaken awake by the driver after they had pulled into the station in Macon. He placed a collect call to his sister Janet's house. Her boyfriend, Kenny, told him that she had already left for the depot on International Boulevard.

He casually walked to the counter and asked the cute little red-head cashier, "How long before the bus pulls out for Atlanta?"